DEATHLIST

Also by Chris Ryan

Non-fiction
The One That Got Away
Chris Ryan's SAS Fitness Book
Chris Ryan's Ultimate Survival Guide
Fight to Win

Fiction
Stand By, Stand By
Zero Option
The Kremlin Device
Tenth Man Down
Hit List
The Watchman
Land of Fire
Greed
The Increment
Blackout
Ultimate Weapon
Strike Back
Firefight
Who Dares Wins
The Kill Zone
Killing for the Company
Osama
Masters of War
Hunter Killer
Hellfire

Chris Ryan Extreme
Hard Target
Night Strike
Most Wanted
Silent Kill

In the Alpha Force Series
Survival
Rat-Catcher
Desert Pursuit
Hostage
Red Centre
Hunted
Blood Money
Fault Line
Black Gold
Untouchable

In the Code Red Series
Flash Flood
Wildfire
Outbreak
Vortex
Twister
Battleground

In the Agent 21 Series
Agent 21
Reloaded
Codebreaker
The Wire
Deadfall
Under Cover
Endgame

CHRIS RYAN

DEATHLIST

CORONET

First published in Great Britain in 2016 by Coronet
An imprint of Hodder & Stoughton
An Hachette UK company

First published in paperback in 2016

1

A CIP catalogue record for this title is available from the British Library

Paperback ISBN 978 1 473 62687 4
Ebook ISBN 978 1 444 78355 1

Typeset in Bembo Std by Hewer Text UK Ltd, Edinburgh

Printed and bound by Clays Ltd, St Ives plc

Hodder & Stoughton policy is to use papers that are natural, renewable
and recyclable products and made from wood grown in sustainable
forests. The logging and manufacturing processes are expected to
conform to the environmental regulations of the country of origin.

Hodder & Stoughton Ltd
Carmelite House
50 Victoria Embankment
London EC4Y 0DZ

www.hodder.co.uk

ONE

Brecon Beacons, Wales.
Friday 8 January, 1999.
0620 hours

The two ramblers hurried towards the peak.

The Brit was the bigger of the two guys. He was six-three and tanned, and built like a Russian tank. The other guy was tall and thin, with a long, narrow face and a bushy goatee. Like a pencil tip turned upside down. Both guys were decked out in matching blue-and-green Gore-Tex jackets and Craghoppers waterproof trousers and Brasher leather hiking boots, and both carried brightly-coloured Berghaus daysacks. If anyone saw them tabbing up the side of the mountain, they would simply assume the two men were hitting the slopes early to beat the crowd. No one would suspect them of a thing.

Not until it was too late.

The ramblers moved at a decent pace. Neither of them spoke. They were blowing hard under their layers, their lungs burning and their leg muscles aching from the steep climb. They had been going at a furious pace when they'd set off fifty-five minutes ago and now they were starting to flag. But they didn't stop to rest. They were getting close now. Two hundred and fifty metres away stood their target: the top of Pen y Fan.

From a distance the peak resembled a giant anvil. It rose out of the granite landscape like a clenched fist, dark and grim and foreboding. The peak was so flat it could have doubled as a bowling green. Cobwebbed mist clung to the tufts of grass and shattered rock, and there was a light dusting of snow across the peak like icing sugar sprinkled on a birthday cake.

1

The bigger of the two men blinked sweat out of his eyes and glanced around the steep and rugged slopes. It was another dark and nasty morning in south Wales. A bitingly cold wind was lashing across the Fan, and the air was so dank you practically had to drink the stuff. The rambler smiled. Nobody in sight. They had the mountain to themselves.

Perfect.

He turned and continued up the sandstone trail leading to the peak, moving ahead of his companion. His heart was beating wildly inside his chest, the blood pounding in his veins. There was a spring in his step now. He forgot all about the deep burn in his muscles and the painful stitch running down his side. His skin tingled with anticipation. They were almost there. Just a little further to go now.

Two hundred metres to go.

A hundred and fifty.

A hundred.

TWO

0621 hours.

'Just our fucking luck, Vic.'

Victor Vowden glanced up from the Clansman PRC-320 radio set he was working on and looked at his mucker. Gary Skimm sat next to the tent, his features worked into a mean scowl as he looked out across the top of Pen y Fan. The wind tugged at the two soldiers' army smocks, stabbing them in the face. Vowden could hardly hear his mate. The wind was howling like a room full of mad women, twisting round the gullies and hitting the grass, echoing across the peak. It was an eerie noise, and Vowden could understand why some people got a bit superstitious up on the Fan.

'What's that, mate?' Vowden said, pretending to give a shit.

'This, Vic.' Skimm waved an arm across the desolate peak. 'RV duty. Fucking typical. Six hours of freezing our bollocks off while the other lads have all the fun.' He shook his head angrily and spat on the ground. 'It doesn't get much more shit than this.'

Vowden gritted his teeth and looked away. The two SAS operators were attached to the Regiment Training Wing, a unit of veteran Blades who ran Selection. SAS Selection was the world's toughest Special Forces recruitment programme. It ran twice a year and lasted for several months, pushing every soldier to the absolute limits of his physical and mental endurance. Of the two hundred or so students who applied to join the Regiment, only a handful would earn the right to wear the famous winged dagger. It was the job of the men on the Training Wing to identify and train up those few special warriors.

Vowden and Skimm had been sent up to the top of the Fan ahead of the day's selection course. A little over an hour from now, the remaining green army students would be tackling the Fan Dance, a gruelling twenty-four kilometre tab up and down the mountains. It was four hours of sheer hell, with each student having to carry a forty-five pound Bergen and a belt kit, and a blank-firing L1A1 SLR rifle. Every course up to this point had been fairly easy, but today was when the hard work really began. By the end of the day, perhaps half the students would find them-selves RTU'd, broken and blistered and physically shattered beyond belief.

Two guys from the Training Wing were required to man an RV at the midway point on the course, on top of Pen y Fan. Vowden and Skimm had arrived fifteen minutes earlier to set up the RV. It was fairly basic. There was a tent and a couple of sleeping bags for keeping warm, and extra supplies of water and a first-aid kit in case any of the students got floppy during the exercise. Once they had the comms link set up, Vowden and Skimm would radio down to the other instructors at the starting point at the bottom of the Fan and confirm that the RV was set up and ready to go. Then one of the instructors would get on the blower to Hereford and inform the Regiment HQ that they were about to release the students. Then the Fan Dance would begin.

'Anything's got to be better than this crap, Vic,' Skimm went on. 'Tell you what. I'd rather pull range duty than freeze my arse off up here.'

You'd rather be down the boozer getting pissed on the Stella, thought Vowden. He glared at his mucker. 'How about you get a brew on the go? It's colder than an eskimo's tits up here today.'

Skimm nodded and fired up the portable hexi stove, muttering under his breath. Vowden turned away, clenching his jaws in anger. Skimm had a well-earned reputation in the Regiment as a bluff-ing twat. The guy was constantly faking injuries to avoid taking the students on the big runs. He'd claim to have pulled a hammy or done his ankle in, saying that he couldn't perform and the CO would have no choice but to let him sit on an RV while the rest of the lads worked up a sweat.

Now I'm stuck up here for the next six hours with this moaning prick, thought Vowden. He wondered how this day could get any worse.

Then he looked up and saw the ramblers dissolving from the mist.

Vowden saw them approach from the edge of the peak, fifty metres away. He counted two of them. They were wearing head-to-toe Gore-Tex, and the pair of them had more layers than an onion. One of the guys was huge. He was maybe the biggest guy Vowden had ever seen. His neck was wide as a lampshade. His legs were like a pair of marble columns and his fingers were the size of Coke cans. A moment later, the second rambler swept into view. He was tall and thin with a goatee, and he was gasping for breath as he staggered the last few paces to the peak. The ramblers both celebrated as they hit the top of the Fan, punching their fists in the air as if they were doing their best Rocky Balboa impressions. Skimm shook his head and laughed.

'Look at these fucking jokers, Vic. Anyone would think they've just climbed Mount Everest.'

Vowden frowned at the ramblers. 'As long as Hilary and his Sherpa leave us alone,' he said, 'I couldn't give a toss what they think.'

Lampshade and Goatee caught their breath then trudged over to the cairn in the north-east corner of the peak. There was a small man-made pile of rocks with a National Trust marker struck on top denoting the height, 886m above sea level. The highest point in southern Britain. Vowden watched the ramblers out of the corner of his eye. Figured they were going to do what every-body did when they climbed the Fan. Pose for photographs next to the marker with the view behind them, maybe have a brew. On a clear summer's day you could see as far as the Bristol Channel to the south and Carmarthen Bay to the west. But on a foggy morning like today, the view was crap. Grey cloud and mist in every bloody direction. The ramblers had picked a bad day for a tab up the Fan.

Then Lampshade stopped in his tracks and glanced slowly around the peak, as if checking that the coast was clear. He noticed the two instructors and marched over to them, grinning.

'Morning, fellas,' Lampshade said in a gravelly accent. Cockney, thought Vowden. Or maybe Essex. 'Nice day for a stroll on the Fan, eh?'

Vowden gritted his teeth. *Here we fucking go*, he thought. There were always one or two civvies who tried chatting to the instructors and students on Selection. That was one of the problems with training in the Brecons. It was public land. Anyone could use the trails. Another problem was the firearms. Or lack of them. None of the instructors carried a weapon on Selection, and the students were only equipped with blank-firing rifles. Too much hassle, the top brass had said. Vowden disagreed. It'd only take one nutter looking to make a name for himself and the whole Regiment could be in trouble. He looked away from the rambler and fiddled with the Clansman, pretending not to have heard him.

'What's going on here, then?' Lampshade asked, stepping closer to the instructors. 'Some sort of secret SAS training, is it?'

Vowden snapped. He turned back to Lampshade and looked him hard in the eye. 'Look, mate. This is an army training exercise. So mind your own fucking business. Got it?'

Lampshade flashed his palms. 'Easy, fella. We don't want any trouble. We're just here to have a celebratory brew. We'll be on our way soon enough.' He turned to Goatee and winked at him. 'Isn't that right?'

Goatee grinned and nodded. He took off his beanie hat and wiped his forehead. The sweat was steaming off the guy's head. Literally.

'Now,' said Lampshade. 'How about that brew?' Goatee smiled back. Said nothing. Replaced his beanie hat. As he took his hand away Vowden noticed that the guy had a tattoo inked on the side of his neck. A distinctive red cross with some letters written beneath it in a language Vowden didn't understand. He wondered about that tattoo as Lampshade and Goatee both dropped to their knees and started rooting around in their daysacks. Then

Lampshade shot to his feet and turned towards the instructors, and Vowden didn't wonder any more.

Lampshade was gripping a semi-automatic in his right hand.

The pistol was a Glock 17. Every Regiment operator was trained in a wide variety of weapons, and Vowden instantly recognised the Glock from its short barrel and polymer design. He'd used the same model dozens of times on ops and down the ranges. And now he was staring at the business end of one.

Vowden froze. So did Skimm. Goatee had also whipped out a Glock. The guy was training it at Skimm's head at point blank range. The colour drained from the instructor's face. He looked like the inside of a potato.

'What the—'

Goatee fired before Skimm could finish the sentence. The pistol barked once and jerked up in his hand. A tongue of flame licked out of the snout and a round slammed into Skimm, punching a hole between his eyes big enough to drop a coin into. Skimm's head snapped back. Blood sprayed furiously out of the exit wound, flinging shattered bone and grey matter all over the place. Skimm went limp. His eyes rolled into the back of his head. Then he fell away. He was dead before he even hit the ground.

Vowden reacted in an instant. He tried to dive out of the way of the pistol. He was fast. But not fast enough to dodge a bullet. Lampshade depressed the trigger twice. In the next moment, Vowden felt something hot explode inside his chest. Like being hit by a two-ton truck. The second round smashed into his right shoulder, pulverising bone and muscle. Vowden fell back and slumped to the cold, wet ground. He tasted something warm and salty in his mouth. Blood, he realised dimly. A kind of green slime closed in around the edges of his vision. Like a camera lens closing. He could feel the blood oozing steadily out of his chest and spilling across the rocks.

Then the camera lens closed.

The bigger of the two ramblers stood over the two dead Blades for a moment and admired his handiwork. So that was what it felt like to kill an SAS operator, Bill Deeds thought. It was a good feeling, he had to admit. Right up there with the pump from a good session on the bench press, or deadlifting a new one-rep max. Better, even. Deeds smiled as he turned away from the dead men and nodded at the guy with the goatee. Markovic.

'Best do something about that,' he said, nodding at the Clansman.

Markovic nodded back. He didn't say much. None of the Serbs did. They weren't really big on conversation. Markovic quickly went to work, trashing the Clansman and ripping out the aerial. At the same time Deeds stuffed the pistols back into their daysacks and scooped up the spent bullet casings. When they were finished he took a final look around the Fan, making sure they hadn't been seen. Then he turned back to Markovic and nodded.

'Right,' said Deeds. 'Let's get a fucking move on.'

Five years, Deeds was thinking as he hurried towards the edge of the peak. Five years he'd waited to get revenge over these fuckers. The SAS had ruined his life once. Now they were going to pay. He smiled as he thought of all the proud young British soldiers who were going to die today. He imagined the bomb exploding, ripping them limb from limb, sucking their bodies inside out. He thought of all the heroes of the SAS lying in pools of blood, screaming for their mothers, and he laughed. In less than an hour the Regiment was going to find itself under attack. Deeds and the Serbs had a plan that was going to blow everybody's mind. And Bill Deeds would finally have his revenge.

He glanced at his watch as he scrabbled back down the side of the mountain.

Fifty-seven minutes to go.

Fifty-six.

Fifty-five.

THREE

It was the blisters that were going to do for him, Joe Kinsella
decided.

I can take the backbreaking tabs through the mountains carrying heavy kit. I can deal with the cold and the hunger, and the
constant exhaustion and anxiety. But if I fail Selection, it's going
to be because of these bloody blisters.

Kinsella could feel them under his training socks and boots.
He'd picked them up during the big runs through the Brecons.
Now there was a huge blister on his big toe, and Christ, it hurt
like fuck. He'd tried to treat the problem by piercing it with a
sterilised needle, but the pain was still there. He could feel it turning septic. Sooner or later he'd have to treat it properly, Kinsella
realised. Otherwise he was in danger of coming down with septi-
caemia. *And then my chances of passing Selection will be well and truly
fucked.*

He was sitting in the back of a Bedford four-tonner army
truck, along with nineteen other green army students. They sat in
cold silence as the four-tonner motored south along the A470,
heading for the starting point for the Fan Dance. Diesel engine
growling, icy wind blasting through the gaps in the canvas and
scraping at the students' faces. None of the guys had said much
since they'd pulled out of the training camp at Sennybridge half
an hour ago. Partly because it was the first week of Hills Phase,
the students mostly came from different parent units and they'd
not yet had time to bond. But mostly because they were dreading
the day's exercise.

For the past five days the students had been beasted rotten by the instructors on the Directing Staff. They had been taken on a series of big runs through the hills around the Beacons, carrying weighted Bergens and rifles. They had done sickening circuits of shuttle runs and push-ups and fireman's carries. Now they were approaching the end of the first week of the Hills Phase, and Kinsella wondered how the hell he was going to make it through the day on his rag order feet. He closed his eyes and repeated the motto that had been drummed into him during pre-Selection training in 2 Para.

Push through the pain. Close your mind to it. Remember, pain is merely weakness leaving the body.

That morning had started like any other for the hundred and fifty guys trying out for Selection. Kinsella and the others had woken up at first reveille at 0400 hours in their dilapidated barracks, the air thick with the stench of piss and sweat. After performing their morning ablutions the students had made their way over to the camp cookhouse to scoff down the vast portions of starch and grease served up by the slop jockeys. They'd returned to the billets to collect their Bergens, then headed over to the armoury to retrieve their dud SLRs using the weapon keys that had been issued to each student on arrival. Then they'd formed up into two separate groups of seventy-five men each for the morning roll call at 0600 hours.

Kinsella had stood there in the icy darkness, listening to the chief instructor's voice as he read out their names. The students all knew what was coming next. They'd been briefed on the day's exercise the previous evening, and a list of names had been posted on the guard room wall so everyone knew which group they were in. After the roll call the students had clambered into the backs of the eight Bedford four-tonners waiting to ferry them down to the Brecons. Now Kinsella could feel his stomach muscles constricting with fear and self-doubt. The endless routine of early rises, hard runs and regular beastings were starting to take their toll on the young Para. He wondered if he really had what it takes to join the hallowed ranks of the SAS.

This is it now. No going back.
Do or fucking die.

'Got a good one for you, mate.'

Kinsella popped open his eyes and looked across at his friend. Lee 'Weasel' Stubbs was a short, squat guy with a heavily knitted brow and a nose with more breaks in it than the *Guinness Book of Records*. Stubbs had joined the Paras at the same time as Kinsella. They had spent the past few years living in each other's pockets in Patrols Platoon, A Company, going out on the lash in Colchester and drinking the town dry. Stubbs was a total gun nut with a dirty sense of humour, and he was the closest thing Kinsella had to a brother. When Stubbs had announced that he planned to try out for Selection, Kinsella had decided to give it a go as well. Seeing a familiar face among the strangers helped ease the anxiety brewing in Kinsella's guts. He smiled warmly at Stubbs.

'All right, Weasel. Let's hear it.'

Stubbs rubbed his hands and grinned like a wanking Jap. The two of them had a tradition of telling each other jokes on the journey to the mountains each morning. It was something they'd started doing in 2 Para, and they found it helped take their minds off the pain they were about to suffer.

'So there's this doctor, right,' Stubbs began, chewing on a mouthful of gum. He was never without a stick or two. 'He's been shagging one of his female patients, and after a while he starts to feel proper guilty about it. He's tormented, right?'

The four-tonner bounced over another pothole in the road, shaking the troops crammed into the back. Kinsella nodded. 'Go on, mate.'

'Now this doctor, he goes to one of his mates and tells him how he's feeling. His mate looks him in the eye and says, "Don't worry. You're not the first medical practitioner to nail one of your patients and you won't be the last. You're not even married, for fuck's sake."'

Stubbs paused. A smile trembled on his lips. Kinsella waited for the punchline.

'Then the doctor speaks to the second friend. And this one tells

11

him, "You might be a doctor, but you're a veterinarian, you sick bastard.'"

Stubbs leaned back and folded his arms across his chest, looking pleased with himself.

'Well?'

Terrible, thought Kinsella.

'Terrific,' he said.

Stubbs grunted. 'Telling you, mate. I missed my calling in life. I should have gone into stand-up.'

'Yeah,' Kinsella replied, widened his smile. 'Put a wig on you and a pair of tits and you're a dead ringer for Dawn French.'

Stubbs pretended to look hurt. 'Take the mick all you want, but I'm telling you. Women like a fella who can make them laugh. I seem to remember it was yours truly who was getting the dirty looks from Becky down the King and Queen last month.'

'Becky Morgan? Sweaty Betty?' Kinsella raised an eyebrow and pulled a face. 'That's nothing to brag about, mate. She's had more pricks in her than a second-hand dartboard. Even the tide wouldn't take her out.'

The two Paras shared an easy laugh. Stubbs popped another stick of gum in his mouth, and for a moment Kinsella forgot about the hell that was waiting for them on the steep slopes of Pen y Fan.

He reminded himself that they'd both trained hard for this moment. For the past year they'd stuck rigidly to the same routine. A ten-mile run before breakfast, circuit training in the afternoons followed by thirty lengths of the swimming pool at the end of the day. In the months leading up to Selection they'd thrown in some orienteering sessions and hill reps, heading down to the Chilterns at the weekends and loading up their Bergens with heavy rocks. They'd race each other up the big hills, empty their Bergens and then scramble back down again as fast as they could. Kinsella and Stubbs were as fit as they'd ever been. The pair of them were literally glowing.

But Kinsella still felt anxious. Everything was on the line today. Fail the Fan Dance and he would be RTU'd, just another Selection hard luck story.

I won't fail. No fucking way.

I've not come this far to give up now.

Suddenly the truck slowed and the engine dialled down to a gentle hum. Kinsella tensed. We must be arriving at the starting point, he realised. Around him the other students gripped their dud rifles and sat up straight. Stubbs was chewing his gum furiously. Then the four-tonner jerked to a halt and the driver lowered the tailgate. From outside the truck Kinsella heard one of the DS guys barking at the students to 'get off the wagons', his throated voice cutting through the gloom like a chainsaw through rusted metal. Kinsella grabbed his Bergen and glanced across at Stubbs.

'You ready for this?'

'Do me a favour. I was fucking born ready.' He flashed a sly grin at Kinsella. 'Tell you what. If it doesn't work out for you today, I'll put in a good word for you when we get back to Colchester. Get Becky to give you a sympathy shag.'

Kinsella screwed up his face. 'You offering me sloppy seconds, Weasel?'

'You know me, mate. I'm all about sharing.'

They exchanged grim smiles. Then Stubbs turned and hopped down from the tailgate after the rest of the students, clutching his Bergen and his SLR. A vicious wind lashed across the blackened landscape and Kinsella felt a chill in his bones as he stepped forward. Then he took a deep breath and dropped down from the truck, ready for whatever Selection could throw at him.

FOUR

0627 hours.

Two miles to the north, a silver Ford Mondeo turned off the A470 and steered into a deserted lay-by.

Kavlak sat behind the wheel. He was the more experienced of the two men. He'd spent ten years fighting in the White Eagles Serbian paramilitary unit and he knew how to stay calm under pressure. Petrovich was the younger guy. This was his first time on the job and he sat in the front passenger seat, sweating like a one-legged man at an arse-kicking contest. His eyes constantly glanced at the rear-view mirror to check that they weren't being followed. His knees were bouncing up and down like a couple of jackhammers. The kid's nerves were understandable, Kavlak figured. After all, they were sitting on a hundred pounds of military-grade C4 high explosive.

There were six men on the op in total, five Serbs and the Brit. They had been divided into three separate teams. Bill Deeds and Sinisa Markovic were the kill team. They were tasked with knocking out the comms link at the RV on top of Pen y Fan. Two more guys were on the overwatch. Their job was to observe the target area at the Storey Arms. That left Kavlak and Petrovich. They were the third team, and they had the most dangerous job of the lot. They were the delivery team.

Kavlak killed the engine and sat back in his chair. Petrovich reached into his jacket pocket and pulled out a pack of twenty Marlboro Reds. His hands were shaking as he plucked out a cigarette from the pack and popped it between his lips. Kavlak turned to him and arched an eyebrow.

'You really think that's a good idea, nephew? Did you forget I only quit smoking last month?'

Petrovich froze. He was several years younger than Kavlak, and it showed. He was all attitude and front. He sported a mohawk and he had a young, podgy face and smooth hands that hadn't done any killing. He probably spent his downtime listening to Dr Dre, playing PlayStation and watching *Scarface*. The kid was out of his depth and Kavlak instantly knew it had been a mistake to bring him along. Realising his error, Petrovich plucked the smoke from his lips and carefully slid it back into the pack. Kavlak breathed a little easier.

'What's the time, uncle?' Petrovich asked, for maybe the thousandth time since they'd set off that morning.

'Try to relax,' said Kavlak. 'We have to wait a while yet, and you're making both of us nervous.'

Petrovich stilled his legs. Kavlak nodded at him, then looked away. Patience, Kavlak reminded himself. The kid needed patience. He was new to the game. Kavlak and the other Serbs had all been soldiers back during the dark days of the Bosnian war. That was how Kavlak got into the bomb-making business. He started off small, fixing up crude explosive mixes in the back of battered old Zastavas and blowing them up outside Croatian government offices. Then he moved on to bigger, more sophisticated devices. He car-bombed Croat leaders and terrorised their supporters. That was when the Tiger had taken notice, and asked him to be a part of a team to carry out an attack right on their enemy's doorstep. Kavlak had jumped at the chance.

The bomb stowed in the back of the Mondeo was a thing of beauty. Fifty clear-white blocks of C4 had been carefully arranged in the boot. Each block weighed 1.25 pounds and looked like a brick made out of putty. Half a dozen one-kilo bags had been placed either side of the C4. The bags were stuffed with ball bearings and eight-inch nails. Shrapnel. The explosive package was rigged with a length of det cord, thin plastic tubing that looked like rope on a washing line. Except the det cord was filled with pentaerythritol tetranitrate, otherwise known as PETN high explosive. One end of the det cord was attached to the bomb. The other end was attached to a battery cell and a radio receiver unit. The detonator was one end of a two-way walkie-talkie, purchased from a hardware store in Newport and set to the same frequency as the receiver unit. Once the remote was activated, it would transmit a signal to the receiver and spark the battery into life, sending a charge down the det cord, triggering the bomb.

It was going to be his masterpiece.

A single block of C4 packed enough of a punch to blow a hole in the side of a wall. Half a dozen blocks could destroy a large truck. Fifty blocks – equivalent to sixty-two-and-a-half pounds – would cause a hell of a bang. There would be an initial outward explosion, a huge orange fireball engulfing everything inside a twenty-five metre radius. There would be a second, even more lethal inward explosion as the gases compressed and sucked everything towards the centre. Anyone who survived that force would be caught in a shower of lethal shrapnel, hot metal shards lacerating flesh and piercing vital organs.

Kavlak smiled to himself. The soldiers wouldn't stand a chance.

He reached into his jacket pocket and dug out a Motorola C250 pre-pay handset. All the guys on the team were using them. It was a trick they'd picked up from Baltimore drug dealers. After each call they would replace the SIM card with a new one and then crush the old card, to cover their tracks. Kavlak figured it was unlikely that the authorities were listening in, but the Tiger had insisted. He didn't want any blowback. He'd been very clear about that.

There were plenty of stories about the Tiger, but Kavlak recalled one in particular. A few years ago the Tiger had learned of a snitch in his organisation. After he'd discovered the identity of the snitch, the Tiger had the man kidnapped and beaten to death. Half a dozen of his trusted lieutenants took hammers to the guy, crushing every bone in his body. When they were finished beating him to death, the Tiger ordered his men to cut up the snitch's body and feed it into a meat grinder. Then he had the minced guts served up for lunch. He ate what was left of the snitch and had the skin on his face made into a mask. It was rumoured to hang in the Tiger's study.

He was not someone Kavlak wanted to disappoint.

Kavlak selected the only number stored in the Contacts list and tapped the call button. There was a long click, followed by a series of light trills. The guy on the other end answered on the third ring.

'We're here,' said Kavlak.

There was a pause. The line hissed and crackled, like someone trying to tune in to a distant radio station. Figured, thought Kavlak. They were in rural Wales, miles from the nearest town. It was hard to get a reception. Two or three bars at least.

'Good,' the voice said at last. 'The soldiers have just arrived.'

'All of them?'

'Not yet.' Another pause. This one was longer. 'We're still waiting for the others. We'll be in touch.'

Click.

Kavlak listened to the dead air for a beat. Then he ended the call. Removed the phone battery and took out the SIM. Opened the car door, dropped the card and crushed it under the heel of his boot. Reached for the tobacco tin in his pocket and took out a new SIM. Inserted it into the back of the Motorola, replaced the battery and rested the phone on the dash. A strange calm washed over Kavlak, as it always did before the start of a mission. They'd gone through the plan maybe a thousand times. The six-man team had spent months poring over maps, calculating times and distances and preparing for every possible scenario. Nothing had been left to chance.

They were ready.

'What happens now, uncle?' Petrovich asked.

'Now,' said Kavlak, 'we wait.'

0630 hours.

Fifty minutes to go.

FIVE

John Porter watched the students as they piled out of the four-tonners into the gloom. A filthy January morning in south Wales, the wind was like ice, whipping down the side of the mountains, and Porter badly needed a drink.

The newest instructor on the Regiment Training Wing had short, dark hair and two stumps on his left hand where his index and middle fingers had once been. He was standing alongside the other half-a-dozen instructors in a car park deep in the heart of the Brecons, ten miles due south of the training camp at Sennybridge and miles from anywhere on a map. In front of them the last of the seventy-five students were spilling out of the backs of the Bedford trucks, gripping their rifles and their weighted Bergens as they prepared to tackle the Fan Dance.

The plan for the Dance was simple. The students had been split into two equal-sized groups back at Sennybridge, with half starting at points at either end of the course. The first group would begin from a wooded area several kilometres to the east of Pen y Fan, not far from the Roman road and the old railway station at Torpantau. The second group would set off from a sandstone trail next to a two-storey building across the road from where Porter was standing. The Storey Arms had once been a café, then a youth hostel. Now it stood empty. Each student's Bergen would be checked for weight. Then they would be split into groups of roughly twenty with their own instructor. Then it was simply up to the students to make sure they kept pace with their instructor during the race up and down the mountain. The Fan Dance was a race against the clock, and against their own limits of endurance.

Porter's group would be leaving first. They would also be joined by half the SP Team, the Regiment's specialist counter-terrorism unit. It was something of a tradition for a few of the SP lads to join in on the Fan Dance. The tab was a good way of maintaining their fitness, and it helped to alleviate the boredom of sitting around Hereford all day waiting for the phone to ring. According to the briefing yesterday afternoon, the SP team lads would RV with the rest of the guys at the Storey Arms at 0640 hours.

My first time leading the students on the Fan Dance, thought Porter. *I'm supposed to be the pride of the Regiment. I should be setting an example to these lads, and all I can think about is my next fucking drink.*

'Get in a line, fellas!' Terry Monk, one of the other instructors, shouted. Monk had been in the Training Wing since the invention of the wheel, and it showed. His face was worn and cracked and rugged, and he had a smile so straight you could strike a cricket ball with it. 'Two ranks deep! Have your Bergens placed in front of you ready for inspection. Get a move on! This is Selection, not some stroll in the park.'

'Lambs to the fucking slaughter, boys,' the chief instructor chuckled, smiling cruelly as the students dragged their knackered bodies over. 'Look at these useless cunts.'

Porter glanced at the chief instructor. Bob McCanliss had a face with more creases in it than an old shirt, and a large birth-mark on his right cheek that resembled a burn mark. Porter had only transferred to the Training Wing a month earlier, joining on a two-year cycle from Mobility Troop. But he'd seen enough already to know that Bob McCanliss was a sadistic bastard.

Most of the instructors knew there was no point being too hard on the students. The bar was already set very high on Selection. Sometimes not even a single student passed. The bar didn't need to be set any higher. It was the instructors' job to select the best men available for the Regiment, and over a period of months guide them through an intense process that would turn some of them from highly capable squaddies into elite operators in the world's leading SF unit.

But some of the instructors acted like glorified drill sergeants. Guys like McCanliss.

Everyone in the Training Wing knew McCanliss had failed Selection at the first time of asking. Fifteen years ago. He'd thrown in the towel. Voluntarily rapped out midway through Selection. He'd tried the next year and passed, but McCanliss couldn't escape the reputation he earned from quitting first time round. They had a special name in the Regiment for guys who chucked in the towel on Selection. *Retreads.* The other Blades had a deep suspicion of retreads. Being an operator was about more than being fit and tough and dedicated. It was about your state of mind. That was the difference between a Blade and a regular squaddie. The guys in the Regiment never quit. They kept going, even when their bodies were screaming at them to stop. The thought of giving up never entered their minds.

Unlike the retreads.

Unlike Bob McCanliss.

Now a retread was running Selection and taking out his rage on the students. McCanliss seemed to think it was his personal mission in life to fail as many of the students as possible. Porter didn't know why. Maybe he thought it added an extra inch to his dick by fucking with the students at every opportunity. On the big runs and circuits the chief instructor beasted them rotten, punishing them mercilessly and generally messing with their minds. They hated his guts.

So did Porter.

'Worst fuckers we've ever had on Selection, this lot,' McCanliss continued in disgust as the students got into line. He looked to the other instructors, rubbing his hands in anticipation. 'I wonder how many of these pricks we'll fail today, eh, lads? At least half, I reckon.'

Porter clenched his jaw as the students formed into a line two ranks deep. He fought a powerful urge to slog McCanliss in the guts. There was tension hanging in the air as Porter ran his eyes across the line of students. Some of the young guys stared anxiously at the forbidding mountains. Others were deep in thought. The atmosphere reminded Porter of the moments before the start of the Grand National. Everyone was tense and bristling with nervous energy. Everyone dreading the pain they were to suffer, but at the same time just wanting to get on with it.

I know the feeling. I was in their boots once.

Eleven years ago Porter had tried out for Selection, passing at the first attempt. Eleven years, but sweet Jesus, it felt more like a lifetime. Back then he'd been a promising young Blade with a loving wife and a newborn baby girl, and a glorious career in the Regiment ahead of him.

Then Beirut had happened, and everything had gone south.

McCanliss cleared his throat and addressed the students.

'Right, lads. This is what's going to happen. Once your Bergens have been checked for weight, you'll be given a colour. That's your group. Staff Porter's group will be leaving first.' He glanced at Porter, shot him a genuine fuck-you. 'Your starting point is that red telephone box.'

He pointed across the empty road at the Storey Arms, thirty metres away. The place looked like a low-grade European youth hostel. A Welsh flag fluttered in the breeze outside and a sign outside read, 'Canoflan Y Bannau. The Storey Arms Centre.' The two Land Rovers the instructors had driven down from Sennybridge were parked up outside the white-walled buildings. The Training Wing CO sat in one of the Landies, working the radio and trying to establish a link with the RV at the top of Pen y Fan.

To the left of the Storey Arms stood a public phone box and an old stile and a waist-high stone wall. Next to the wall was a sandstone trail that snaked up the side of the mountain, twisting through heather and long grass. The starting point of the Fan Dance.

'The course completion time is four hours ten minutes,'

McCanliss went on. 'You lucky bastards get the extra ten minutes because it's Winter Selection. Be back at that gate with your DS in exactly that time, or under. Anyone who comes in late, even by a minute, tough shit. You're binned.'

McCanliss searched the students' eyes. They were staring apprehensively at the gate. He cleared his throat and continued.

'Your Bergens will be weighed throughout the course. So any smart fuckers thinking of trying to empty their Bergens along the way, don't even try. Anyone found to be in possession of an underweight Bergen will be given one of these beauties.'

The chief instructor hefted up a rock he'd been holding. It was the size of a brick. He raised it high above his head, so all the students could get a good look at it. McCanliss's expression suddenly darkened and he fixed his gaze on a stocky student in the front rank. Porter recognised the lad. Stubbs. The instructors were constantly making notes on the students, identifying the ones who had the qualities necessary for thriving in the SAS. Stubbs had it in spades. And now McCanliss was glowering at him with obvious rage.

Silence fluttered across the car park as McCanliss stepped towards the student. The chief instructor narrowed his eyes to knife slits. His facial muscles twitched, as they always did when he was on the verge of losing his rag.

'What the fuck was that?' he snarled.

Stubbs blinked. 'Staff?'

'Did you just drop a piece of litter, Stubbsy?'

Stubbs glanced around him. Swallowed hard. 'No, staff.'

McCanliss simmered. His face twitched horribly. 'Calling me a liar, is it?' He pointed to a foil chewing gum wrapper on the tarmac. 'What the fuck do you call that, then?' He stepped closer to the student. 'Is that what you do on an op, Stubbsy? Be scruffy and leave signs all over the fucking place? Sacking offence that, Stubbsy.'

Stubbs's mouth opened and shut but no words came out. Around him the other students shifted anxiously on their feet. McCanliss glared at Stubbs and pointed to the ground.

'Cunt,' he hissed. 'Get in the position, and don't stop until I say so.'

Stubbs opened his mouth to protest. Then he thought better of it and reluctantly dropped to the ground and started banging out the push-ups. At the same time McCanliss swivelled his gaze towards the other students, his eyes burning with hatred.

'Which one of you dopey wankers saw Stubbsy drop that litter, then?' No one spoke. McCanliss's face shaded red. The veins on his neck bulged like tense rope. 'None of you? Right, either you're all blind or you're not fucking alert. You can't be half asleep in the Regiment. This is the SAS not the fucking Boy Scouts. Get in the position right now. All of you.'

The other seventy-four students grudgingly hit the deck. One or two shot angry stares at Stubbs. Then McCanliss gave his back to the students, smiling with satisfaction. He nodded at Terry Monk.

'Do us a favour, Terry. Once these cunts get to fifty, get 'em on their feet and weigh their Bergens. I need to check in with the CO. See if we've heard anything from those two idiots at the RV yet.'

As he shaped to turn away McCanliss caught Porter eyeballing him. The chief instructor turned towards him. He shot Porter a look like he was sucking on a bag of dicks.

'The fuck are you looking at, Porter?'

Porter shrugged. 'I thought the idea was to pass people on Selection, Bob. Not fail them all.'

McCanliss said nothing for a beat. His facial muscles twitched.

'Did you, now?' he spat. 'Well, I've got some fucking news for you, Porter. We're not here to have tea and biscuits with these tossers.'

'We're not here to fuck with them either, Bob.'

McCanliss glowered at him. Porter stood his ground. The chief instructor stepped closer. The veins on his neck threatened to explode. He dropped his voice so low it could have crawled under the belly of a snake.

'I'll tell you something, Porter. Even the worst of these pricks would make a better operator than you. I wonder what our

Keith would have said, if he'd heard you were on the Training Wing.'

Something like a knife moved through Porter. The memories came flooding back, stabbing at him. *Beirut, 1989.* A hostage rescue op. Porter's first mission after he'd finished continuation training. A British businessman called Kenneth Bratton had been taken hostage by Hezbollah operatives demanding missile systems in exchange for his release. The government refused to negotiate and called in the Regiment to sort out the mess. The mission should have been a straightforward evacuation job, but it had quickly descended into a giant clusterfuck. In the sweat and chaos of the firefight Porter had spared the life of one of the Arabs guarding the Brit hostage. A kid, no older than twelve or thirteen. Instead of slotting him, Porter had knocked the kid unconscious.

Only the kid hadn't stayed down. Minutes later he was back on his feet and putting down rounds on the rest of the team. Three good Blades had died that day. Steve Rashford. Mike Jones. Keith Dunleavy. Porter had blood on his hands. Regiment blood. The kind you could never wash away.

Every now and then Porter saw their faces. Sometimes it was nothing more than a flash of blood. Other days he'd see their brains splattered across the windshield, or their twisted bodies lying slumped in the streets in Hereford. So he turned to the bottle to block out the nightmares. Self-medicating, Regiment-style. On a good day he took a bottle of Bushmills to numb the pain. On the bad days, he needed two. He'd managed to hide his drinking from the other lads, but Porter knew he couldn't keep it up for much longer. He was struggling to hold it together.

'You're nothing but a cunt,' McCanliss hissed at Porter under his breath. 'A sad, washed-up old cunt with two missing fingers. Our Keith would be turning in his grave if he knew you were on the team.'

Porter suddenly exploded. He grabbed McCanliss and took him to one side and shot the instructor a cold, hard look. He spoke in a low voice so the students wouldn't overhear the two Blades arguing.

'Listen, you fucking retread. Mention Beirut again and I'll knock you back to that time you were on easy duty, sitting in that nice comfy office while we were out doing the proper ops. Got it?'

McCanliss twitched with rage. Porter had hit a nerve and he knew it. The guy had avoided seeing action in Iraq and Bosnia. He'd spent his career on the sidelines while the other lads got all the glory, and that niggled McCanliss. The chief instructor simmered, but kept his fists by his sides. There was no way he'd lash out. Not in front of the students. He stepped into Porter's face and scowled.

'Don't forget who you're fucking talking to, Porter.'

Porter smiled. 'Is that a threat, Bob?'

McCanliss simmered. 'Nah. It's an invitation. After the Fan Dance. I'll see you in the gym. Me and you'll sort it out then. I'll drop you so fucking hard you'll be pissing blood for the next month.'

'A retread with a pair of balls on him. Got to be a first, that.'

Porter released his grip and turned away from McCanliss before the guy could get another word in. He'd taken enough shit from the chief instructor for one day. McCanliss didn't know what he'd gone through. None of the lads did. He'd been put in a sticky situation that day in Beirut. *If I'd slotted the Arab kid, I would have been prosecuted for war crimes for killing a minor. I had no fucking choice.* Bottom line, it was down to Porter to live with his inner demons. But he wasn't putting up with anyone else passing judgement on him. And definitely not some jumped-up retread who'd been sipping coffee in a nice warm office while the other guys in the squadron had risked their lives.

McCanliss beat a quick path over to the Landies, glancing back at Porter and starring daggers at him. Terry Monk ordered the students to their feet and stepped towards the first guy in the line, holding out a set of handheld scales. He handed the student the scales. The lad attached the hook to his Bergen and hefted it up. Monk checked the weight, making sure he was within the regulation limits. Then he took the scales and moved onto the next guy in line. At the same time one of the other instructors set up a tea urn in the corner of the car park.

It started to rain. Porter looked up and squinted at the clouds. They were black and low and heavy, like bulging sacks of coal about to split down the middle. It was going to piss it down this morning, Porter realised. That icy January rain that cut right through to your bones.

SIX

0641 hours.

Nine minutes later, the twelve guys on the SP team arrived at the Storey Arms.

They pulled up in three civvy Range Rovers they'd driven down from the Regiment HQ. Engines chainsawing, headlamps burning in the bleak winter light. The Range Rovers skidded to a halt close to the four-tonners at the far end of the car park, twenty metres downstream from the students. A few moments later, the twelve operators climbed out from the motors and grabbed their helium-filled Bergens from the backs of the Range Rovers. They were decked out in a mixture of civvy and army clothing, and each of them was packing a Sig Sauer P226 semi-automatic pistol strapped to a thigh holster. Among the operators was a Jock with a shock of prematurely greying hair. He wore a deep frown and small, dark eyes that peered out at the world as if from behind a veil of cigarette smoke. John Bald, the meanest Blade in the Regiments, was spitting mad. And it was all Eddie Stoop's fault.

Twenty-four hours ago Bald had been looking forward to his first training exercise as assault team commander on the Red half of the SP Team. The Regiment's counter-terrorist unit was split into two groups of equal size, Blue and Red. The Blue guys were the three-hour response team. That meant they had to be rolling through the gates at Hereford within three hours of a terrorist incident being reported. Blue had the guys from Mountain and Air Troop. Red was the thirty-minute team. Their guys came from Boat and Mobility Troop. Both teams regularly trained at the Killing House down at Pontrilas, a multi-storey mock-up building that the SAS used to practise deliberate action drills using live rounds. Bald had been desperate for his first op at the Killing House to run smoothly. And then Eddie Stoop had gone and fucked things up.

Stoop had been fooling around with the wife of one of the other guys on the team, Bill Bowen. Nailing another Blade's missus was a big no-no in the Regiment, for obvious reasons. Blades operated in tight-knit groups. The last thing you needed was one guy holding a grudge against someone else on the same team. Eddie Stoop found that out the hard way. He'd taken a round to the back of the head during the training exercise. Bowen had put the drop on him, claiming that Stoop had stepped into his line of fire. Which Bald knew was bullshit, but there was no way of proving it either way.

Red Team had been suspended, pending an internal investigation. And now Bald was being hung out to dry. His first test as assault commander had gone south. Big-time.

'Good morning for the Dance, eh, Jock?' the operator next to Bald said, grinning inanely. Bald turned and glared at him. Steve Stoner was a burly Sheffield lad with a permanent smile plastered across his mug, and an easygoing manner that really pissed Bald off. Stoner was the kind of guy who could find the silver lining in any cloud. Even when those clouds were grey as fuck and it was pissing it down across the Brecon Beacons.

'If you say so,' said Bald.

He sighed and shook his head. He'd only agreed to join in with the Blue Team guys on the Fan Dance to clear his head after yesterday's shitstorm. But as the skies turned grey as coal and the icy rain stabbed him in the face, Bald was starting to think that this was a really bad idea.

Should've stayed at home, John. Stayed away from Stoner and the other twats. They'll be gloating over your failure. Taking the piss out of you.

They passed the students. Some of the guys glanced in awe at the veteran Blades in their midst. Bald just ignored them and strolled on.

Stoner nodded at the students and said, 'McCanliss had better go easy on these lads this morning. Can't push the students too hard in these conditions, Jock. One of 'em might come down with hypothermia.'

Bald shrugged. 'Yeah, well. Nature's way of saying you've failed Selection.'

'You're a mean bastard, Jack.'

'Someone's go to be.'

They beat a path across the tarmac towards the instructors. Half a dozen of them were standing in a loose group around the tea urn, helping themselves to steaming hot brews. Among them Bald noticed a vaguely familiar face. Noticed the two stumps on the guy's left hand. Bald then did a double-take. Turned to Stoner.

'Christ,' said Bald. 'Is that Porter? What's he doing here'

Stoner nodded. 'Didn't you hear? He transferred to the Training Wing a few weeks ago.'

'Fuck me sideways. He's aged a lot.'

And he had, thought Bald. The last time he'd seen Porter the pair of them had been on an op in Serbia. Just over half the squadron had been deployed to the region during the Bosnian war, wearing UN berets and armed with SA80 rifles to blend in with the regular squaddie units. Their orders had been to hit the paramilitary units that had been propping up Milosevic's regime, slaughtering Muslims in the surrounding villages. That had been almost eighteen months ago. Bald hadn't seen him since.

'He looks like crap,' said Bald. 'Like a five-pound shit stuffed inside a one-pound sack.'

'His missus just left him,' Stoner explained. 'Took his kid and all. Word around Hereford is that he's been hitting the bottle. Big-time. I'm surprised the guy's keeping it together.'

Bald gritted his teeth. 'He shouldn't be on the Training Wing, then. You've got to be fit as fuck to lead those lads on the big runs. How's he going to handle the workload, looking like that? I've taken shits that are in better shape than him.'

Stoner said nothing. Bald strolled on, clenching his jaws and shaking his head. He had zero sympathy for guys like Porter. As far as he was concerned, whenever life kicked you off the log you dusted yourself down and climbed right back on it. No matter how many times, no matter what. When you cut through all the bullshit, that was what being a Blade was all about. Refusing to give in. Sitting around and feeling sorry for yourself, that was for posh housewives in Surrey, and the French.

'Morning, lads,' Bob McCanliss said, greeting the SP team guys as they marched over to the tea urn. 'Good to have you along for the stroll.'

The chief instructor took a sip of his brew and turned to Bald. His lips parted into a wicked grin. He arched his eyebrows, feigning surprise.

'Wasn't expecting to you see here this morning, Jock. Thought you might be resting up a bit after that nasty business down the Killing House.'

Bald gave a shrug of his broad shoulders. Stared at McCanliss. 'Yeah, well. Thought I'd come down here and clear my head on the Fan. Get away from all the paperwork. You know how it is.'

'I do, John, I do.' McCanliss was still grinning. There was a gleam in his eyes that made Bald angry. 'Still, it's a bloody shame what happened yesterday with poor Eddie. Fucking tragic, that.'

'Accidents happen,' said Bald. Blood boiling in his veins.

McCanliss made a face. 'Accident now, was it? I heard different, Jock. I heard that Eddie was slinging one up Bowen's missus. So Bowen gave him a bullet for his troubles. That's what I heard.'

'You know what they say. Don't believe everything you hear, Bob.'

McCanliss smiled. Bald felt a compulsive desire to rearrange his face. He somehow stood his ground and composed his features. 'Sure, Jock, sure. Still, if it wasn't an accident, it served Eddie fucking right. You don't fool around with another Blade's bird. First rule of the Regiment, that.' His smile twitched at the corners. 'Just a shame you'll take the fall for what happened. Real shame.'

Bald kept his lips pressed shut. The voice picked at the base of his skull. The one telling him he should've stayed at home. Now he was having to put up with McCanliss's shit. 'It was an accident,' he said woodenly. 'Nothing more than that.'

'You daft cunt,' McCanliss said. He chuckled heartily. 'Try telling that to the CO when they're done with their investigation. The top brass will need a scapegoat, and guess who's neck'll be on the line? Yours, Jock. Yours.'

McCanliss laughed again. Before Bald could reply, a figure marched briskly over to the instructors from the direction of the Landies parked outside the Storey Arms. Bald recognised him as the CO of the Training Wing. Cameron Borthwick had a face like a freshly polished pair of leather brogues, and a nose as' wide as a wind tunnel. With his heavily furrowed brow and reddened cheeks, he looked more like an Oxbridge Latin scholar than a soldier. Borthwick cleared his throat and looked at each of the instructors in turn.

'Gents,' he said too loudly, as if he was addressing a lecture hall of students rather than a few hardened Blades. 'I'm afraid we have a problem.'

'What's that, boss?' McCanliss asked.

'We're still unable to establish contact with our chaps at the RV. We've been trying for the past fifteen minutes, and there's still no answer.'

'What the fuck are they doing up there?' Terry Monk wondered aloud. 'Inventing a longer-lasting light bulb?'

Porter scratched his cheek. 'Radio's probably knackered. You know what those Clansmans are like. About as reliable as a Nigerian bank account.'

'Either that,' McCanliss offered, stroking his face. 'Or one of those twats has fallen into a ditch and broken a leg. Wouldn't put it past those two jokers.'

Borthwick considered. 'Unlikely. If that was the case, one of them would have radioed down for help, surely?' He shook his head firmly. 'No. Porter's right. It's far more likely to be a technical problem of some kind.'

'What's to be done, then?' McCanliss asked.

Borthwick pursed his lips. 'I'm sure you're all familiar with the protocol. I'm not authorised to release the students until we have the all-clear from the RV. There's only one thing for it. One of you will have to go up and investigate. Find out what's happened and sort out the Clansman so we can get things moving at this end.'

'Go up?' Porter asked, incredulous. 'An extra trek up and down that bastard?'

Borthwick shrugged. 'It's either that, or we sit here and wait for Vowden and Skimm to establish contact, or return from the RV. Which could be hours. And I don't particularly want all the students standing around in the cold. Especially after what happened last year.'

Everyone nodded grimly. An officer had died during the previous Winter Selection. Bald remembered the shitstorm that had caused at Whitehall at the time. The guy had gotten separated from the main group during the Long Drag, and died of hypothermia. Mountain rescue had discovered his corpse on the frozen mountain days later. There had been a media leak. Questions had been asked. The Regiment top brass was already coming under pressure to change some of Selection's practices, such as forcing the students to forage for their own drinking water once they ran out, and no one wanted a repeat in case the Whitehall pen-pushers tried to make Selection easier.

'Well?' Borthwick continued, searching each instructor's face in turn. 'Any volunteers?'

No one offered a hand. Which wasn't exactly a surprise. Trudging up the Fan, sorting out the RV and possibly having to fix a knackered Clansman was going to be a royal pain in the arse, Bald figured.

Suddenly McCanliss's eyes lit up and he turned to Borthwick. 'Porter should go, boss,' he said. 'He's new to the Training Wing. He could do with putting a few more miles in his legs.'

Borthwick swivelled his arrogant gaze towards Porter. 'Well, man? What's your answer?'

Bald looked at Porter. The guy was wrestling with the decision. He clearly didn't fancy it, but McCanliss had called him out in front of the other lads. There was no way Porter could turn him down without looking like he was trying to cry off his duties.

'Fine, boss,' he said at last. 'I'll do it.'

Borthwick clapped his hands and nodded stiffly. 'Good man. You'll need one of the other lads to go with you, of course, in case one of your fellow instructors is injured.' He creased his smooth brow. 'But we're two men short as it is. We really can't afford to spare another instructor or we won't have enough men to begin the exercise.'

He looked around at the guys. Waiting for a response. Bald thought for a moment. Then he stepped forward. 'Fuck it, I'll go.'

'Excellent, Jock!' Borthwick exclaimed. He cleared his throat and looked at Porter and Bald in turn. 'Right, then. Leave at once. And for God's sakes hurry. I don't want to leave the students waiting here for a moment longer than necessary. Got it?'

The CO nodded at the two Blades before turning on his heels and marching back over to the Landies. McCanliss followed in his wake like an obedient dog. Terry Monk made his way over to the students and barked at them to sit down on their Bergens and help themselves to a brew while they waited. Porter turned to Bald.

'Ready, mate?'

'The excitement's killing me,' said Bald.

The two Blades set their Bergens down and beat a quick path across the main road. A fierce wind picked up as they approached the old red telephone box fifteen metres to the left of the Storey Arms, driving the rain into their faces. Bald shook his head angrily.

'Wait till we find Vowden and Skimm,' he snarled. 'I'm gonna give the pair of them a slap for making us go up this bastard.'

Porter turned to him and smiled. 'Thought you wanted to clear your head, Jock?'

'Did I fuck.' Bald made a face and spat on the ground. 'I just wanted to get away from that twat McCanliss. Ten seconds longer round that wanker and I'd have given him a Glasgow kiss. With fucking bells on.'

Porter suddenly stopped in his tracks a few metres before the phone box and the start of the trail. His eyes were drawn to the first floor of the main Storey Arms building. Something moved in the third window from the left. A glimmer. A fleeting shadow. It was there one second and gone the next.

'I thought that place was supposed to be empty over the winter,' said Porter.

Bald grunted. 'Yeah? So?'

Porter didn't reply. He looked back to the window. In the summer the Storey Arms was an outdoor education centre. School kids and youth groups stayed in the dormitories while they earned their Duke of Edinburgh certificates in basic rock-climbing and white-water rafting. But over Christmas, the building stood empty. Or at least, it usually did. As far as he knew. *So who the fuck did I just see in the window?*

Bald scanned the window. Shrugged. 'I don't see anything.'

'It was just there. I definitely saw something, Jock.'

'Maybe they've got the cleaners in?'

Bald shrugged again. Porter could tell what he was thinking. It's the drink. He's hallucinating. *The drunken old bastard's seeing things.* Maybe he's got a point, Porter conceded. Maybe my mind is playing tricks. All that booze is finally catching up with me. *Christ, I'm starting to lose the plot.*

Bald said, 'Let's get a move on. The sooner we get up the Fan, the quicker we can get this shite sorted.'

He turned away and headed for the stile next to the phone box, arms swinging. Porter hesitated for a moment, still searching the windows. Looking for the shadow. But he couldn't see anything. He looked away. Then he turned and followed Bald up the trail.

SEVEN

Stankovic watched the two Blades disappear from sight.

'They're gone,' he said. 'Back to work.'

Dragan crept back towards the window. The two Serbs resumed their task of observing the crowd of soldiers across the car park. The Serbs weren't using telescopes or military optics to watch their targets. There was no need. They were less than fifty metres from the car park, kneeling in front of a south-facing window on the first floor of the Storey Arms. The dormitory room looked like a cheap imitation of a Swiss chalet, but it offered them a perfect vantage point. From their position Stankovic and Dragan had an unobstructed view of the students and the instructors lining up on the other side of the road.

They'd moved into position two hours ago, in the dead hours. Something they had learned during their time in the army. The best time to carry out an attack is 0400 hours. Statistically, most people were likely to be asleep then. Too early for the early-risers, too late for everyone else.

Breaking into the building had been easy enough. The Storey Arms was closed over Christmas and the place was empty except for the on-site housekeeper, a balding man in his fifties with a bad leg who got free accommodation in lieu of a salary. He lived alone, in the smaller house to the side of the Storey Arms. Dragan had knocked on the door while Stankovic waited in the shadows to the side, a Glock 17 semi-automatic in his right hand. A knock on a door in the middle of the Brecons usually meant one thing: someone was in trouble on the mountains. So the housekeeper had been quick to answer the door, even at gone four in the morning. He hadn't suspected a thing. Not until he cracked open the door. Then Stankovic stepped out of the darkness and put the Glock to the side of his skull and pulled the trigger. He'd dumped the housekeeper's body in the crappy kitchen at the back of the house while Dragan grabbed the keys to the main building and disabled the alarm system. The whole operation had taken less than three minutes.

Then they went to work.

The overwatch team had a simple job. OP the soldiers and relay int to the guys on the delivery team. Movements, timings, anything unusual. They were also looking for the optimum place to park the bomb. It was a job they were ideally suited to. Both Stankovic and Dragan had trained as army snipers back in the day. They had plenty of experience of lying prone for hours on end, doing nothing but observing the enemy. They were four hours in and so far, everything had gone according to plan.

'Students sitting down on their Bergens,' Stankovic reported. 'Distance, thirty-five metres. Time, six-thirty-six hours.'

Dragan made a note and said, 'What are you going to do? With the money?'

The Tiger had promised each man on the team a reward on completion of the job. Half a million dollars, American. Stankovic took a swig of Red Bull and kept his eyes on the students.

'I haven't decided yet. You?'

'Miami,' Dragan replied without a moment's hesitation. 'I'm gonna move to Miami. House on the beach, a boat, pussy. All that shit. Man, I'm gonna live like a fucking king.'

Stankovic nodded but said nothing. He'd heard it all before. Dragan was always going on about moving to Florida. The guy had a peculiar fascination with America. Peculiar, because America was the enemy. But Dragan had found some way to separate it inside his head. He followed basketball and wore Nike Air Jordans and smoked Lucky Strikes. Ever since they'd started preparing for the mission, he'd been obsessed by the whole Miami thing. Personally, Stankovic thought it was dangerous to think too far ahead.

They'd planned the attack meticulously, but there was always the chance that something might go wrong. He didn't want to tempt fate.

The bomb would do the heavy lifting. Some of the guys had been in favour of a gun attack, but bombs were more terrifying and would give the two of them a better chance of escaping unscathed. The car bomb would detonate at 0720 hours, cutting down most of the soldiers. Then the team would switch to the second phase of the attack. Stankovic and Dragan had a stack of weaponry laid out on the tables in the staff kitchen downstairs, all of it sourced from the old Yugoslav army. Half-a-dozen AK-47 assault rifles, Glock 17 semi-automatic pistols chambered for the 9x19mm Parabellum cartridge, plus a box of hand grenades and six sets of Kevlar body armour.

The weapons had been smuggled into the UK the same way as the C4 explosives, secreted inside a hidden compartment in a knackered old Polish van they had driven over from Rotterdam via the car ferry. Once they'd passed through customs the Serbs had motored west to the meeting point, an old stone cottage outside Crickhowell, several miles due east of the Brecons. No one at the rental office had raised any eyebrows about six out-of-towners renting the cottage for the week. After all, this was rambling country. It wasn't unusual for groups of hikers to base themselves in a cottage while they explored the mountains. Happened all the time.

Once they had arrived at the cottage, the Serbs had ripped apart the van, retrieving the weapons and the explosives hidden inside the panelling. They'd spent the past three days fine-tuning the plan and recceing the area, running through the plan one last time. The timing was critical, Stankovic knew. As soon as the bomb went off, they'd have approximately eight minutes until the first emergency responders arrived on the scene. There wasn't a whole lot of margin for error.

Their getaway vehicle was a white Ford Transit van parked up at the side of the Storey Arms, with the name of a fake maintenance company splashed down the side. If anyone strolled past and noticed the van, they'd assume the housekeeper had called in the plumbers for an emergency job over the holidays. Once the attack had gone down, they'd ride the van to an abandoned iron-works on the outskirts of Merthyr Tydfil, ten miles to the south of the Storey Arms. Then they'd change up vehicles, torching the Transit and switching to a couple of Vauxhall Astras with clean plates. From Merthyr it was an eighty-mile drive west to the port at Fishguard and a ferry across the Irish Sea to Rosslare. By the time the security forces were getting their shit together, Stankovic and the other guys would be flying out of Dublin airport.

The rain was now falling in a constant dull rhythm, greying the land. Big drops were spattering against the window, sliding like melted gelatine down the glass. Stankovic looked on as the students sat down on their Bergens in a wide circle in the middle of the car park, twenty metres away from the four army trucks. He smiled to himself.

Everything was going according to plan.

'Time?' he asked.

'Six-forty-five,' Dragan said.

Stankovic nodded. Thirty-five minutes to go.

EIGHT

The mist was rolling down like spray from a wave as Porter and Bald tabbed up the mountain. The cold scraped like knives against their faces, tugging at their windproof smocks and needling their bones. Fifteen minutes after they'd set off up the trail and Porter could literally feel the booze sweating out of him. His throat was drier than a Mormon wedding. The thumping inside his skull was relentless. But he kept going. In spite of his heavy drinking he had a decent level of fitness from going on the big runs on the Training Wing, and the old muscles were soon working overtime as the two Blades pushed on up the steep and rugged slopes.

The first kilometre had been steady uphill work, rising on a sharp incline past a densely wooded area to their right before it dropped down to a grassy valley with a small stream running across it. The ground around the Blaen Taf Fawr was scattered with damp, slippery rocks and the air was thick with the smell of fresh heather and churned mud. There was no one else about, Porter saw. Not at this hour. There was nothing but a dull stretch of wet rock and tufts of long, brownish grass.

No sign of Vowden and Skimm.

They're probably on the top of the Fan. Clansman's probably shafted. All this way for a poxy radio.

He thought back to McCanliss. He'd have to deal with the chief instructor after the Fan Dance. Porter had already been looking forward to beating the crap out of McCanliss. But now he had an extra motivation to hurry up and get back down to the

Storey Arms. Porter would bide his time until the Fan Dance was over. *Then I'm going to batter the cunt.*

Bald was blowing hard. He blinked sweat out of his eyes, his face shading red with the strain. In the Regiment, everyone blows in different ways. There were the greyhounds, the guys who were superfit and lean and could run for hours without breaking into a sweat. And then there were the bigger guys like Bald. The ones who were more muscular, but who struggled more when it came to the runs. But they kept going. They kept pushing. Because they were Blades, not retreads like Bob fucking McCanliss. Because it wasn't in their nature to quit.

'Fuck's sake,' Bald gasped. 'It's true what they say. No matter how many times you climb this bastard, it never gets any easier.'

Porter grinned. 'You've been hitting the weights down the gym too hard, Jock. Should've worked on your cardio a bit.'

Bald glared at his mucker and caught his ragged breath. 'That's rich coming from you, mate. The only thing you've been lifting is a whisky bottle to your lips. Christ, I can smell your breath from here.'

'I had a few jars last night,' Porter replied.

'A few shelves, more like.' Bald snorted and shook his head. 'Sod it. A few hours from now I'll be getting shitfaced too. Smudge Staunton is having his leaving do tonight down the Newmarket Arms. Half the Regiment's gonna be there. I could do with a drink after that shite at the Killing House.'

Porter frowned. 'What really happened up there, Jock?'

Bald paused again in his tracks. He stared levelly at Porter. 'It was an accident.'

'But if something did happen . . .'

'It didn't, all right?' Bald snapped. 'But that prick McCanliss is right. The top brass are looking for a scapegoat. Someone to hang this mess on. My arse is on the line here, mate.' He fell silent for a beat as the two Blades moved on up the trail. 'Maybe I should take a leaf out of Smudge's book. Get out of Hereford before the CO gives me the boot. Cash in my chips and go on the Circuit.'

Porter looked at his mucker. 'That's what Smudge is going to do?'

'Too fucking right,' said Bald. 'He's got himself a gig down at Templar, the lucky sod.'

Porter listened keenly. Templar. The name vaguely rang a bell. He'd heard of them somewhere before. A secretive PMC based down in swish Mayfair, headed up by an elusive former CO of the Regiment by the name of Marcus Keppel. Templar was big money. Or so Porter had heard.

'Ten grand a month,' Bald said between erratic draws of breath. 'That's what Smudge reckons he'll be on at Templar. Think about it, mate. Ten large. That's some proper wedge. Way more than we'll ever earn if we stick around Hereford.'

Porter cast a doubtful look at Bald. 'You'd really turn your back on the Regiment?'

'For that kind of money, I'd turn my back on my own mother.' Porter opened his mouth to reply but Bald quickly threw up a hand. 'Before you get started, don't give me all that crap about loyalty. The top brass don't know the fucking meaning of the word. I should know, after what those pricks did to me in Belfast.'

There was a dangerous gleam in his cold blue eyes as he spoke. Porter nodded and said nothing. He knew about Belfast. All the Blades did. A few years back Bald had crossed the Irish border, risking his life to rescue an MI5 handler who'd been kidnapped by the Notting Squad, the IRA's internal security unit. The illegal crossing had very nearly triggered an international incident, and instead of being congratulated on saving the handler's life, Bald had been severely reprimanded by the head shed. His actions had turned him into a pariah and almost cost him his career.

'Maybe I'll join you at Templar,' Porter said with a smile. 'Maybe it's time for us both to get out.'

'You'll have to sort your breath out first,' Bald said. 'Jesus, mate. You could strip the paint off the Sistine Chapel with breath like that.'

Porter looked away. Hated to admit it, but Bald was right. His drinking was out of control. He'd hit the bottle soon after Beirut.

The CO had ordered him to take six months' leave. Officially it was to allow Porter to decompress and recover from his injuries. Unofficially, he was being blackballed. On his return to Hereford there had been a clear-the-air meeting and Porter had been exonerated of any blame. Killing children was against the Geneva Convention and there was nothing the top brass could do. But that didn't stop the accusing looks from the other Blades in the Hereford boozers. Guys he'd once counted as good mates giving him wary glances. Porter knew what they were thinking. He could see it in their eyes.

We can't trust this guy. No way. When push comes to shove, Porter won't have our backs.

He could have left the Regiment, but being a soldier was all Porter knew. So he carried on, a Hereford outcast with the blood of his muckers on his hands. Then the nightmares started, and he turned to the bottle. At first it was a few liveners first thing in the morning, just a little something to help him get through the day. Then it turned into a bottle of Bushmills every day, washed down with a crate of Stella. Diana found out about his drinking. She threatened to walk out on him if he didn't stop. Porter drank more. Then one day he came home to find a handwritten note on the kitchen counter.

I've leaving, the note had read. The words were stencilled in his mind. *I'm sorry, John, but I can't take it any more. I'm taking Sandy with me. Please don't try to contact us. Take care. Diana.*

Sandy. His daughter. She was seven. She had hair the colour of sunshine and eyes as big as poker chips, and a laugh so infectious it belonged in a government laboratory. There was no bond like that between a father and his daughter. Some of the other guys in the Regiment struggled to bond with their kids, but Porter had never had that problem with Sandy. She had all of her mum's good looks and none of her old man's cynicism. She was the one person who made life worth living.

And now she was gone.

He had nothing left. He wasn't even a true soldier any more. The closest he'd ever get to combat again would be instructing the students on how to assault a building six months from now. His stint on the Training Wing was to be his last posting in the Regiment. What will I do then? Porter wondered. Knock on the door at Templar and ask them to give us a job? He smiled in amusement. One phone call to Hereford and they'd laugh me out of the building. No. The only job I'll be able to get will be working the doors at a dodgy Romford nightclub.

He tried to block out the drilling pain in his head and pushed up the mountain. They were a hundred metres beyond the stream when Porter saw the two ramblers.

They were charging down the track like a couple of bats out of hell, seventy metres ahead of Bald and Porter. They were decked out in matching blue-and-green jackets and beanie hats, Porter noted. One of the ramblers was much bigger than his mate. His chest was wide as a forty-gallon drum. His arms were like a pair of hams stuffed in a sack. His legs were as big as grain silos. The second guy ran along a few paces behind Tank. He was tall and scrawny and he sported a shabby goatee.

Suddenly Goatee lost his footing and stacked it, crashing to the ground ten or so metres ahead of Bald and Porter. Tank about-turned and hurried over to his mate, helping him to his feet. As he stood up, Tank caught glanced down at Porter and hesitated. Something like recognition flashed behind his eyes. As if he'd seen Porter somewhere before. Then he turned and carried on down the trail with Goatee staggering after him, wincing with pain. Porter watched the pair of them scrabble down towards the Blaen Taf Fawr stream. A few moments later they were lost to the mist.

'Why were those two in such a hurry?' Porter asked nobody.

Bald shrugged. 'Maybe they're worried they're going to miss Kilroy.'

Porter let his gaze linger on the trail a moment longer. Maybe it was nothing. But something about the two ramblers had been off, he thought. A niggling concern picked away at the base of his skull like an icepick. He thought again about that look in Tank's eyes. Something about that had been familiar.

'Fuck 'em,' said Bald. 'Let's get moving. There's a beer with my name on it down the Newmarket Arms, and I don't want to keep it waiting.'

They moved on. The incline quickly steeped beyond the stream. Porter could feel his legs burning with the effort. Beads of sweat clung to his face. The mist thickened. It was like walking through a cloud. Five hundred metres further on Porter spotted a small stone obelisk to the north. The Tommy Jones memorial was named after a miner's son from Maerys who'd died a hundred years ago after getting lost on the Fan. On a rank winter's day it was a useful marker. Porter knew they were getting closer to the point where the track split into a V and led towards Pen y Fan. He kept thinking back to the two ramblers they'd passed by. Why had they been tearing down the trail? It wasn't like walkers to be in such a rush. They usually took their time to walk down, admiring the view. Usually the only people in a hurry on the Fan were the students taking SAS Selection.

Porter was still wondering about them when Bald stopped dead in his tracks.

'Shit,' he said.

Porter looked up. Then he stopped too. He spotted three figures stumbling along the track, fifty metres ahead. A man and a woman in bright-yellow jackets, edging along either side of a heavyset figure wearing army fatigues and a sweater. The man and woman had their arms slung around his shoulders. Even at this distance, Porter could see the guy was a mess. His head hung low, and his arms were limp at his sides. Blood glistened down his front, spattering his legs. Then Porter took a few steps closer to the man, and his blood froze in his veins.

He was looking at Victor Vowden.

NINE

0703 hours.

Dread seized hold of Porter. Like a hand clasping tight around his throat. He sprinted up the trail, racing towards Vowden and the ramblers. Bald rushed after him, blowing hard. Up ahead the woman caught sight of the two Blades and frantically shouted at them, waving them over. At the same time the other guy was setting Vowden down carefully at the side of the track. The wounded Blade's arms were hanging by his sides, big and heavy and limp.

'Out of the way!' Porter barked at the ramblers as he drew close.

The man and woman stepped back from Vowden, giving Porter room. He could feel his heart pounding as he dropped to one knee beside the wounded sergeant and examined his injuries. Straightaway Porter could see that Vowden was in a bad way. His eyes were dancing wildly in their sockets. His left shoulder had been pulverised and there was a ragged hole in the middle of his chest wide as a tube of Smarties. Blood was bubbling around the wound, disgorging steadily and running down his front. Porter detected a wet sucking noise every time Vowden breathed in. He snapped his gaze to the man and woman.

'What the fuck happened?'

The pair of them swapped worried looks. For a moment they were too stunned to respond. Then the man spoke. He was a grey-haired guy with the doughy build of someone who spent most of his life sitting in an open plan office. His lips were visibly trembling.

'We found him over there,' the man said, pointing up the trail, in the distant direction of Pen y Fan. 'He was on the peak. They both were.'

'Both?' Bald demanded. 'Where's the other one?'

'Dead.' The man shook his head. 'My wife, she checked his pulse.'

'So you just left him there?'

The man hesitated. He looked defensively at Bald. 'There was nothing we could do for him.'

Porter glanced quickly at his mucker. The Jock's fists were so tightly clenched that the knuckles had shaded white. He swung back to Vowden. The guy was making a gargling noise in the back of his throat. He was drowning in his own blood, Porter realised grimly. There was no point trying to grill him. Vowden could hardly breathe, let alone try to speak. Porter looked up at the couple.

'Did you see who did this?'

The husband said nothing for a long, cold beat. He was staring at Vowden. Watching the blood bubble and hiss around the bullet wound, like water gurgling out of a blocked sink. He was transfixed. The guy had probably never seen a bullet wound in his life, Porter told himself.

'We've only seen two ramblers,' the woman replied falteringly. 'We saw them leaving the peak, not long before we found him. They were running down, real fast. Like they were in a hurry.' She turned to the man. 'Isn't that right, Gary?'

Gary nodded. 'Yeah. A couple of ramblers.'

'Nobody else?' Porter said.

'Nobody,' said Gary.

Porter looked at Bald. Bald looked at Porter. Both of them thinking the same thing.

The ramblers we just passed.

Had to be.

And suddenly he understood why they had been in such a blind hurry to get down the side of the mountain. Because they had just shot two SAS instructors. He looked back to the woman and tried to keep his voice calm and controlled. 'What did they look like?'

The woman thought for a beat. 'One of them was tall. Shabby-looking? He had a beard. The other one, he was bigger. Like a wrestler, you know. That kind of big.'

Porter glanced down the track, his mind racing ahead of him. Working the angles. The two ramblers had been tearing down the trail towards the Blaen Taf Fawr stream. That trail led only one way, Porter knew. Back up a low rise before it descended steeply towards the Storey Arms.

Towards the instructors and the students.

Porter turned towards the husband and wife. There was no time to lose. He cocked his head at the man.

'Have you got a wallet on you? Driver's licence, credit card, anything like that?'

The man blinked. 'What for?'

'Just hand it over!'

The husband nodded anxiously, then dug his wallet out of his jacket pocket. His hand was shaking as he passed it to Porter. The Blade flipped open the wallet and fished out the husband's driving licence. Then he took the small laminate card and placed it over the gaping hole in Vowden's chest. Like all SAS operators Porter had a secondary level of expertise alongside his specialist skill, and he'd done training as a medic during his time at Hereford. The strip of plastic would act as an emergency occlusive dressing, letting in enough air to help Vowden breathe, but at the same time stopping any excess air from escaping and causing his lungs to collapse.

'Stay here,' Porter said to the man, handing his wallet back minus the blood-stained licence. 'Keep the wound sealed and whatever you do, don't move him or you'll fuck up his spinal cord. Got it?'

The man stared at Vowden for a beat. Then he snapped out of his stupor and looked at Porter. 'Where are you going?'

'To send for help. Mountain rescue will have to get up here and lift him out.'

If the poor fucker isn't already dead by then, Porter didn't add.

The man nodded. Porter shot to his feet and looked to Bald. They didn't need to say anything. They both knew the score. What had to be done. At that moment two armed SAS killers were scrambling down the side of the mountain and heading directly for the students and their instructors. Porter didn't know what they were planning. He didn't know who they were, or why they'd put the drop on two Regiment sergeants on a bitter windswept morning in the Brecon Beacons. All he knew was that his mates were in danger, and he had to stop the ramblers before they got to them.

He spun away from Vowden and hurried back down the track in the direction of the Storey Arms, praying that he wasn't too late.

TEN

It was time.

Stankovic crept back from the window and left Dragan on OP duty. He took out his phone, pulled up the basic menu showing the last incoming call and hit Dial. His heart was starting to beat faster now. He could feel the adrenaline coursing through his veins. Dragan and a couple of the other guys had taken a load of speed to keep themselves alert, but Stankovic didn't need drugs to stay focused. Never had. The thrill of the mission was enough for him. The thought of how many men were going to die, that was like the world's best high. It made him horny.

The driver of the Mondeo answered on the third buzz.

Stankovic said, 'We're ready. Targets all in place.'

There was nothing to commemorate the moment. No big statement, no one saying, 'Well, this is it, now,' or any other crap, like they did in all the big Hollywood movies Stankovic used to watch in his apartment in Belgrade.

Kavlak simply said, 'Okay.'

Stankovic said, 'Park in the south-west corner. As close as you can get to the students. Just make sure you steer clear of the trucks.' He hesitated, anticipating the other man's concern. 'It's going to attract attention, parking that close. But it's our best point of attack.'

'Don't worry. I'll find a way.'

Stankovic killed the call. Then he checked the time.

0706 hours.

Fourteen minutes to go.

★   ★   ★

49

Twenty seconds later, Kavlak fired up the Mondeo and steered out of the lay-by. He headed south on the A470 towards the Storey Arms. He kept his eyes on the road and kept the Mondeo purring along at forty per, well below the speed limit. He was Zen calm.

This was it. There was no going back. After six months of planning, poring over maps and figuring out routes and possible scenarios, they were moving forward now. The ball was finally rolling.

It felt good.

Petrovich sat up straight in the front passenger seat. His knees were bouncing twice as fast now. The speed in his bloodstream mixing with the adrenaline and the anxiety he was feeling. Kavlak ignored his jumpy nephew and focused on the road. The rain was drumming its fingers against the windscreen. They passed a few cars heading in the opposite direction. They passed a lorry parked in a lay-by on the other side of the road next to a greasy mobile food van. They passed trees and hills the colour of granite.

Three minutes later, the Storey Arms slid into view.

Kavlak slowed the Mondeo down to fifteen per and hung a right into the car park. It wasn't hard to spot the students. They were sat in a big group ten metres or so from the entrance next to the two Land Rovers. The four Bedford army trucks and three Range Rovers were parked up in a line twenty metres or so further along from the students. They sat mostly in silence, some sipping at their brews from their metal mugs. They were soaked to the bone and looked thoroughly miserable. Kavlak smiled to himself. A few minutes now, the rain was going to be the least of their worries.

He pulled up as close as he dared to the students, eight metres from the group. He angled the Mondeo so that the front end was facing away from the students and facing out across the Fan Fawr mountain to the west. He glanced up at the rear-view, checking that the car boot was pointing directly at the students. Eight metres. Close enough to wipe out most of the students, and a good number of the instructors too. He shunted the Mondeo into Park and killed the engine.

Almost there.

He was about to climb out when he saw the instructor marching over. Kavlak clocked him in the rear-view. A short, stumpy Brit with a large birth-mark on one side of his face and tiny black eyes that gleamed menacingly, like the points of a couple of sharpened knives. The instructor beat a path around to the driver's side of the Mondeo and rapped his knuckles on the window. Kavlak thumbed the automatic slider and lowered the glass halfway. He looked up and smiled. The instructor glared at him. His facial muscles were twitching. He looked pissed off.

'You can't park here,' the instructor said, pointing to the students. 'This is an army training exercise. Got it? Go a couple of miles down the road. There's another car park there. You can use that one.'

Kavlak stared blankly at the instructor and shrugged as if to say, *No speak English*. The instructor gritted his teeth. He leaned through the window, and glared at Kavlak.

'Are you deaf? I said, move your fucking vehicle.'

Kavlak kept on playing the dumb foreigner, it was a good act. The instructor snorted through his flared nostrils and eventually turned away from the Mondeo. 'Fucking foreigners,' he muttered under his breath.

Kavlak watched the instructor as he trooped back over to the students. He looked to Petrovich. The guy had stopped bouncing his knees. He was quiet now as the enormity of what they were about to do finally hit home.

'Do you remember the plan?' Kavlak asked.

'Yes, uncle,' Petrovich said. 'Stay calm, act normal and don't do anything to make the target suspicious.'

'Good. You're learning.' Petrovich smiled warmly at his uncle's approval. There was hope for him yet. 'Let's go.'

They stepped out of the Mondeo into the driving rain. The cold hit Kavlak like a fist. He swung open the rear passenger door and grabbed one of a pair of dark-blue Montane rucksacks stowed in the back seat. Petrovich took the other one. The two Serbs shouldered their rucksacks and strode across the car park towards the main road. Kavlak forced himself to move at a casual pace, ignoring the frantic thumping of his heart. He needn't have worried. The rucksacks and the walking gear worked perfectly, just as they'd predicted. No one gave the Serbs so much as a second glance. As far as the soldiers were concerned, Kavlak and Petrovich were just another pair of walkers about to begin their early morning pilgrimage up Pen y Fan.

They crossed the road. The wind close to the start of the trail was deafening. Like being in the path of a Boeing 767 cleared for take-off. Once past the red telephone box they moved through the gate and started pounding up the sandstone trail. Kavlak didn't look back. He forced himself to stare dead. He counted his paces and steadied his breathing. Don't do anything to drawn attention to yourself.

The trail snaked up a steady incline and dissolved into the mist beyond the wooded area. From the telephone box to the edge of the forest was a distance of roughly a hundred metres. To the right of the track there was a jagged line of conifer trees screening a camping area to the rear of the Storey Arms, some forty metres away.

The two Serbs paced up for sixty metres until they reached a slight curve in the track. Kavlak glanced over his shoulder, checking they were shielded from view of the car park by the treeline. Then he broke off the track and slipped through the treeline and hooked around towards the camping ground. Petrovich followed close behind, the rain spattering against their jackets as they quick-walked past the empty site and the outdoor toilets and approached a door at the rear of the Storey Arms, fifteen metres due south of the wooded area. As they arrived at the door Kavlak paused and glanced back at the track to check no one was watching them. Then he turned and stepped inside.

They entered an unheated room with bare walls and a wrinkled linoleum floor. The air was choked with dust and there was a rank smell of sweat and mould. Petrovich and Stankovic were inside the room, running checks on the various guns laid out on a table in the far corner. Next to the weapons there were six sets of fake passports and matching drivers' licences, plus six stacks of cash amounting to three thousand pounds each, and Visa credit cards issued to the same names as the fake IDs with £5,000 credit limits. Also, pre-paid Nokia mobile phones plus six AerLingus plane tickets for various flights out of Dublin.

Sixty seconds later, Deeds and Markovic, aka Tank and Goatee, swept through the door.

The pair of them were red-faced and soaked through with sweat from their blistering sprint down the mountain. Deeds unloaded his daysack and threw off his beanie hat. Then he took in a long draw of breath and looked at each of the five Serbs in turn. A smile crawled out of the corner of his mouth. His eyes burned bright with excitement.

'Okay,' said Deeds. 'Let's fucking do this.'

0715 hours.

Five minutes to go.

ELEVEN

0716 hours.

Porter hurried up the slope. Bald raced after him. They were setting a crazy pace, massacring their legs as they pounded up the trail. They'd cleared the stream at Blaen Taf Fawr six or seven minutes earlier. Now they were tearing up the gradient towards the crest overlooking the Storey Arms. They were a hundred metres from the crest. Porter could hear the blood rushing in his ears above the furious cut and thrust of the wind and rain. A painful stitch was making itself felt down his right side and he could feel his heart beating frantically inside his chest. Porter shoved aside the pain. He thought only of stopping the ramblers.

Ten years ago he'd failed to protect his muckers. Steve, Keith and Mike had died that day. Porter had been paying the price ever since. Ten years of living with the nightmares and the visions. Ten years of feeling the eyes of the dead men boring holes in his back. He wasn't about to let it happen again.

Not this time. No fucking way.

He upped the pace, surging towards the crest, the stitch feeling like a set of knives twisting inside his obliques. The rain was slicking the ground and making the trail slippery underfoot. Twice Porter almost stacked it as he hurried along. His mind was racing ahead of him. They'd passed the ramblers five or six minutes before they'd discovered Vowden. Which meant the ramblers had a five-minute head start on them. Which meant they might already be too late, Porter realised grimly. They might have already reached the Storey Arms by now. There was nothing for it but to go hell for leather and hope they weren't out of time.

Fifty metres to the crest. Now forty.

Porter ran on. Questions scratched at the base of his skull. Who the fuck were the shooters, and why had they brassed up Vowden and Skimm in the first place? His first instinct had been that the ramblers were a couple of nutters with a grudge against the Regiment. That had been the big fear of some of the instructors when it came to running Selection exercises in the Brecons. But he dismissed the idea almost as quickly as it entered his mind. The attack had been too well planned. This wasn't the work of a couple of random crazies listening to the voices inside their heads. The ramblers had been armed. They'd tabbed up that mountain knowing that Vowden and Skimm would be up there setting up the RV.

So the ramblers must have known that the Fan Dance was happening today, Porter thought to himself. But the only people who knew about the specifics of Selection were the instructors on the Training Wing and the other guys at Hereford. And the students, of course. So where had these ramblers managed to get their int?

Only one way to find out.

He chopped his stride up the last steep section of the incline. He looked over his shoulder. Bald was breathing hard, gasping with the strain. The two Blades had hardly said a word to each other since they'd set off after the ramblers.

'So much for clearing my fucking head,' Bald rasped.

'Hurry it up, Jock. If we catch these bastards, first round's on me.'

Bald smiled grimly. 'Now you're talking my language, mate.'

Porter hit the crest a few strides ahead of his mucker. He willed himself forward, the blood pounding in his veins as they closed in on the final stretch of the trail. Beyond the crest the track dropped down for a kilometre, all the way to the telephone box next to the Storey Arms. The mist had started to clear lower down the slope and Porter could see the land rolling out in front of him. Six hundred metres away Porter spotted the dense wooded area they'd passed on the way up. Beyond the forest, he glimpsed the Storey

Arms. A thought flashed up in front of him, and he felt his stomach muscles tighten into a vicious knot.

God, no.

The whole way down Porter had been asking himself why the ramblers had been heading in this direction. If that was me, having just brassed up a couple of operators, I'd be looking to put as much distance between myself and the rest of the SAS as possible, he thought. I sure as fuck wouldn't leg it down the side of the Fan towards the exact point where the other instructors and students were busy forming up. But now Porter set eyes on the Storey Arms, and he remembered the fleeting movement he'd glimpsed in the first-floor window.

And right there and then, he instinctively knew that whatever he'd seen in the Storey Arms had something to do with the two ramblers and the shooting on top of the Fan. He didn't know what it was. But his guts told him that if he didn't hurry up Vowden and Skimm wouldn't be the only casualties that day.

Porter took a deep breath and charged down the track.

TWELVE

0717 hours.
Three minutes to go.

The six-man team made their final preparations. Weapons were checked. Clips were inserted into mag receivers. Rounds were chambered, charging handles pulled, body armour strapped on and spare clips stashed in pockets where they could be easily accessed. They put on black three-holed ski masks to hide their faces. Each man also pocketed his fake passport, driver's licence and credit cards, and straps of cash. The IDs had been sourced from a professional art forger called Schmidtt who ran a side business in faked documents. They were the best on the market. Even a seasoned border official wouldn't be able to tell the difference.

The men kept their chatter to a minimum. There was no reason to speak now. Everyone knew their job. There was just the sharp mechanical click and clatter of six men preparing to go to war.

At 0718 hours, Stankovic left the five others and exited the building through the rear door. He stepped out into the camping area immediately behind the Storey Arms, screened from view of the main road and the soldiers resting in the car park. In his right hand Stankovic carried a juice bottle filled with half liquid soap flakes and half petrol. In his left hand, he carried a large gym bag filled with half a dozen pairs of trousers and shirts and shoes. The clean clothes were for changing into once they'd bugged out of the Brecons and reached the RV at Merthyr Tydfil. The juice bottle was for torching the van, their old clothes and weapons, erasing any trace of the six men.

Stankovic paced round the back of the Storey Arms and made a beeline for the small parking area to the side of the building, fifty metres to the east. Several wheelie bins were racked up like bowling pins across the back of the blacktop, next to a Transit van. The Transit was one of the new models with the 2.5-litre diesel engine and the curved-box design. It had been paid for in cash and the plates were clean. Stankovic swung around to the back of the van. He popped open the back doors, dumped the gym bag and the juice bottle in the back. Closed the doors, paced around to the driver's side door and climbed behind the wheel. Shoved the key in the ignition, gripped the wheel, and waited.

At 0719 hours, Bill Deeds and the other four guys made their way to the front door. Even Kavlak started to feel nervous now. He could sense the invisible rope tightening around his chest, the sweat leaking out of his palms. The men formed up either side of the door. Kavlak and Petrovich to the right, Markovic, Dragan and Deeds to the left. In addition to his AK-47 and Glock-17, Kavlak carried a set of portable traffic spikes to lay across the road and delay the cops. He set down the spikes and checked his watch.

Twenty seconds to go.

Petrovich was anxious. The assault rifle was shaking in his grip. It was time for his nephew to man the fuck up, Kavlak decided. Time to stop pretending to kill people in video games, and do it for real. To show that he was worthy of being in the gang. He dug out the remote-controlled detonator from his pocket and offered it to Petrovich. The kid froze, not comprehending.

The dumb fuck.

'Uncle?'

'Here,' said Kavlak. 'You do the honours.'

Petrovich didn't move. He swallowed hard and looked wide-eyed at the walkie-talkie, breathing hard inside his mask. 'Me? But shouldn't someone with experience do it, uncle? Why not Dragan? Or you?'

Kavlak sighed. 'Do you like fucking, nephew?'

Petrovich nodded obediently. Like a dog. 'Yes, uncle.'

'Then press the damn button, and tonight you'll have the greatest fuck of your life. This much I promise you.'

Petrovich stayed very still for a moment. Kavlak could see his eyes working furiously behind his mask, trying to build himself up to the moment. His shoulders were pumping furiously up and down with the tension. He reluctantly took the detonator. His thumb hovered over the Push-to-Talk button. Kavlak checked his watch.

Ten seconds.

'Do it,' he urged. 'Become a man.'

Petrovich still hesitated. He kept staring at the walkie-talkie. The other four guys watched him in stony silence. Kavlak could see his nephew's thumb shaking.

Five seconds.

Four. Three.

Two seconds.

'Now!' Kavlak urged.

Petrovich closed his eyes, breathing hard.

Then he pushed the button.

THIRTEEN

0720 hours.
Joe Kinsella didn't hear the bomb.

He was sitting on his Bergen amongst the other students, shivering cold and soaked through to the bone, nursing a hot brew. He was listening to Stubbs tell another one of his naff jokes and pretending to laugh. He was trying hard not to show his nerves. He was trying not to think about the excruciating pain from his blistered feet.

Ten metres behind him, a radio receiver unit in the boot of the Ford Mondeo picked up a signal from the direction of the Storey Arms and ignited the det cord. A split second later, the C4 exploded. There was a momentary flash of hot white light that blinded Kinsella. In the next instant he was thrown back by a scorching hot blast of wind and smoke, burning his hair and flesh and crushing his rib cage like a fist closing in around an empty Coke can. Then the smoke and the heat roared over him, hurling him off his feet, and as the flames engulfed Joe Kinsella his last thought was, *God help me.*

Then nothing.

Porter was three hundred metres away when he heard the blast. A distinct whump, followed by a low angry rumble that shuddered like thunder across the mountain. Bright orange flames spewed into the sky high above the car park, like a flare stack on an oil rig. Fists of thick smoke mushroomed out of the flames, throwing up a million pieces of debris and shrapnel. Behind the roar of the outward explosion and the clatter of the falling debris, Porter heard a scream.

He stood rooted to the spot next to Bald for a cold moment, his breath trapped deep in his throat. Like someone had pulled a noose tight around his neck. Everything seemed surreal. He looked on in disbelief at the tendrils of smoke billowing up into the air, raining down debris across the road like ash pouring down from an erupting volcano. Two cars had been gliding down the main road, coming from the west. From the direction of Brecon. They were fifty metres away when the bomb kicked off. The lead car hit the brakes and skidded to a halt in front of the explosion. The rear motor was too late. It slammed into the saloon's rear bumper in the middle of the road. Glass shattered. Car alarms wailed.

'Jesus,' Bald whispered at his side. 'Jesus Christ. Oh, fuck.'

This can't be happening, Porter kept thinking, over and over. *This can't be fucking happening.*

Then the realisation hit him, like a fist to the guts. Car bomb. Had to be. Nothing else could cause a bang like that, Porter knew. He'd seen dozens of the fuckers detonate during the time he'd spent serving in Northern Ireland. Someone's just detonated a car bomb in the middle of Selection, he realised. The Regiment's been hit.

We're under attack.

Porter shook his head clear. His training instincts suddenly kicked in. Ten years as an SAS operator, his reactions to danger were hardwired into his muscle memory and he knew instantly what he had to do. Get to the bomb site, assess the situation and send for help for the soldiers. The ones who weren't already dead. The thought flashed across his mind that the fuckers responsible for this might still be nearby. And at least two of them – the ramblers – were armed. And I don't even have a pistol. But Porter couldn't worry about that now. His mates needed him.

'Fucking move!' he yelled at Bald as he sprinted down the trail. 'Let's go!'

Bald sprang into action. The two Blades hurtled towards the main road, racing past the wooded area to their left, their legs scrambling for purchase on the rain-swept track. Two hundred and fifty metres from the telephone box, Porter heard the agonised screams of the wounded splitting the air. He quickened his stride, running for all he was worth, ignoring the savage pain between his temples and the burning in his leg muscles.

As he drew closer to the road he tasted the acrid tang of blood and burning metal in the air, and the pungent stench of charred human flesh filled his nostrils. He could see the gusts of smoke swirling across the road, blocking his view of the car park. He could hear the shattered glass from the Storey Arms as it showered the tarmac, making a noise like thousands of coins being spat out of a slot machine. A little further on the smoke had cleared and he spotted the pools of blood glistening on the tarmac on the other side of the road. He saw the twisted bodies of the dead sprawled on the ground, and the twisted metal carcass of the car, still churning black smoke into the air. Porter and Bald ran on.

They were two hundred metres from the phone box when the gunfire started.

FOURTEEN

0720 hours.

Ten seconds after the initial blast, the five masked gunmen burst out of the front of the Storey Arms and fanned out across the driveway. They moved quickly but calmly across the road, brandishing their AK-47 assault rifles. Shattered glass crunching under their boots, smoke swirling around their ankles as they headed towards the car park. Towards the screams, and the wounded soldiers.

They had sixty seconds.

Deeds led the way. The car park was carnage. He could feel the heat from the blast as he approached, the sweat sliding down his brow under his ski mask. The temperature at ground zero was a million degrees. It was like walking into a furnace, and Deeds found it hard to believe that anyone could have survived such a massive explosion. But as he crossed the road he noticed a few survivors amid the body parts and the charred corpses. Those closest to the Mondeo had been literally ripped apart. There was nothing left of them except chunks of blackened flesh and ruptured organs like diced meat on a chopping board. The instructors and their mates on the SP team had been further away from the blast. Some of the SAS operators had been cut down by the vicious hail of shrapnel that accompanied the bomb. Others were lying on the ground, disorientated and groggy, their hands and feet covered in blood.

Deeds turned his attention to an operator lying on his side. The guy was easily identifiable in his mixture of civvies and combat fatigues, and his thick beard and military Gore-Tex jacket. The guys on the SP team were the only soldiers carrying pistols. Which made them more of a threat, Deeds knew. The students had nothing but SLRs chambered with blank rounds. And the instructors were defenceless. But the SP team operators had pistols loaded with live ammo. They could shoot back. Deeds and the Serbs had taken that into account when planning the attack. *After the bomb, go for the SP team first. Neutralise the biggest threat.*

The operator lying in front of Deeds was in a bad way. His stomach had been torn open and his bowels were spilling out in front of him, like a bulging inner tube out of a slashed car tyre. The guy was desperately trying to shove his vitals back inside his stomach. Deeds coolly approached the wounded operator and thumbed the safety selector on the side of the AK-47 to 'J'. The AK was an old Yugoslav army variant and the 'J' indicated the semi-automatic fire setting. The rifle felt good in his grip. Sturdy. Deeds had thirty rounds in the mag, plus two spare clips in his back pockets, giving him ninety rounds of 7.62x39mm brass. More than enough to get the job done and slot the remaining soldiers.

Deeds lowered the AK-47 so that the rear sight notch and front sighting post were trained directly at the operator's head. The guy looked up at Deeds. Not pleading. Not begging for his life. He didn't say anything. He just blinked in some sort of vague acceptance that he was into the last seconds of his life. Then Deeds depressed the trigger. The barrel lit up. The operator spasmed violently. Blood spat out of a hole in the back of his head in a furious red spray, like someone had just shaken a bottle of Dom Perignon then popped the cork. He was still falling away as Deeds turned his attention to the next target.

He caught sight of a heavily-bleeding soldier lying five or six metres away, slumped against the side of one of the Range Rovers. The guy was reaching down to his thigh holster and fumbling with his Sig. Deeds arced the AK-47 towards the guy. The operator raised his hands.

'Are you going to kill me?' the man croaked.

'Yes, chief.'

Deeds gave him a three-round burst to the chest before he could retrieve his pistol. The operator slumped backwards like a marionette with all the strings cut. His right leg twitched. Deeds paced over to him and put another round between his eyes for good measure. His leg stopped twitching.

Across the car park the other four gunmen were putting down the other survivors with sharp bursts, slotting the wounded where they lay. The air was quickly filled with the incessant crack of rifle reports and the chink of spent jackets as they spat out of ejectors and tumbled to the asphalt, and the groans of the dying. Some of the wounded students tried to drag themselves away from the car park in a desperate attempt to escape the killing frenzy. The gunmen dropped them in quick succession. They were merciless.

Deeds saw one instructor staggering towards a Volkswagen Golf that had stopped fifty or so metres to the north of the car park. It was easy to spot the instructors. They were older than the students, and they weren't wearing the mini-belt kits issued to soldiers taking Selection. Some of the instructors even wore their SAS berets. This guy's leg was in rag order. He shouted at the terrified woman behind the wheel, screaming for help. Deeds lined up the instructor's back and let rip. The first two rounds thumped into his spine. The third punched into the nape of his neck and the fourth took out a chunk of his scalp. The guy dropped a couple of metres from the Golf, blood and brain matter spattering the bonnet. His beret fell to the ground beside him. From behind the wheel, Deeds heard the woman screaming as she hit the deck.

Thirty seconds to go. From across the road Deeds heard a loud rumble as Stankovic sparked up the getaway vehicle. Four seconds later, the white Transit van rolled out of the parking area to the side of the Storey Arms and turned left out of the driveway. A sign painted on the side of the van read 'Newport Plumbing and Heating Solutions Ltd'. The Transit veered onto the main road and then jerked to a halt seventy metres away from Deeds and the four Serbs. Engine racing, ready to bounce south as soon as the gunmen finished executing the remaining soldiers.

Three seconds after that, the two Regiment men raced into view at the telephone box.

FIFTEEN

0721 hours.

Porter saw the gunmen as he bolted forward. There were five of them, spread out in a wide arc across the car park, forty metres downstream from the red phone box. They wore black ski masks but Porter recognised two of them from their Gore-Tex jackets and trousers. The ramblers who'd raced down the side of the Fan. Tank was the nearest of the gunmen. He was putting down rounds on the Volkswagen to the right of the phone box, fifty metres from Bald and Porter. Goatee stood three metres further back, pissing bullets at the wounded students.

The other three gunmen were dressed in matching black fatigues. They were all clutching AK-47s and unloading their clips into anything that moved.

A third gunmen stood near to Tank and Goatee, a bulky guy wearing a pair of scuffed white Nike trainers. The guy was moving swiftly over to Bob McCanliss. Porter saw the chief instructor crawling along the tarmac. The lower half of his left leg had been blown clean off and there was a trail of glistening blood behind him. Nike rolled McCanliss over onto his front and drew the AK level with his face. McCanliss screamed something at the gunman. Nike fired twice, blowing McCanliss's brains out.

The gunman spun away from McCanliss as he spied Bald and Porter rushing towards the road. In a blur of motion Nike brought his weapon to bear and pulled the trigger. Porter turned and shouted at Bald.

'Get down! GET FUCKING DOWN!'

There was a waist-high stone wall next to the phone box. Porter threw himself forward, diving for cover behind the wall just as the AK-47 muzzle flashed. Bald dived behind a separate section of the wall as the first rounds hit and ricocheted off the stone, spitting dust and stone fragments into the air. The gunman let off another sharp three-round burst. Bald cursed under his breath as the bullets slapped into the wall no more than six inches above his head.

'Where did the rest of these bastards come from?' he spat.

There was a brief lull in the gunfire. Porter peered out from the side of the wall and looked towards the Storey Arms. The front door was hanging open. *So that's where the gunmen were hiding*, he realised. His mind hadn't been playing tricks on him. They'd been holed up inside the building all along. Down the road from the Storey Arms he spied the white Transit van, eighty metres from their position and parallel to the far end of the car park. The two gunmen nearest to the Transit were already racing over to the van. Another ten or fifteen seconds, Porter realised, and the shooters would be gone.

They had to act now. Porter snapped back behind cover as Nike unleashed another three-round burst at the wall. He heard the bullets glancing off the stone pile. Then he heard Nike shouting at the other gunmen, alerting them to the two Blades across the road. Nike turned away from the car park and raced towards Tank and Goatee. The two other gunmen were emptying their clips into the wounded soldiers. A few of the students were still alive. Some were screaming in pain. Others were trying to drag themselves away from the shooting. Porter looked back to Bald.

'We've got to get the drop on this lot,' he said urgently.

Bald nodded. 'You just read my mind, mate.'

The Jock had already retrieved his Sig Sauer P226 from its holster. Now Bald thumbed the decocker on the right-hand side of the receiver and manually cocked the hammer. There was no safety mechanism on the Sig, just a decocker that varied how much pressure you needed to apply to the trigger to discharge a round. With the decocker off and the hammer cocked, Bald would only need to give the trigger the slightest squeeze in order to loose off a round. Porter watched him ready his weapon and wished to God that he had his own tool to hand. *We're going up against five heavily-armed gunmen, and I don't even have a fucking pea-shooter.*

Beyond the wall, the two ramblers brought up their weapons and loosed off a pair of three-round bursts. The first three bullets struck the wall. The second grouping whizzed over Porter's head and hit the telephone box, shattering the glass panels and ricocheting off the phone unit in a mad flurry of sparks. Bald waited for another lull in the fire. Then he rolled out of cover to the right of the wall, his weapon drawn in a firm two-handed grip with his support hand resting under the left side of the slider and his left thumb pointing forward to help him line up his target. In the same instant Porter glanced around his section of the wall, giving him a line of sight to the ramblers. He saw Nike on a knee in the middle of the road. The guy had hurried over to the two ramblers. Three gunmen were now focused on Bald and Porter while the other two guys were on mopping-up duty. Nike was slapping a fresh mag into his AK-47. Porter watched him and worked the angles. From the stone wall to the gunmen was a distance of maybe forty-five metres. The Sig had a maximum effective range of fifty metres. Bald was operating right on the threshold.

Nike had almost finished reloading his AK-47. He had the clip fully inserted. He tugged on the charging handle, chambering the first round. Then he shot to his feet, raised the assault rifle so that it was level with his shoulder and peered down the sighting post.

Just in time to see Bald pull the trigger.

The Sig fired twice. Bald's aim was surgical, the result of thousands of hours he'd spent on the ranges. The first round of 9x19mm Parabellum hit Nike square in the groin. The guy jerked back, howling in agony. Blood splashed across his trousers. The second round thumped into his neck, sending Nike into a tailspin. He dropped like his body was weighed down with lead. His weapon tumbled from his grip, clattering to the ground next to his slack frame, the blood pooling around him and mixing with the hard rain.

One down, Porter thought. *Four left to kill.*

Tank saw what was happening and swung his AK-47 towards the wall. Bald and Porter ducked behind cover as Tank depressed the trigger. Rounds hammered against the stone pile in a relentless staccato rhythm. Porter counted the shots. One, two, three.

Four, five, six.

There was a break in the rifle reports. From the other side of the road Porter heard voices shouting. He peered over the wall. Saw the Transit eighty metres away. The other two gunmen finished emptying their clips into a couple of wounded students crawling across the car park. They heard the getaway driver shouting at them and then turned and bolted towards the Transit. One of the gunmen made for the back doors while the other guy laid out a line of traffic spikes widthways across the road, five or six metres behind the Transit. If any cop cars tried chasing after the gunmen, the spikes would slash open their tyres and put the brakes on their pursuit.

The first gunman popped the back doors and climbed inside the van. The second gunman finished setting up the spikes and joined him. They started shouting at Tank and Goatee, frantically beckoning them over. The ramblers took the hint. They turned and started making a run for it. Porter reckoned they were forty metres from the Transit, maybe forty-five. With the ramblers' backs turned Bald now sprang out from behind cover and drew his Sig level with the nearest target. Goatee. He aimed for the torso, the largest centre of mass. At forty metres a hit wasn't a sure thing. Bald fired twice. The first shot missed, sparking off the tarmac like a matchstick striking against the side of a box. The second round smashed into Goatee's left leg just above the knee joint, punching through his flesh and shattering his femur. A mist of blood and shattered bone spat out of the wound. Goatee howled in pain and crumpled to the ground.

Tank stopped. Dropped to a knee beside his mucker and put down a quick burst at Bald and Porter. His aim was off. The rounds landed short, slapping into the wet turf and throwing up fists of dirt. Goatee was writhing in agony on the ground beside Tank, squealing like a stuck pig as he tried to staunch the flow of blood from the trauma wound to his leg. There wasn't a great deal of blood, which meant the bullet hadn't severed the femoral artery. Bald fired again. Once. Missed.

The getaway driver panicked. He gunned the engine and the tyres screeched as the Transit began pulling away from the Storey Arms. Tank glanced over his shoulder and saw what was happening. He let off another frantic burst at the wall then spun away and raced after the van. But the Transit was too far ahead and picking up speed. In a matter of seconds the van was sledding south on the A470, hurtling into the distance, leaving Tank and Goatee behind in a trail of exhaust fumes. Tank hesitated, his head darting urgently left and right as he searched for another escape route. Then he hurried over to the four-tonners. They were parked up in a line at the far end of the car park. The windows were shattered and the paintwork covered in dust and smoke, but otherwise the four army trucks had survived the bombing.

'Move it!' Bald shouted. 'NOW!'

He leapt over the wall. Porter followed hard on his heels. The two Blades surged across the road. Ahead of them Goatee had struggled to his feet. He was limping towards the four-tonners. Hobbling after Tank. His trouser leg glistening with blood. Porter dropped down beside Nike's limp body and grabbed the AK-47. The weapon felt good, and heavy. Porter knew the AK-47 was fully loaded. He'd seen Nike seat a fresh mag in the rifle right before Bald sent him over to the dark side. There were thirty rounds of 7.62x39mm brass in an AK-47 mag. Throw in the nine rounds Bald had in the Sig, and they had enough firepower to take down the two gunmen. They had the two ramblers trapped in the car park, with nowhere left to run.

Now we're in fucking business.

A huge cloud of smoke was still pouring across the car park. The air was thick with the stench of cordite and burnt plastic, fusing with the hot stink of blood. Porter could hardly breathe. His eyes watered. His throat burned. Everywhere he looked he could see body parts and splashes of blood. Some of the dead students were on fire. Others had been ripped apart by the sheer force of the explosion. Arms had been torn from their sockets. Faces sucked inwards. Bowels slashed open by pieces of shrapnel. In the corner of his eye Porter noticed Kinsella sprawled like a rag doll on the tarmac. His torso had been severed at the waist. His intestines were slopping out of the ruptured stump where his legs had once been.

Up ahead Goatee glanced over his shoulder. Saw Bald and Porter tearing towards him, and hesitated. He glanced back at the trucks. Like he was measuring the distances. Weighing up whether his best bet was to make a run for it, or stand and fight. Goatee chose the second option.

Bad call.

Goatee trained his AK-47 at the onrushing Blades and let rip. Flames spat out of the rifle snout. Hot lead spattered the ground inches from Bald and Porter. They scrambled for cover behind the Range Rovers parked fifteen metres further back, closer to the main road. They ducked behind the front and rear wheels as a volley of bullets hammered against the bodywork. Like a thousand hammers banging against a lead pipe. Then the shooting stopped. Porter looked up. Spied Goatee kneeling by the front of the army truck, gritting his teeth through the pain as he shunted a new clip into the AK-47. Porter shrank back from view as he put down a furious burst of gunfire at the Range Rover. There was a deafening clatter as bullets punched through the vehicle, shattering the glass and pinballing through the chassis.

There was no sign of Tank. Porter figured the guy was still hunched down behind the truck. Probably reloading his weapon. Probably waiting for Goatee to catch up with him.

'They've got us pinned down!' Bald shouted above the clamour.

Porter thought for a beat. 'Give me some covering fire. I'll hook around the truck and give this prick the good news.'

Bald nodded. They did a three-count. Then Bald sprang up from behind cover and started putting down suppressive fire at the four-tonner in a controlled rhythm. The bullets struck the front end of the truck in a close grouping, keeping Goatee pinned down. In the same movement Porter broke to the left, kicking aside the spent brass as he moved to swing around the side of the four-tonner. He had the AK-47 raised, the metal stock tucked tight against his shoulder and his index finger resting on the trigger. His booze-soaked heart was beating so fast it felt like it might burst out of his chest at any moment.

Porter was twelve metres to the left of the Range Rover when Bald reached the end of his clip. Porter heard the dreaded *click-click*. The Jock dropped down to his haunches behind the vehicle. Then Goatee sprang out from behind the four-tonner. He didn't see Porter. His focus was purely on the shooter behind the Range Rover. Porter lined up Goatee down the AK-47's metal sights. He didn't panic. He'd fired thousands of rounds before, on the ranges and in combat. Shooting a bad guy came as easily to him as brushing his teeth. He tightened his core, relaxed his shoulder. Exhaled.

Then he depressed the trigger.

The AK-47 jerked. The muzzle flashed. Two rounds spat out of the snout in quick succession and thumped into Goatee. The guy spasmed. Like someone had struck him in the back with a sledgehammer. Blood spayed across the front end of the truck. He dropped like a sigh, the AK-47 clattering to the ground next to him. Porter and Bald sprinted towards him. Porter got there first, kicking away the rifle. He raced past the wounded gunman and headed for the other side of the truck, the blood pounding savagely in his veins.

One rambler down. One to go.

He was surprised that Tank hadn't put down any covering fire for his companion. Maybe the guy had suffered a stoppage, Porter thought. Or maybe he was out of ammo. He moved cautiously around the front end of the truck. Weapon raised, eyes peering down the sights. Finger tense on the trigger. Tank had to be hiding on the other side of the four-tonners. Porter's heart skipped a beat. Got him now.

Got the bastard right where I want him.

Then he swept around to the other side of the truck and froze. Tank wasn't there.

Porter stood rooted to the spot for a long moment. He kept his weapon raised as he glanced frantically around the trucks. Bald joined him a moment later, a puzzled expression etched across his face. Porter looked out beyond the car park. Thinking, *Where the fuck is this guy?* He was right under our noses, and now he's gone.

Then he spotted something in the middle distance. A smudge of colour faintly visible beyond the billowing smoke. The smoke cleared, revealing a heavyset figure in a brightly-coloured jacket four hundred metres away, charging up the ridgeline at Fan Fawr. A cold dread sank through Porter as he watched the figure legging it towards the mist-wreathed peak.

Shit.

Tank was getting away.

SIXTEEN

0724 hours.

Bald turned to race up the slope. Porter didn't move. He could see Tank pounding towards the ridgeline. Another couple of seconds and the guy would be out of sight behind the ridge. He was too far away to try and drop with a couple of rounds. Anything over four hundred metres, the AK–47 was about as accurate as a Chinese fortune cookie.

Bald stopped and looked back to Porter, clenching his brow.

'The fuck are we waiting for?'

Porter shook his head and said, 'I know where he's going.'

'Where?'

'That trail leads one way.' Porter pointed to the ridgeline along Fan Fawr. By now Tank had disappeared from view behind the ridge. 'It drops down the other side of that ridge and brings you out to the Beacons reservoir. That's where he's headed. He's gonna double back on himself and hit the road to the south of here.'

'Maybe,' said Bald. He chewed on the thought like it was gum. 'Or maybe he's pissing off in another direction. There's no way of knowing.'

Porter shook his head again. 'There's fuck-all to the west of that ridge. The only way he's getting off that mountain is by going south and hitting the main road. Trust me, mate. He's headed for the reservoir. If we head south on the main road we can cut him off at the other end before he legs it.' He tipped his head in the direction of the main road then looked back to Bald. 'He won't be expecting that.'

A broad grin played out on Bald's mug again. 'We'll give the fucker a nasty surprise.'

They turned and hurried past the trucks. Bald stopped beside Goatee and grabbed his AK-47, plus a spare clip from his jacket pocket. There was blood all over him, oozing out of the two exit wounds on his back and forming a slippery puddle of blood. Porter stepped around the body and sprinted towards the main road, Bald hurrying after him. They passed the debris and the dead soldiers and the spent brass. Ahead of them a Ford Escort had stopped in the middle of the road. Porter flagged down the driver, a civvy in a windbreaker. The guy sat frozen in horror behind the wheel, staring at the carnage in front of him. It took him a couple of seconds to peel his eyes away from the body parts strewn across the asphalt. He cranked open his door as Porter rushed over. His eyes were wide with terror.

'Got a phone?' Porter yelled.

The man nodded slowly.

'Get on the blower to the police. Tell them there's a fucking emergency at the Storey Arms. There's been an attack on 22 SAS. Multiple dead. Armed gunmen spotted leaving the scene in a white Ford Transit. We need everyone down here, five fucking minutes ago. Got all that?'

The man nodded again. Quickly this time. He was reaching for a brick-sized carphone as Porter and Bald turned and hurried on down the road. Help wouldn't be on the way for a while, Porter knew. They were slap bang in the middle of the Brecons, thirty miles due west of the Regiment HQ and ten miles from the nearest police station. It would take the cops eight or nine minutes to show up. It would take another twenty minutes for the cops to raise the alarm at Hereford and the Regiment CO to get the Red Team guys briefed and deployed. Say, thirty minutes to get mobilised. By that time, the gunman could have gone to ground. In half an hour the van could have motored down to Pontypridd to the south-west, or Neath to the south. In fifty minutes they could reach Cardiff airport or catch the ferry from Swansea to Cork. Only Porter and Bald could stop him now.

They slung round a wide bend in the road and raced south. It was still raining. Drops spit-polished the road and tapped against the barrel of Porter's AK-47 in a steady dull patter. The mist had started to clear now, and past his right shoulder Porter could see the outline of Fan Fawr as it descended steadily towards the reservoir. Four cars had stopped in the middle of the road. The drivers had stepped out of their motors. Three of them were staring ahead in disbelief, or fear. The fourth driver was reaching frantically for his phone. No one paid any attention to the two SAS operators gripping their assault rifles and hurtling down the side of the road. The civvies were all transfixed by the huge column of smoke and fumes still rising above the Storey Arms.

Past a wooded area to the right Bald and Porter hit the reservoir. The treeline gave way to a wide expanse of water, flat and grey as a sheet of steel. The surface rippled under the constant rain. The reservoir stretched out parallel to the road for five hundred metres. At the far bank Porter could see the water tower marking the reservoir's edge, separating it from the dam and the spillway on the far side. Porter knew from the days spent running Selection exercises on the Brecons that there was a stone path running past the water tower. That path led from the bottom of Fan Fawr and exited onto the A470 a short distance ahead of a busy lay-by. Porter could see the lay-by up ahead. Dozens of civvies were crowded outside their VW camper vans and caravans, staring in the direction of the Storey Arms. Porter summoned one last effort in his tired muscles. We're almost there, he told himself. Don't give up now. Another two hundred metres. Then we'll cut Tank off from the main road. He'll have no choice but to retreat back up Fan Fawr. There won't be anywhere else for him to go then. He'll be trapped in the mountains.

Then we'll teach the fucker a lesson he won't live long enough to forget.

Porter was a hundred and fifty metres from the tower when he spotted Tank.

The gunman surged into view past the water tower and staggered towards the main road, ninety metres away. Even at this distance, Porter could see that the guy was spent. He was moving along in big lumbering strides, like he was negotiating a bunch of car tyres on an obstacle course. The frantic race up and down Pen y Fan, the firefight and his rushed escape, all of it taking its toll on his body.

Tank ran on. Porter was a hundred and twenty metres from Tank now. The guy crashed through the gate at the edge of the footpath and limped into the road. Porter brought his AK-47 to bear and went to loose off a round. Tank caught sight of the two Regiment men charging towards him and let off a quick burst at the civvies in the lay-by. His muzzle flashed six times. Half a dozen rounds zipped past Porter and Bald, smashing into the caravan parked to his immediate right. Bullets shattered the windows and blew the tyres. Air hissed violently out of the punctures. A woman shrieked in terror. Some of the civvies hit the deck. Others scurried for cover behind the camper vans. Several people legged it in the opposite direction of the gunfire, spilling across the road and blocking Porter and Bald's path.

'Out of my way!' Bald roared, shoving aside a screaming woman. 'Fucking move!'

A hundred metres ahead, Tank turned towards a dark-blue Vauxhall Vectra motoring towards him from the south. He stood in the middle of the road and pointed the AK-47 at the windscreen. As if he was shaping to spray the driver. The Vectra hit the brakes a couple of metres ahead of Tank. He shouted something at the driver. A second later, a dark-haired woman in jeans and a sweater stepped out from behind the wheel. Porter still couldn't get a clean shot off at the gunman. Tank grabbed the woman roughly by the arm and shoved her aside. Then he flung open the driver's side door. Glanced up. Saw Bald and Porter finally breaking free of the crowd of panicked civvies and racing towards him. Tank arced his AK-47 slightly to his left. Pointed the barrel in the direction of the terrified bystanders scattered across the lay-by. Pulled the trigger.

'Get down!' Porter shouted at the civvies. 'NOW!'

Tank emptied his clip at the lay-by. He wasn't even aiming at anything. Just praying and spraying. He just wanted to cause as much chaos as possible. Round after furious round struck the camper vans. A podgy middle-aged guy jerked as he took a bullet to the nape of his neck. He skidded to the ground like he'd slipped on ice. A nearby woman screamed hysterically. Her cries were drowned out by a throated grunt as another man was shot in the guts. Several people rushed over to the guy, screaming for help as he bled out on the rain-spattered tarmac. Everyone else scrambled for cover, rushing past Porter and Bald and slowing them down.

Porter shoved aside a guy in jogging gear. For a split second he had a clear line of sight to Tank. He brought his AK-47 to bear. Zeroed in on the gunman. Tank was fifty metres away. He'd slotted the driver. She was lying in a bloodied heap on the ground a few steps away from the Vectra, pawing at her gunshot wound. Porter returned his focus to Tank. The guy was folding himself behind the wheel, preparing to take off. Porter took aim and fired twice. The bullets starred the windscreen. *Chink-chink*. Both rounds missed. Tank ducked out of sight below the dash and gunned the Vectra engine.

Two rounds fired, plus two back at the car park. I'm down four bullets, Porter told himself. Twenty-six left in the clip.

He threaded his way past the crowd, trying to get another clear shot. Bald was at his three o'clock, shouting and desperately elbowing aside anyone who got in his way. Forty-five metres to the Vectra now. The engine roared as Tank started to reverse back down the A470. Away from the lay-by. Away from Bald and Porter. There was a sudden loud crunch as the back of the Vectra slammed into the front bumper of the car to the rear. The Vectra ground to a temporary halt. Porter broke free of the crowd and saw Tank through the spiderwebbed windscreen.

Now's my chance, thought Porter. *Nail this prick.*

There was no time to fuck about with the sights. He had to rely on pure instinct. Porter closed his mind to the outside world and narrowed his eye at Tank. The AK-47 felt like an extension of his arm. He took a shallow draw of breath and depressed the trigger.

The shot cracked through the windscreen. A split second later,

Tank's shoulder exploded in a gout of blood and bone. Before Porter could adjust his aim the gunman shunted the wheel hard to the right and hit the accelerator. The tyres were spinning madly, snorting out streams of white smoke as the Vectra made a sharp U-turn in the middle of the road. The front end of the Vectra cut across the grass verge next to the road before it straightened out and faced south. Then Tank put his foot to the floor. Porter let off three more rounds, hoping to blow the tyres. But his aim was off. The rounds struck high, glancing off the boot and shattering the right brake light. The Vectra shrieked as it rocketed south.

Porter kept on running after the Vectra, even as it shrank into the distance. A moment later the car disappeared behind a sharp bend in the road, and Porter finally stopped running. The growl of the engine faded behind the treeline. He was too late.

Tank was gone.

SEVENTEEN

0751 hours.

It took Deeds fifteen minutes to hit the abandoned ironworks outside Merthyr. He'd hammered it down the A470, mashing the pedal. The pain clawing at his skull, twisting like a knife point inside his rag-order shoulder. Those two fucking Regiment operators. They'd nearly ruined the entire plan. Only Deeds's quick thinking had saved him. He'd remembered the route up Fan Fawr, the trail winding down to the Beacons reservoir to the south. That's why he was still breathing, and Markovic was lying dead in the Storey Arms car park.

I should have killed them when I had the chance, Deeds thought. When we were bombing down the side of Pen y Fan. *I should have dug out my Glock and popped both those fucking Blades.*

He wasn't sure what had stopped him back then. He replayed the scene in his mind as he raced south in the stolen Vectra. Markovic had stumbled and fallen over a rock. Deeds had stopped to help his companion to his feet. Then he'd looked up and seen the two Regiment men tabbing up the Fan. And hesitated.

He'd thought about reaching for his rucksack and digging out the Glock. Emptying his clip into the two SAS operators. Sweet Jesus, that would have felt good. But the mist was lifting and the slopes were starting to fill with ramblers. A gunshot might have raised the alarm down at the Storey Arms, jeopardising the mission. Then Deeds had spotted the pistol grip jutting out of the leg holster of the second Blade. That made up his mind. The guy might have put the drop on Deeds and Markovic before they'd retrieved their pistols. So he took the decision to leave the two Regiment men and focus on the core mission.

That had been a mistake.

Now Markovic and Dragan were dead. *And I nearly fucking joined them.*

Deeds was a hundred metres short of the ironworks when he saw the flames. Bright orange fists, spewing out of the charred skeleton of what had unmistakably been a Ford Transit. Both Vauxhall Astras were gone. Deeds hit the brakes and punched the wheel in frustration. The bastards. Stankovic, Petrovich and Kavlak had driven off without him. It took Deeds a few moments to calm down and coldly assess his situation. He decided it could have been much worse. He still had his forged passport and driving licence. He still had his Visa card, the three grand in cash and the AerLingus ticket.

Okay, think.

He reversed out of the ironworks and sped back towards Merthyr. He'd noticed an old Ford Escort parked near a huge council estate on the drive up, a mile or so east of the ironworks. One of those battered old motors with ninety thousand miles on the clock and a handwritten 'FOR SALE' sign tacked to the windscreen. Which meant no one would notice the car gone. At least not for a while. Deeds retraced his steps and parked up next to the Escort. He glanced around to make sure no one was watching him. Smashed open the side window of the Escort with the butt of his AK-47. Cleared away the fragments with the rifle barrel. Dumped the weapon on the front passenger seat and slid behind the wheel. In less than two minutes Deeds had the ancient Escort hotwired and the engine purring.

He raced west. Mapping out the plan in his head. He'd stop at a pharmacy in Neath. Buy himself a pack of painkillers, a roll of stretch dressing and adhesive tape. Clean out the wound and seal the fucker up. The pills would only dampen the pain in his shoulder, but it didn't matter. A few hours of hurt was nothing. He could handle it. He could be on the ferry at Fishguard in less than two hours. On a plane out of Dublin in less than seven. With luck

he'd land at his destination at around eight o'clock this even.
There was a croak, a veterinary surgeon he knew who could
patch him up, for the right price.

And an old friend who could help him out.

08.29 hours.
The sirens wailed their mechanical screams.

Sixty-nine minutes after the attack happened, Porter and Bald
stood at the side of the road and looked on as another ambulance
shuttled south, taking the wounded towards Prince Charles
Hospital in Merthyr Tydfil. The ambos had been arriving and
leaving in an almost continual flow since the emergency services
had first arrived on the scene forty minutes ago. Officers from
the National Crime Squad had been quick to secure the site of
the attack, establishing a cordon either side of the Storey Arms.
White tents had been erected. Neon blue lights cracked and
popped in the light rain as dozens of scene-of-crime officers
dressed in white overalls sifted through the thousands of pieces
of evidence. Every shard of debris, every spent bullet jacket and
shred of fabric, had to be collected, zip-locked, tagged and logged.
It was a painfully slow process to watch, but any scrap of evidence
might provide the clue that could ultimately help identify the
perpetrators.

Choppers circled the grey skies overhead. The Regiment had
deployed its two Augusta helicopters as soon as word reached the
head shed of the bombing. They were joined by a Eurocopter 145
in blue-and-yellow police livery. For the past thirty minutes the
three birds had been scouring the Brecons by air, searching for
any sign of the escaped gunmen. It was a pointless exercise, Porter
knew. You don't just plan an attack that sophisticated without also
having a watertight escape plan. By now the gunmen were probably long gone.

'Training Wing's being stood down,' the Regimental Major,
Pete Maston, said. 'With immediate effect. Whatever's left of it.'

Bald sniffed and looked away. Porter said nothing. He just
stared out across the carnage. The rest of Sabre Squadron had

rocked up a few minutes earlier. The other guys were helping out in any way they could. Some were sorting out food and temporary shelter to treat the wounded. Others were assisting in the recovery of the bodies. Or bits of bodies, Porter reminded himself grimly. With the Regiment CO having to brief the Prime Minister, Maston had been detailed to sort out the mess in the Brecons.

'I said Training Wing's being stood down,' Maston said.

'Heard you the first time, boss,' said Porter. 'But if it's all the same, I'd rather stay on duty. I'm not abandoning my muckers.'

Maston looked him hard in the eye. 'That's not a request, Porter. That's a bloody order. Stand down now.' He glanced at Bald. 'Both of you.'

'And do what?' Bald growled. Rage boiled behind his eyes. 'Sit around with our dicks in our hands while we wait for the cops to catch whoever did this? That's a load of bollocks. We should be out there hunting these cunts down.'

Maston sighed wearily. 'Look, don't blame yourselves for what happened. There was nothing more you could have done. Either of you. Christ, you got two of the bastards. That's something, at least.'

Maston was trying to put a spin on it. Bald looked away from the Sergeant Major as he replied. 'It wasn't enough, boss. We should have dropped every last one of those pricks.'

'What about Vowden?' Porter asked.

Maston lowered his head. 'Didn't make it. Died of his injuries up on the Fan.'

'How many dead is that, total?'

'Fifty-two. Another three aren't expected to make it. That's not including the civvies who were shot over at the reservoir. And the housekepeer's body the police found inside the Storey Arms.' He paused. 'That reminds me. The police will want a statement from you two in due course.'

'Whatever,' said Bald. 'The Old Bill must have me on speed dial by now.'

Porter looked back towards the police as they methodically

combed through the crime scene. It was going to take ages to sort through it all, he realised. Months to compile the evidence. Even longer to build a case and bring the attackers to justice. They were looking at years before they had the perpetrators in silver bracelets. Perhaps never. Porter clamped his eyes shut. All he could think about was getting revenge over the men who had killed his mates.

'There's nothing more you can do here,' Maston said after a long pause. 'Go home. You too, Jock. I'll be in touch with any developments.'

Porter nodded.

Said nothing.

If we had just got there a few seconds earlier, we could have stopped it.

That was the bottom line, thought Porter. Six gunmen had killed over fifty British soldiers. They'd executed Regiment men in cold blood, right in front of Porter's eyes. And three of the killers had managed to get away.

I should have stopped them, the voice at the back of Porter's head told him as he trudged alongside Bald towards the army car waiting to ferry them back to Stirling Lines. If only I'd been quicker down that mountain setting. If only I'd stopped the ramblers from getting to the Storey Arms, then Terry Monk and Stubbs and the rest of the lads would still be alive. If only. A hollow feeling ran through Porter just then. Once again, he'd failed his muckers when they needed him the most. Bald must have seen the look of despair in his eyes because he placed a hand on his mucker's shoulder and looked him hard in the eye.

'We'll get them,' said Bald. 'Mark my words, mate. We'll find the fuckers who did this, and we'll make them pay.' He looked back to the ambo and gritted his teeth. 'Whoever did this is gonna regret the day they took us on.'

EIGHTEEN

Whitehall, London.
The next day. 1759 hours.

Cecilia Lakes, the recently-promoted Assistant Chief and Director of Operations and Intelligence at SIS, had done well for herself. It had taken her the best part of twenty years, but the daughter of the former head of the Civil Service had finally escaped her father's shadow. Lakes was now one of the most powerful women in the country, the second-in-command at MI6. She reminded herself of this fact as she quick-walked down the flight of stairs leading to the basement beneath the Cabinet Office. She had faced many challenges in her life. She had dealt with Provo terrorists, Russian oligarchs and Colombian drug barons. Not to mention the old boys' network at MI6 that resented having to work with a woman smarter than most of them put together. Now she was having to deal with the biggest crisis of her life. Lakes was going to need to call on all of her experience to get through it.

She tried to compose herself as she strode down the bland corridor leading towards Cabinet Office Briefing Room A. There were in fact a dozen COBRA rooms. Most were cramped back rooms the size of broom cupboards, each assigned to a dedicated government department to allow them to get live int in the middle of COBRA briefings. One room was used by the intelligence services. Another belonged to the Home Office, a third to the Army. And so on. Lakes knew the layout well. It had practically been her second home in the hours since the attack in south Wales. There had been COBRA briefings every hour since news of the attack. Everything had moved very fast. The general threat level had been raised to amber. The army placed on high alert. All major ports and airports put on standby, with officials checking who was leaving the country. Separately, another team was back at Vauxhall, checking the whereabouts of every person of interest to the security services. Meanwhile, the National Crime Squad detectives were sifting through the masses of evidence at the crime scene, cataloguing every fragment of shrapnel and searching through thousands of hours of CCTV footage. It had been a frenzy of activity, and Lakes had only slept four hours in the past two days. And now she'd been called in for another COBRA pre-meeting.

She entered the room at the far end of the corridor. The main COBRA briefing room didn't look much like a place where matters of national security were discussed. It looked more like a conference room in a dingy lawyer's office. There was a long table in the middle with twenty cheap seats huddled around it. Dim panel lights coloured everything sickly yellow. The walls were the colour of mustard. There were boxes of files stacked either side of the table, and telephone cables running all over the place.

Five men were sitting around the table.

The man at the far end of the table was Osbert Bell, the Home Secretary. He was a slender man with long manicured hands and a smooth complexion. Next to him sat a dour-looking man with jowly cheeks and a face ready to work itself into a scowl at the slightest provocation. He sipped tea from a chipped West Bromwich Albion coffee mug. Dudley Granger was the Downing Street press officer, and he wielded an unusual amount of power over the Prime Minister. To the right of Granger was Michael Sutter, the Chief of the Defence Staff. Next to Sutter sat Lake's boss, Sir Alan Pettigrove, the Director-General of MI6. Next to Pettigrove there was a man Lakes didn't recognise. He was younger than the rest, with a baby face, and he wore a pair of thick horn-rimmed glasses. He smiled briefly at Lakes as she took her seat.

'Right on time,' Osbert Bell said. His voice was so smooth you could have broken out the Pimms and played croquet on it. He gestured to the other faces seated around the table. 'I'm sure you're familiar with everyone here, Miss Lakes. Except perhaps Clarence Hawkridge. He's our Director of Counter-terrorism Operations over at Thames House.'

Lakes nodded at Hawkridge then slid into the chair, wondering why this pre-meet had been called. All the major defence and security chiefs in one place. And no one else from the cabinet, Lakes noticed.

She had no time to idly speculate. Bell cleared his throat and stared down the barrel of his long nose at her. 'Before we begin, I assume there have been no further developments since we last convened?'

Lakes glanced at her boss, then shook her head. 'Nothing so far, Home Secretary. But we're working on it. There's a lot of ground to cover, as you can imagine.'

Bell nodded. 'We still don't have confirmed identities on the bodies we recovered from the scene?'

'Not yet, Home Secretary. We've run their fingerprints through our systems. No matches. As we suspected, the passports and driving licences they were carrying are faked. Interpol and the NSA are cross-referencing their profiles with their own databases. But we're not hopeful.'

'That leaves us with the tattoos,' Hawkridge cut in.

'Tattoos?' Granger enquired.

Bell smiled at Lakes. 'Perhaps you'd care to bring Dudley up to speed.'

'Both gunmen had the same tattoo,' Lakes said, looking to Granger. 'A red cross pattée.'

'It's been used by various orders down the centuries,' Hawkridge added. 'The Teutonic Knights, the Crusaders, and so on. Indeed, the Germans borrowed the style for the Iron Cross.'

'How the hell does that help us?' Granger muttered.

Lakes cleared her throat. 'It could be that the tattoo means something. Maybe the gunmen belong to some kind of a group. Like the mark of a gang? Or it could mean nothing at all. Maybe the shooters just got the same tattoo for a joke.'

'Do we know of any terrorist groups using this pattée cross today?'

'To the best of our knowledge, no,' said Hawkridge. 'But that doesn't mean they don't exist, of course. It could belong to some new fringe organisation that hasn't shown up in our radar yet. It's a possibility.'

Granger looked unimpressed. 'Is that all we have? A bloody tattoo that may or may not belong to a group that may or may not exist?'

'There is something else,' Bell added. 'Perhaps you'd care to explain, Miss Lakes.'

Granger looked at her. So did everyone else at the table. 'Well?'

'We have a positive ID on one of the gunmen who escaped.'

'How?'

'We got lucky. Someone flagged him up. He's on our watch list.'

'One of the gunmen was known to us?'

Pettigrove stepped in now. 'Thousands of people are known to us, Dudley. The watch list changes all the time. Some people are added, others drop off. We can't track all of them, all of the time. The man in question dropped off a while ago.'

'How many people know about this?'

'No one outside this room,' Hawkridge said. 'We're not saying anything publicly, of course, other than the number of casualties and the involvement of British armed forces personnel.'

'And we'd very much like to keep it that way,' Granger said. 'As far as the PM's concerned, the less information the redtops have the better on this one.'

'For operational reasons, of course,' Bell chipped in. 'We don't want the people who did this to know that we're on to them.' His lips curled up at the edges as he glanced around the room. 'Do we, chaps?'

Lakes flashed a quizzical look at her boss. Sir Alan said nothing. Bell removed his glasses and rubbed his tired eyes.

'Let us speak frankly,' he continued. 'This attack was unprecedented. We can all agree on that. Terrorist attacks are to be expected once every so often, of course. One of the perils of being a free society. One can't stop them all, sadly. But a couple of swarthy Arab types killing a few civilians with their home-made bombs is something we can absorb. They present no great threat. But this . . . this attack is different. The people who did this were sending a message to us.' He dug out a handkerchief from his pocket and wiped his spectacle lenses. 'Wouldn't you agree, Miss Lakes?'

It was more of a statement than a question. Everyone stared intently at Lakes. She swallowed hard and nodded. 'It certainly appears that way, Home Secretary.'

Bell paused. He put his glasses back on, looked to Granger as if seeking permission. Then he looked back to Lakes. Said, 'Then, in that case, perhaps it's time we sent a message of our own.'

He let the last sentence hang in the air for a beat. Lakes sat very still as Granger leaned forward and spoke. He was thumbing a coin in his right hand. One of those coins they handed out in Alcoholics Anonymous to celebrate another year of sobriety. Lakes recognised it, because her father used to keep a set in a desk drawer in his bedroom. He'd managed to collect twenty-eight such coins before he took his own life.

'Let's cut to the chase, gentlemen,' said Granger. 'Politically, the attack's a fucking disaster. Fifty-five of our best young servicemen killed, right on our bloody doorstep. Losing our brave boys abroad is unfortunate, but, well . . . It's not the same. We expect a few casualties when we're fighting in some godfor-saken shithole in the Middle East. But an attack here, in Britain? It's unheard of. The Prime Minister looks weak. We all look fucking weak.'

Granger paused as he swung his dead-eyed gaze across the room. Everyone visibly squirmed. Christ, this guy's got a lot of clout, Lakes thought. No one else could speak in that tone to the intelligence chiefs and get away with it.

'Dudley is correct, of course,' Sutter put in, cautiously looking at Granger. 'I understand that our friends across the pond are starting to question the value of our relationship. They're openly wondering whether 22 SAS can be relied upon any more, if they're not even safe in their own back yard.'

Lakes nodded, grasping the point. It was the world's worst-kept secret that the Yanks found Britain useful for two reasons: GCHQ, and the SAS. And one of them had just suffered the deadliest attack in its history.

Now it was Bell's turn to speak. He shifted in his chair, like maybe he was sitting on a pile of broken glass. 'We've spoken with the PM. He's keen to explore the possibility of alternative action.'

Lakes cleared her throat. 'Alternative action?'

Bell nodded again. 'It's our understanding that a full investigation could take months. Years, even. It took over a decade to bring the Lockerbie bombers to trial. We don't have that long in this situation. We need action now.' He stared hard at Lakes. 'We need these men gone.'

Lakes swallowed. Her throat suddenly felt very hot and heavy. Granger watched her, drumming his fingers on the table. 'You want us to find the men who carried out the attack?'

'And take them out,' Bell added uncomfortably. 'Using whatever means necessary.'

'By "take them out", you mean—'

'Kill,' Bell cut her off. 'We want you to kill the men who did this. All of them.' He gestured to Pettigrove. 'Sir Alan assures me you're the perfect person for the job.'

Lakes looked quickly to her boss. He smiled weakly, then hack-coughed.

'There must be a layer between us, of course,' Granger cut in moodily as he scribbled on an A4 pad in front of him. A pair of tits, Lakes noted with a slight measure of disgust. 'Plausible deniability. That's the buzz word for this operation.'

'Of course,' Lakes said. 'I understand.' Thinking, *There's more layers on this thing than a Hollywood pre-nup.*

Hawkridge said, 'I'll have a list drawn up. Hereford men who fit the criteria.'

Bell nodded busily. 'Fine. But I don't need to know the details.' He looked around the table to underline his point. 'Michael will keep me informed on the big picture. As for the details, that's up to you lot to sort out. We don't want to know. We don't even want to know that we don't know. Am I clear?'

Lakes nodded curtly at the Home Secretary. Typical Whitehall buck-passing. Osbert Bell was a master of washing his hands of responsibility whilst simultaneously taking all the credit.

'Yes, Home Secretary,' she said.

'Good.' Bell promptly stood up and straightened his back, signalling the end of the briefing. He paused and looked around the room. 'It goes without saying that this conversation never happened.'

'Naturally,' said Hawkridge.

'I leave the planning details to you,' Bell added, looking at Hawkridge and Lakes in turn. 'Clarence here will work with you on the particulars. He's good at this sort of thing. Now, if that's everything, gentlemen?'

No one had any questions. The men in suits slid out of their chairs and made for the door, each of them wearing grim faces. Lakes turned to follow them but then Bell moved towards her, intercepting her before she could reach the door.

'A quick word, Miss Lakes. If you wouldn't mind.'

Lakes stood by the door. Bell waited until everyone else had stepped outside. Then he closed the door behind them. He paced around the table, tutting and shaking his head.

'Damned terrible news about Alan.'

'News?' Lakes asked, not following.

Bell feigned ignorance. 'Haven't you heard? Poor bugger's got the cancer. Started out in the liver, now it's spread to his lungs and brain. He's refused chemo, the stubborn old fool. Doctors have given him three months to live. Absolutely tragedy.' Bell stared at the floor, sounding about as genuine as a four-pound note. 'I imagine this must be hard for you.'

Lakes let her eyes fall to the floor. 'Alan's been something of a mentor to me.'

'That's tough.'

An uneasy moment of silence hung over the room. Then Bell

leaned in close to Lakes and lowered his voice. She caught a whiff of his stale breath. It reeked of garlic and red wine.

Bell said, 'Between you and me, we'll have to start looking for Alan's replacement very soon. These things can't wait.' He paused and a smile played out on his face like a knife slitting through silk. 'Should this operation run smoothly, then your candidacy would be hard to ignore, Miss Lakes. *Very* hard indeed.'

NINETEEN

Hereford.
Two days later. 0811 hours.
Porter reached for the Bushmills. There were still a few drops of the good stuff left in the bottom of the bottle, along with the remnants of a stubbed-out cigarette. He shrugged and pressed the bottle to his lips. He tipped the whisky dregs down his throat. Then he reached for his pack of Bensons, sparked up a tab and took a long drag. Ah, better.

Breakfast.

Three days had passed since the attack, and Porter had done nothing but drink and stare at the grisly footage playing out on the news channels. Empty whisky bottles were scattered around the living room, along with several crushed fag packets and a couple of greasy takeaway cartons he'd barely touched. He hadn't set foot outside since the Training Wing had been stood down. There was a media blackout in place. Orders from the CO. Every surviving guy on the Training Wing had been told to stay low and avoid going into town unless it was absolutely essential. Reporters from the national rags were out in force in Hereford, talking to all the local shags and punters in the hopes of finding out a few scraps of information and piecing together an exclusive. So Porter had shut himself indoors with the curtains drawn, drinking and trying to forget.

But he couldn't escape. The news channels were having a field day. In the absence of hard facts, everyone was engaged in feverish round-the-clock speculation. The TV in the corner of the living room was tuned in to Sky News. A sombre-faced brunette reporter was standing in front of a police cordon down the road from the Storey Arms. Helicopters were buzzing overhead and a couple of local bobbies were standing watch on the other side of the cordon, keeping the hacks at bay.

'Sources at Whitehall have confirmed fifty-five soldiers were killed in Friday's attack,' the reporter said in a grave tone of voice. 'As of yet, no terrorist group has claimed responsibility for the bombing. Many are, of course, speculating that this may be the start of a new campaign by the IRA to undermine the Good Friday Agreement. Others believe that Islamic fundamentalists may be behind the attack. Earlier, the Prime Minister had this to say.'

The camera cut to the steps of 10 Downing Street on a grey afternoon. A million paparazzi bulbs flashed as a middle-aged man with wavy black hair stood in front of a wooden podium. Prime Minister Andrew Massey's trademark cheerful smirk had been utterly wiped from his smooth face. Now he stood in front of the world's press, brow heavily furrowed, wearing a look of grim sobriety.

'Three days ago, Britain suffered an unprecedented attack on her armed forces,' the Prime Minister began in a grave tone of voice. 'My thoughts and prayers go out to the victims and their families, and all those affected by this barbaric act. Let me be clear. Those behind the attack, whoever they are, wish to destroy our society. But we are stronger than that. Our resolve is firmer than the terrorists. At present, we do not know who was responsible for killing our brave young soldiers. But in due course, we shall find those responsible and bring them to justice, as a civilised nation...'

Porter hit the mute button. Finished his cigarette and chucked the butt into the empty bottle. Then he reached for the phone. His hands were shaking as he punched in the number. He put the receiver to his ear and glanced at the clock. 0812 hours. They'd be heading out the door on the school run any minute now. The phone rang and rang, and for a moment he thought no one would pick up. Then a young, bright voice answered on the fifth ring.

'Hello?'

Porter smiled. 'Happy birthday, love.'

There was an excited shriek on the other end of the line. 'Daddy!'

Something warm swept through Porter at the sound of his daughter's voice. Eight years old. His little girl. He could hardly believe how quickly the time had passed. He pressed the receiver closer to his ear. In the background he could hear someone rushing around.

'Did you get lots of presents?' Porter asked, his voice choked with emotion.

'Oh, Dad, you *have* to see them all,' Sandy went on breathlessly. 'Mum got me a Barbie dream house and two Barbie dolls. And Stuart got me a pony. He's amazing. I'm going to call him Dancer.'

Porter frowned. Stuart. The bloke Diana had been seeing after she'd relocated to Nottingham. Some moneyed-up big-shot who made his fortune in shopping centres in the north-west. Guy was forever splashing the cash on Sandy. You can't buy love, thought Porter. But this prick was having a damn good go.

'Is that so?' he asked through gritted teeth, rage brewing inside his chest.

'I have to go to school now, but you're coming to my party this weekend? Dad?'

Before Porter could reply a sharp voice in the background said, 'Pass the phone to mummy.'

Porter sparked up another tab. There was a fumbling noise, and he could hear Diana telling Sandy to go and wait in the car. Then his wife's voice came clearly down the line. 'You shouldn't be calling here, John. Not without letting me know first. That's what we agreed.'

'I just wanted to wish her a happy birthday,' Porter replied. 'That's all.'

Diana sighed. It came down the line more like an angry hiss. 'I was meaning to call you. I saw the pictures on the news. Those poor soldiers. God, it's so awful. Are you—?'

'I'm fine,' Porter replied flatly. 'Can't really talk about it.'

Silence. He took another pull on his tab and blew out smoke. He could hear Sandy's faint voice in the background, pleading with her mother to give the phone back so she could speak to Daddy.

Porter said, 'I was thinking, maybe I could come down for the birthday party. Give Sandy her present, like.'

And to see her face, he thought. Sweet Jesus, I miss her.

There was a long pause. Then Diana said, 'I really don't think that's a good idea.'

'I wouldn't be any harm. I'll be in and out in five minutes. Christ, Di. I'm not asking for much here.'

More silence. Porter could feel it hanging in the air. Like fruit from a tree.

'Stuart and I have been talking,' she said at last. 'We think it's for the best if you stay away for a while. What Sandy needs in her life right now is stability. When she hears your voice, it – it confuses things.'

Porter gripped the phone so hard he thought it might crack. 'I'm her old man, for fuck's sake.'

'Right now she needs a *father*, John. Not some stranger who occasionally shows up blazing drunk at two in the morning. Stuart's here for her. For both of us. I'm sorry, but that's just the way it is.'

Porter said nothing. He smoked some more. He thought of all the angry things he could hurl down the line at Diana, but when you drilled down to it, there was only himself to blame. He'd fucked it up. Maybe Diana was right, the familiar voice prodded at him. Maybe Sandy was better off without her old man in her life. A rich twat like Stuart could give her a good life. She could have everything she ever wanted. What could he give her?

Fuck-all.

'John? Are you still there?'

Porter hung up the phone. Stubbed out his tab and looked down at the clumsily wrapped present he'd bought for Sandy. A cuddly penguin he'd picked up at the local toy shop for twenty quid. And there was Stuart buying her a pony. A fucking *pony*, for Christ's sake. How the hell could he match up to that?

Face it, John. You might be Sandy's old man, but you're just a washed-up old cunt.

The pounding between his temples returned. God, he needed another drink. He got up, rooted around the flat and came up empty. He was flat out of booze, and the shops weren't open yet. The only thing he could find was a bottle of mouthwash in the bathroom cabinet. There was some alcohol in it, according to the label. Right now, that would have to do. Anything to numb the pain. Porter screwed the top off. He was about to take a long swig when the phone rang.

He set the mouthwash down and paced back over to the phone. Probably Di. Probably mad at him for hanging up just now. She'd give it to him with both barrels. He picked up the phone and said, 'Yeah?'

'Porter, it's Stones here.'

Porter sat up straight. He recognised the voice of the Regiment ops officer. Stones sounded serious, thought Porter. But then again, he always sounded serious with that deadpan Brummie accent.

'Boss?'

'Listen, the CO wants you to come in for a chat.'

'What for?' Porter asked.

'No bloody clue,' said Stones. 'But he's been pacing up and down all morning. If I were you, I'd get my arse down here right fucking now.'

Twenty-five minutes later Porter was rolling through the gates at RAF Credenhill. He eased his motor into the packed car park and unfolded himself from behind the wheel.

The atmosphere inside the camp was restless. Porter could sense it as he marched across the parade ground towards the main Regimental HQ, a plain building overlooking the parade ground. The Regiment was on high alert. The SP team was back at Hereford, with a second squadron overseas on stand-by for further action. All the guys were milling around the camp and bumping guns, their kit squared away, ready to move out at a moment's notice. No one said much. They were spitting mad for vengeance.

Porter trudged past the guard room. It was eerily quiet. Normally all the lads would be sitting around watching pornos and taking the piss, but this morning the guys were grim-faced and silent. Porter paced up the stairs and hurried down a narrow corridor leading towards the Kremlin, the Regiment's inner sanctum. As he swept past the ops rooms Porter wondered again why the CO had called him in this morning. It couldn't be anything to do with the Training Wing, he knew. Selection had been suspended indefinitely, with the remaining students being processed back to their parent units and the head shed conducting a root-and-branch review of the SOPs to try and prevent a similar attack happening in the future. Besides, half of the instructors were dead. There would be no new Selection courses for a while.

So why does the CO want to see me now?

Porter arrived at the door of Lieutenant-Colonel Graydon Ruck. He straightened his back and knocked on the door. There was a slight pause. Then a booming voice carried through the wood.

'Enter.'

Porter stepped inside a small, sparsely-furnished room. The Commanding Officer of 22 SAS sat behind a metal desk piled high with manila folders and printed-out documents. Graydon Ruck was a tall man, pencil-thin, with eyes the colour of stainless steel knives and lips that were pressed tight, like he was trying to crack nuts with them. Ruck was one of the new breed of officers in the Regiment. The guy looked more like a manager at a branch of Barclays, or maybe a regional head of sales for an office supplies company. He was political, corporate. Safe. Ten years from now Ruck would probably be making six figures in a cosy position as head of security for an oil firm, living with his trophy wife in a Buckinghamshire mansion while Porter rooted around for loose change down the back of the sofa.

There were two chairs opposite Ruck. The one on the left was empty.

Sitting in the chair on the right was John Bald.

'Glad you could join us.' Ruck fixed a smile at Porter. 'Please, John. Take a seat.'

Porter hesitated for a moment. The fact that Bald was here confirmed his earlier suspicions. This definitely wasn't anything to do with the Training Wing. He figured maybe the CO wanted to run over their statements before they spoke to the police. Make sure they were singing from the same hymn sheet. He shrugged casually, dropped into his chair and turned to Ruck. The guy had heavy bags under his eyes. He looked like he hadn't slept in a week. Which probably wasn't far from the truth.

'I'll make this quick,' Ruck began impatiently. 'I've got a mountain of paperwork to get through, as you might well imagine. Whitehall's been on my case every hour since the attack. On top of that, trying to manage this media blackout is a bloody nightmare.'

Porter saw something in Ruck's eyes. Something he'd never seen before. It was fear, he realised. The Regiment found itself in unchartered territory. The loss of a few Blades during an op would have been bad enough. But to have so many of their own slotted a few miles from the Regiment headquarter, was a shock that everyone was struggling to deal with. Including Ruck.

'You're being seconded to MI6,' Ruck went on. 'Both of you. Effective immediately.'

He leaned forward and planted his hands on the desk, waiting for a response. Porter frowned. Bald stared at Ruck, puzzled.

'What for, boss?'

Ruck rolled his eyes. 'Take a wild guess.'

'The attack?'

Ruck nodded. 'I'm not privy to the ins-and-outs. Vauxhall wasn't exactly forthcoming with the particulars, as you can probably imagine. But reading between the lines, it looks like they're putting together a covert team. Downing Street wants action, gentlemen. Apparently the chaps over at Vauxhall are being given carte blanche to get the bastards who did this. It seems they've requested you two to help out on the ground.'

'Why us?' Porter asked.

Ruck shrugged. 'Frankly, your guess is as good as mine. All I know is, they asked for you two specifically.' He added bitterly, 'They must have their reasons, I suppose.'

Porter said nothing. From the look on Ruck's face he guessed that the suits at Vauxhall had kept the CO out of the loop as far as possible. Nothing would have pissed him off more, Porter realised with an inward smile. Ruck was comfortable kissing Whitehall arse and ingratiating himself with the Westminster set. Being kept in the dark on a top-secret op involving two of his men must have really been eating away at the guy.

'Military transport's sending a car down at 1300 hours. They'll pick you up from the gates out front and drive you down to London.'

'Where's the RV?' Bald asked.

'The Wainwright Hotel in Marylebone. An MI6 liaison will meet you at the Piano Bar at 1700 hours.' Ruck leaned back in his chair and steepled his fingers on the desk. 'That's as much as I know and as much as they were willing to tell me. Questions?'

Porter pursed his lips. There were a million questions pinballing around inside his head, but there was no point asking Ruck any of them. Clearly whoever was running things over at Vauxhall wanted to share as little as possible with the CO. Which suggested that whatever the suits wanted from Bald and Porter, they wanted it to be strictly off the books. If that was how the Firm wanted to play it then fine, thought Porter. They'd get their answers soon enough.

'None, boss,' he said.

'Good.' Ruck straightened his back and gestured to the door. 'Then I suggest you both get a bloody move on.'

TWENTY

1300 hours.

The car was waiting for them at the camp gates. A Rover 400. Possibly green, although it was hard to tell beneath the six inches of dust and bird shit. Which made it perfect for transporting a couple of Regiment men down to London. Bald climbed into the back. Porter folded himself into the front passenger seat. After the briefing with the CO he'd returned home and taken a hot shower and then shaved and changed into his civvies. Now he wore a pair of dark-blue jeans and a grey leather jacket over a wrinkled flannel shirt and t-shirt combo, as well as a scuffed pair of Merrell boots. He felt vaguely more human than a few hours earlier.

The driver was a prematurely balding guy in a crumpled suit who introduced himself as Glover. He didn't say much, and Porter didn't bother pressing him for details. If Ruck knew the sum total of fuck-all, Glover was likely to know even less. The three men were silent as they headed south out of Hereford and hit the A40 just outside of Gloucester. Every few miles Glover checked the rear-view mirror, no doubt to make sure they weren't being tailed. They weren't, as far as Porter could tell.

He tuned out and watched the landscape ticker-taping by. He found his thoughts drifting back to the meeting with Ruck. What the fuck did the Firm want with a couple of outcast Regiment men? Whatever it was, it had to be questionable, Porter decided. If the spooks had wanted the SAS for an above-the-board op, they would have fully briefed Ruck rather than keeping him in the dark. They would have asked the CO for his best men, and they would have asked for more than two of them. So whatever the Firm had in mind for Bald and Porter, it wasn't going to be a regular security detail. Porter found his curiosity building as they raced towards London.

After maybe a hundred miles the landscape shifted to a palette of greys and dirty browns. They were heading into Porter's old neighbourhood now. Glover turned off Western Avenue and steered the Rover onto the Westway, rolling past Wembley Stadium. They motored down a three-lane stretch of worn black-top flanked by rows of council houses that looked like a set of rotten brown teeth. Everything was instantly familiar to Porter. The drab industrial estates and halal food shops, the neglected parks half-filled with teenagers pushing prams and migrants clutching plastic shopping bags. They shuttled along the flyover past Shepherd's Bush and White City and a bunch of other places choked with traffic until they emerged onto the sprawling inter-section at Edgware Road. Then Glover took a road that funnelled them down towards Marylebone.

It was like moving from one city to another. All the tower blocks and council estates disappeared from view, replaced with a neatly-arranged grid of elegant red-brick townhouses inter-spersed with gleaming glass-and-steel towers. The streets were lined with quaint trees, and scrubbed clean of bird shit and gum. The cars were all Maseratis and Bentleys and Mercedes CLK coupés. The only black face Porter saw was the guy sweeping the steps of the old Marylebone Town Hall. All the people wore tailored suits and carried leather briefcases. They walked quickly, like they had somewhere important to be.

Eight minutes later, Glover pulled up outside the Wainwright.

Porter was light-blinded as he stepped out of the Rover. He stretched his legs and gave the hotel the once-over. It was a great big red-brick place the size of a medieval castle. It looked like something out of a Harry Potter film. A row of trees screened the entrance from the main road. There was a tower mounted in the middle of the rooftop with a clock face on the front, like a minia-ture Big Ben. The ageing doorman cast a long look at Porter, as if weighing up whether he should admit the trampish-looking Blade. With a doubtful expression the doorman opened the grand mahogany door and Bald and Porter stepped inside a lobby full of suited-up rich types speaking in busy voices. Porter glanced around. To his right stood a bank of lifts, with the main reception desk in front of them. To the left was the Piano Bar.

The RV.

Porter led the way. They strode into the bar and sank into a couple of leather armchairs and casually scanned the joint. It was a dimly-lit room with retro furnishings and a big mirror behind the bar with a rack of luxury Scottish single-malts arranged on a shelf in front of it. Most of the punters were red-faced men in pin-striped suits. Their throated laughs filled the air, drawing out the classical music. There was a young woman sitting on her own in the far corner of the bar, next to a door leading to the toilets. Porter noticed her because she was the only one sitting by herself, and because she looked a little cheap compared to her surroundings. Her hair was dyed peroxide blonde, and she wore tight jeans and high heels. She was smoking a cigarette and flicking through a glossy magazine. In the corner of his eye Porter noticed Bald casting a dirty look at the blonde.

'Any sign of our man?' Bald asked, looking away.

Porter checked his watch. It said 1647 hours. He shook his head. 'We're early.'

'Best get a round in, then. Don't want to stand out next to all these sloppy Herberts.'

A bored-looking waitress with a thick eastern European accent wandered over to the table and took their order. Bald went for a bottle of Yank lager. Porter settled on a double measure of Bushmill. The waitress came back with their drinks, and the bill. Bald made to reach inside his jacket. Then a frown creased his face and he looked to Porter, clicking his tongue.

'Shit. Left my wallet at home, mate. Do us a favour and pick up the tab.'

Porter grudgingly reached for the bill. He looked down at the total and did a spit-take. Jesus, he thought. Twenty quid. You could buy a crate of Special Brew for less than that. The waitress tapped her foot and waited. Porter dug out his wallet and handed over his last crumpled twenty-pound note. The waitress almost looked sorry for him as she handed back a few coins in change.

As soon as she had moved away, Bald got up from his seat.

'Need a slash,' he said. 'Been busting for a piss ever since we left Hereford.'

Porter nodded. He watched Bald as the guy threaded his way towards the toilets at the rear of the bar. He took a detour, hooking around the edge of the bar and swinging directly past the blonde. The woman looked up, saw Bald and quickly stubbed out her cigarette. Then she grabbed her leather handbag and moved towards Bald as he approached the toilets. Bald stopped by the entrance and said something to her. The blonde glanced nervously around, then reached into her handbag. Porter's view was partially blocked by the crowd of Hooray Henrys but for a split second he thought he saw the blonde passing something to Bald. A package of some kind. Before he could get a better look the blonde had turned away and was moving at a brisk pace towards the second exit at the rear. At the same time Bald disappeared inside the toilets. Five minutes later he strolled out, puffed out his cheeks and swaggered back over to the table wearing a big grin.

'What was all that about?' Porter asked.

Bald clenched his brow. 'What do you mean, mate?'

'That blonde bit. The one you were chatting to just now.'

'Her? That's nothing, that. Just some tight bird trying it on. Happens all the time.' Bald winked at him. The grin widened. 'You know what they say. Them posh birds love a bit of rough.'

Porter smiled and took a sip of his drink. Thought about pressing Bald over the blonde. But he couldn't be sure what he'd seen. He parked the thought. Necked the rest of his Bushmills in a single gulp.

'Jesus, mate,' said Bald. 'And I thought the Scots could fucking drink. The rate you're going, you could drink half of Glasgow under the table.'

Porter put down the glass. 'What'd you mean by that, Jock?'

'Nothing. Just saying.'

But the look in his eyes gave Bald away. Porter knew what he was thinking. *The guy's a full-blown alcoholic. How the fuck is he supposed to perform?* Porter knew, because he was thinking the exact same thing. He was at the fag end of his career in the Regiment, and whatever the Firm had lined up for them he would need to be sharp. If he didn't stop boozing, he wouldn't be much use in the field.

Six minutes later their liaison walked into the bar.

Porter clocked the guy straightaway. He looked almost as out of place as the blonde. But for different reasons. He had a six-quid haircut and cheap-looking shoes, and his brown suit looked like it came straight off the discount rack at Burtons. He sported the tiniest amount of bumfluff on his chin in some pitiful attempt to make himself look older than he really was. But it was the eyes that gave him away. They swept across the room in that way that only suits working for the Firm did. Scanning, they called it. Taking in everything in sight at a moment's notice. The liaison's gaze quickly settled on Bald and Porter. He strode over to their table and greeted them with a slight nod.

'Either of you gentlemen know a chap called Steve Mann?' he asked. 'Steve from Doncaster?'

'Sorry, mate,' Porter replied, giving the prearranged response. 'We're both from Chelmsford. Never been to Doncaster in our lives.'

The liaison nodded again, their identities established. He lowered his voice. 'I'm Nealy,' he said flatly, giving them the usual warm and friendly Firm welcome. 'Follow me, please. They're waiting.'

'Who?' Bald asked.

'You'll see.'

Porter sank the dregs of his Bushmills, putting the lid on the hangover drilling between his temples. Then he and Bald followed Nealy out of the bar. They paced across the spit-polished lobby and took the next available Otis lift to the twelfth floor. Thirty seconds later they were following Nealy down a wide, stuffy corridor lined with old paintings. Eventually Nealy stopped outside a room with a discreet brass plaque next to it that read PRESIDENTIAL SUITE. He took out a keycard from his jacket pocket and swiped it through the reader. The reader clicked and the lock light flashed green. Then Nealy cracked open the door and motioned for Bald and Porter to step inside.

They entered a hallway that smelled of potpourri and money. There was a private dining room ahead, and a bathroom to the right that seemed to be constructed entirely of white marble and gold. Nealy ushered them into a large room to the left. They swept into a lounge twice the size of Porter's flat, and maybe a thousand times more expensive. An Egyptian rug covered the polished marble floor. The furnishings were antique and the paintings hanging from the walls looked like they belonged in the Louvre. If Sotheby's rented a storage unit, Porter figured it would look something like this.

Three figures were sitting around a coffee table in the middle of the room. Two men and a woman. They stood up to greet the two Blades as they entered. Porter sized up the woman first. She had dark brown shoulder-length hair and wide green eyes. She wore a black skirt suit and low heels and although she appeared to be in her late forties, Porter could tell from her figure that she kept herself in good shape. She greeted Porter with a professional smile. The kind you get when you walk into Coutts to open a bank account, maybe. Her whole demeanour suggested someone who knew exactly where she was going in her life, and what she had to do to get there.

'Thank you, Nealy,' the woman said.

Nealy took the hint. He turned on his heels and paced out of the suite, closing the door behind him. Once he was gone the woman turned back to Porter and Bald. She still wore the professional smile, but it was wavering slightly at the edges.

'Thank you for joining us, gentlemen. My name is Cecilia Lakes, Director of Operations at MI6.' She gestured towards the nearest of the two men. 'And this is Clarence Hawkridge, MI5.'

Porter swivelled his gaze towards Hawkridge. The guy frowned at him, as if Porter was something he'd just scraped off the bottom of his shoe. Hawkridge had a childlike face and horn-rimmed glasses and thinning hair. His lips curled up at the edges slightly in a sneering expression.

He said, 'Thank you for coming, chaps. Hope you had a pleasant journey.'

Bald grunted and said, 'It was fucking wild.'

Hawkridge adjusted his glasses. Smiled uncomfortably. Lakes moved on. Gestured to the third man. 'This is Marcus Keppel. CEO of Templar International.'

Porter recognised the name immediately. The ex-CO of 22 SAS. He had a square jaw and bright, piercing blue eyes. He wore a charcoal two-piece with a crisp white shirt and a popped collar button, no tie. His shoes were polished to within an inch of their life. His cufflinks gleamed. The guy was so crisp it was like he'd walked straight out of the fridge. Keppel looked posh as fuck, but hard as nails. One of those Ruperts with an uber-competitive streak, Porter figured. The guy probably climbed mountains and competed in triathlons in his spare time.

What's Keppel doing here? Porter wondered. *I thought this was an MI6 op, not some private gig.*

'Always good to see a couple of Regiment men.' Keppel talked in a deep and matter-of-fact voice that was rough around the edges. 'You were in Beirut, if I recall?'

Porter nodded. 'That's right.'

'Bloody mess, that. After my time, of course, but I heard about what happened on the grapevine.'

Porter felt his hand instinctively clench. He glanced around the room, hoping to see a rack of drinks or maybe a mini-bar. There was nothing except the tray of tea and coffee and posh mineral water placed on the coffee table in front of him.

'It was a long time ago,' he said.

Keppel nodded professionally. His eyes were cold and grey and hard. Like wet stones on a winter beach. 'Still. These things stay with a man. We've all been there, lad. Nothing for it but to stand tall and soldier on through.'

There was a pause of silence, and then Lakes gestured to the empty sofa next to the coffee table. 'Please. Sit down. Coffee? Tea? Biscuits?'

'Fine, love,' said Porter as he parked himself on the sofa. He almost asked for a shot of Bushmills. Almost, but didn't.

Lakes reached for a pack of Parliaments from her handbag and sparked up with a silver Zippo lighter. She took a long drag. Exhaled. Porter noticed a thick manila folder lying next to the ashtray on the coffee table. Lakes took another pull on her smoke then reached for the file and flipped it open to the first page.

'John Porter,' she began, as if doing a book reading. 'Born in Ealing on 7th May, 1962. Served in the Irish Guards from 1980 to 1988. Transferred to the SAS the same year. Served until '92, then given a six-month sabbatical before returning to the Regiment in 1993. Lost two fingers during a hostage-rescue operation in Beirut in '89. Separated from your wife, Diana, and your eight-year-old daughter Sandy.'

Porter listened impassively as Lakes read out his file. This was a typical Firm play, he knew. The Vauxhall suits get you nice and comfortable. Then they read out your file in front of you, showing you how much they know about you, from your primary school reports right down to what brand of toothpaste you use. Their aim was to intimidate you. It was the Firm's way of saying, *See how easily we can find out about the tiniest details of your life? Don't try hiding any aces up your sleeve, because it won't work.*

Lakes flipped the page and turned to Bald. Gave him the same treatment.

'John Fraser Bald. Born 20th June, 1971 at the Maryfield Hospital in Dundee. Attended St John's Roman Catholic High School. Left at sixteen and joined the Black Watch. Passed Selection to 22 SAS in 1993. The same year, faced charges for almost triggering a diplomatic incident by crossing the border in Northern Ireland and killing several Provisional IRA suspects, as well as an MI5 informant.'

'To be fair,' Bald said, grinning, 'those Irish fuckers started it.'

Porter raised a half smile. Lakes just stared at the Jock. Like she was suffering from a total sense-of-humour failure. She took another drag on her tab and blew smoke towards the ceiling.

'Before I continue, I must point out that everything that is said in this room is classified information. Under no circumstances will you mention our conversation to anyone else. Not to your family, not to your friends. Not now, not ten years from now. Am I clear?' She noticed Bald looking warily around the room and added, 'The room's secure. Our guys swept it thoroughly.'

'Fine,' said Bald, giving a casual shrug of his shoulders. 'What's the craic, love?'

Lakes looked at the two men carefully. 'Do you know why you're here?'

'Because someone told us to get in a car.'

Lakes arched an eyebrow at Porter. 'Is your friend always this funny?'

'Only when I'm sober,' Bald deadpanned. 'You should see me after a dozen Stellas. I'm fucking hilarious then, lass.'

Hawkridge poured himself a glass of sparkling water and took a long gulp, as if trying to calm his nerves. Keppel just sat there, carefully studying the two men and giving away nothing. His mouth was like the stroke of a knife across a throat.

Lakes said, 'You're here because of Friday's events. But you probably guessed that already.' She watched Porter. He nodded. She smoked and continued. 'The government's stance on this matter is perfectly clear. An attack of this nature cannot be tolerated, and the people behind it must be made to pay. We're putting together a team, and we want you both to be part of it.'

'What kind of a team?' Porter asked. But he already knew the answer to that question.

Lakes smoked and said, 'We want you to find the people who did this. And we want you to kill them.'

There was a pregnant silence in the room. No one said anything for what felt like a very long time, but was probably no more than four or five seconds. Then Lakes continued.

'It'll be an outside job. You'll resign from the Regiment with immediate effect, both of you. Officially you'll be working for

Templar as private contractors on the Circuit, with Marcus's blessing. Unofficially, you'll report to myself and Clarence.'

'Give up our jobs in the Regiment?' Porter spluttered. 'You can't be serious.'

'We are,' Hawkridge replied. 'Deadly, old fruit.'

Bald said, 'What about our pay? Our pensions?'

'You'll be paid by Templar, as if you were contractors on their payroll. The pay will be equal to what you currently receive at Hereford. As for your pensions, they'll be funnelled into private accounts. No one will have access to them as long as you're employed by Templar. They'll gather dust, and interest, until such a point as your contracts are terminated.'

Lakes saw the sceptical looks in their eyes and said, 'That's non-negotiable. This operation has to remain at arm's length from Whitehall. Orders from the very top. If you want in, that's how we have to play it.'

Porter pressed his lips shut. Said nothing. Now he understood why Keppel was there. To keep the Firm out of it. To disguise their involvement. Someone higher up the food chain than Lakes or Hawkridge didn't want any government fingerprints on the job. The whole thing sat uneasily with Porter. His gut instincts told him to get up and leave. *Walk away from the job, John. While you still have the chance.* Porter didn't like the idea of throwing in the towel and giving up the only job he'd ever known.

But then an image flashed in front of him. Joe Kinsella's mutilated body slumped in the road, the air choked with the putrid stench of burning flesh and metal. The garbled screams of his dying muckers carrying through the cold air. He thought of the dead soldiers' families. He thought of the police investigators collecting up the bits of bodies, and the anger flared up inside him, like someone had thrown a switch in his chest. As much as he distrusted Keppel, he couldn't leave. He'd pulsed with the desire for revenge. Now Lakes was offering him a chance to slot the guys responsible for the attack. It wasn't the kind of offer you turned down, no matter what strings were attached.

Hawkridge and Lakes exchanged a quick look. The MI5 man leaned forward, resting his hands on his knees. 'Chaps, I realise this is a big decision. If you need some time to think it through—'

Porter cut him off with a wave of his palm.

'I'm in,' he said.

Hawkridge nodded. He turned to Bald. 'And you, John?'

'I was never fucking out, mate. Who's the target?'

Lake's lips curled up slightly at the edges. Porter figured that was as close as she ever got to breaking out into a smile. She stubbed out her cigarette and cleared her throat. 'There will be several.' But right now we just have the one.'

She plucked a photograph from the folder and slid it across the table. Porter and Bald both leaned forward to get a closer look at the snap. It was a grainy shot of a heavyset guy dressed in army combats, posing in front of the camera with his shirt off. He had a tattoo of the St George's flag inked across his chest, and a distinctive red cross on the side of his neck. The cross was narrow at the centre and curved at the edges. It looked like the kind of thing knights wore over their chainmail armour in the Crusades. The guy's face was round and hard and smooth, like a bowling ball. His small eyes peered out from their deep sockets like a couple of coins glinting at the bottom of a deep well.

Porter looked at the face and recognised it with a jolt.

It was the face of the rambler he'd seen bombing it down the side of Pen y Fan. The gunman who'd escaped the Storey Arms and given Bald and Porter the slip at the Beacons reservoir. The guy Porter had nailed in the shoulder.

Tank.

TWENTY-ONE

1714 hours.

'His name is Bill Deeds,' Lakes said. She paused and reached for another cigarette from her pack. 'He's ex-Parachute Regiment. Born in Clacton in 1969. Deeds got in trouble for a string of petty offences as a teenager. He flunked his exams but earned money working as a doorman in various clubs in the East End. In 1991 Deeds joined 2 Para. Three years later, he applied for SAS Selection. He failed the distance on the Fan Dance. The following year he tried out again, but he was kicked out for failing a drugs test. His failure left him with a lifelong grudge against the Regiment.'

'What's new?' Bald said. 'Half the crap hats hate our guts.'

'Perhaps. But Deeds' hatred runs deeper than most. After he failed Selection the second time around he fell in with an Essex-based crime syndicate run by a guy called Curtis Scarsdale. The syndicate is made up of former football hooligans and old East End gangsters who got into the cocaine smuggling business. Deeds needed the money. He did a few jobs here and there for Scarsdale.'

Porter listened in silence. There were always one or two bent squaddies in the ranks. Guys who were willing to sell out their muckers in order to make a few quid. The other rankers had a special hatred for those cowards. Lakes blew out smoke as Hawkridge took up the story.

'In early 1997 Deeds went from low-life criminal to arms smuggler. Soon after he was deployed to eastern Bosnia with 2 Para, he established a contact with the local Serbian mafia. They came to an arrangement. Money in exchange for shipping arms

113

off the local army base. The Serbs readily agreed. They needed arms, and several of their weapons caches had been intercepted by NATO forces. As for Deeds, he owed money to some Albanians. A gambling debt he'd racked up.'

Hawkridge crossed his legs. Lakes puffed away on her Parliament. Keppel sat frozen. Like a statue.

'We're talking a considerable arsenal of firepower, chaps. SA80 assault rifles, Browning Hi-Power pistols, Accuracy Internal sniper rifles and LAW anti-tank projectiles. Not to mention several crates of hand grenades.' Hawkridge adjusted his glasses before continuing. 'Enough to keep the paramilitaries in business for quite a while. The plan was to smuggle the weapons off the army base at Sipovo and transport them to the border at Potocari, where the Serbian mafia had established a stronghold.'

Porter said, 'So what happened?'

Lakes stubbed out her cigarette and said, 'We found out about the plot through a local intelligence asset inside Sarajevo. We set up a sting operation alongside the RMP. Two of Deeds's associates were arrested, Dave Treadwell and Steve Blakeway. But Deeds himself never showed at the meeting point. Someone must have warned him. We put out an all-forces alert, but by then it was too late.'

Porter nodded slowly. His guts clenched like ice. Now he remembered where he'd seen Deeds's face before. In the Regiment ops room. In Bosnia.

Back then Porter had been in the country for several months, as part of a team tasked with bringing down the gangs loyal to Milosevic. By that point the paramilitary gangs had become a serious problem. In return for being badged up and put on the Interior Ministry payroll, dozens of gangs had been given free rein to butcher Bosnian and Croat Muslims. The gangs could do as they pleased, and they took the offer and ran with it. Their men killed thousands of civvies in the villages up and down the border. In response, the Regiment had been covertly inserted with orders to put a stop to the gangs and decapitate their leaderships. Porter had been awarded the Distinguished Conduct Medal for his part in the op to smash the paramilitary gangs.

But he couldn't remember much about Deeds. Far as he could recall, the guy had been a side-issue to the main event. A bent Para trying to offload stolen weapons wasn't exactly a big deal when there were Serb warlords to bring down. There had been no concerted efforts to locate Deeds. His photograph had been distributed with orders to bring him in if spotted, but he'd never been the number-one target. The guy wasn't memorable enough to warrant serious attention.

'What happened to Deeds?' asked Bald.

Lakes sighed heavily and toyed with the Zippo lighter. 'We never caught him. We looked everywhere, but Deeds just went off the grid. He simply disappeared.' She hesitated. 'Until last week.'

She reached into the folder and took out another snap. Then she placed the photograph alongside the shot of Deeds striking a bodybuilding pose. This one was a black-and-white still from a CCTV feed. The image wasn't exactly clear, but Porter could just about make out the muscular guy in a hooded sweatshirt and sneakers, standing next to a knackered truck. The figure had his hands stuffed in his jeans pockets and he was looking away from the camera, but it was unmistakably Bill Deeds. Same build, same size. Same widow's peak atop his round head. There were five other guys next to him and a bunch of numbers and letters at the top that Porter didn't understand. At the bottom there was the date and time.

06:34:00. 05:01:99.

Six days ago, Porter thought.

'This was taken three days before the attack,' Lakes explained. 'Deeds and five other men entered the country at Harwich. They took a ferry over from the Hook of Holland using false papers.'

'Do we know who the other guys are?' said Porter.

Lakes gave a rueful shake of her head. 'We're still in the process of identifying the bodies. No luck so far on a match. They're not on any of our watch lists. But we know for damn sure that Deeds was involved in setting up the attack.'

There was a long silence. Porter stared at the photos, trying to process everything. When Deeds had bugged out from the Storey

Arms up Fan Fawr, he'd known to take the back route down the Beacons reservoir. Only someone with deep experience of the Brecons would know about that route. Now Porter understood. Deeds would have known that mountain well from the big runs on Selection. A hot rage swept through his veins just then. Deeds would pay. They all would. But there was still something else that bothered Porter.

'I don't get it.'

Lakes frowned. 'Get what?'

Porter tapped a finger against the snap. 'Deeds hates the Regiment. So bloody what? He's not the first idiot to think that, and he won't be the last. You're not telling me he went out, recruited a bunch of guys and set up a bomb, just because he hates our guts. I'm not buying that.'

Lakes and Hawkridge swapped uncomfortable looks. Then Lakes spoke. 'Of course not. We're not treating that as a possible motive.'

'Then why'd he do it?' Bald demanded.

Now Hawkridge spoke. 'We're not sure, old fruit. Not yet, anyway. What we can say for sure is that Deeds wasn't the brains trust of this operation. Our profile on the man suggests he was never more than a foot soldier in his activities. Besides, this attack has all the hallmarks of a sophisticated military operation. We're talking months of planning. Funds, weapons procurement, blue-prints. Deeds was probably recruited because he knew about Selection, and he probably agreed in part because of the resent-ment he has towards you chaps in the SAS. What we can say for sure is that Deeds is part of something much bigger.'

'You just don't know what, or who,' said Bald, folding his arms. 'I thought you lot were supposed to be in the intelligence business?'

Hawkridge glared at him. Then Lakes coughed and said, 'We're working on a number of theories. After Deeds went AWOL he went underground with the criminal networks running the Balkans. It's possible the Serbian mafia was somehow involved. Maybe he's just one link in a very long chain.' She leaned across the table and met Bald's gaze. 'But my point is, there are two ways of bringing the perpetrators to justice. There's the long way. A formal investigation. That would probably take years. In the meantime, the attackers are free to do as they wish. If they're smart, they'll be going to ground even as we speak. By the time we have names, it'll be too late. They'll be out of our reach.'

Porter leaned back. Scratched his jaw. 'So that makes us the shortcut option.'

Lakes nodded. 'We want you to get to Deeds. Find out what he knows and then kill him. And then go after the others. Anyone who played a part in the attack is a viable target. Anyone involved in the planning or execution. But we want the ringleaders, not the foot soldiers.'

As he soaked it all up Porter could feel his left hand starting to shake. Christ, he needed a drink. *As soon as we're out of here I'll get a drop of something,* Porter told himself.

'Do we know where Deeds is?'

'Puerto Banus. Marbella. Since the day after the attack.'

'You managed to trace Deeds, but none of the other gunmen?'

'We got lucky,' said Lakes. 'Scarsdale's gang has a Spanish operation.'

'Scarsdale?' Bald repeated. 'The gangster Deeds did jobs for back in the day?'

Lakes nodded. 'The same. His guys are major players in the European cannabis trade. They bring up shipments from Morocco, land it at Puerto Banus and then despatch it north by truck to France before it goes on to the UK. The problem is so bad that the local authorities have set up giant spotlights across the beach to catch the speedboats. Not that it does much good. Most of it comes in on luxury yachts now. The police are never going to search those boats. Not if they don't want to piss off a load of oligarchs and sheikhs.'

'What does this have to do with Deeds?'

'The Met have been running a joint operation with their Spanish counterparts to try and bring down Scarsdale and his lieutenants. We're talking years of undercover work. They've got a guy on the inside. Gathering evidence, tipping off the police.'

'Three days ago they get a call from their inside man,' Hawkridge explained. 'Saying he's found one of the shooters behind the attack on Selection.'

Lakes said, 'Our guy overheard one of Scarsdale's associates in an expat bar. Bill Deeds. He's got connections with Scarsdale. They still do business together, once in a while. You could say that they're tight. So Deeds gets drunk and starts bigging himself up. Claiming he was involved in the attack.'

Porter said nothing. None of this surprised him. Not after Northern Ireland. It had never ceased to amaze Porter how many seasoned IRA guys opened their mouths after a few jars of Guinness and start shooting their mouths off what jobs they'd done, or what jobs they were about to pull off. Without realising that their ranks had been infiltrated and the intelligence would invariably land on a desk somewhere in Whitehall. The security services relied heavily on IRA guys touting themselves at every opportunity. If every guy in the IRA kept their mouth shut, they would have had a lot more success in carrying out operations.

Lakes continued, 'Our guy on the inside figured Deeds was bullshitting. Obviously. Guys like that are always bigging themselves up after a few drinks.'

'Trying to buy himself some street cred,' Bald said. 'Typical.'

'But then Deeds mentioned a couple of details. Things that no one else could have known about, because we've had a media blackout in place. Like the fact that there were six shooters. And that two instructors had been killed on top of Pen y Fan an hour before the main attack took place. Our guy passed the intelligence on to his handler.'

'And the police alerted you,' Porter said, joining up the dots.

Lakes nodded. 'We checked it out. Had our teams trawl through CCTV footage. We have Deeds catching a ferry out of Fishguard approximately eight hours after the attack. We have him boarding an AerLingus flight from Dublin to Malaga seven hours after that, under the name Jack Holland. Once we confirmed the ID, we told the cops to sit on it and do nothing. Just watch Deeds and keep us informed of his movements.' Lakes shrugged. 'Like I said, we got lucky.'

Bald frowned. 'Why didn't the others follow him? To Spain.'

'Maybe they had orders to disperse across Europe,' Lakes speculated. 'Three guys in three separate countries is a lot harder to track than three guys on the same flight. Or maybe Deeds panicked and headed elsewhere after he got cut off from the others. Either way, Deeds is there and he's our only link to finding the other gunmen, and whoever organised this attack.'

'Bring him in yourself, then,' Bald suggested. 'If you know where he is, slap a pair of silver bracelets on the cunt and get him talking.'

Lakes shot Bald a look that was half amused and half despairing. 'I admire your thinking, John. But that won't work. In fact, that hasn't worked in about a decade. This is 1999, in case you hadn't noticed. We rough up a suspect today, tomorrow he's on the front page of the *Guardian*. By the end of the week there's a sit-down protest at St Paul's. We're bound by law.'

'But we're not,' said Porter.

'Precisely.'

Hawkridge took out a handkerchief and blew his nose. He continued. 'The formal way of doing things is longer and more painstaking, naturally. But we'd make a breakthrough sooner or later. Either way, your job will be to carry out multiple hits. Your team will remain active for as long as it takes to bring the enemy to justice.'

'In Europe only,' Lakes said. 'Avoid Russia. We're trying to repair relations with Moscow, we can't have anything messy over there. Nothing in the US, of course. They don't know a thing about this operation and the last thing we want to do is to piss off our American friends. It goes without saying that civilian casualties are to be avoided at all costs, as well as local law enforcement.'

Bald said, 'Do you want us to make them look like accidents? The kills.'

Lakes shook her head and said, 'The opposite. We want them to suffer. We want every terrorist piece of shit to pick up the morning paper and see what happens when you attack us. The bigger the impact, the messier the death—'

'The louder the message we send,' Porter finished. 'I get the idea, love.'

Lakes sparked up her third tab of the meeting. Tendrils of smoke drifted lazily towards the ceiling. Hawkridge said nothing. Keppel just sat there, watching Bald and Porter with his granite eyes. Lakes turned to him.

'Marcus, if you wouldn't mind.'

Without saying a word Keppel reached down to his brown leather briefcase and produced a pair of documents. He handed them over to Lakes. She took the documents and placed them on the coffee table. One in front of Bald, the other in front of Porter. Then Keppel passed her a couple of Montblanc fountain pens. She placed them next to the documents. Bald glanced up at Lakes, clenching his brow.

'The fuck is this?'

'It's your contract. Actually, it's two contracts. The first is a resignation letter. It states that you are being discharged from the Regiment, effective immediately. As soon as you sign that letter, your status will change to civilian. You will be removed from the government payroll, your bank cards will be changed and your military ID rescinded. To all intents and purposes it will look as though you've resigned from active duty. Only you haven't.'

'It's called sheep-dipping,' Hawkridge butted in. 'It will appear to anyone on the outside that you've been stood down and are now on Civvy Street. But you will still be employed by HMG. We'll place you both into Templar as clean assets. That's your second contract. A boilerplate agreement between yourselves and Templar, hiring you as security contractors. You'll have a new identity, new documents, new bank accounts. New everything.'

'Think of it as money laundering,' Keppel said with a smug smile. 'Except with people instead of currency.'

Lakes glanced at her colleagues then turned back to Porter. 'Nobody will know your past. Where you've been, what you've done. Who you were. You'll be entirely clean, or as close as it's possible to get in today's world.'

'We haven't talked money,' said Bald.

'Yes,' said Lakes. 'We have.'

Bald shook his head. 'You're trying to fob us off with the same salary we were getting in the Regiment. But this isn't some regular op. You want us to do your dirty work, fine. But you need to pay the going rate.'

Lakes attempted a smile. 'You care more about money than revenge?'

'Who says we have to choose? We're up for slotting the fuckers behind the attack, love. We're up for that all day long. But if we're gonna put our necks on the line, we should be getting paid properly.'

'Out of the question. Money's tight at the moment. The budget's being squeezed.'

'You can always find some more. This is the MoD. You practically have a licence to print the stuff.'

Lakes glanced at Hawkridge. Shifted. Looked back to Bald. 'Fine. We'll pay you one-and-a-half times your salary.'

'Triple it,' said Bald.

'Double your salary,' said Lakes. 'That's our final offer. Do we have a deal?'

Porter stilled his trembling left hand and looked down at the contracts. They were giving him the big sell, Lakes and Hawkridge and Keppel, but there was no need. He was already sold on the idea. His name, his past, everything that had happened to him in Beirut. Finally he was being given the opportunity to draw a line in the sand. Put it all behind him and start again. Twelve hours ago Porter had been drinking himself into an early grave and trying to figure out where it had all gone wrong. Now they were offering him the chance to wipe the slate clean.

Lakes said, 'Marcus will be your go-to man during the operation. Anything you need will come via Templar. Safe houses, vehicles, hardware. We'll supply the intelligence and the money, but to all intents and purposes this is a private Templar venture, independent of – and unknown to – HMG.'

And no doubt Keppel will pocket a small fortune and a knighthood in exchange for doing Whitehall a favour, thought Porter.

No wonder the guy wore such a big smile. He was going to be fucking minted, even more so than he was now, probably.

Hawkridge leaned forward and dropped his voice so low it could've fallen off a cliff.

'Of course, if either of you gets caught, then you're on your own.'

Porter smiled faintly. It was the same old Vauxhall deal, then. The contract might be in a different font but the small print was still the fucking same. He didn't like the idea of working for Keppel. But he didn't have much of a choice. Either they shook hands with the devil, or they passed up the opportunity to take down the guys who'd slotted their mates. When you framed it like that, it wasn't any kind of a choice at all.

'Well?' Lakes asked. 'Are you going to sign?'

Porter didn't hesitate. He took the pen. Scribbled his signature at the bottom of the resignation and then flipped to the high-lighted page at the back of the Templar contract. Signed on the dotted line, then set the pen down. Bald did the same. Once they were done, Lakes took the contracts and handed them back to Keppel. She passed the resignation letters to Hawkridge. Then she straightened her back.

'Nealy will take you to a safe house across town. You'll spend three days there until your new documents have been processed. In the meantime, I suggest you tie up your affairs and work on memorising your new identities.'

'What about the other lads on the team?' Bald asked.

'Patience, old chap,' said Keppel. The guy had an annoying habit of always sounding pleased with himself. 'They'll RV with you at the safe house. They're two of my best men.'

'Regiment?' Porter said.

Keppel shook his head. 'But they're both former SF. They've been vetted by our friends over at Thames House. I can vouch for them personally.' He glanced quickly at Lakes as he spoke.

Bald frowned. 'Why the outsiders? Why not just get two other fellas from Hereford?'

Porter already knew the answer to that question. 'Deniability,' he said, looking at Lakes. 'The less of a connection us lot have to Hereford, the easier it is for you lot to claim you don't have anything to do with us.'

Lakes almost smiled. 'Exactly.'

At that moment the main door clicked and Nealy entered. Lakes stubbed out her cigarette in her empty coffee mug and rose smoothly to her feet. 'I'll be along in a couple of days to present your papers and brief you further. Unless you have any questions?'

'Just the one,' Porter said. 'Why us?'

Lakes considered for a beat. 'We needed someone who fitted our profile and was close to retirement. Someone who could disappear from the grid without attracting much attention.'

Porter smiled wryly. 'You'll have to do better than that, love. There are plenty of other Blades in the same position as me. Lots of ex-Regiment men kicking their heels on Civvy Street too.'

Lakes hesitated. Hawkridge shifted awkwardly. 'We wanted someone obstinate. Someone who doesn't quit. I've seen your file, John. You could have walked away after Beirut. But you didn't. You decided to stick it out. And you took down two gunmen at the Brecons and very nearly stopped Deeds. That tells me you've got guts.'

Porter shook his head. 'I'm no hero.'

'We're not looking for heroes,' said Lakes. 'Heroes are no good when you're trying to keep a low profile. We're interested in the men who never give up, even when the odds are stacked against them. Men like you.'

'What about me?' Bald put in.

'Your CO recommended you, John,' Lakes replied. 'In fact, he couldn't wait to get rid of you. I understand that incident over at the Killing House was the final straw in your rather chequered Regiment career. If you'd turned down our offer, they would've booted you out of Hereford for good.'

Bald stood there, stewing. 'Bastards,' he muttered under his breath.

The meeting was over. Nealy ushered Bald and Porter out of

the suite. They rode the Otis back down to the hotel lobby in cold silence. For the first time in a long time, Porter felt alive. He could feel his muscles beginning to pump with adrenaline. Against all the odds, someone had tossed him a second chance. It was a chance to avenge his dead muckers, and a chance to make up for that day in Beirut ten years ago when he'd failed Keith, Mike and Steve.

He wouldn't fail. Not this time. He would find Bill Deeds and the others. And he would settle the score.

Permanently.

TWENTY-TWO

1827 hours.

The safe house was a fifteen-minute ride east of the Wainwright. Nealy drove them in a slick black BMW 3 Series that still had that new-car smell. Porter eased back in the leather seats as they trundled east on Euston Road, past Madame Tussauds and Regent's Park and tree-lined streets overflowing with gawping tourists. Everywhere Porter looked there was a lot of rebuilding work going on. Urban regeneration. Cranes towered in the distance. Roads had been sealed off for construction. Old London giving way to the new. They swept past King's Cross and its cramped rows of shabby pubs and decrepit betting shops and prowling hookers. After another twenty minutes in traffic they hit the City Road, a chaotic spiral of sixties buildings and artists' warehouses rubbing shoulders with big new glass office blocks.

'You're very lucky to be working for Miss Lakes, you know,' Nealy said.

'Yeah?' Bald arched an eyebrow. 'Why's that?'

'She's on the up. Lakes is really going places. There are rumours that she's being lined up to be the next chief of MI6.'

'Good for her.'

'Par for the course for her family, I suppose.' Nealy was making small talk now, filling the silence in the Beemer. 'They've done well for themselves down the years. Highly connected, if you know what I mean.'

'How so?' said Porter.

'Her grandfather was a political commentator in his day. Very influential. Lots of friends in Westminster. Good friend of Oswald Mosley, apparently.'

'Mosley? The guy who led the British Fascists?'

Nealy nodded awkwardly. 'I think there's a bit of mystery there. How much did he really believe all that stuff, you know? Anyway, her father didn't seem to have any trouble getting a job because of it. Sir Terence. He worked his way up the civil service ladder and ended up being Cabinet Secretary under Ted Heath. Like I said, lot of connections in that family.'

'Fascinating,' Bald said drily.

Nealy slowed down past the roundabout at Old Street and made a couple of quick turns down a one-way system. Heading west in the direction of Farringdon and Barbican and Chancery Lane. Halfway down the street he pulled up outside a modern apartment block wedged between a pair of crumbling Georgian townhouses. He steered into a parking space and climbed out of the Beemer. Porter and Bald unfolded themselves and followed Nealy as he beat a path towards the entrance to the apartment block. A sign above the frosted glass doors said, 'TWENTY-TWO FEATHERSTONE STREET'.

'Templar own a number of properties in and around town,' Nealy said cheerily as he fished out the key from his pocket and fiddled with the lock. 'Serviced apartments for their clients, secure locations for meetings and so on.'

'Must cost a packet,' Bald said as he took in the shiny exterior.

'Oh, Templar aren't your usual one-man-band security company. Far from it. They have offices all around the world. New York, Boston, Mexico City, Delhi, Tokyo. They're big business, you know. Very lucrative. Keppel's an extraordinary man.'

Nealy sounded in awe of Templar, thought Porter. Next he'll be trying to sell me shares in the bloody company.

They stepped into the foyer. The on-duty doorman greeted Nealy with a polite smile then went back to his paperback Grisham. The three men made for the lift and took the first available one to the third floor.

'The clientele here is travelling businessmen,' Nealy explained as he led them towards the apartment at the end of the corridor. 'No one stays here for more than a few days, and most of them visit three or four times a year. That means you're not going to raise any questions. No one's going to pay any attention to four guys coming and going.'

They arrived at the door to number 9. While Nealy twisted the key in the lock, Porter found himself wondering if there was any booze stashed away inside. With a bit of luck Keppel kept the place stocked up with expensive whiskys for his clients.

They stepped into an apartment that looked almost as new as the Beemer, and had the same kind of smell. Nealy gave them the grand tour. There was a huge living room with a twenty-eight-inch Sony TV in one corner and a pair of matching white leather sofas. The kitchen had a Nespresso machine and a black retro Smeg fridge. The laminate wooden flooring was so polished Porter could see his own face in it. The apartment looked more like a showroom than a place where people actually lived. Probably cost north of two million, he figured. And Templar owned dozens of apartments like this, according to Nealy.

'We're in the wrong bloody business,' Bald said, reading his mucker's mind.

'There's a gym in the basement,' Nealy said as he handed the two Blades a set of keys each. 'Pool, weights area, treadmills. The fridge is stocked up with food and there's coffee and tea if you need it.'

'What are we supposed to do in the meantime?'

Nealy shrugged. Like he pretended to care. Bald said nothing. He was used to sitting around doing nothing. There were long stretches in the Regiment when you were just hurrying up and waiting.

'What about a drink?' Porter asked hopefully.

'Afraid not,' Nealy said. 'Company policy. You're on Templar's clock now. Keppel runs a tight ship and doesn't like his men drinking on the job unless it's to blend in with their environment. For now there's water, iced tea or coffee.'

Porter gritted his teeth. Maybe signing his life over to Templar hadn't been such a good idea after all.

Nealy pointed to a set of A4 folders lying on the kitchen table. He handed one to Porter, gave the other one to Bald. 'Backgrounds for your new identities. Names, dates, where you were born. What school you went to, what beer you drink. The works. The backgrounds of the other guys on the team are there as well. Memorise your identities. Every detail. The slightest inconsistency could make somebody suspicious.'

Porter browsed through the folder. His assumed name was David Mulryne. Someone had gone to great effort to flesh out a full background for his character. Which told him one thing. The Firm planned on using theses identities for a while. This wasn't going to be an in-and-out job. They were in it for the long haul.

Porter looked around. 'Where are the other guys?'

'They'll be here shortly,' said Nealy. 'They've been briefed separately by Keppel so they know what they're walking into. Oh, before I forget.'

Nealy took out a pair of crumpled white envelopes from his jacket pocket. Handed them over to Porter and Bald.

'There's two hundred quid in there. That should cover any essentials. Clothes, food. That kind of stuff. Any belongings you need from your homes, let us know and we'll have a driver go pick them up.'

Porter took a peek inside the envelope, then pocketed it. Two hundred quid. Now that's more bloody like it. I could buy half a dozen bottles of Bushmills with that. Or a crate of White Lightning.

'Right,' Nealy added. 'That covers everything. I'll be off. Lakes will brief you again once your documents are ready. In the meantime, sit tight.'

Then he gave his back to them and left. As soon as the door had shut behind him Porter rummaged through the fridge and kitchen cupboards, hoping that someone had left a bottle of booze somewhere. But Nealy was right. The place was drier than a camel's armpit. After a while Porter admitted defeat and fixed himself a double shot of espresso from the coffee machine. Then he sat down at the table overlooking the balcony and lit up a Bensons. The smoke flowed through his veins. It wasn't as good as a slug of Jameson's, but it was the next best thing. Porter smoked and drank his coffee and flicked through the folder Nealy had given him while Bald sat on the sofa, hopping channels. He eventually settled for Sky News.

The main item on the news was still Friday's bombing. The reporter managed to spin out a six-minute piece on what they already knew. Which amounted to very little. They regurgitated the same old shots of smoke pouring into the sky above the Brecons, helicopters circling the cordoned-off area around the Storey Arms. With no new angle to cover, the news turned to events in Kosovo. Serbian police had rounded up a bunch of local farmers, taken them to a hill and given them the double-tap. There was a shot of a pile of corpses slumped in a mass grave. Most of them were naked. Their flesh had putrified and their faces were caked in mud. Then the screen cut to a NATO conference with various foreign ministers standing before the cameras. According to the reporter's voiceover there was talk of Milosevic being indicted on charges of war crimes. There were shots of US fighter planes being scrambled off aircraft carriers, and protests on the streets of Belgrade. Everyone seemed to be gearing up for another round of war.

It never ends, thought Porter. First the Bosnian war a couple of years ago. Now this. It's like they can't bloody help themselves.

Roughly an hour later a car pulled up outside. Porter spotted it through the balcony window as he smoked another cigarette. A white Mercedes-Benz E-class sedan, rolling into the parking space directly in front of the block. Two figures clambered out of the back of the Merc and made for the entrance. Less than a minute later Porter heard the click on the front door. He drained the rest of his espresso and stood up to greet the two guys as they strode into the hallway. They dumped their gym bags on the floor and glanced around, giving the place the once-over. Stood together, the two figures looked like opposite ends of a matryoshka doll set.

The bigger one finally rested his eyes on Porter and frowned at the sight of his missing fingers.

'You must be Porter,' the guy said.

He had a throated, rusty voice that sounded like a car that wouldn't start. His face was leathery, with prominent crow's feet at the corners of his eyes. Like someone had carved his face out of a block of petrified wood. With his lantern jaw and huge physique, he gave the impression of guy who could drink a dozen cans of Fosters and still drop a couple of heavies.

Porter waved a hand at the folder on the table. 'We were told not to use those names.'

The bigger guy adjusted his crotch and snorted. 'Ah, sod it, mate. We're not on the mission. Not yet.' He thrust out a hand. 'Mick Devereaux.'

Porter shook it. The guy had a firm grip. Like a boa constrictor tightening around its prey. 'You're from Oz?'

'Darwin born and bred, mate,' Devereaux replied. 'Did eight years in the SASR down at Swanbourne.'

Porter nodded. The SASR was the Australian equivalent of the Regiment. Their lads shared the same training principles and even the same motto. Porter had taken part in a few joint training ops with the SASR guys and they'd proved themselves a bunch of tough hard-drinking bastards. Also more than capable of handling themselves in a fight.

'How long have you been with Templar?'

'Couple of years now. Best decision I ever made, handing in my notice. If I hadn't joined Templar I'd be back in Darwin right now, fixing up old Fords for cents.'

'Cars?' Porter asked. 'That's your thing?'

'Anything on four wheels, mate. Or two. If it has an engine, I'm your man. I can fix up any motor there is. When I'm not racing the heck out of 'em, that is. Guess that makes me your transporter.'

Bald cocked his head at the shorter guy standing next to Devereaux. The smaller half of the doll set. 'What's your story?'

'Name's Davey Coles,' the guy responded in a distinctive South African accent. 'You're Bald, right? They warned us about you, chief.' He winked at Devereaux. 'Said you were a bit of a cunt.'

Bald frowned at Coles. 'Who the fuck said that?'

'Does it matter, chief? We're all here now.'

Porter sized Coles up. He was a scruffy bastard. He had tanned skin the colour of mahogany and the lean, angular physique of someone who exercised outdoors rather than in the comfort of an air-conditioned gym. He gave away six inches in height to Devereaux and maybe fifty pounds in muscle. He had a wild look in his eyes, as if he was constantly gunning for a fight. He was the walking definition of small man syndrome.

'You're ex-SF too?' Porter asked.

'Among other things,' Coles replied evasively. 'I started out in the Recces. Back in the days when the darkies knew their place.'

Porter looked at Bald but said nothing. The Recces were South Africa's Special Forces outfit. Porter had never worked with their guys, but in the SF world the Recces carried a reputation as some of the toughest warriors in the business. They'd fought in nasty local conflicts in Angola and Namibia, operating in some of the most hostile places on the planet.

'What brought you over here?'

Coles scratched his balls. 'Not much work for an old Recce in South Africa these days. Not when you've got the darkies running the fucking shop. I came over here, spent six months pulling pints in a boozer over in Fulham. Then one day I get a call from a guy at Templar. Saying he wants to make me an offer I can't refuse. Turns out he was right.'

Bald made a face. 'What are you talking about?'

'The money we're getting for this job, chief. Half a million large each.' Coles grinned, revealing a set of small, stained teeth. 'Can't argue with that. It's a hell of a lot better than pulling pints for six quid an hour.'

Porter swapped a look with Bald. Thinking, the mission's not even started and the Firm is already shafting us. We're doing the job for peanuts while these two guys and Coles are raking in the big bucks.

'Once this is over, I'm going to get myself a beach pad in California,' said Coles. 'Somewhere in LA. Away from all the darkies, like. Santa Monica, maybe.' He nodded at Bald. Grinned. 'Ever been to California, chief?'

Bald clenched his jaws so hard Porter could hear the enamel grate. 'No.'

'You should, chief. You fucking should. It's wild out there. And the women.' Coles whistled. 'They're unreal. I'm talking tits out to *here*.'

Coles cupped his hands and held them about twelve inches in front of his chest to demonstrate. He kept on grinning at Bald. But if the guy was looking for a reaction, he didn't get one. Bald just pressed his lips shut and said nothing. Neither did Porter. They didn't want to let on to the other lads that they were being taken for a ride by their Vauxhall paymasters. Besides, Porter told himself, it was too late. Lakes had given them the hard sell. They'd already signed on the dotted line, signed their lives away to Templar. There was nothing they could do about it now.

They were locked in.

TWENTY-THREE

Two days later.
0911 hours.
'Deeds is still in Puerto Banus,' Lakes said.

They were sitting around the living room. Bald, Porter, Devereaux and Coles. Lakes was sitting opposite them. Nealy guarded the door. This was it. The final briefing before the team began their mission.

For the past two days Porter had settled into a decent routine. In the mornings he worked on his phys down at the gym, pounding the treadmill and hitting the weight machines, doing all the compound exercises. Squats, deadlifts, bench presses. In the afternoons Porter and the other guys on the strike team committed their identities to memory and studied maps of Puerto Banus and the surrounding terrain. In the evenings, Porter drank.

There was no booze in the flat but on the first evening he'd found a corner shop two minutes away from the block where you could get a bottle of cheap vodka for under a tenner. The bloke behind the counter gave him a brown paper bag without Porter even asking. He must get a dozen blokes like me in here every day, thought Porter. Alcoholics. Blokes slowly drinking themselves into an early grave. There was a park behind the block of flats with a burial garden and a few benches. Porter sat there drinking his vodka. Then he'd head back to the safe house and sit in front of the TV, smoking and flicking between Sky News and BBC News 24. With no new developments on the Selection attack the media was beginning to lose interest in the story. Their attention was turning to the imminent war in Kosovo.

On the third morning Porter returned from his gym session to find Lakes in the living room. She was pacing up and down, a cigarette dangling from her lips and a cup of coffee in her right hand. Porter had quickly towelled the sweat off his face then pulled up a pew as Lakes had dug a folder out of her tote bag. Nealy stood in the hallway while Lakes spread a dozen photographs across the coffee table. The snaps were slightly out of focus, as if they'd been taken with a long-range camera lens. Each one showed Deeds entering or leaving various bars and establishments.

'These pictures were taken twenty-four hours ago,' Lakes continued. 'Deeds is staying at the Romano Hotel on the Golden Mile, five kilometres to the north of Puerto Banus. According to our guy on the inside, Deeds has a fairly regular routine. During the day he sticks to the hotel. He hangs by the pool, working on his tan and drinking cocktails.'

'So we lift the prick from his hotel room,' said Devereaux. 'Easy.'

Lakes shook her head. 'The Romano is a five-star hotel with its own security detail. Plus security cameras in the lobby and lifts. You wouldn't stand a chance of getting to Deeds there. Not without the hotel's security staff knowing about it. Even if you did lift Deeds, there's still the security footage. Your faces would be all over the news before you could get out of the country.'

'Doesn't he ever leave the hotel?' Porter asked.

'Only in the evenings,' said Lakes. 'Around seven o'clock he heads over to Jimmy's, an Irish joint where all the expats meet to talk shop over Guinness. Deeds usually sticks around til closing time. Sometimes he stops off for a few drinks at Hollywood's, a trendy bar down by the marina. One of those places where all the local celebrities and footballers hang out.' She tapped her finger at another photograph, showing Deeds slipping out of a dingy doorway with a glitzy neon sign above it. 'Later, he heads to a nearby strip club, the Pony Lounge.'

'Same routine?' Devereaux enquired, stroking his chin. 'Every day?'

'Deeds is a creature of habit. He doesn't go anywhere he doesn't know. Far as we can tell, his tastes are pretty narrow. He likes a full English, a pint of Stella and a stripper called Brandy.'

'A man after my own heart,' Bald said.

Lakes shot him a look. A thought took hold of Porter. He leaned forward and pointed to one of the photographs. 'What's wrong with this picture?'

Lakes sucked on her cigarette. 'I'm not sure I follow.'

'Deeds has just slotted a load of British soldiers, right? If I was in his boots, I'd be trying to keep a low profile. I'd keep my head down as much as possible. I wouldn't come up for air unless I had to. And I sure as shit wouldn't be strolling around the Costa del Sol without a care in the world.'

There was a pause. A cloud of cigarette smoke hung in front of Lake's face. Like a veil. 'Deeds doesn't need to hide. He's being protected.'

'By who?'

'Scarsdale.'

Bald and Porter exchanged a look. Bald turned back to Lakes. Frowned. 'Scarsdale wants to protect Deeds? Why?'

'Two reasons. First, because Scarsdale and Deeds go way back. Deeds did a few favours for Scarsdale back in the day. Now he's calling them in. Plus Scarsdale comes from the old school of British criminals. He's from that generation that hates snitches. He's not the type to rat on an associate.'

Porter said, 'What's the second reason?'

'Business. According to our guy, Scarsdale and his associates are trying to get into the weapons smuggling racket. It's a logical move. The Russians have been muscling in on the drug trade in Marbella, and everyone knows you don't mess with them. A lot of their competitors have wound up dead. You don't get to be where Scarsdale is today by being stupid. He's read the writing on the wall and wants to move into a less crowded trade.'

'And Deeds is his way in,' said Porter. 'He's an asset.'

Lakes nodded. 'But it also means that trying to get to Deeds is going to be difficult.'

'Why?' Devereaux asked. 'You're not telling me that Scarsdale's people have got the whole town on lockdown?'

'I'm saying exactly that,' Lakes replied. 'The gangs are highly active in and around Marbella. They own a lot of bars and restaurants, they supply drugs and hookers to tourists and they have eyes on most of the town, because their shipments come directly in to the marina from Morocco.'

'What about cops?'

'The police are there just for show. To make the tourists feel better. It's bad publicity if word gets out that Marbella is basically run by criminal syndicates. The tourists would dry up and the place would go under. So the cops turn a blind eye most of the time and no one investigates shootings or disappearances too closely. Their number one priority is making sure stuff says out of the news.'

'Good for us, then,' Bald cut in. 'Makes it less likely that Deeds's face will be in the papers after we've grabbed him.'

'What protection does he have?' Porter asked.

Lakes said, 'Whenever he's out and about in town, Deeds has usually got a couple of Scarsdale's toughs along with him. Low-grade thugs. You could probably handle them, but Puerto Banus is a busy place, even at this time of the year. We'd like to avoid things getting noisy.'

'How do we get to him, then?'

Lakes held up her hand. 'I'll leave the operational details to you. Just make sure you take Deeds alive. He's our only link to the people behind the attack. If he dies, it could take months to turn up another solid lead.'

A wave of anger pulsed through Bald as he cast his eye over the photos. 'We'll get the bastard,' he said to Lakes. 'Don't you worry about that, lass.'

'I'm not worried,' she said matter-of-factly. 'Otherwise we wouldn't have chosen you for the job.' Lakes took a last pull on her smoke and stubbed it out in the ashtray. 'Marcus has arranged accommodation for you. You're checked into an apartment on Calle Ramon Areces. It's not far from the marina. Under your assumed names, of course. Your cover story is that you're four middle-aged guys on a drinking jolly. You're looking to have some fun and enjoy being away from your wives for a few days.'

'That'll hold up?' Coles asked.

'It's Marbella. The place is wall-to-wall cheap bars and strip clubs and kebab shops. Middle-aged guys on boozy weekends are their biggest customers.'

Lakes reached under her jacket and came out with four slim burgundy passports. She slid them across the table.

'Your new identities.'

Porter picked his up and flipped it to the information page. It was one of the shiny new digital passports with a computer chip stitched into the back page containing all his personal data. The passport was under his new name, David Mulryne, and listed his place of birth as Luton. It had been backdated to two years ago, and someone at the Firm had the foresight to put a few visa stamps in the front pages. Turkey, Canada, Mexico. That made sense, Porter figured. A brand new passport would raise suspicion with the border stiffs.

Lakes then took out four slim white envelopes and handed them out to the four guys. Porter opened his envelope and peeked inside. There was a driving licence made out to his new name, along with an HSBC bank debit card and a credit card made out to Templar, both with the words 'BUSINESS A/C' stamped along the bottom.

'The cards are for small expenses,' Lakes said quickly. 'There's a daily cash limit on them of £250. It should be enough to cover your basic needs. Flights, hotels, car rentals, that sort of thing.'

'What about when we need to buy hardware?' Porter said.

'We've arranged for a safe deposit box at the Rehmer International Bank in Zurich. There's two hundred thousand pounds in sterling in the box. You can wire the money to local accounts as necessary. Every time you make a withdrawal, the box fund will be automatically replenished.'

She saw the greedy look in Bald's eyes and her expression hardened.

'I want receipts, gentlemen. This isn't some government jolly.

Every expense has to be accounted for. Anything else will be deducted from your retainer upon completion of the mission.'

Porter said, 'We'll need contacts.'

'What for?'

'The hardware. If we have to source all our kit locally, it'll take time.'

Lakes tipped her head at Devereaux. 'That's Mick's area of expertise. Templar has access to a number of contacts across Europe. Suppliers. Mick has their details. They can get you whatever you need at short notice. Guns, cars, armour, forged documents.'

'What if we need to get in touch with you?' Porter asked.

'Generally speaking, you won't need to,' Lakes responded. 'The way we've set up the team, you should be self-sufficient. All of you have the skills and financing to operate independently of a command unit.'

'What if the situation changes, though?' Devereaux said. 'What if your people come across new int that you need to share with us?'

'In that case, we'll communicate through a telephone service. It's one-way. The number will put you through to a secure line. You'll hear a brief tune, then a series of numbers in code. Think of it as a numbers station, but using telephones. Anything we need to alert you to, we'll leave as a coded message, so you should check in frequently.'

'What if there's an emergency?' Porter said. 'Something we need to communicate to you.'

Lakes nodded impatiently, as if she'd already thought of that. She took out four business cards and placed them on the table. Porter picked one up. It was plain white with some kind of textured surface. There was a name embossed on the front in black lettering: KOVACS ANTIQUES. Below the name there was an address on Friedrichstrasse, Berlin, and a telephone number.

'The dealer's a front,' said Lakes. 'No one will ever pick up the phone, but if you leave a message there, one of our guys will pass it on. Otherwise you're on your own.'

'Tell us something we don't know,' said Bald.

Lakes flashed him a dirty look. 'You might think we're washing our hands of you, John. But that couldn't be further from the truth. We're all taking a risk here. Just make sure you don't screw it up.' Then her features softened at the edges and she added, 'Get this right, gentlemen, and we could start talking about a more permanent arrangement.'

'How do you mean?' Porter asked.

'Let's just say that there might be one or two senior openings at the top end of Templar. Think about it. Director of a global PMC. Six-figure salary, private travel, benefits. Complete your mission, and we'll talk some more.'

Bald's eyes lit up. He rubbed his hands at the prospect of a job on the board. Porter watched Lakes follow Nealy out of the door, his stomach muscles tightening into an anxious knot. Then he looked back to Bald. The Jock had dug out his old Nokia mobile and was busy tapping out a message.

'Get the feeling they're not telling us something?'

'What else is new?' Bald tucked away his phone and sighed. 'You know what the Firm's like. Slippery bastards. I'd rather shit on my hand and clap than believe a word they say. Fuck it. We've got a chance to kill Deeds, and anyone else who had a hand in the attack. That's all I give a toss about.'

Bald stood up and popped on his trainers. Coles and Devereaux had already left the apartment and headed down to the gym.

'Going for a session with Saffer and Crocodile Dundee.'

Suddenly Porter was alone in the apartment. He thought about putting in a call to Sandy. Tell her he was sorry for not making it to her birthday party. Promise that her old man would find some way of making it up to her. But Lakes had given them explicit orders not to reach out to anyone connected to their real-world identities. Phone calls were off-limits. They weren't even permitted to have their own personal mobiles for as long as the mission lasted. It would be a long while before Porter heard his daughter's voice again.

We think it's best if you stay away for a while. That's what Diana had told him. *Stuart's there for her.* Not me. My one shot at a happy family, and I blew it.

His hands started to shake. *I need a drink.* Porter grabbed his coat and made for the door. He headed out of the building, turned right on Featherstone and paced towards City Road. Half past ten on a gritty Friday morning in London, and it was as if the Selection attack had never happened. People were just getting on with it. Businessmen were striding briskly to work, looking equal parts aloof and harrassed. Japanese tourists stood around taking snaps of old buildings. The streets were bustling with students and dog walkers and nannies doing the school run.

Porter was getting ready to kill a bunch of people.

The corner shop was just off Old Street, situated between a sushi bar and an organic coffee house. Porter ducked inside and approached the sweaty bloke behind the counter.

'The usual,' he said.

The guy took a bottle of cheap vodka from the shelf along with a pack of twenty Bensons. Porter handed him fifteen quid, grabbed the brown paper bag and stuffed the cigarettes in his pocket. Stepped outside. Unscrewed the cap and took a swig from the vodka bottle. God, but that felt good. He took another gulp. Then a third. His hands stopped shaking. Porter screwed the cap back on and started across the street, heading back down Featherstone towards the burial garden. A bottle of vodka and a pack of fags to start the day. *And I'm supposed to be leading a fucking kill team.*

What the hell happened to you, John?

He reached the corner of City Road and Featherstone and stopped in his tracks. Sixty metres away he saw Bald stepping out of the apartment block and crossing the road, a brown envelope tucked under his arm. He was heading away from Porter and didn't appear to have noticed his mucker. Porter hung by the corner and looked on as Bald approached an apartment building on the opposite side of the road. A blonde-haired woman stood in the doorway, her coat flapping in the sharp breeze. From where Porter was standing he couldn't get a good look at her face. Bald stopped next to the building. Glanced up and down the street. Then he handed over the envelope to the blonde. She hurriedly stuffed the envelope into her handbag. Like she didn't want anyone to see it. Bald nodded at her. Hurried back across the road. Then the blonde stepped out of the doorway and into the street. She turned right, heading east towards City Road. She walked right past Porter. That's when he finally got a look at her face.

He recognised her immediately.

It was the same blonde he'd seen in the Piano Bar.

TWENTY-FOUR

Puerto Banus, Spain. Four days later.
2348 hours.
Ten days after the attack on Selection, Porter took a sip of his pint and waited for the man they'd been sent to lift.

He was sitting next to Bald at a table at the front of the Paradiso Bar, midway along the main strip and thirty metres up from the marina. Outside a cool wind blasted in from the Mediterranean, shaking the awnings above the restaurants and tumbleweeding cigarette butts across the cobbled street. Close to midnight and Puerto Banus was heaving with stag groups and tourists and bored-looking Russian models with their Louis Vuitton handbags and Jimmy Choo high heels. Marbella in January was a lot like Essex in July, thought Porter. Only with less fake tan.

Thirty metres away on the other side of the street stood the Pony Lounge. The strip club was discreetly tucked away on the first floor of a whitewashed building at the corner of the strip, at Porter's two o'clock. A set of steps led from street level up to a whitewashed building with a plain brown door and a small neon sign above it in bright pink lettering, and the svelte silhouette of a topless dancer. There were no windows looking into the club. Maybe the Pony Lounge was going for the discreet end of the market.

From where Porter and Bald were sitting they had an unob-structed view of the area immediately surrounding the strip club. They could see everyone entering and leaving. The two operators had been observing the joint for the past twenty minutes. Ever since Bill Deeds and his mates had entered the club. Now all they had to do was wait. If everything went to plan, ninety minutes from now Deeds would be bound and gagged in the back of a getaway van.

'Can't believe you're actually drinking that piss,' said Bald, nodding at his mucker's pint.

Porter looked at his glass. He was drinking a shandy. Bald had gone for a bottle of low-calorie American lager. They weren't supposed to be drinking on the job, but two middle-aged blokes drinking Cokes in a bar would look suspicious. So they drank to blend in with the crowd of expats and holidaying Brits. The Paradiso had a Brit theme. Union Jacks all over the place, Stella on tap and Proclaimers tunes blaring out of the dusty speakers. The joint reeked of stale sweat and piss and roll-ups. It looked like it hadn't been cleaned since the invention of the internet. Match of the Day was showing on a big TV in one corner of the bar. Chelsea versus Spurs. Chelsea were winning one-nil. George Weah had just scored.

'I've had worse,' said Porter.

And I have. A lot bloody worse.

He took another sip of his shandy. Could hardly taste the alcohol in it. *I could do with something a bit stronger right now, he thought. Something to calm my nerves. A double measure of Bushmills would go down nicely.*

'Better make that pint last a while,' said Bald. 'You can't get pissed on the fucking job, mate.'

'That's fucking rich, coming from you,' Porter growled. 'You're no slouch when it comes to the drink. I've seen you put it away.'

'Maybe,' said Bald. 'But I know when to drink and when to stop. That's the difference between you and me, mate. You can't stop. The lads at Hereford were bang on the money. You're out of control.'

Porter took a gulp of his pint and set the glass down. Gripped it tightly and eyeballed the Jock. 'I'm not the one with the fucking problem here. I'm not the one sneaking around behind everyone's back.'

'What's that supposed to mean?'

'That bird you bumped into at the hotel,' Porter said. 'I saw you and her outside the safe house. You were giving her some sort of package. What the fuck was that all about?'

'Her?' Bald made a face. 'She's my solicitor.'

'Bollocks,' said Porter. 'That's not what you said at the Piano Bar. You reckoned you didn't who she was then.'

Bald hardened his expression. His face looked like a slab of concrete. 'It was private business. Nothing to do with you. I was handing over the signed deeds for a new flat in Hereford, that's all. Now fuck off.'

He took a pull on his beer and looked away. Porter glanced at his Casio G-Shock Mudman watch. It said 2350 hours. Deeds had a fairly regular routine, a blessing for the guys on the hit team. According to their int, Deeds bugged out of the strip club at around 0030 hours every night. He headed straight back to the hotel he was staying at on Calle Torre Verde, a mile to the east of the marina. Instead of catching a taxi, Deeds usually took a ride back to the hotel from one of Scarsdale's lieutenants. Which meant that in around forty minutes' time Deeds would be leaving the strip club. And then the strike team would make their move.

A wave of tiredness settled like a fog behind Porter's eyes as he kept a mark-one eyeball on the strip club. The team had arrived in Spain three days ago, entering the country at different times and locations. That had been a necessary precaution, to make it more difficult for the authorities to trace the other guys on the team in the event that one of them got into trouble. Devereaux and Coles had taken the land route, riding the Eurostar from Waterloo down to Gare du Nord in Paris then taking the TGV to Barcelona. From there they'd rented a Honda Accord using their new papers and made the ten-hour drive south to the safe house. Meanwhile Bald had taken an easyJet flight out of Luton, landing at Malaga International Airport at around the same time as Devereaux and Coles hit the RV.

Porter had been the last to arrive. He'd stopped over in Zurich, making a withdrawal from the safe deposit box at the Rehmer

Bank on Seefeldstrasse in the heart of the city. He'd taken a hundred thousand in cash out of the box, stashing the thin bands in a black briefcase he had been carrying. He spent the afternoon opening current accounts at four separate commercial banks using his fake ID, depositing twenty-five thousand pounds in each account. The sums of money were too small to attract the attention of the banks and the team would be able to draw on each of the accounts wherever they were operating. In the evening Porter had taken an airberlin flight to Malaga, landing twenty-four hours after Bald and the rest of the team. He breezed through immigration control and took a cab direct to the safe house on Calle Ramon Areces in downtown Puerto Banus, RV'ing with the other guys. He checked in with the phone number in Austria that Lakes had given him, but there was no message waiting for them from the numbers station. Just a tune that played over and over and sounded like the title music from a Nintendo game.

Then the team went over the plan to lift Bill Deeds.

The plan was simple. While Porter had been moving money around in Zurich, Coles and Devereaux had been running surveillance on Deeds, with Bald carrying out a detailed recce of the marina and surrounding streets. The team had agreed that the optimum time to grab Deeds was when he slipped out of the Pony Lounge shortly after midnight. On each occasion Deeds and his driver took the same route back to the Range Rover, heading down a narrow alley that acted as a shortcut between the strip and the main road along Avenida Julio Iglesias. Bald had scoped out the alley during the daytime, checking it for security cameras and activities at the balconies above. The alley was thirty metres long, about as narrow as a Chinaman's smile and dimly lit by streetlamps at either end. There were no CCTV cameras and only two balconies, both of which were empty.

It was the perfect place to make the snatch.

Once the team had agreed on a plan, Devereaux got on the case with the hardware. He reached out to Templar's local contact, an Algerian gun-runner who operated out of San Pedro Alcantara.

Devereaux met him at an abandoned luxury development further along the Costa del Sol. One of those places that the government had sunk millions into, hoping to transform an empty beachfront into a tourist mecca. But for whatever reason the investment had dried up and the government had got cold feet, and now the half-finished concrete blocks were left to mothball under the lazy Mediterranean sun.

Devereaux purchased three Glock 17 semi-automatic pistols and two boxes of ZQI 9x19mm Parabellum, each with fifty rounds. He also bought three shoulder holsters, plus a Heckler & Koch MP5SD 9mm submachine gun fitted with a suppressor in case things went noisy. The bill for the hardware came to five grand. Expensive, but that was the going rate on the black market. And the weapons were in good nick. No scratches, no obvious damage. Devereaux paid for the tools in cash in Spanish pesetas, from one of the accounts Porter had opened in Zurich.

Porter and Bald had their Glocks concealed in the shoulder holsters beneath their leather jackets. They were armed, and ready.

'How long's it been?' Bald asked.

'Thirty-nine minutes,' said Porter.

Bald took a pull on his Yank brew and shook his head in disgust. 'Ain't right. Those poor fucking students are six feet under, and we're having to sit here while that tosser gets a lap-dance special.'

They had their differences, but Porter shared his mucker's rage. In the days since the attack he'd been trying to process it, and failing. No matter how much he tried, he couldn't forget what he'd seen. He remembered Kinsella's lifeless corpse, the guts spilling out of his severed torso. He remembered seeing the gaping hole where Terry Monk's face had once been. Bald and Porter hadn't talked about it. They weren't about to open up and get all softy-softy. That wasn't the Regiment way. There was only one way to heal those wounds.

Vengeance.

Porter said, 'I can't get my head around it.'

'Around what?

'The attack. How the fuck did they manage to pull it off, mate? Christ, we couldn't have planned it better ourselves.'

'What's your point?' Bald growled.

'Nothing, maybe. Only that Lakes is right. Deeds is part of something much bigger. We're dealing with some serious people. Deeds probably is right at the bottom of the food chain. Whoever's at the top, they've got some balls on them going after the Regiment like that. They're not going to be easy to get to.'

'I don't give a shit who they are. Those lads were ripped to shreds. Now we've got an opportunity to do the same to them. And I'm going to rip every one of those bastards up. Starting with this tosser.'

At that moment a shout came from the direction of the strip club. Porter looked across the street and clocked a group of about twenty blokes on a stag do trying to get into the Pony Lounge. The stag was steaming drunk and the burly-looking bouncer at the door wasn't having any of it. After a few half-hearted protests the blokes turned away and moved on.

Twenty metres to the west of the Pony Lounge, Davey Coles looked up from the newspaper he was reading and glanced at the tourists. Coles was the third man on the OP. He was sat outside a late-night restaurant, smoking and sipping a Diet Coke while he pretended to read the *Daily Mirror*.

The team had run through the plan a dozen times back at the safe house until everyone knew exactly what they were doing. As soon as Deeds swept out of the strip club with his driver, Coles would move fifteen metres ahead of them down the alley. Porter and Bald would exit the bar and follow the target, keeping an equal distance behind. Bald would deal with the driver while Porter focused on grabbing Deeds. Coles would block the alley exit, stopping the target from escaping.

While they were busy lifting the target, Devereaux would be sitting behind the wheel of a Mercedes-Benz Sprinter van parked on the corner of Avenida Julio Iglesias and Calle Jesus Puente, sixty metres due west of the alley. The van had been painted to look like it was from a local cleaning firm, and Devereaux had the MP5SD submachine gun stowed in the front passenger seat. He would be keeping eyes on the alley, waiting for Coles to emerge. Once he saw Coles, he'd know that Deeds was right behind. That was the signal for Devereaux to fire up the Sprinter. He'd steer the van across the street, stopping directly in front of the alley. Then Bald and Porter would pop open the main door and shove Deeds inside the back before anyone else realised what was going on. Then they'd speed out of Puerto Banus, changing getaway vehicles a few miles outside of town before driving to a separate safe house they'd rented in Fuengirola, twenty-five miles to the east.

The plan relied on coordination, and timing. The team didn't want things to get noisy. Gunshots meant cops, and in a place like Puerto Banus with a lot of tourists and celebrities, the police would be on the scene within minutes. From start to finish, the grab should take no more than ninety seconds.

Porter took another sip of his beer and glanced down at his watch.

It said 2356 hours.

Thirty-four minutes to go.

Not long.

Not long at all.

0039 hours.

'Fuck's sake,' said Bald. 'What's taking him so long?'

Porter shrugged. 'Probably getting a happy ending.'

Bald was still on his first bottle of beer. Porter had switched to something a little stronger. He'd ordered a triple measure of Bell's while Bald had nipped to the toilets and tipped the shots into his pint glass. He could feel the booze already working its magic, glowing in his veins and easing his nerves. Drink was his crutch, and Porter wasn't afraid to admit it. Alcohol slowed other people down, but not Porter. That's what he told himself, at least. It helped to settle his anxieties. Helped him forget the fear brewing in his guts. They were taking a big risk with this op. If it went south, the guys could end up spending the next ten years in a Spanish prison.

They'd been OP'ing the door at the front of the Pony Lounge for the past hour and Deeds still hadn't emerged. Outside the streets had started to empty shortly after midnight and most of the action had switched to the clubs further to the west along the strip. Across the street hookers and drug dealers had crawled out of the woodwork and were openly touting for business. Which was fine with Bald, because he had a thing for hookers. Mainly high-class ones with posh accents, but right now he had his eyes on a leggy blonde shrink-wrapped in a red latex miniskirt and a pair of white stilettos that wouldn't look out of place on a Romford dance floor. She had high cheekbones and pouting lips and piercing light blue eyes. Slavic, thought Bald. Czech, maybe. Or Slovakian. She blew him a kiss then strolled off up the street, hips swinging seductively from side to side. Maybe he'd come back to Puerto Banus after the mission, Bald thought. Look her up.

Over on the TV the programme had switched to a late-night boxing match in between a couple of Ukrainians Bald had never heard of. Most of the punters had cleared out and the few that remained were sitting around at the bar, hunched over their lagers while they moaned about mortgages and ex-wives in their slurred voices. The regulars all seemed to know each other and Bald was conscious of the fact that he and Porter stood out like a pair of bishops at the morning call to prayer. He hoped to fuck that Deeds showed his face soon. It was only a matter of time before the punters started to take notice of the two guys by the window, slowly sipping their beers.

Bald said, 'If he doesn't come out soon, I'll go in and find the cunt myself.'

Porter gritted his teeth and said, 'No one's going anywhere, Jock. We stick to the plan.'

Bald stewed. Porter checked his G-Shock for the hundredth time in the last five minutes.

It said 0042 hours.

Twelve minutes late.

Where the fuck is he?

The staff at the Paradiso were beginning to close up for the night. They were collecting empty glasses and wiping down the tables and emptying ashtrays. Some of the bigger joints stayed open until four or five, but the clientele here was mostly Brits and the bar closed at one o'clock on the dot. Other than Bald and Porter only a handful of hard drinkers remained. In another ten or fifteen minutes they would have to leave the OP and find another spot with a good vantage point overlooking the street. But most of the other boozers at this end of the strip were also shutting up for the night. If Deeds didn't emerge soon then they'd have to abandon the mission and try their luck again tomorrow. Porter was starting to think they'd have to abort.

Three minutes later, Bill Deeds stepped out of the club.

'Here's our boy,' said Porter.

'About fucking time,' grumbled Bald.

Deeds swaggered out of the door at the front of the Pony Lounge, thirty metres away from the Blades' position at the bar. He looked pleased with himself, a massive grin plastered across his ugly face. He also looked even bigger than Porter remembered him. His biceps bulged out of the sleeves of his Lacoste t-shirt like a pair of basketballs stuffed into sacks. His thighs were as wide as tree trunks inside his dark blue jeans. His skin was the colour of mahogany from all the fake tan. Deeds's left arm was strapped up in a dressing. Porter recalled shooting the ex-squaddie in the shoulder, moments before he'd sped away from the Beacons reservoir.

A heavy stood at his flank. Porter recognised him from the dry runs they'd made on the target over the last two days. A low-level operator in Scarsdale's organisation. The driver. He was also thickly-built, but stood next to Deeds he looked like a contestant trying out for a Mr Muscle ad. He wore a baggy Burberry polo that hung like a tent from his wide frame and knee-length cargo shorts. His eyes were like buttons pressed into the folds of his face. He looked like the kind of guy who bench-pressed a hundred and fifty kilos at the gym and thought that made him tough. He was big and mean and dumb.

Low-grade thugs, Lakes had said. *You could probably handle them.*

But Porter wasn't worried about the driver. The real difficulty was going to be getting away without alerting any of the other gang affiliates. He recalled what Lakes had said about Scarsdale's people owning half of Puerto Banus. They operated several bars along the strip and had VIP lounges in all the clubs. Their foot soldiers worked the doors and supplied the drugs to the clubbers. From their surveillance Porter and Bald knew that there were at least a dozen of Scarsdale's people inside a hundred-metre radius of the alleyway. No wonder Deeds was acting so chilled. He was in Scarsdale's back yard. The idea of someone lifting him would simply never have occurred to him. But if Deeds did manage to sound the alarm, Porter reckoned they would have thirty seconds at most to bug out of the marina before things went south. Everything depended on the grab being quick and clean and smooth. Any delay risked turning the op into one big clusterfuck.

He looked on as Deeds pounded down the stairs alongside Burberry. As soon as the Brits hit the street level they turned and headed west along the strip, making for the darkened alley twenty metres away at Porter's twelve o'clock. At the same time Coles calmly stood up from his table across the street, left his newspaper and a couple of notes for the bill, and paced ahead of Deeds and the driver. He hit the alley fifteen metres ahead of the target. Twenty metres ahead of Bald and Porter. Six seconds later, Deeds and Burberry stepped into the alley.

Then Bald turned to Porter.

'Let's grab this cunt.'

The two operators slid out of their chairs and made for the door.

A cool breeze hit Porter as he stepped out into the street, running its fingers through his hair and thrusting down the bones of his face. There was a salty chill in the air and the streets were spit-polished with the look of recent rain. They fast-walked towards the alley, fifteen metres behind Deeds and Burberry. By now most of the nearby joints had almost emptied out. The streets were brimming with dealers and pimps, jostling for custom with pissed tourists. Bald and Porter were now twelve metres behind Deeds. They had to force themselves to move at a slower pace in order to keep at a reasonable distance from their quarry. As they approached the alley Porter could feel his heart beating like a snare drum inside his chest. His muscles instinctively tensed. His guts tied themselves into a vicious knot, mixing with the alcohol glowing in his chest. They were getting close now. Another thirty seconds and Bill Deeds – the first name on their deathlist – would be in the bag.

Ahead of them Deeds strolled casually down the alley, laughing at something Burberry had said. Porter and Bald stayed fifteen metres back, eyes scanning the balconies and terraces that jutted out of the apartment blocks either side of the alley. Empty. None of the locals would dream of sitting outside in this crap weather, Porter thought. He lowered his gaze and saw that Coles was now approaching the far end of the alley. The South African would stop once he hit the exit, blocking off the only escape route for Deeds and Burberry. They would have nowhere left to run.

Porter felt his pulse quicken. Any second now Devereaux would kickstart the Sprinter and steer the van into position.

Twenty seconds.

He glanced over his shoulder, scanning the alley at his six o'clock to check that they weren't being followed. Then he slid a hand under his leather jacket and reached for his holstered Glock. So did Bald. Porter tightened his hand around the polymer grip, his index finger resting on the trigger mechanism. He liked the heft of the loaded Glock, the weight of it with a full clip of brass. A hot thrill swept through his veins as they increased their stride and approached the target. The net was closing around Deeds now. He'd slipped through their grasp once before. But he wouldn't get away. Not tonight. This time they were going to nail the fucker good and proper.

They were ten metres from the target when a figure stepped out of the shadows.

Bald froze. Porter froze too. For a cold second both operators stood rooted to the spot as the figure slipped out of one of the doorways lining the alley and moved towards Bald. His eyes adjusted to the gloom and he realised it was the hooker he'd had his eye on back at the Paradiso. The one who'd blown him a kiss. The Slavic stunner. Her bright blue eyes glowed like a couple of coins in a wishing well. She smiled wickedly at Bald.

'You want good time, baby?' the hooker said.

She had a husky eastern European accent. Bald's favourite. She also had a cracking pair of tits on her, and on any other day he would have been tempted to take up the hooker's offer. But not tonight. He tried to slide past her.

'Maybe tomorrow, love.'

But the hooker wasn't taking no for an answer. She stepped closer to Bald. She was so close Bald could smell her cheap perfume. Strawberries and sex. She ran her delicate hand over his crotch.

'Suck and fuck, baby? I give you good time. Best fuck in all of Spain. Hundred thousand peseta.'

Porter gritted his teeth. He still had his right hand inside his jacket pocket, gripping his Glock. Bald had already retrieved his weapon. Deeds and Burberry were ten metres ahead of Bald and Porter. Ten short of the alley exit. But this hooker was going to wreck the mission. She stood blocking the operators' path. Delaying them. Deeds and Burberry were twelve metres ahead. Now thirteen. Coles had already hit the end of the alley. He stopped and reached inside his jacket for his weapon. Porter and Bald had to act now. Otherwise it was going to be two on one. Coles against Burberry and Deeds. Porter flared with anger. He shoved the hooker aside with his free hand.

'Out of my fucking way,' he snarled.

The hooker let out a high-pitched shriek as she stumbled backwards on her high heels and crashed against the doorway she'd stepped out from, knocking over a bin overflowing with rubbish. The sudden noise made Deeds and his driver stop dead in their tracks four or five metres short of the alley exit. Deeds looked past his shoulder. Caught sight of the hooker in the door-way, spitting curses at Bald in her foreign accent. Deeds stared at her curiously for a cold beat, a question mark forming in his narrow eyes. Then he swivelled his gaze towards the two operators. He saw their faces in the reflected glow of the lights from the main strip. Saw the Glock in Bald's right hand.

For a half second nobody moved. The world just stopped. Deeds stood there next to Burberry and stared at Bald and Porter. Then his eyes went wide with recognition. Then he looked really fucking scared.

Then Deeds turned and ran.

TWENTY-FIVE

0046 hours.

Everything happened fast. At the end of the alley, Coles heard the hooker's scream and turned towards his six o'clock. Towards Bald and Porter and Burberry and Deeds. The South African was digging out his holstered Glock as Deeds broke into a run. The target was five metres from Coles. Too close. Not enough distance. Not enough time for Coles to retrieve his weapon, extend his gun arm, aim at the target and shout for him to stop. He was still retrieving his weapon as Deeds crashed into him, knocking Coles back and following up with a sharp knee to the groin. Coles stumbled backwards, grunting. He dropped his Glock. Deeds and Burberry bolted past him and raced towards the alley exit.

Bald reacted quickest. He snapped his right arm level with his shoulder. Trained the Glock on Deeds. Tensed his index finger on the trigger. Ready to loose off a shot.

'Jock, no!' Porter shouted. 'We need him alive.'

Bald hesitated. A split second later, Deeds and Burberry were ducking out of sight. They swept past Coles and headed east on Avenida Julio Iglesias. Bald lowered his weapon and cursed under his breath. Then he broke forward, sprinting ahead of Porter and Coles and surging towards the end of the alley.

Bald swept out onto the sprawling main street that straddled Puerto Banus. Sixty metres away to his left on the corner of Calle Jesus Puente, Bald could see Devereaux gunning the Sprinter engine and steering the van onto the main road. Coles was on his feet, grabbing his dropped pistol. Bald swivelled his gaze to his three o'clock. He was looking east down Avenida Julio Iglesias.

The road stretched on for maybe three hundred metres all the way to the fringe of the beach along Playa de Levante, downstream from the marina and the super-yachts. Twenty metres away Deeds and Burberry were charging down the wide pavement, barging past tourists as they hurried towards the Range Rover parked fifty metres away, directly outside a fast food joint.

Bald turned to Coles. 'Stay here! Watch the alley!'

Coles nodded. Then Bald turned and chased after Deeds. Porter stumbled alongside the Jock. Still fumbling to deholster his weapon. He's rusty, thought Bald. The guy's been out of the game for too long. Not for the first time he wondered if Porter was really up to this mission.

Bald raced after the target. Adrenaline flooding his veins. His heart pumping furiously. Everything was a blur. Like watching a shaky home video. He was running on instinct, and fumes. Every sense was heightened. Bald scuttled past the stunned tourists. Some of them caught sight of the Glock in his right hand and screamed, diving for cover in the nearest doorways or ducking behind their cars. Others stood rooted to the spot in terror or confusion, or maybe both. Bald blanked them out and focused solely on grabbing Deeds. He had to close the gap and stop the fucker from bugging out. If he gave them the slip now, he'd be spooked, Bald knew. He wouldn't stick around in Spain. He'd go to ground, somewhere way under the radar. Somewhere the Firm would never be able to find him. The chances of locating Deeds again would be virtually nil. The mission would be fucked.

If Deeds gets away now, it's over.

The ex-Para pounded down the pavement as fast as his huge legs could carry him. Which wasn't very fast at all. All that heavy muscle weighed the guy down. His injured left arm slowed him down even further and forced him to move along in a lumbering gait. Burberry was just as slow. The guy was fifty per cent muscle and fifty per cent body fat.

Bald quickly closed the gap on the target. He could hear Porter's breathing behind him as he hurried along a few paces further back. They were fifteen metres away from the target now.

Deeds and Burberry were forty metres from the Range Rover. Bald ran on, his lungs burning. Like someone had poured petrol down his throat and then tossed in a struck match. The wind was blowing hard, shivering the fronds of the palm trees lining both sides of the road, and he could feel drops of rain spattering against his face. He raced down the street. Past the tacky clubs and the designer outlets and the strip bars. Towards the man who'd killed fifty-five British soldiers.

Up ahead Burberry risked a glance past his shoulder. Saw the two operators bearing down on him. Realised he wasn't going to reach the Range Rover in time, and panicked. That was his first mistake. He stopped. Did a one-eighty. Reached under his shirt and dug out a pistol stashed in the waistband of his cargos. Bald got a glimpse of the tool. A hefty-looking handgun with a stainless-steel barrel and gaping mouth at the end, the kind of thing you bought just because it looked good. Maybe a Taurus PT92, thought Bald. Something like that. The Porsche 911 of handguns.

Burberry shaped to take aim at Bald. That was his second mistake. The fatal one. Bald punished him lethally. He didn't panic. He had ten thousand hours of Regiment training drilled into him and he knew exactly what to do. He dropped to a crouch and raised his Glock in a fast but controlled movement, his muscles tensed but not overly stiff. Then he lined up Burberry's torso between the front and rear sighting posts on the Glock. He didn't need to a flick off a safety. There wasn't one. On the Glock, your safety was your trigger finger. You didn't fire the gun unless you pulled the trigger, and you didn't pull the trigger unless you wanted to fire the gun.

Bald exhaled.

Squeezed the trigger.

The muzzle flashed. The Glock barked.

Bald had cocked the weapon before leaving the safe house. Meaning, there was already a round nestling in the snout. The slider shunted back and then rocketed forward, spitting out the chambered bullet. He fired twice more. Three rounds in deadly, quick succession. The bullets hit Burberry in a close grouping, slamming into his upper chest with a dull wet *whump*. Like fists smacking against a punchbag. Burberry jerked wildly, doing the dead man's dance. He made a deep grunt in his throat as he dropped like a sack of hot potatoes. The semi-automatic clattered to the ground beside him as the blood spurted out of an exit wound in his neck in a hot red gush. The discharges echoed like thunder across the street. A passing taxi picked up speed and bulleted away. Somewhere across the street, a woman screamed.

Bald smiled inwardly and felt good about himself, and life generally.

I've still fucking got it.

As soon as the first shot had discharged, Deeds instinctively hit the deck. Now he scurried towards the semi-automatic lying next to Burberry. Deeds was twenty-five metres from the Range Rover and four or five away from his slotted mate. Twelve metres ahead of Bald. Which meant Bald had more than twice the distance to clear if he was to get to Deeds before the guy put the drop on him. He dug deep and sprinted forward, straining every sinew in his body. The blood rapidly pooled under Burberry's lifeless corpse, running in the gaps between the flagstones. Deeds crawled forward and reached out a hand, making a play for the semi. Six metres to the target. Bald lunged madly forward. He bore down on Deeds as the guy clasped his thick fingers around the weapon grip.

Deeds shaped to raise the weapon. He never got the chance. Bald leapt forward and aimed his right foot at the guy. There was a satisfying crunch as the Jock's Timberland connected with the ex-Para's jaw. Deeds groaned and rolled onto his back. His grip automatically released the pistol. Bald swiped another kick at him, this time driving at the guy's ribs. He hit him with such force that the air exploded out of his lungs. Bald kicked him again. He heard a sound like a branch snapping in two and figured he'd broken a couple of ribs. A shattered rib or two was nothing compared to the pain Deeds would be feeling by the time Bald and the others went to work on him. But it was a damn good start.

Deeds tried to fight back. He had a lot of muscle. But like most bodybuilders, it was all slow muscle. The kind that you got after spending hour after hour working on your one-rep max on the bench press. Bald had the other kind. Fast muscle. Less bulk, but more explosive power. The kind of muscle that, as any boxer will tell you, wins you fights. All slow muscle does is win you the occasional glance on a beach. Deeds kicked out at Bald, throwing all of his power into his leg muscles as he aimed for the Jock's groin. Bald saw the move coming. He shifted quickly on his feet and dodged the blow, punching out with his gun arm and smashing the Glock barrel into the bridge of Deeds's face. Then he dropped down and pressed the Glock into Deeds's side, digging the muzzle hard into his broken ribs. The guy howled in pain.

'On your feet,' Bald ordered.

Deeds didn't move. He glowered up at the Jock, blood trickling down his chin from his fucked-up nose. Beside him the blood continued to pump steadily out of Burberry's multiple exit wounds. Bald drove the weapon harder into Deeds's ribs, drawing another pained cry from the guy. By now Porter had reached them, his weapon drawn and the business end trained on Deeds. There was a flash of defiance in the ex-Para's eyes as he staggered to his feet.

'You're making a big mistake,' he rasped nasally.

'Shut up,' said Bald, keeping the Glock pressed to the guy's broken ribs.

'A big fucking mistake. You don't know who you're messing with, pal.'

'Shut it. Get moving.'

Porter and Bald shoved Deeds back down Avenida Julio Iglesias. Towards the Sprinter. Around them people were screaming at the sound of the gunshot. One man lay on his front, hands over his head and begging Bald not to shoot him. Others ran for their lives, darting inside the nearest restaurants and screaming for someone to call the police. Bald hurried Deeds along. He figured they had maybe two or three minutes before the cops showed. Devereaux had drawn the Sprinter to a halt just before the alley, forty metres ahead of Bald and Porter. Coles stood between the alley and the van. Gesturing for the other guys to hurry up.

They were thirty metes from the van when Bald heard voices coming from the direction of the main strip. More than one of them. Maybe six or seven. Scarsdale's people, he realised. The foot soldiers must have heard the gunshot on the main road. Another ten or fifteen seconds and the guys would be swarming over the alley like flies on shit. Bald pushed on alongside Porter, manhandling Deeds towards the Sprinter. The target stumbled forward, wincing in pain and clutching his busted rib. They were fifteen metres from the Sprinter now. It seemed to take an age to reach the van.

'Move it!' Coles yelled. 'We've got company!'

Bald willed himself on. Muscles burning. Heart thumping so fast he could feel it pulsing in the back of his throat. The voices from the strip were getting louder now. Bald figured the foot soldiers must have reached the alley. Ten metres to the Sprinter now. Nine metres. Eight. Coles hurried over to the Sprinter and yanked open the side door. Ready to bundle Deeds inside the van.

Seven metres to go.

Six.

Five metres from the van, Bald heard a shout at his nine o'clock. He looked across his shoulder. Spotted four guys tearing down the alley. Racing towards him. One of the foot soldiers had seen Deeds and pointed him out to his mates. The nearest tough was fifteen metres away when he reached for his weapon. He was a thickset guy with a crew cut and a beer belly. He looked like a testicle with arms and he wore an England 1990 World Cup replica football shirt.

It was no contest. Bald already had his weapon drawn and ready to use. He twisted at the waist and simultaneously hefted up the Glock at England. There was no time to properly aim. No time to put the guy in focus between the weapon sights. Bald gave the trigger a quick squeeze. The muzzle lit up like a dope smoker at Christmas. The bullet struck England dead centre in the chest. Bald gave him a neat bullet hole to go with the Three Lions on his shirt. The guy crumpled. He dropped to a heap amid the scattered rubbish. Fuck him. Bald didn't like England anyway.

Coles scurried over to the alley and put down three more rounds on the advancing foot soldiers. Covering Bald and Porter. The rounds glanced off the alley walls and sent the guys scattering. They darted for the nearest available cover. In the doorways, behind the bins. Wherever they could find somewhere to hide. They wouldn't stay down for long, Bald knew. But the strike team only needed a few seconds. He turned and dragged Deeds the last few steps to the Sprinter. Porter had his Glock pointed at the nape of the guy's neck. They hit the van in three breathless strides and shoved Deeds inside. Climbed in after the target. Porter slapped a pair of plasticuffs around the guy's thick wrists and pulled a hessian sack over his head. Coles let off a final warning shot down the alley then jumped into the Sprinter and wrenched the side door shut.

'Go!' Porter shouted. 'FUCKING GO! NOW!'

Devereaux didn't need a second invitation. The Aussie put his foot to the accelerator and gunned the Sprinter engine. The van growled angrily into life as they slid out of the parking spot and lurched onto the main road. The shooting had emptied the streets of traffic and they quickly began to pull away. Through the rear window Bald could see the remaining three foot soldiers racing out of the alley, weapons drawn as they shouted at the van. They were twenty metres away, then thirty. Then forty. One of the guys fired twice at the back of the Sprinter. Porter heard the bullets hammering against the rear door. Then the Sprinter picked up speed and the foot soldiers finally gave up the chase. After three hundred metres Devereaux made a hard right on Avenida de las Naciones Unidas and they raced past the beach, the sands purple under the reflected glow of the moon. The rain was falling hard as they raced north towards the Autovia del Mediterraneo. Behind them, Puerto Banus started to shrink from view.

Then it was gone.

They were a mile outside Puerto Banus when Bald finally lost his rag.

'The fuck was that about?' he snapped angrily. He was looking at Porter. 'Shoving the hooker. Jesus, you almost let the bastard get away.'

'She was in the way,' Porter hit back. 'What the fuck was I supposed to do? Let Deeds escape?'

Bald simmered. It took every ounce of self-control to stop himself from lashing out. 'You were supposed to not fuck up the mission. You were supposed to not make a ton of noise and warn the target before we had him cornered. That's basic, that.'

'We got him, mate,' said Porter. 'That's all that matters.'

Bald snorted through his nostrils. 'But we nearly fucking didn't. Deeds was a cunt hair from giving us the slip. If I hadn't slotted the driver, he might have escaped. That would've been on you. Mate.'

He looked away. Porter stared silently out of the window. He hated to admit it, but Bald was right. Porter had nearly shafted the mission. He was in serious danger of losing his touch. He didn't respect Bald as a personality, but the guy was a first-class operator in the field. Porter had just seen that with his own eyes. The guy was sharp. Surgical. Lethal. But seeing the Jock's skills reminded Porter of just how far he'd let his own standards drop.

You got lucky this time, the voice in the back of his head said. But you won't get a second chance. *If I'm going to complete the mission, then I'm gonna have to sharpen up my act.*

TWENTY-SIX

0128 hours.

The safe house in Fuengirola was a thirty-minute ride away, on the AP-7 motorway that ran between Guadirao to the west and Malaga to the east. Devereaux drove under the limit, keeping the Sprinter purring along at fifty miles per. They stopped to change vehicles at Ojén, a nothing town a couple of miles north of Marbella. There had to have been at least a dozen witnesses to the shooting in Puerto Banus and the van would soon be hot, if it wasn't already. They pulled into the back of a disued garage on Calle Avellano, bundled Deeds out of the Sprinter and shoved him into the boot of a white SEAT Toledo that Devereaux had stashed the previous day. Then Coles took a jerry can filled with petrol, doused the Sprinter and lit the fucker up. Thirty seconds later they were pulling out onto the main road and motoring east to the safe house. By the time the cops showed up, any DNA evidence or fingerprints would have gone up in smoke.

Twenty-one minutes later the strike team pulled up outside an address on the outskirts of the town, away from the souvenir shops and the London-themed boozers along the bustling seafront. Places with names like the Elephant and Castle, the Mods and Rockers, the Nag's Head. The safe house was a basement apartment set at the end of a rubbish-strewn street, flanked by ramshackle high-rises and shuttered shop fronts. The walls of the apartment had been soundproofed and they were half a mile from the centre of town. No one would hear Deeds once he started screaming.

The apartment was filthy. Bald had visited it two days before the mission to get the place ready for the grab. There were piss stains on the floor and bars on the windows, and a large brown stain covered most of the ceiling in the living room. The team had laid out clear plastic sheeting on the floor to cover any blood splatters. A single metal chair stood in the middle of the main room with a naked lightbulb hanging directly above. There was a fold-out DIY table to one side of the room with a bunch of tools laid out on it, along with a piece of 2 x 4 and a Bosch cordless power drill. There was also a portable blowtorch and a can of lighter fluid and a box of matches. They had more tools than Homebase, but they wouldn't be putting together any kitchens tonight.

Bald ran his hands slowly over the tools while Porter and Devereaux hustled Deeds into the room. They stripped him naked and shoved him down onto the chair. Then they wrapped duct tape around his chest to bind him to the chair and tied his ankles to the chair legs with a length of paracord.

'You can't fucking do this,' Deeds snarled. 'You hear? I got friends in high places, pal. I'm talking serious fucking players. People will be out looking for me.'

They didn't say a word. Porter and Devereaux finished tying Deeds to the chair. Then Devereaux left to stow the car in a back street while Coles waited outside to keep watch. Suddenly Bald and Porter were alone with the ex-squaddie. He groaned nasally. They'd slapped Deeds up a bit in the back of the Sprinter and now he looked like crap. Blood bubbled under his bruised nose. His bottom lip was purpled and badly cut. His right eye had swollen to the size of a walnut. Deeds spat blood on the floor then lifted his eyes to Bald and glared at him.

'You're a fucking dead man.' He looked to Porter. 'You too. You're all fucking dead.'

Bald said nothing. Porter lit up a cigarette, watching the Jock as he calmly picked up a set of heavy-duty Stanley bolt-cutters. The two operators had agreed on a strategy before heading to the safe house. Bald would handle the torture, while Porter would play the role of the good cop. That way Deeds would naturally look towards Porter as the more reasonable of the two interrogators.

Bald tested the bolt-cutters. They made a delicate snipping noise that quickly got Deeds' undivided attention. He glanced at the bolt-cutters then looked back to Porter, his face twitching with fear.

'You got the wrong man,' he said. He was trying to put on a brave face, but his voice was cracking around the edges. 'I don't know shit. That's the truth, I swear. I can't tell you nothing.'

Porter smoked some more, the nicotine helping to settle his nerves. Bald still said nothing. He turned his attention to a Spear and Jackson hacksaw. He held the blade up to the light and ran his fingers gently over the stainless-steel teeth. Deeds started shaking like a Scouse at a job interview.

'Scarsdale will find you. Mark my words. He knows every nook and cranny between here and Malaga. He'll find you and he'll cut the pair of you up. You'll fucking see.'

Porter went on giving Deeds the silent treatment and stubbed out his cigarette on the bare floor. Over at the DIY table, Bald set down the hacksaw and returned to the bolt-cutters. He picked them up along with the blowtorch and without saying a word paced over to Deeds. Porter took a dirty soiled rag and stuffed it in the guy's mouth. Then Bald dropped to a knee in front of the ex-Para and placed the toe on his right foot between the steel jaws, making sure the edges were at a right angle to get a nice clean cut. The colour drained instantly from Deeds's face. His eyes went so wide they looked like they might pop out of their sockets. He hadn't been expecting this. He'd probably figured that they would start off with a few questions, rough him up a bit more first.

He figured wrong.

Bald gripped the cutter handles and spread them apart as far as they would go. Then he brought them firmly together. Deeds gave a muffled scream as the jaws sliced clean through his toe, clipping bone and gristle and flesh. Blood spurted out of the torn ragged stump, spilling across the plastic sheeting. The guy kept on screaming, breathing furiously through his nostrils. Bald reached for the blowtorch. He turned on the gas. Took a matchstick from a box of matches, lit it. Held the naked flame to the torch nozzle. There was a sharp hissing noise as a bluish flame lit up. Then Bald took the blowtorch and held the flame close to Deeds's bleeding toe, cauterising the wound. Deeds screamed again through the rag in his mouth. The smell of burning flesh filled the room as he thrashed wildly in his chair, rocking back and forth and convulsing with pain. He struggled to breathe. Then Bald took the flame away and Porter tore the dirty rag out of Deeds' mouth. He promptly leaned forward and puked up, emptying his guts onto the floor.

Bald stood back and watched. The blowtorch flame was still running. Deeds spat out blood and made a weird sound that was somewhere between a dry heave and a moan. The flesh around his big toe was charred black. He groaned again.

'Jesus, okay. Christ. I'll talk. I'll tell you fucking everything. Just please, no more.'

Porter stared at the guy in puzzlement. 'Tell us what? We haven't asked you a fucking question yet.'

There was a glimmer of fear in Deeds' eyes. His lips quivered. The guy was absolutely bricking it. His imagination was working overtime now as he wondered how much worse the pain was going to get before he got the chance to spill his guts.

Porter stuffed the rag back in Deeds' mouth. Bald reached for the bolt-cutters and fit the jaws snug around another of the guy's toes. Deeds tensed as he braced himself for the pain. Porter clamped his hands down on the guy's shoulders to keep him still while Bald worked the bolt-cutters and cut through his second toe. Blood oozed out of the stump, spattering the sheet dark red. Deeds screamed hysterically. Piss was running down his legs now, forming a puddle between his feet. Bald took the blowtorch to the wound and the sickly sweet odour of burnt flesh mingled with the rancid stench of urine. When he was finished, Bald stepped back and took a moment to admire his work. Deeds's foot was in rag order. He wouldn't be turning out for his Sunday league team anytime soon.

Porter stepped forward and dropped to a knee in front of Deeds. He took out the rag. Fixed his gaze on the guy.

Said, 'Listen to me carefully, because I'm only going to say this once. You're going to die tonight. That's going to happen, and there's fuck-all you can do about it. How you die, that's up to you.'

Deeds started crying. Tears streamed down his face. He was muttering under his breath, begging for help. From God or his torturers, Porter couldn't tell. Either way it wouldn't do him much good.

'Bill,' he said. 'Look at me.'

Deeds stopped bawling like a baby. He lifted his eyes to Porter. They were big and wide and scared.

Porter said, 'Here's what's going to happen, Bill. You've got one chance to tell us the truth. Not some of the truth. We want all of it. Do you understand? If you level with us, then I'll give you a soldier's death. A bullet to the head, nice and quick. It'll be painless. You won't feel a thing. You have my word.'

Porter paused. He was deliberately using Deeds' first name. Trying to make the guy think that the two of them had an understanding. That he could trust Porter. Bald stood close by, wielding the bolt-cutters.

'But if you lie to us, or if you hold back, then my mate here will rip you apart.' Porter tipped his head at the Jock. 'He'll cut off the rest of your toes first. Then your fingers. Then your bollocks. By the time he's finished you'll have more stumps than the rainforest. It'll take you days to die, and it'll hurt like fuck.'

Deeds hung his head low. He was utterly broken now. He wept uncontrollably, shaking his head and whimpering. 'This isn't fucking happening,' he kept saying, over and over. 'This isn't happening. It can't be.'

'It is,' said Porter. 'And if you want me to make it quick, you'd better start talking.'

Deeds clamped his eyes shut and clenched his brow. His face was a picture of torment as he wrestled with the agonising decision. 'Fuck it. What do you want to know?'

'You know who we are, Bill?' Porter asked.

Deeds nodded. Barely. 'You're Regiment. You were there that day. At the Brecons.'

'Then you know why we're here.'

Deeds didn't say anything this time. He didn't need to. His face gave him away.

'Who else was involved?' Porter demanded.

'There were six of us,' Deeds said between ragged draws of breath.

'Who were the others, Bill?'

'Serbs. They were Serbs.'

Porter glanced at Bald in surprise. He thought back to what Lakes had said. About Deeds going underground after he'd tried to smuggle weapons. *It's possible the Serbian mafia was involved,* she'd said.

Maybe he's just one link in a very long chain.

Jesus, thought Porter.

Did the Serb mafia order the hit on the Regiment?

He looked back to Deeds. 'All of them? They were all Serbs?'

Deeds managed a nod. His eyes were dim and he was slipping in and out of consciousness. The adrenaline was starting to wear off and the pain was kicking in. Any moment now the guy would go floppy.

'Where are the others now?' Porter said. 'Are they here, in Spain?'

'Scattered,' said Deeds. 'All over. That was the plan. That's what we were told to do.'

'By who?'

But Deeds didn't answer. His head fell forward and his shoulders sagged. Spittle dangled out of the corners of his slack mouth, forming a neat pool on the floor. Porter gestured to Bald.

'Wake this fucker up.'

Bald returned to the table and picked up the can of lighter fluid. He flipped up the red nozzle and paced over to Deeds. Gave the can a squeeze and poured fluid on his chest. Then he struck a match and chucked it at Deeds. His chest went up in flames. Deeds jolted upright. He howled, writhing in pain. When the guy was nice and toasted Bald unscrewed the cap on a bottle of water and chucked it over Deeds, dousing the flames.

'Jesus,' he gasped, clenching his teeth. 'Oh fuck, oh Jesus. Fuck!'

Bald went to light Deeds up again but Porter shot him a look that said, *That's enough.* They needed Deeds awake. Not dead. Not yet, anyway. Bald reluctantly lowered the can of lighter fluid and took a step back. Porter swung his gaze back to Deeds. The guy looked all kinds of fucked up.

Porter said, 'Who gave the order?'

Deeds groaned and said, 'These people. They're not fucking amateurs, like. They're big time. They've got serious balls on them. You don't want to mess with them.'

'I'll take my chances. Tell me now, or you lose another toe.'

Deeds hesitated. Bald snapped. He moved towards the ex-Para, his face shading white with rage as he wielded the bolt-cutters. 'You killed our mates, you cunt. You'd better fucking talk.'

Porter ignored his mucker and focused his gaze on Deeds, appealing to the guy's judgement. He was playing a craftier game than Bald. The Jock was pure anger. Porter knew it was better to try and tease the int out of Deeds by offering him the incentive of a soldier's death. He was still going to rip the guy to shreds once they'd got all the information out of him. But Deeds didn't know that.

'His name,' Porter said. 'Tell us who planned the attack, and I'll make it quick.'

Deeds took a deep draw of breath. Then he spoke.

'It's Brozovic,' he said. 'His name is Radoslav Brozovic, but everyone calls him the Tiger.'

A long moment of stunned silence played out in the room. Deeds slumped in his chair. Porter felt a cold dread run down his spine. He looked to Bald. Saw the colour draining from his mucker's face, like water running down a plughole. Neither of them said a word. They didn't need to.

Radoslav Brozovic.

They'd both heard that name before.

TWENTY-SEVEN

0204 hours.

The silence went on for what seemed like a long while, but was probably no more than two or three seconds. Porter just stood there, an invisible band tightening around his chest. Then Bald spoke.

'The Serb warlord?' He cocked his head at Porter and frowned. 'Isn't that the cunt you went after in Bosnia?'

Porter nodded and said, 'Yeah. That's him all right.'

The memories came rushing back at him. Like a fist to the solar plexus. Images he'd spent the past eighteen months trying to erase. Bosnia, 1997. Porter had been part of a four-man team sent out to put a stop to Radoslav Brozovic. The self-styled Tiger of the Balkans commanded a notorious paramilitary unit, the Red Eagles. His soldiers had been running wild, butchering Muslims, raping women and burying kids alive in the villages along the border with Bosnia. Reports flooded in daily of new atrocities linked to Brozovic and his goons. There were rumours the guy took a golf bag and a caddy wherever he went. Instead of clubs, the golf bag was filled with weapons. A length of wood with rusted nails driven through it. A baseball bat. A pickaxe, a crowbar. All different kinds of weapons. Whenever they entered a town Brozovic's men would round up any Muslims and force them to their knees. Then Brozovic would turn to his caddy and ask for the nine iron, or the wedge or the putter. The caddy would hand over the right club. Then Brozovic would batter the victim until their brains were seeping out of their skull. The Red Eagles made Arkan's toughs look like the Care Bears.

It had taken months to track Brozovic down. Int suggested the guy was holed up in a remote town close to the border at Zvornik. All the young men had left the village to go and fight for the various sides, leaving the old boys behind. Brozovic's men moved in and turned the village into a living hell. They lined up every Muslim and had them shot. They kidnapped girls from both sides of the divide and took them to a house on the outskirts of the village. Then they took turns to rape the girls, renting them out to Serbian soldiers who needed to let off steam. When they were done, Brozovic had his men slit the girls' throats and dump their bodies in a separate room. Porter's team had gone in covertly and OP'd the village from a lying-up point just to the south. Once they had eyes on the toughs, Porter had called in an artillery barrage right on top of his position, risking his own safety to nail the fuckers. The fast air had narrowly missed Porter. Brozovic had left the village moments before, but most of his lieutenants had been blown to pieces.

Including his younger brother, Bosko.

Everyone in the Regiment knew about the op. Every Christmas all the various squadrons got together for the annual cross-brief. Decorations were handed out, missions were discussed and some of the lads from Delta or the SEALs often joined in, giving briefings on ops they'd run. After the Regimental rugby match the lads had a massive scoff and then got shitfaced in the squadron bars. So Bald knew all about Porter's DCM. He knew all about the op to take down Brozovic. And he knew that Porter had been warning the head shed of the massacres taking place in Bosnia, long before anyone in Whitehall had stared to sit up and take notice.

Bald shook his head angrily. 'Why the fuck would Brozovic carry out an attack on the Regiment?'

He looked to Deeds as he spoke. The guy was still groaning in pain, struggling to keep his head up. The skin on his chest was blistered. He parted his cracked lips and said, 'The same reason you're here. Revenge.'

'For killing his brother?' Porter said.

Deeds nodded. 'For killing Bosko. And for wiping out half his gang. Brozovic wanted to make the SAS pay. An eye for a fucking eye.'

'So he had you carry out the attack?'

'Brozovic had his own men lined up for the gig. But he needed someone local. Someone who knew about Selection, all the ins and outs. Someone who could show his guys the ropes.'

Porter glared at Deeds. A spark of rage flared in his chest. 'And you just went along with it?'

'I had no fucking choice,' Deeds said. There was a pleading look in his eyes as he spoke. 'Jesus, I needed the wedge. After they kicked me out of the Paras, I couldn't get a job. I had sod-all. I didn't even have a pot to piss in.'

'Spare us the fucking sob story,' Bald put in. 'You should have thought about that before you started trading weapons to the Serbs.'

Porter rubbed his jaw and said, 'How did Brozovic know it was the Regiment who carried out the attack? That op was covert. No one knew we were out there. All the lads were undercover.'

'Brozovic hired a private investigator,' said Deeds. 'Some Serb down in London. Ex-security services. He cross-checked the records of the *London Gazette* looking for anything that matched the date of the bombing. He found that there had been a DCM awarded for a lad in the Irish Guards on that day. And the Irish Guards weren't even in Bosnia then.'

The temperature in the room plummeted. The hairs on the back of Porter's neck stood on end as he cast his mind back to the notice in the *Gazette*. He remembered every word of it. The notice had appeared under 'Honours and Awards'.

The Queen has been graciously pleased to approve the award of the Distinguished Conduct Medal to 24479620 Sergeant John Porter Irish Guards 21 October 1998 in recognition of gallant and distinguished services in Bosnia, 14 February 1997.

Blades who got decorated were never listed as currently serving in the SAS. That was too risky. Instead they were listed as belonging to their old unit. In Porter's case, the Irish Guards.

The room got colder. Deeds went on.

'It didn't take long for the investigator to work out that the SAS were involved. He checked out the birth records and marriage certificates. Looking for anyone who went by the name John Porter who'd served in the Irish Guards. Found out this Porter guy had got married in a registry office in Hereford a few years back.'

Deeds hacked and coughed, going red in the face. His eyes were bloodshot and there was white crap at the corners of his mouth.

'Water,' he croaked.

Porter reached for a bottle of water and pressed it to Deeds's lips. At the same time the door swung open behind them and Devereaux returned. He took one look at Deeds and the blood splatters and his severed toes and did a double-take. Porter took the water bottle away.

'Keep talking, Bill,' he said.

Deeds licked his lips and composed himself.

'This Serb, he asked around a few Hereford boozers. Discreetly, like. Nothing heavy-handed, so word wouldn't get back to the Regiment. He didn't have any luck at first. Then some pissed old Blade let slip that the fucker who got decorated was serving on the Regiment Training Wing. So Brozovic came up with the plan. He'd take out the guys on Selection. We'd slot the instructors, and wipe out the next generation of operators as well. Two birds, one stone. That's when he reached out to me.'

Porter glanced at his mate. Bald was bristling with animal rage. His hands were balled into tight fists and his veins were bulging on his neck. He was on the verge of losing his rag, thought Porter.

He looked back to Deeds. 'Where can we find Brozovic?'

'I don't know. I swear.'

Bald dangled the bolt-cutters menacingly in front of Deeds.

'You sure about that?'

'It's the truth!' Deeds exclaimed, his voice trembling with panic. 'Please. You don't believe me, ask around. Brozovic went deep underground after the bombing. I'm talking way off the radar.

The guy's got a warrant out for his arrest, for fuck's sake. No one's been able to find him. Not the Brits. Not the UN. Not even the Yanks.'

'If that's the case, how did he stay in touch with you?' Porter asked.

'He didn't. We never met. We did everything through his 2i/c. Some guy called Ninkovic. He used to serve in the Red Eagles under Brozovic, so I heard. But I only met him twice. I don't know where he is. I couldn't even tell you what fucking continent he's on. That's everything I know.'

Porter kept his mouth shut and searched Deeds's eyes. He was shitting himself, alright. But there was a glimmer of defiance in his eyes too. *He's holding something back*, thought Porter. *He knows something else.*

He gave his back to the ex-Para and tipped his head at Bald. 'We're done here. He's all yours, Jock.'

Bald hefted up the bolt-cutters and moved towards Deeds.

'Wait, wait!' Deeds spluttered.

Porter stopped. Did a one-eighty and looked back at Deeds. The guy didn't look defiant any more. He just looked shit-scared. He waited for Deeds to unglue his eyes from the bolt-cutters.

'The other gunmen,' he said. 'The Serbs. I know where they're hiding. Two of 'em, anyway.'

Porter said, 'I need names, Bill.'

Deeds closed his eyes, riding another wave of pain. 'Niko Kavlak and Dejan Petrovich. They're laying low in a safe house in Malta.'

'What the fuck are they doing there?' Bald demanded. 'Why not just head back to Serbia?'

'It's a double feint,' said Deeds. 'Sooner or later, the Brits will find out that the Serbs were responsible for the attack, right? So they'll have their people looking all over Serbia for the gunmen. Brozovic figured it would be safer if his guys were outside the country when the shit hit the fan. Once the dust's settled, they'll move back to Serbia. Like I said, it's a double feint.'

'Do you have an address?' said Porter.

'It's a penthouse in Valleta. The old town. 215 St Paul's Street. Brozovic used it for hooking up with his mistresses. The Serbs, they've got orders not to leave unless it's an emergency. They're just holed up there, bingeing on coke and hookers.'

'There were four gunmen who escaped the Brecons,' said Bald. 'You and the two Serbs in Valletta makes three. Where's the fourth guy?'

'Stankovic? I don't know. The guy kept to himself. He never told me his plans. That's all I know, I fucking swear.'

Porter stayed quiet for a beat. Then he nodded and said, 'Okay, Bill. I believe you.'

He dug out his Glock from his holster. He still had all seventeen rounds in the clip and one in the chamber. Deeds caught sight of the piece and closed his eyes. Straightened his back and exhaled. Bracing himself for his soldier's death.

Then Porter lowered the Glock and turned to Bald. 'Kill this cunt.'

Bald grinned. Deeds popped his eyes open. He looked confused. Then his confusion gave way to fear as he saw Bald set down the bolt-cutters and reach for a metal ground spike next to the power tools. The spike was maybe thirty centimetres long and had a sharpened tip at the end that glinted under the intense glare of the naked lightbulb. Deeds looked back to Porter, his face crumbling into absolute terror.

'No! No, no! Shit. You promised. You said you'd make it quick.'

Porter shrugged. 'I lied.'

'Jesus, no. Christ, please, don't do—'

Porter stuffed the rag back in Deeds's mouth. Then he stepped back, giving the stage to Bald. Deeds gave out a muffled scream as the Jock clasped a hand around his skull and plunged the sharpened spike tip directly into his left eye. There was a sickening wet crunch as the tip punched through his eyeball. Deeds started convulsing madly as Bald jerked the spike around, doing all kinds of damage to the guy's frontal lobe. His arms and legs started to shake. He looked like a guy on the electric chair right after the executioner had flipped the switch. His screams hit a new crescendo. Then Deeds voided his bowels. Bald drove the spike deeper and angled it up, boring deep into his brains. Deeds jerked some more. Then he stopped screaming.

Then he went still.

Bald stepped away, leaving the spike buried deep in Deeds's skull. Blood trickled out of his eye socket and ran down his chin, dripping onto his chest. There was blood all over the place. There was a steaming brown pool of piss and shit and vomit between his feet.

'Jesus,' said Devereaux, sucking the stale air between his teeth. He was staring at Deeds. 'Jesus bloody Christ. The fuck did you do that for?'

Bald answered for both of them. 'He had it coming. They all do. Brozovic and his lieutenants. They're dead men, Mick. That's what we're here for, in case it's slipped your mind.'

'Fair enough, he had to kick the bucket. But this . . . ?' Devereaux waved a hand at the metal spike.

'You weren't there,' Porter said back. Surprising even himself at the anger in his voice. 'You didn't see your mates getting shot and blown to shit. We did. Take it from me, that's something you won't ever forget.'

Devereaux thought about pressing the issue further, but in the end he just shrugged and flashed his palms at the two operators. 'I get it, fella. You want these wankers to hurt. But it's your call. That's all I'm saying.'

There was another cold beat and then Bald turned to Porter and said, 'What you want us to do with this prick?'

Tipping his head at Deeds. Porter looked at the ex-Para. Blood dripped from the end of the spike lodged in the guy's head, hitting the floor in a dull wet patter. Porter thought for a beat. Then he looked to Devereaux.

'Bring the car round once we've cleared this mess up. We need to get rid of Deeds.'

Bald made a face. Like he was chewing on a block of tar.

'I thought we were supposed to leave him here for everyone to see, mate? Set an example, like.'

Porter said, 'I've got a better idea.'

Thirty minutes later Devereaux steered the Toledo to the front of the apartment. Coles checked that the coast was clear, then signalled to Bald and Porter by rapping his knuckles on the door twice. Then the two operators emerged from the apartment with Deeds. He was bound up inside a breathable Gore-Tex bivi bag sealed at the hood with a strip of duct tape. They dumped the body in the boot of the Toledo and rolled west for three minutes on Calle Rio Grande, pulling up next to a row of tumbledown shops. A pharmacy. A convenience store. A couple of empty lots with to-let signs out front. Porter had noticed them on the drive up from Puerto Banus.

There was a big storm drain at the end of the street, next to a broken streetlamp. Devereaux killed the engine. Then Coles got out and did a quick recce of the street. At gone three o'clock in the morning they were in the dead hours. Every house light was switched off and the street was dark and deserted except for a couple of feral cats sniffing for scraps around a dumpster. The cats scuttled away as soon as Bald and Porter debussed from the Toledo. The two operators swung around to the back of the motor while Coles dropped down beside the storm drain and lifted the large metal grate. Then Bald and Porter lugged over the bivi bag with Deeds in it and rammed the body head-first into the drain opening. Deeds was heavier dead than alive, and it was a tight squeeze. Once they had shoved him inside, Coles replaced the grate.

Burying Deeds in the storm drain was technically going against orders, but Porter considered it a necessary precaution. They needed to keep Deeds hidden for a while. At least long enough to move onto the next names on the list without alerting them. The last thing they wanted was to give the two Serbs advance warning that they were being targeted. Deeds would stay hidden for a couple of weeks, or until the rain came and the storm drain overflowed. Which meant his name wouldn't be in the papers. There was still the firefight in the streets to worry about, but there were plenty of inter-gang rivalries and shootings in and around Marbella, and Porter was confident that the local police wouldn't investigate too closely. Even if they did, the authorities would want to keep the shooting out of the news. They always did. Crime was bad for business on the Costa del Sol. Everyone knew that. Tourists didn't like to read about gangland slayings over their midday sangria.

At 0344 hours the Toledo quietly steered out of Calle Rio Grande and motored east out of Fuengirola on the A-7, heading for the back-up safe house the team had rented in downtown Malaga.

Seventeen hours later they headed to Valletta.

TWENTY-EIGHT

Six days later.
Valletta, Malta. 1928 hours.
Niko Kavlak reached for the bottle of Grey Goose and poured himself another slug.

Fifteen fucking days.

The penthouse in Valletta was situated on the fourth floor of a five-hundred-year-old crumbling block, a hundred metres from the city's cathedral and the main square at San Gwann. It was the perfect blend of the old and the new. The balcony had a panoramic view of the old town and the grand harbour and the sea, deep, deep blue against the pale sky. It was like looking out across an open-air museum. Quaint, if you gave a crap about that kind of stuff. Which Kavlak didn't.

Inside the penthouse, it was a different story. Everything was brand new, from the leather sofas and the huge TV right down to the exotic fish in the tank next to the kitchen. There was everything a guy could ever want. A fridge stocked full of beer. Flagons of vodka and whisky in the drinks cabinet. Satellite TV with a couple of hundred channels including Sky Sports. A rack of movies and a separate stack of porn DVDs. A PlayStation and a Nintendo 64. They had cartons of cigarettes and menus for a dozen local takeaways. There was even a games room with a pool table and a dartboard.

But after fifteen days, even the best penthouse can start to feel like a prison.

Kavlak and Petrovich had been bottled up in the apartment ever since the attack on Selection had gone down. Orders from

Brozovic himself. They were to stay low and not leave the apartment. *Not under any circumstances.* And Kavlak knew better than to disobey a direct order from the Tiger of the Balkans. But still. Fifteen days straight inside these four walls was enough to drive anyone stir-crazy. Especially when you were sharing with Petrovich.

The kid was on edge. Had been since the moment they'd bugged out of Merthyr Tydfil and headed to Fishguard, taking the ferry across the Irish Sea. Kavlak didn't know why. The kid should have been celebrating. They'd got away with the attack, against the odds. Kavlak had feared the worst when the two SAS soldiers had rocked up to the Storey Arms and killed Markovic and Dragan. But he'd managed to get into the Transit just in time, along with Petrovich. So they had lived, while their companions had died. But Petrovich didn't seem to appreciate his good fortune. Instead he was pacing up and down the living room, chain-smoking a pack of Marlboro Reds and working a trench line into the hardwood floor. He had bags under his eyes the size of hockey pucks, and his hair was a mess. It didn't help that he was caning it on the Bolivian marching powder.

'How much longer we gonna be here?' Petrovich asked.

Kavlak shrugged and knocked back his Grey Goose. Poured himself another measure. 'As long as it takes, nephew. As long as it takes. Calm down. The Tiger will tell us when it's over.'

Petrovich pulled on his Marlboro, scratched his four-day-old stubble. 'What if they're onto us? What then?'

Kavlak smiled. 'They're not. If they were, our faces would be on the front page of every newspaper and TV station from here to Moscow. Trust me. We're in the clear. We covered our tracks. Now we just have to wait.'

'I don't like it. We shouldn't be here. We should be back in Belgrade.'

'No, we shouldn't. Not unless you want the Tiger to feed you into a meat grinder.'

Petrovich smoked and paced. 'I'm just saying, uncle. I don't like it.'

Kavlak sighed. Blowing up those Brit soldiers should have

toughened his nephew up. Put a set of balls on him. Instead Petrovich had turned paranoid. The kid had seen too many Hollywood films. Now he constantly panicked that the cops would come crashing through the door at any moment to arrest them. Kavlak knew better than to entertain such thoughts. He'd done this kind of thing before, and he knew the score. They'd been careful not to leave any loose ends. The hard part was over. Now they simply had to wait. But Petrovich didn't see it that way. Kavlak was finding it hard to stay calm despite the stack of porno mags and bottles of vodka and cocaine on tap. About the only thing keeping him from going mad was the steady supply of hookers.

There were plenty of good whores in Valletta, and in the past fifteen days Kavlak had been an enthusiastic user of their services. The high-end ones, mostly. He liked his women clean and obedient, and for a few extra lira the premium ones would let you slap them about a bit. And since they were on the Tiger's clock, they didn't have to spend a cent of their own money. They could have a woman or two whenever they wanted, for free.

For the past two weeks Kavlak had spent his days knocking back Grey Goose, doing lines of coke and watching EuroNews on the TV. He passed the daytime thinking about all that money sitting in his off-shore bank account in the British Virgin Islands. Kavlak liked to think about how he'd spend his money. On whores, mostly. He was thinking he'd move to Nicaragua once this was over. Or maybe Belize. Half a million dollars could buy a lot of whores in a place like Belize. Maybe all of them. Maybe for life. These were the sort of thoughts that occupied him during the day.

In the evenings, Kavlak fucked whores.

There were three decent agencies in town. They worked at the classy end of the market, catering for the wealthy Russian and Chinese businessmen who'd recently put down roots in the city. As such, their services were reliable and discreet. Kavlak alternated between the three agencies, because if too many girls left with bruises and nosebleeds the agency madams would maybe stop taking your calls.

Kavlak necked his vodka and felt the stirring in his groin again. He poured himself another drink and reached for the landline. Then he punched in a number. It was seven-thirty in the evening and Kavlak needed another whore.

Nine hundred metres to the east, Porter waited for the phone to ring.

He was sitting in the kitchen of a rundown apartment on the first floor of a block on the corner of St Joseph's Street and North Street, spitting distance from the bleached ruins at Fort Saint Elmo. Bald sat across the table from Porter, eyeballing the phone. As if he could make it ring just by staring at it. They'd been waiting for the call to come through for the past three hours, and still they hadn't heard a peep.

'How much longer?' said Bald.

'No idea,' said Porter. 'Could be a while yet.'

'Fuck's sake.'

Porter took a sip from his bottled water and said nothing. Six days had passed since the Puerto Banus job. Six days since they'd tortured Bill Deeds and dumped his body in a storm drain. Six days since Porter last had a drop of booze.

Spain had been a wake-up call. A sign. On the flight out of Malaga he'd ordered a Jack Daniels and Coke from the stewardess. He cracked open the miniature and went to tip the contents down his throat. But then something had stopped him.

The voice.

The one telling him, *You can't afford to fuck this up.*

There are no more chances, John. It's time to clean up, or go home.

Porter had listened to the voice. Reluctantly. For the last six days he'd been sticking to water and black coffee. The first forty-eight hours had been pure torture. But after the third day, the shaking in his hands and the sick feeling in the pit of his stomach began to pass. Slowly, Porter could feel some of his old sharpness returning. The puffiness on his face disappeared. His eyes started to glow again. He felt leaner. Clear-headed. Ready to perform.

All four guys on the strike team had taken separate flights out of Malaga. They'd changed at Zurich, taking connections to the airport at Luqa, six miles due south of Valletta. Then they'd RV'd at the apartment. Devereaux had sourced the place courtesy of one of his contacts at Templar. A local fixer and retired cop who ran a side-business selling unregistered weapons and forged documents. Under instructions from Devereaux, the fixer had paid cash to rent the apartment in the old town under his own name, handing the keys over to the Aussie as soon as he'd landed at Luqa.

As soon as the strike team had RV'd at the apartment, they started running surveillance on Kavlak and Petrovich. There was no time to lose. Deeds's body might be discovered any day now, and the team had no idea how long the Serbs were planning on staying holed up inside their penthouse. But it didn't take them to long to realise that Deeds had been bang on the money. Kavlak and Petrovich never left the penthouse. Not for a stroll, not to check out the local watering holes. Not even to take out the rubbish. They were more locked down than Wormwood Scrubs during a prison riot. Getting to them outside the penthouse was out of the question.

'What about triggering the fire alarm?' Devereaux had suggested three days earlier, when the team had sat down to study the layout and the int they'd gathered on the targets. 'Force 'em out into the open, mate.'

'That's a non-starter.' Porter pointed to the blueprints. 'There must be seventy people living in those apartments. Even if half of them are out when we trip the alarm, that still leaves us with a bunch of witnesses at the emergency gathering point. And Valletta's small. We're talking four hundred thousand people in an area the size of Camden. If someone hears a gunshot, we'll have every fucking cop on the island on our case in the time it takes to make a brew.'

'What about people going in, chief?' Coles had asked.

'There's two we know about. A cleaner, and a runner who delivers supplies to the Serbs every few days. The runner's some local thug. He delivers vodka, beer, fags, dirty mags, pizzas. All that shit.'

'Can we use him to gain access?' Devereaux asked.

'No chance,' said Bald. 'He doesn't have a regular schedule.'

'That leaves us with the hookers,' Porter said. 'Kavlak and Petrovich get them in every other night, as far as we can tell. They always order two of them, and it's always a couple of blondes.'

Devereaux said, 'Same agency?'

'No. They use a couple of different ones. But they always ask for the same type. The Serbs like their tarts leggy and blonde, and they like them European. They don't go for anything exotic.'

'Amen to that, brother,' said Coles. 'White is right.'

Bald had arched an eyebrow at the South African. 'Says the bloke who comes from the rainbow nation.'

Coles made a screw-face. 'Piss off, chief. That's just some crap the darkies came up with. Make themselves feel better about stealing all our land and jobs.'

'Now you know how we feel about the English.'

Devereaux shook his head and said, 'So what's the plan?'

Porter said, 'There's only one thing for it. We can't lure the fuckers out. And we can't go in noisy. We're going to have to use the hookers to get in.'

They moved quickly after that. Porter had reached out to Lakes via the emergency number she'd given them at the mission briefing. The number put him through to the antique dealer in Berlin. Kovacs Antiques. No one answered the phone, just as Lakes had said. The call went through to voicemail. Porter left a message outlining their plan and hung up. Then he waited for the Firm to pick up the message and respond.

While Porter was making the call, Devereaux met with Templar's local fixer. An ex-cop called Cabinelli. The Aussie purchased four Beretta 92 pistols fitted with Silencerco Osprey suppressors. The silencers wouldn't hush the gunshots to a whisper like in the movies, but they would muffle the deafening crack and reduce it to something more polite. If someone heard a silenced round discharging inside a building, they wouldn't automatically think, *Gunshot*. The suppressors would buy the team a few precious seconds in the event that they needed to make a quick escape. Along with the guns Devereaux also bought four boxes of Fiocchi 115-grain full metal jacket 19x19mm ammo, with fifty rounds to a box. Plus a few grams of a yellowish powder called GHB, otherwise known as liquid ecstasy. An odourless and colourless drug, in small doses GHB gave a person a dreamlike high. But a higher dosage could knock someone out in a few minutes.

At the same time, Bald and Coles headed over to Rabat on the other side of the island. They found an independent car dealer and paid cash for a blue Ford Transit and a red Alfa Romeo 146. On the way back to the safe house they stopped at a hardware shop in Qormi. Bought a selection of power tools and zip wire, plus a snap gun for picking locks. Snap guns had originally been designed for law enforcement but they were freely available from any locksmith. The gun would come in useful in case the plan went wrong and the team had to force their way into the penthouse.

Twenty-four hours later there was a new message on the numbers station. Porter listened to it twice before decoding it. It simply said, *Message received. Assets en route. Landing tomorrow at 0949 hours. GCHQ listening in.*

There were two parts to the plan the team had cooked up. The first part arrived the following morning at Malta International Airport. Two intelligence officers sent down from the Firm, Ophelia Starling and Evelyn Cross. At first glance the two spies didn't look like much. They were both dark-haired and pale and severe-looking. With their Barbour jackets and dark-blue jeans and suede shoes they looked like a couple of PhD students on a weekend getaway. But slap a couple of blonde wigs on them, some fishnet stockings and a touch of make-up, and they would instantly grab the attention of every full-blood-ied male in sight.

Six hours after the two spies arrived the second part of the plan was up and running. Porter had requested that GCHQ tap directly into the Serbs' landline. It was easy enough to do, even at a distance of two thousand miles. GCHQ had the capability to tap into any phone, anywhere in the world, by accessing the local telephone company's substation. For the past twenty-four hours an intelligence analyst had been sitting in front of a screen in a drab open-plan office somewhere in Cheltenham, listening in to every phone call the Serbs made and received.

As soon as Kavlak and Petrovich put in a call to one of the escort agencies, GCHQ would pick up the chatter. They would get straight on the blower to the strike team. Then Porter would reach out to Devereaux and Coles. The two guys were waiting in the Transit fifty metres west of the penthouse. Once they had eyes on the hookers, Devereaux and Coles would move to intercept them. At the same time Ophelia and Evelyn would approach the penthouse posing as the whores. Once they were inside they would spike the Serbs' drinks with GHB and wait for the drugs to take effect. Then they'd let in Porter and Bald. Half an hour or so later, the Serbs would wake up. Then the operators would introduce Kavlak and Petrovich to a world of pain.

'Them lasses are taking their time,' said Bald.

He was nodding at the bathroom. Ophelia and Evelyn had been locked away in the bathroom for the past half hour, getting themselves slagged up. Porter took a sip of his water and shrugged.

'Long as they look the part.'

Bald stared at him for a beat. 'You sure you're up for this, mate? Maybe you should sit this one out. Swap places with Davey or Mick.'

'I'll be fine,' Porter growled.

'Yeah, mate. Because you looked fine in Spain. You looked sharp as fuck when you were shoving that hooker out of the way.'

'I said I'll be fine. I've still got it.'

'I should fucking hope so,' said Bald. 'Because if you're sloppy again, I won't be there to bail you out.'

Porter looked away from Bald. Took a swig of his water. I might be old, he thought, but I'm still a bloody good soldier. I'll show Jock. I'll show them all. You don't spend eleven years in the Regiment without having the skills to perform.

At 1938, the phone rang.

TWENTY-NINE

1938 hours.

Porter grabbed the receiver and pressed it to his ear.

'We've got the buggers,' the voice on the other end of the line said.

Porter recognised the voice at once. Hawkridge.

'They put in a call?'

'Roughly six minutes ago, old fruit.' Hawkridge paused. There was the sound of paper rustling in the background. 'To a company called Divine Pleasures. They're based in Paceville over in a town called Saint Julian's. North of your location.'

'What time did they ask for the girls?'

'Soon as possible, old fruit.' Hawkridge cleared his throat. 'It seems our Serbian friends are an impatient bunch. They're sending out two ladies at this very moment. Blondes.'

Porter glanced down at the detailed map of the area spread out across the kitchen table. Saint Julian's was situated five miles to the north of Valletta. He found the address and quickly calculated the route. A cab ride from the Paceville district to St Paul's Street would take twenty-five minutes, max. It would take Porter and Bald maybe five minutes to drive down to St Paul's from the apartment. Maybe eight minutes in traffic. They'd have to bug out of the apartment in the next few minutes in order to set everything up in time for the intercept.

He said, 'What are their names?'

'Sapphire and Charity. Not real. Obviously.'

Porter said, 'Nationality?'

'Romanian.'

189

'Got it.'

Porter hung up. Punched in a ten-digit number and put in a call to Devereaux on the mobile burner the Aussie was packing. Gave him the description of the two hookers and their ETA.

'Just make sure those girls don't reach the penthouse,' said Porter.

'On it, fella.'

Then Porter killed the call. Turned to Bald.

'Well?' the Jock asked.

'We're on,' Porter said.

At that moment the bathroom door swung open and the two Firm lasses swaggered out in their whore kit. Bald took one look at them and dropped his jaw so far it almost thudded against the kitchen floor. The girls were unrecognisable from the two plain birds who'd stepped off the plane at Luqa. Ophelia wore a skin-tight red mini-skirt and a pair of six-inch platform heels, with a tight black crop-top that barely stretched across her smooth breasts. Evelyn wore a pair of knee-high leather fuck-me boots and a black lace-fringe dress that reached teasingly down to her arse. The pair of them had more curves than a Monte Carlo racetrack. They were caked in make-up and the blonde wigs completed the look. Bald could feel a boner coming on as he checked the spies out.

'Okay,' Ophelia said coolly, brushing a strand of hair behind her ear. 'We're ready.'

Bald grinned. 'That's one way of putting it, love.'

Evelyn shot him a look. She had a stern, businesslike manner about her. Professional. But something about her told Porter that she could put on a sexy pout when the mission called for it. That's what made them so dangerous. And why they were so good at their job. They understood that a compelling disguise was about more than slapping on some eyeliner and a blonde wig. These lasses could change their entire personalities at the drop of a hat.

Ophelia turned to Porter and said, 'Do you want to tell us who's who?'

It took Porter a moment to compose himself. Just staring at the spies reminded him that it had been a while since he'd last got a bird in the sack. Not since the breakdown of his marriage. A hot feeling stirred up inside him just then, but he quickly blocked it from his mind. He had a mission to complete, and a pair of Serbs to grab and torture. Everything else was secondary to revenge. That's how it would remain until they had avenged all those who had died in the Brecons.

He said, 'One of you is Sapphire. The other one's Charity.'

Evelyn rolled her eyes. 'With names like that, who'd ever think they were prostitutes?'

Ophelia said, 'Anything else we should know?'

'The girls are from Romania. You'll have to wing it. Say there's been a mix-up at the agency.'

'What's the name of it? The agency.'

'Divine Pleasures. They're based over in Paceville.'

'Imaginative,' said Evelyn.

Porter stiffened his jaw and said, 'Just focus on getting us inside the apartment. We know that Kavlak and Petrovich like to crack open a bottle of vodka and have themselves a party before they get down to any action. That's your best window of opportunity to spike their drinks.'

'We know.' Evelyn sounded impatient. 'We've been through this already.'

'Then we'll go through it again,' said Porter, forcefully. 'It shouldn't take more than seven or eight minutes to knock the Serbs out. Make sure you don't overdo it on the drugs or you'll put them in a coma. Once they're out cold, get on the blower and ring the number for my burner. Hang up as soon as I answer. Then we'll enter the building. We'll be close by in the getaway car. If there's any problems, activate the transponder in your purse.'

'Thanks,' said Ophelia. 'But we can handle ourselves.'

Porter stepped towards the spy. Placed a hand on her shoulder and fixed his gaze on her.

'These guys are fucking killers. They shot dead Regiment men in cold blood. Take it from me, love. If they find out who you are, they won't hesitate to put a bullet between your eyes.'

Ophelia adjusted her bra and said, 'You don't need to worry

about us. We know what we're doing. We've done this sort of thing before.'

'I bet you have,' said Bald. 'What are you doing after this?'

'Getting on a plane,' Ophelia replied. 'And definitely not calling you.'

'You're missing out, lass. Us Scots are harder than those poofs from down south.'

'I'll have to take your word for it.'

'It's time,' said Porter, checking his watch. 'Let's do this.'

The two operators slid out of their chairs. Ophelia grabbed her clutch purse, containing the two small vials filled with GHB and an emergency transponder.

Then they made for the door.

1959 hours.

Twenty-one minutes later an unmarked taxi pulled up on the corner of St Paul's Street and Saint Lucia. Two women climbed out of the back seats and stepped out into traffic. One of them paid the driver, and the guy took off. Then the women crossed the street and strutted towards the apartment block at number 215.

Devereaux saw them from his position thirty metres to the west of the taxi, behind the wheel of the Ford Transit. He'd been sitting there for the past two hours, watching and waiting. Coles sat alongside him, cracking his knuckles and chewing tobacco furiously. They were parked directly outside the apartment building, at the side of a steep and narrow street flanked by ancient baroque buildings. In the distance Devereaux could see the streets leading on a sharp decline all the way down to the old fortifications that ringed the city. Like a ski slope made out of concrete. Beyond the fortifications stood a narrow band of sea, gunmetal and choppy in the January gloom.

The apartment block looked like any of the other buildings lining Valletta's cramped streets. Five storeys high with a limestone façade that had faded in the sun, overhanging balconies on each floor and Venetian blinds on the windows. The main entrance was a two-metre-high wooden door with a pair of stone lion heads fixed either side of it. The street was deserted. Had been for the past forty-five minutes. The government workers had clocked off for the day. The tourists had migrated to the bars and cafes on Old Theatre Street a hundred metres or so to the north. Everyone else had gone home.

Devereaux saw the two whores immediately. Hookers dressed the same the world over. They didn't go for subtle. Not unless the clients were paying big bucks for the girlfriend experience and taking them out on a date. Most punters wanted something trashy-looking in something leather and tight that didn't leave a whole lot to the imagination. These two more than fit the bill. They were dressed in matching black mini-skirts and platform heels and low-cut tops. One of them was maybe five-five and had the whole petite thing going on. Her fake breasts were tightly packed into her strapless white tank top. The other one was taller and slightly darker. She was all legs. Every inch of the two women screamed *hooker*.

'They're here,' said Devereaux. 'Let's go.'

They slipped on their black ski masks. Sprang open their side doors and debussed from the Transit. Glanced up and down the street. All clear. The hookers were five or six metres away. Strutting towards the entrance to the apartment block. They moved slowly. They had to. Wearing heels that high, moving fast wasn't an option. Petite was rooting around in her clutch purse. Legs was fiddling with her mini-skirt, hitching it even higher.

Neither of them saw the two masked men in dark clothes pacing towards them.

Not until it was too late.

'Hey,' Devereaux called out.

Legs turned to face him. An instinctive reaction. Someone calls out to you, you stop and turn to see who it is. Devereaux stepped forward and flattened his right hand into a solid palm. He thrust out with his arm as his front foot hit the deck, pushing through and throwing his body weight into his palm strike. He aimed for the hooker's solar plexus, at the top of the abs and just below the sternum. Devereaux kept his arm muscles relaxed. He didn't need to hit her very hard. A solar plexus strike isn't flashy, but the best attacks never are. Devereaux had once seen a guy knock a Muay Thai fighter out cold with a single well-aimed palm strike.

The blow stunned Legs. Devereaux's palm struck her just below the breastbone with a jarring blow, causing her diaphragm to spasm. She formed an 'O' with her mouth and doubled over. Coles struck out at Petite before she could let out a scream. She folded at the waist and dropped to her knees, retching and gasping. Devereaux grabbed Legs by the arm. Yanked open the side door on the Transit and shoved her roughly inside. Legs didn't fight him. She couldn't. She was too busy trying to breathe. Coles hauled Petite to her feet and bundled her into the back of the Transit alongside Legs. Then the two operators climbed in after the hookers and pulled the side door shut. They bound the whores' wrists and ankles with zip wire. Stuffed rags in their mouths and pulled blindfolds over their eyes. Legs started to scream through her gag, kicking out at the Transit's back door. Devereaux knelt beside her.

'We don't want to hurt you,' he said calmly. 'If you stay quiet, you'll be free in a couple of hours. You have my word. But if you make trouble, you won't leave us any choice. Nod if you understand.'

Legs stilled. Then she nodded. It made sense. A Romanian hooker in her thirties working in Valletta. She'd probably been threatened on multiple occasions. By boyfriends. By pimps. Probably by some of her clients too. Probably had a gun pointed at her before. She'd made it this far in life. Therefore she was a survivor. Therefore she wouldn't do anything to upset her captors. She would cling to the promise of freedom and concentrate all her energies on surviving through to that moment. Petite took her lead from Legs and stopped struggling as well.

Devereaux climbed back out of the side of the Transit. Left Coles to watch over the two hookers. Then he hopped into the front cab, fired up the engine and bulleted west down St Paul's Street. If the girls were going to struggle it would be in the first few minutes after they'd been snatched. Devereaux would do a couple of loops of the old town, so that their cries would be drowned out by the Transit.

The first part of the operation was complete.

2002 hours.

Forty metres to the east, Porter and Bald watched the Transit pushing west down St Paul's.

They had moved into position twelve minutes earlier. The two operators sat up front in the Alfa Romeo, with the two spies in the rear passenger seats. They'd parked on the crossroads of St Paul's and Triq L'Arcisqof, next to a retro British sweet shop called Bertie's and a tacky jewellers called Kaufmann & Co. Both men were packing their Beretta 92s, strapped to shoulder holsters concealed beneath their sherpa-lined denim jackets.

Porter nodded at Ophelia and Evelyn in the rear-view.

'We're on,' he said. 'Get moving.'

The spies grabbed their clutch purses and stepped out of the Alfa. Then they crossed the street and beat a brisk path towards the apartment block. Bald got an eyeful as they approached the entrance. The pair of them had cracking arses. The birds were stern and posh and sexy all in the same breath. They weren't normally his kind of woman, but Bald could swear that the one in the leather boots had been giving him the eye back at the apartment. He whistled.

'Fuck me. Those lasses look the part all right.'

Porter grunted. 'Let's hope those Serbs have got a solid lead on the 2i/c. Because if they don't, we've hit a fucking dead end.'

Bald grunted. 'They'll know. If those Serbs fought under Brozovic back in the day, they'll have a handle on where the lieutenant's hiding.'

'And if they don't?'

Bald shrugged. 'Then we'll slot the fuckers anyway.'

There was a hardness to his voice that told Porter he meant every word. Porter still wasn't sure what to make of Bald. He respected the Jock's abilities as an operator. But the more he thought about what Bald had said in Puerto Banus, the more he was convinced that the guy had lied to him.

There was no way that blonde in the Piano Bar was a solicitor. She didn't look the type. Even if she was, why would Bald meet her in the bar of a posh London hotel and outside the safe house, instead of her own office? No. Something else was going on with Bald. Porter was certain of it. Maybe there were drugs in the envelope? Dirty money? He couldn't know for sure. But he'd heard the rumours doing the rounds at Hereford. The ones that said Bald had his fingers in more pies than Mary Berry. He wasn't to be trusted, the other lads said. He's dodgy.

Maybe he is. Maybe he isn't. There's only one way to know for sure.

Keep a close eye on him.

Sooner or later he'll slip up.

Porter looked back to the apartment building. The spies had reached the main entrance. Ophelia paused by the panel next to the entrance and thumbed the buzzer. For a few seconds nothing happened.

Then the door opened, and the two spies stepped inside.

2006 hours.

Kavlak answered the door with a sly grin. His grin widened as he laid eyes on the two blondes standing in the hallway, pouting and looking tarty as hell. The hookers they'd been ordering had been decent quality. Young, good racks, and they weren't bad to look at. But these two were way off the chart. They belonged in a damn Britney Spears video.

Ophelia smiled teasingly back at the Serb. 'You going to just stand there, sweetheart? Or are you going to show us in?'

Kavlak rediscovered the power of speech. 'Yes. This way. Please. In.'

Ophelia and Evelyn swaggered inside the penthouse, the Serb's greedy eyes following them every step of the way. The place was big and airy and had a minimalist feel to it. The walls were all exposed brick. There was a large black sofa in the living room with a cold white coffee table in front of it and a TV in the far corner. A ceiling fan whirred lazily above their heads. Weak shafts of light crawled in through the gaps in the blinds pulled across the windows. There were empty vodka bottles all over the place, and a stack of dirty plates and glasses next to the sink. Ophelia noticed several half-eaten takeaway portions on the coffee table, along with a dozen empty cans of Cisk Extra Strength lager and a glass ashtray pile high with cigarette butts. *Casino* was playing on the TV. A couple of guys were beating the shit out of Joe Pesci with baseball bats.

'Nice place,' said Ophelia. Hoping she sounded sincere.

The younger Serb was sitting on the sofa with his legs spread wide. He had a mohawk haircut and more gold jewellery than a Hatton Garden safe. Petrovich glanced over at the hallway. Kind of nodded at Ophelia and Evelyn and grunted. Ophelia didn't like the look of the kid. He was moody and quiet. Disengaged. He didn't seem interested in the hookers. He didn't seem interested in anything at all.

Kavlak was still wearing a grin wide as the Brooklyn Bridge so Ophelia decided to make the introductions. 'I'm Sapphire,' she said, before gesturing to Evelyn. 'And this is Charity.'

She was putting on her best French accent. Both spies were fluent French speakers. That was part of their cover. Most of the high-class escorts in Malta were Russian, or Romanian, or French. There were a few Spanish girls, and one or two Portuguese. But absolutely no English. If they'd walked in with their natural Thames estuary accents, that would have been an instant red flag to the targets. Their French accents weren't perfect. But they were passable. Good enough to fool a couple of Serbs who'd probably never set foot in Paris.

Petrovich narrowed his eyes at Ophelia. 'You're French?'

'*Oui*. From Lille.'

'We asked for two Romanian girls.'

Ophelia wore a blank expression and shrugged indifferently. 'There must have been some mistake at the agency or something.'

'They would have called.' Petrovich looked to Kavlak. 'They would have said something, uncle. Surely?'

Kavlak hesitated. Ophelia moved towards him. Reached down with her hand and stroked his balls. 'Relax, honey. We're much better than those Romanian girls. I'm sure we could teach you big boys a thing or two.'

Kavlak's eyes lit up. 'I've never fucked a French woman.'

'Then you're in for a treat tonight.'

Kavlak smiled. He managed to tear his gaze away from the women and looked back at Petrovich. 'Dejan. Show some fucking manners and make these ladies a drink, eh?'

Ophelia and Evelyn planted themselves down on the sofa while Petrovich rooted around in the kitchen cupboards. The kid returned a few moments later with a bottle of Russian Standard Gold vodka and four smeared tumblers. He set down the tumblers on the coffee table and poured a generous measure into each one. Kavlak scooped up his glass and nodded at the hookers, still grinning.

'First we drink. Then we fuck. *Zivio Ziveli*, as we say in Belgrade.'

He tipped half the drink down his gullet and ahhhed. Ophelia and Evelyn sipped their drinks, not wanting to blow their cover but trying to stay as sober as possible. Then Petrovich set down his glass and stood up.

Kavlak looked up at him and said, 'Where the fuck do you think you're going?'

Petrovich said, 'Need to take a piss, uncle.'

'Make it quick, eh? Don't keep these ladies waiting. They're on the clock.'

The kid trudged down the hallway leading to the bedrooms and bathroom at the far end of the penthouse. Ophelia watched him slip inside the toilet. Then she looked carefully at Evelyn and indicated Kavlak with her eyes. Evelyn understood immediately. She took another swig of her vodka then manoeuvred around the coffee table, swinging her hips and smiling teasingly as she took Kavlak by the hand.

'Come on, big boy. I want to dance.'

Kavlak let Evelyn guide him to the space between the sofas and the hallway. There was a hi-fi on the wall and she hit Play. Eurodance music started pumping out of the speakers. Ophelia recognised the tune. 2 Unlimited. 'No Limit'. Evelyn started grinding up against the Serb, running her hand down to his groin and fondling his crotch. Kavlak's face was one big grin. He grabbed Evelyn's arse and buried his head in her tits. He had his back turned to the sofa.

Now, thought Ophelia.

She reached for her clutch purse and quietly popped it open. Her heart beat faster as she retrieved the two vials from her bag. Each vial was filled with a couple of grams of GHB. The dosage was hard to get right, but one or two grams would be enough to put the Serbs into a dizzying spiral of nausea and violent convulsions and loss of motor function. By the time they realised their drinks had been spiked, it would be too late for them to do anything. They would be out cold.

Ophelia glanced up quickly at Evelyn, making sure she was keeping the older Serb distracted. She took the first vial and unscrewed the cap, carefully tapping the powder into Kavlak's half-finished drink. Then she took the second vial and tipped it into Petrovich's glass.

Ophelia was almost done emptying the vials when she heard a voice at her three o'clock.

'What the fuck . . .?'

She froze. Looked up. Saw a figure standing in the hallway, staring at her.

Petrovich.

THIRTY

2019 hours.

A cold beat passed between the spies and the Serbs. 2 Unlimited kept playing. Singing about how there's no limit. Over and over. Kavlak let go of Evelyn's arse. He looked inquiringly at his nephew. Then he turned towards Ophelia. Saw the empty vial in her hand. Blinked. Ophelia could almost see the gears grinding behind his dim, small eyes. His face contorted with sheer rage. The muscles on his neck bunched. His veins looked like bulges in a couple of water hoses. He breathed heavily through his flared nostrils, his shovel-like hands closing up into fists the size of kettle bells.

'The fuck is this? You trying to drug us, bitches?' Kavlak swung his gaze towards Evelyn, stepped towards her. 'That's your fucking plan, eh? Knock us out and steal our shit?'

Evelyn tried to back away. Before she could move out of range Kavlak took a swing at her, driving his balled fist into her stomach. Evelyn jackknifed and let out a pained gasp as the air rushed out of her lungs. She staggered backwards, clutching her tummy. Kavlak took a half-step towards her and dropped his right shoulder, slamming his fist into the spy's face. Evelyn groaned. Her head snapped back, her jawbone crashing into the roof of her skull. Her legs buckled and she fell backwards, crashing into the hi-fi unit.

Ophelia reacted in an instant, reaching for her purse. In the same blur of motion Petrovich pounded across the hallway and flew at her with his fists. He was on Ophelia in a flash, knocking her away from the coffee table before she could grab the transponder. A sharp pain exploded down her spine as she crash-landed on her back on the hardwood floor. Petrovich rushed forward before Ophelia could scrape herself off the floor and kicked her in the ribs, screaming at the top of his voice.

'Fucking bitch! Lying whore!'

Petrovich swung his foot at Ophelia again. This time she read the move and kicked out at him, driving her heel up into his balls. Petrovich whimpered in agony and folded at the waist, hissing between his clenched teeth as his face shaded red with pain. Now Ophelia scrabbled to her feet and grabbed one of the glasses from the table, smashing it against the side of the Serb's head. The tumbler shattered into tiny fragments. Petrovich stumbled backwards, the blood pouring out of the wound to his temple in a hot red gush. The Serb clamped a hand to his head to stop the bleeding. Ophelia knew she had a second to activate the transponder. Maybe less. She grabbed her purse while Petrovich hissed with pain, swearing under his breath as he shook his head clear. Ophelia's hands were shaking as she fumbled inside for the transponder. She found it. Clamped her hand around the button.

She activated the transponder a split second before Petrovich shoved her to the ground.

This time Ophelia couldn't fight back. Petrovich stamped on her guts then clasped a huge hand around her wrist, yanking her roughly to her feet. The blood was still trickling down his face. His ugly, thin features were screwed up into a look of twisted rage. He gripped Ophelia tightly and nodded at Kavlak. The older Serb had Evelyn pinned against the wall, a hand clamped around her throat. She was struggling to breathe.

'What should we do with these bitches, uncle?' Petrovich asked.

Kavlak eased his grip a little on Evelyn's throat. 'Tie them up and take them into the bedroom.' He smiled. 'We'll teach these whores not to fuck with us. We'll teach them good.'

2021 hours.

Forty metres away, Porter saw the transponder light flashing red.

For a second he didn't move.

Shit, he thought.

'Shit,' said Bald.

The blinking light could only mean one thing. The spies were in deep shit. The op had gone south. They needed to move, and fast.

'Fucking go!' Porter shouted.

The two operators scrambled out of the Alfa and pounded across the street towards the apartment block. From the team's previous recces of the surrounding area Porter knew there was a fire escape located at the rear of the building, down an alley that ran between St Paul's and Triq Il-Merkanti. They could use the staircase to climb up to the rooftop and drop down to the balcony outside the penthouse.

Porter bolted around the side of the apartment block and hung a right, moving at a fast pace towards the alley. He could feel his heart beating furiously inside his chest. He hit the alley in a dozen quick strides and ducked into it a few steps ahead of Bald, sweeping past the dumpsters overflowing with rubbish and the brownish puddles. There was no lighting down the alley and he could barely make out the ladder at the bottom of the fire escape fifteen metres away. Porter broke into a run towards it. Thinking, *Thirty seconds since the spies sounded the alarm.*

The Serbs wouldn't fuck about, he knew. Not once they realised that Ophelia and Evelyn had been trying to dope them. They'd start beating the spies senseless, demanding answers. It wouldn't be long before the wigs came off. Once that happened, the Serbs would realise they'd been deliberately targeted. They would show no mercy to their victims then. They'd put the drop on the pair of them.

Porter raced towards the ladder, the stench of rubbish choking the mild evening air. There was a bricked-up window on the ground floor of the building, just below the fire escape ladder, with a small ledge jutting out at the bottom. Porter boosted himself up onto the window ledge and then reached up with both arms, grabbing the overhanging ladder rail and planting his feet firmly on the bottom rung. Then he started clambering up the ladder towards the lowest horizontal platform on the escape.

Forty seconds since the spies had sounded the alarm.

He climbed fast, hauling himself up to the platform and then vaulting up the stairs to the next platform. The rusted steel gratings rattled and jolted with every step. A week ago he would have been blowing hard and literally sweating out the booze. But now Porter moved with speed and determination. He still had it. He could feel his muscles pumping, the old strength coming back. Back in Spain, he thought he'd lost it for good. He'd fucked up, and the team had nearly lost Deeds as a result. But now he felt strong. It felt good to be back in the game.

He pounded up the last staircase and reached the top platform with Bald a few metres behind. Porter pulled himself up the low ledge leading to the flat rooftop. He sprinted across the rooftop and headed towards the eastern side of the building. Fifty seconds now. Porter could hear his heart pounding in his ears as he raced towards the ledge twenty metres away. Sixty seconds. He hit the far ledge and looked down, scanning the balconies below. He spotted the one leading to the Serbs' penthouse. It was on the eastern corner of the block, on the top floor below the rooftop. Most of the other balconies were in a state of disrepair but the parapet on the Serbs' place had been given a fresh lick of paint and it stood out from the rest. There was a drop of seven or eight metres from the rooftop to the balcony, Porter figured. He caught his breath then swung his right leg over the ledge, glancing below to check that he was directly over the balcony. The platform was narrow, no more than a metre wide and three metres long. Then he started to lower himself down the side of the building.

The guttering was loose and Porter could feel it sagging as he eased himself down. This side of the apartment block looked out across a dimly lit side street and there was no noise from below except for the distant rumble of traffic coming from the main road to the south. Porter dropped down the last five metres to the balcony and landed on the platform with a heavy thud. Then he signalled for Bald to follow. The Jock promptly swung a leg over the rooftop ledge and began to ease himself down after his mucker.

Suddenly there was a loud crack as a section of the gutter buckled under Bald's weight and sprang loose from the railing. Bald lost his grip and plummeted down, crashing to the balcony and landing a few inches away from Porter with a dense thud. His trailing leg clattered into a neat arrangement of potted plants, shattering the clay pots and making a ton of noise. Bald scrabbled to his feet as an angry shout went up inside the penthouse. Porter could hear the voice getting louder, accompanied by the sound of footsteps fast approaching the balcony door. Footsteps and the incessant rhythm of eurodance music. Porter snapped his suppressed Beretta 92 out of his shoulder holster and wrapped his fingers around the pistol's walnut grip. Then he kicked open the wooden balcony door and crashed inside the penthouse.

The door wasn't locked. It swung back violently on its hinges. Porter looked up. Saw Kavlak three metres in front of him. The Serb was charging towards him, ready to wade in with his fists. He was fast. But Porter was faster. He lunged forward in a light-ning motion and arced his gun arm across, clipping the Serb in the face with the Beretta. There was a pleasing crunch as the stainless-steel barrel clattered into the bridge of Kavlak's nose, shattering the bones and grinding up cartilage. Kavlak let out a pained grunt as he stumbled backwards and pawed at his mashed-up face, the blood streaming out of his nostrils. Porter stepped inside Kavlak and unloaded a low jab, twisting at the torso and slamming the flat of his fist into the Serb's ribs, winding the fucker.

Kavlak stumbled back a heavy step, caught himself and then launched a punch at Porter. It was big and slow, and it had more warnings on it than a cigarette packet. Porter sidestepped the blow. Kavlak's fist steered east of Porter and connected with thin air. Then Porter jerked his head forward, butting the Serb square in the face. Kavlak grunted as the hard dome of his opponent's skull bulldozed his broken nose. Porter followed up with a kick at the guy's ankle. Kavlak lost his balance and fell backwards, his flailing arms grappling hopelessly. He crashed into the coffee table, spilling vodka and cigarette ash and takeaway cartons across the floor.

Porter noticed a flicker of movement in his peripheral vision. Coming from his nine o'clock. From the direction of the hallway. He spun towards the figure. Saw Petrovich charging at him.

A kitchen knife in his right hand.

THIRTY-ONE

2023 hours.

Petrovich was four metres away. He was close. Too close for Porter to bring the Beretta up and discharge a round at the guy. Too close to evade the attack. For half a second Porter was convinced that the Serb was going to gut him. He would die, right here and now. And there was nothing he could do about it.

Then Porter saw a flash of sudden movement at his nine o'clock again. Bald rushed forward from the balcony door and hurled himself at Petrovich. The Serb turned towards the onrushing Jock, his face registering a look of dumb surprise. Bald charged shoulder-first into Petrovich, knocking the guy backwards. Petrovich slammed against the kitchen counter. The knife clattered to the floor beside him. Petrovich made to grab it but Bald burst forward and beat the Serb to the weapon, trampling his hand underfoot and grinding up the guy's knuckles like he was stubbing out a cigarette butt. Petrovich howled in agony. Bald released his foot from Petrovich's crushed right hand. Like taking his foot off the pedal. Then he bent down and drove his elbow into the back of the guy's head. Petrovich groaned. He looked up. Saw Porter training the Beretta on him. The fight drained out of the kid.

Porter kept the Beretta targeted at Petrovich and said, 'Where are the girls?'

'Bedroom,' Petrovich croaked. 'End of the hall.'

Porter tipped his head at Bald. 'Go check on them, mucker.'

'Aye,' Bald nodded.

He turned and disappeared down the hallway. Kavlak was writhing on the floor. His hands and face were badly cut up from the shattered glass. *Let's see if Bald's got anything to say about my performance now.*

Thirty seconds later, the Jock returned with Ophelia and Evelyn. They were bruised and a little shaken up, but they could stand upright and neither of them appeared to be bleeding.

'You okay?' Porter asked.

'We're fine,' Ophelia answered.

They didn't look fine. But they were dealing with it. Like professionals. Risking their lives was part of the job description. If they couldn't handle it, they would never have made it past the Firm's rigorous vetting process. Porter looked back to the Serbs. Petrovich was glancing up at them. The blood glistened from the deep cut on the side of his head, matting his hair together in thick clumps.

'Who the fuck are you?' Petrovich spat.

Kavlak gave a dry laugh as he scraped himself off the floor and propped himself against the wall. 'You fucking idiot, nephew. Don't you recognise their faces? These are the pieces of shit who killed Dragan and Markovic.'

Petrovich's eyes immediately widened with fear. Porter ignored him and fished out his burner, a Sagem 815 handset he'd purchased from a local electronics shop in downtown Valletta. He drew up the only number in the contacts list, hit Dial and waited. Devereaux answered on the third buzz.

Porter said, 'Everything's under control. Any trouble down there?'

Devereaux said, 'None, fella. The girls are quiet. Not a word out of 'em. Just swinging back around to St Paul's now.'

'Good. Park close by and get Coles up here. Tell him to bring up the toolkit.'

'Roger that, fella.'

Petrovich's eyes widened a little more. Porter killed the call and tucked away the burner. Bald shut the balcony doors and manoeuvred around to the sofa, his Beretta deholstered and pointing at Kavlak. Ophelia and Evelyn sat at the kitchen table, smoking Marlboro Menthols. Petrovich winced in pain. Kavlak glared at the two spies. Two minutes passed. Then the intercom sparked into life. Bald thumbed the entry button on the panel next to the front door and buzzed Coles up, releasing the latch on the door. Thirty seconds later Coles marched inside, carrying a large black Stanley toolbox in his right hand and a bucket filled with domestic cleaning products in his left. The South African paced over to Porter. Set down the cleaning products. Popped open the toolbox.

There was a flash of fear in Petrovich's eyes as he caught sight of the contents. Inside was a claw hammer, a Stanley knife and a bunch of nails, along with a Black and Decker cordless power drill and several drill bits. There was also a roll of black masking tape, plus some soiled rags and a couple of pairs of plasticuffs.

'The fuck are you doing?' Petrovich said in a pleading tone of voice.

Porter and Bald said nothing. Coles slapped a pair of plasticuffs around the Serbs' ankles and wrists. Petrovich looked anxiously at the operators. His eyes were bouncing from one guy to the next like a couple of pinballs in an arcade.

'I said, what are you doing?'

'The fuck does it look like?' Kavlak answered. 'They're going to torture us, nephew. Then they're going to ask us what we know.' He stared defiantly up at Porter as an evil grin spread across his mug. 'These fucking sacks of shit think they can make us talk. They think we're weak.'

Bald shook his head slowly. 'Nah. You're not weak. You're just a couple of sick cunts. Only a twisted bastard could have murdered those lads at the Brecons.'

'Murdered?' Kavlak repeated. He sniggered. 'But you are mistaken. Those men were legitimate targets. They were British soldiers trying out for the SAS. That makes them our enemies. They deserved to die.'

Bald could feel his blood rising again. 'They were unarmed. They didn't stand a chance.'

'Like our brothers, then,' Kavlak spat. 'Like the soldiers you bombed at Zvornik. There is no difference.'

'Yes,' said Porter. 'Yes there fucking is. You lot were slaughtering women and children. Butchering them and dumping their bodies in mass graves. Them lads we blew up were cowards. Just like your boss. Brozovic.'

Kavlak glared at the operator. A look of rage spread across his face. 'Brozovic is a hero. He was the only one prepared to stand up to the Muslims . . . to save our homeland from extinction.' He looked at Bald and snorted. 'When the Tiger finds out what you've done he'll cut you up into little pieces and feed you to his hunting dogs. He'll find you, no problem.'

'Good,' said Porter. 'It'll mean killing him that much sooner.'

Kavlak looked away and snorted again. Porter looked the Serb up and down. He noted the red cross tattoo on the side of his neck. The same tattoo Porter had seen on Bill Deeds's neck. He saw, too, the look of cold hatred in Kavlak's eyes. Most people gave up the hero act once they were face-to-face with the reality of death. They started pleading for their lives, or begging to whatever god they believed in. But not Kavlak. He just watched his captors with an expression of utter contempt. Which told Porter that the guy was rock-hard. Fearless. Breaking him down wasn't going to be easy. He took Bald to one side so that they were out of earshot of the two Serbs and spoke in a low voice.

'What'd you think, mucker?'

Bald grunted. 'That older one's gonna be a tough nut to crack.'

Porter nodded in agreement. 'He's got balls on him.'

'For now,' said Bald, grinning. 'I can take care of that, mate. Hammer a few nails into his bollocks. That'd break the cunt down.'

Porter paused and then said, 'I've got a better idea.'

Bald grinned, reading his mind. Porter spun back towards the Serbs. He paced across the room to Coles and passed him the

Beretta. Coles kept the pistol levelled with Kavlak while Porter dropped to his knee beside the toolbox and picked up the power drill. He took a nine-inch metal drill bit and set it straight in the chuck. He thumbed the gear setting to high and twisted the clutch to the drilling position. Then he took the drill and swung back around to face Kavlak. Bald stuffed a dirty rag in the Serb's mouth. Kavlak tried to protest but all that came out was a muffled cry. He kicked out with his legs, trying to wriggle free. Coles moved over to help restrain him, leaving Evelyn and Ophelia to guard Petrovich.

The younger Serb looked on in horror as Porter knelt beside Kavlak and pressed the drill bit to the side of his skull. Kavlak was screaming wildly now. His eyes were the size of pitching balls. Every vein in his body was pulled tight with tension. His nostrils were working overtime, trying to flood his body with oxygen. Bald pinned Kavlak to the floor, holding him in place so the drill wouldn't slip. Ophelia and Evelyn just watched, expressionless and businesslike. Like they knew what was coming and were both cool with it. Like they'd seen this kind of thing before.

Kavlak clamped his eyes shut, bracing himself for the pain. Then Porter depressed the trigger.

The drill whirred. Kavlak howled in agony as the bit bored into his skull, grinding up bone. The Black and Decker made a distinctive, shrill sound like a dentist's drill. Porter pushed down hard, keeping his grip firm as he drove the bit deeper into the Serb's cranium. The drill jerked a little and there was a wet sucking noise as Porter pierced through the bone, scrambling his brains. Porter kept drilling. Bits of cranium spat out of the hole in the Serb's head like wood chips flying out of an industrial chipper. Kavlak shuddered violently. His eyelids twitched. Blood oozed out of his nostrils. His legs kicked out, the soles of his shoes scuffing the polished floor.

Then he stilled.

Porter took away the Black and Decker. The drill bit was smeared with sticky blood and bits of diced-up brain matter, and the air was thick with the sharp tang of blood and hot metal. He turned his attention to Petrovich. The guy was staring at Kavlak, his lower lip quivering. His face went whiter than the lines on a freshly painted football pitch. Porter could smell the fear coming off him in waves. Fear, and urine. There was a large dark patch on his trousers from where he'd pissed himself. The plan had worked a treat. The younger Serb had just seen his brave-as-fuck uncle take a gruesome trip to the dark side. Now he was terrified. And ready to spill his guts.

Porter looked at him and said, 'You've got two choices. You can talk, and tell us what we need to know. Or I can give you a home-made lobotomy like your uncle there. What's it going to be?'

Petrovich gulped. Said nothing. An uncertain look flickered in his eyes.

Bald said, 'Think hard, pal. Think very hard about your next move.'

Petrovich nodded. 'Okay, okay, I talk.'

Porter lowered the drill. 'There were four gunman who got away from the Brecons. Bill Deeds, you and your uncle. Where's the fourth guy?'

'Tell us,' Bald added, 'if you don't want a fucking hole in your head.'

Petrovich glanced at his slotted uncle. At the blood disgorging from the ragged hole in the side of his head. Then he looked back to Porter. Swallowed.

'Stankovic. His name is Milan Stankovic.' The words came out in a rapid-fire burst. Like the kid had too many words in his throat and he had to spit them all out before he choked on them. 'He's in a safe house in Budapest. Same deal as the rest of us. He's not to leave until he gets the green light from the Tiger.'

'Why Budapest?' Bald said. 'Why not here, with you two?'

'Brozovic told us it was better if we were split up.' He spoke with a mouthful of blood. 'He said we'd be harder to find ... if anyone came looking for us.'

'Not that hard,' Bald replied. 'We fucking found you, didn't we?'

Petrovich said nothing.

Porter said, 'What's the address?'

'It's a block on Népszínház Street. Sixty-one. He's on the third floor. Number twelve.'

'That's all you know?'

Petrovich nodded. 'That's it, man. I swear.'

Porter nodded back. 'That's too bad.'

The Serb shot him a quizzical look. Porter ignored him and looked towards Ophelia. She was still pointing the Beretta at Petrovich, gripping the semi-automatic in a confident manner that implied she'd used a piece more than once in her lifetime. Which she probably had. Porter gestured for her to hand over the Beretta. Porter clasped his finger around the Beretta trigger mechanism. Swung back towards Petrovich.

'No,' the Serb said. 'No, no, no.'

Porter grabbed a pillow from the sofa and stepped towards Petrovich.

'Wait!' he screamed. 'I know where he is!'

Porter hesitated. 'Who?'

'Dusan Ninkovic. He's the Tiger's right-hand man. They're close, you know? They fought together. In the Red Eagles.'

Ninkovic. The name rang a bell. Deeds had mentioned the guy, Porter recalled. *We did everything through his 2i/c,* Deeds had said. *Some guy called Ninkovic. He used to serve in the Red Eagles under Brozovic.*

'Close enough that he might know where Brozovic is?' he asked.

Petrovich shrugged. 'Maybe.'

'Where can we find him?'

'He's got a log cabin. Out in the countryside. Word is, Ninkovic fled to the cabin after the war. Right after NATO put out the warrant for Brozovic's arrest.'

'Where's the cabin?'

'In the west of Serbia. Close to the border with Bosnia. A place called Zlatibor.'

Bald grunted. 'How are we supposed to find a log cabin in the middle of bloody nowhere?'

'There's a trail,' Petrovich said. 'South of Zlatibor. It leads up to the mountains. There's a lake nearby. Lake Ribnica. That's where you'll find the cabin.'

'You're sure?'

Petrovich nodded quickly. 'My uncle used to take me fishing there years ago. I remember it.' He looked up at Porter with frightened eyes. 'That's all I know, I swear to fuck. I don't know anything else.'

Porter said nothing for a beat. Weighed it up. The kid was too young to be a serious player in Brozovic's operation, and the look of terror stencilled across his face told Porter that he'd given up every shred of int he had. There was no point grilling him over the whereabouts of Brozovic himself.

'Okay,' said Porter. 'I believe you.'

The kid looked relieved. As if he thought the operators might actually let him go. Then Porter took the pillow and gun and moved towards Petrovich. The Serb immediately understood what was happening and opened his mouth to protest. He didn't get the words out in time. Porter smothered his face with the pillow then shoved the suppressed Beretta into the fold and depressed the trigger. There was a dull crack as the suppressor absorbed all of the muzzle flash and some of the noise, with the pillow diluting the sound further. Petrovich jerked. Like someone had pressed a couple of defibrillator pads to his chest and flicked the switch. Then he went as still as the dead Serb by his side. Porter stepped back. Tossed the pillow aside. Dug out his car keys and tossed them to Coles.

'Bring round the Alfa,' he said. 'Park under the balcony. Me and Jock will start bagging these fuckers up.'

'On it, chief.'

Coles departed. Porter grabbed a box of latex surgical gloves from the bucket of cleaning products. He took one pair for himself and chucked another pair at Bald. They each grabbed a waterproof plastic bag from the bucket and pulled them over the dead Serbs' heads, fastening the bags with black masking tape around the necks and sealing off the only points of bleeding on both victims. Then they dragged Kavlak over to the balcony doors. Bald stepped out onto the balcony and peered down below, checking to see that Devereaux had steered the Alfa Romeo into position. He glanced up and down the street to make sure it was clear of witnesses. Then the two operators grabbed Kavlak by his ankles and hoisted him up and over the wrought-iron parapet. The Serb's head dangled over the side of the balcony, the plastic bag rustling in the frigid breeze.

Bald and Porter did a three count then released their grip. Kavlak tumbled to earth like cargo spilling out the back of a plane. He landed with a thud on a heap of black bin bags twenty metres below. Devereaux and Coles immediately hopped out of the Alfa and swung around to the back, popping open the boot. They hefted up Kavlak by his arms and legs and shoved the dead Serb in the back of the Alfa while Porter and Bald grabbed Petrovich from the living room. They hurled his dead weight over the balcony and watched him nosedive to earth, crash-landing in the same spot among the bins. Devereaux and Coles somehow crowbarred him into the boot alongside his uncle. Then they piled back inside the Alfa and sped off in the direction of the airport.

They would dump the motor in a spot in the long-term parking bay, leaving the Serbs stashed in the boot. The bodies would stay hidden until the team had killed the rest of the names on the deathlist. Once the mission was over, one of the guys would make an anonymous phone call to the local cops. Read out the Alfa licence number and report that there were a couple of bodies hidden inside. The delayed discovery would send a message to the world. *This is what happens when you fuck with the Regiment.*

After Devereaux and Coles had peeled off, Porter headed back inside the penthouse. He looked to Evelyn and said, 'What have you touched?'

'We've done this before,' Ophelia replied, rising to her feet. 'We'll take care of it.'

She stubbed out her cigarette and grabbed a pair of gloves. So did Evelyn. They went to work alongside Porter and Bald, wiping down every surface with a bottle of bleach and a roll of paper towels they'd raided from the bathroom. Ophelia found a hand-held vacuum in the kitchen and hoovered any stray hairs and shards of broken glass. Evelyn dusted down the tumblers they'd handled. They were meticulous. Anything the forensics teams might try and get a fingerprint or DNA sample from.

While the spies cleaned, Bald and Porter rearranged the furniture and put everything back in its place. They placed a bottle of half empty Grey Goose on the coffee table and topped up a couple of dirty glasses. Arranged a few lines of coke next to the bottle. Closed the balcony doors and put the lock back in place. Stuck a hardcore porn film in the DVD player and hit Play. By the time they were finished the bloodstains and shattered glass were gone and the porn flick was playing at full blast. To a casual observer it looked as if Kavlak and Petrovich had been sitting at home getting hammered on the toot and booze, and at some point in the evening had simply decided to check out of the penthouse in search of some action.

As if they had vanished.

2124 hours.
They left the penthouse and stepped out into the quiet street. Porter, Bald, Ophelia and Evelyn. It was dark outside. The air was cool but clammy. The two operators and spies made their way over to the Ford Transit parked on the other side of the road from the apartment block. Porter took the wheel. Bald sat up front. Ophelia and Evelyn clambered into the back with the tied-up hookers.

Seven minutes later they were shuttling out of Valletta.

They stayed under the speed limit. Drove south-west. Past a bunch of places with strange names like Marsa, Tarxien and Hal Ghaxaq. They continued south for six miles until the freeport slid into view on the horizon. Porter took a right turn and motored past ancient ruins and barren fields for another quarter of a mile before he pulled over. He killed the engine, stepped out of the Transit and swung around to the side door. Grabbed the handle, sucked the door open. Took out the Stanley knife he'd grabbed from the toolbox back at the penthouse and cut through the zip wires strapped around the hookers' ankles and wrists. Then Ophelia and Evelyn removed the gags from their mouths. They left the blindfolds on. The spies helped the hookers out of the Transit. There was nothing but dirt and rocks for miles in every direction.

Porter dug out two envelopes from his jacket pocket. Two bands of a hundred thousand dollars apiece. He gave one to Legs. Gave the other to Petite.

'The fuck is this?' Legs said in a thick eastern European accent, feeling the envelope.

'For your troubles,' said Porter. 'This should more than cover what the Serbs owed you.'

He turned the blindfolded hookers around until they were facing south on the road. Like spinning a kid before a piñata game.

'Walk down that road and count to a hundred. Then take off your blindfolds. There's a taxi rank about two miles south of here. No hard feelings, love.'

Legs laughed drily. 'Fuck you, mister.'

She spat on the ground. She cursed him and called him every name under the sun. But she kept hold of the money. They always did. Porter slammed the Transit's side door shut and folded himself back behind the steering wheel. Legs and Petite were already shuffling off down the road, taking small steps and counting to a hundred in their heads. Porter steered onto the main road. Left the hookers behind and headed north towards the airport, where they would RV with Devereaux and Coles. He considered it unlikely the hookers would go to the cops. But he didn't want to take any risks. The way things stood, the hookers were an hour from civilisation. By the time they managed to alert the cops, the strike team would have already bugged out of the country.

'What now?' said Bald.

'First we go after Stankovic,' Porter replied. 'Then we'll get to Ninkovic.'

THIRTY-TWO

Two days later. Budapest, Hungary.
1843 hours.

'He's not home,' said Bald.

They were sitting in a rented Toyota Corolla on the corner of Népszínház Street and Galajda Street, in downtown Budapest. Coles and Devereaux in the back seats, Porter up front with Bald behind the wheel. At their nine o'clock was a concrete tower block, grey and bleak and monolithic. The product of the warped imagination of some over-enthusiastic Soviet planner in the fifties. To their right was a shabby parade of downtrodden cafes and shuttered bars and porn shops with a rusted Trabant parked outside gathering dust. Twenty metres away at their twelve o'clock stood the apartment block at number 61 Népszínház Street.

For the past twenty-four hours the team had been running surveillance on the safe house, working in two-man teams and changing shifts every six hours. They'd arrived in Budapest at 0900 hours the previous morning, taking a Turkish Airlines flight out of Malta to Istanbul. There was a nine-hour stopover in Turkey before the team could take the next direct flight to Budapest. They agreed that Ophelia and Evelyn would stay on in Istanbul and rent a room at the Marriott close to the airport. They wouldn't be needed for the Budapest op, but they would come in useful again when the time came for the team to go after Ninkovic.

Twelve hours after they breezed out of Valletta, the strike team touched down in Budapest. They'd bought a bunch of maps of the city from a souvenir shop at the airport and rented the Corolla from the Europcar rental desk. They booked into a cheap hotel on a narrow side street a hundred metres from the bustling main thoroughfare along Andrassy Utca. Budapest's equivalent of Fifth Avenue or Oxford Street. Designer fashion outlets jostled for space with upmarket coffee shops and Argentinean steakhouses. It was like Communism had never existed.

Devereaux quickly established contact with Templar's local guy. They met outside an abandoned factory in the 21st district, on the Buda side of the Danube. It wasn't hard to find weapons in Hungary. And they were cheap. The country was practically over-run with old Soviet guns. Devereaux bought four PA-63 semi-automatic pistols, chambered for the 9x18mm Makarov round. The Makarov was the standard bullet used by Eastern Bloc countries during the Cold War and roughly equivalent to the 9x19mm Parabellum round. Including ammo and holsters, the total bill came to five hundred quid. Cheaper than a night out at Spearmint Rhino. By the late afternoon they were ready to start OP'ing the target.

Twenty-four hours later, there was still no sign of activity in the apartment.

Coles had carried out a detailed recce of the block. From the layout of the building, they knew that number 12 faced out onto the main street. Porter and Bald could see the living room window above the small balcony, with the kitchen and bedroom windows either side of it. But the lights had been off the entire day, and the previous night. There had been no movement inside the flat. No comings or goings. Nothing at all. It was as if there was nobody home. Just like Bald had said.

'He has to be in there,' said Porter. 'You heard what Petrovich said. These guys are under strict orders not to leave their safe houses.'

'Maybe Brozovic gave the order,' Bald thought aloud. 'Or maybe he just got cold feet.'

Porter mulled over it. Shook his head. 'No, mate. These guys wouldn't cross Brozovic. They're shit-scared of him. If Stankovic has been told to stay put, he'll do exactly that.'

Bald shrugged. 'Just saying. If he is in there, he's being fucking quiet.'

'I agree with Jock,' said Coles. The South African and Devereaux had climbed into the back of the Corolla a few minutes ago to take over their OP duty from Bald and Porter. 'Something ain't right. This is a good location. Discreet. Not many tourists. No darkies. He wouldn't abandon it. Not without a bloody good reason.'

Porter nodded and thought some more. They had a simple choice. Stay put, carry on observing the apartment and hope for some movement. Or go proactive and check out the place for themselves. There were risks attached with going in through the front door. They might alert Stankovic. Or they might be walking into a trap. But there was no point staking out an empty gaff. One way or another, they had to know if the target was in there or not.

He looked to Bald. 'Grab the snap gun, Jock. Let's check it out. Davey, Mick. Wait here.'

They stepped out into the street. Bald retrieved the snap gun from the boot of the Corolla. He'd carried it with him from the job in Valletta, in case the team needed to break into a room or a house belonging to one of the other targets. Now it was going to come in handy. He followed Porter across the street towards the apartment block. It was dark outside, the bright winter sun replaced by the sickly apricot glow of city streetlamps. A putrid smell of piss and sewage wafted across the air, violating Porter's nostrils. They hit the block and stepped through the entrance leading to the ground-floor foyer. It was cool and damp inside. The cheap fluorescent lights flickered on and off. Porter smelled detergent. He could hear dripping from somewhere close by. There was no elevator inside the block, presumably because money was tight under the old regime. Or maybe the Communists didn't believe in elevators. Maybe there was more solidarity in walking.

The operators climbed two flights of stairs and hits a dimly lit landing with damp on the walls and a mosaic floor with half the tiles missing. Bald and Porter moved down the landing until they reached the door to number 12. Bald took out the snap gun from his jacket pocket and gave the door the once-over. Plain green, no spyhole. Deadbolt lock. Not Yale, but something cheaper. More cost-effective, but easier to break. Bald took out the snap gun. It was a small metal thing about the size of a pocket pistol. Like a drill that had been shrunken down in the wash. Bald took the tension wrench from his jacket pocket and inserted it into the bottom of the door lock. Then he adjusted the striking speed by rotating a wheel on the back of the snap gun. Porter stood to the side of the door while he worked, watching the landing. He kept his right hand resting on his shoulder-holstered PA-63 semi-automatic in case of trouble. He could hear voices from the bottom of the stairwell. Kids screaming. A parent shouting at them.

'Hurry up, Jock.'

Bald drove the screw-needle mounted at the end of the snap gun into the lock just above the tension wrench. Then he pulled the trigger. The snap gun made a loud clapping noise, striking the pins inside the lock and jolting them up, applying tension until they hit the shear line. Using a snap gun was faster and less complicated than the old method of raking the pins individually. But the gun sometimes needed to be fired several times before it could bypass the lock. The voices in the stairwell were getting louder. Bald kept pressing. The snap gun kept snapping. After maybe a dozen clicks the lock sprang open and the operators stepped inside the apartment and closed the door behind them.

A vicious smell hit Porter as he entered the hallway. The odour of rotting flesh and expunged gasses.

He lowered his gaze.

Saw the body.

Froze.

Stankovic was lying face-down with a hole in the back of his head big enough to sink a golf ball into. Porter recognised the Serb from the description Petrovich had given them. He had a curved cross tattoo on the side of his neck. The same one he'd seen on the other gunmen. A puddle of blood had formed beneath Stankovic. His body was puffy and bloated. Like someone had pumped him full of air. There was no smell of cordite in the air. Porter guessed the guy had been lying there for at least a day.

'Shit,' said Bald.

'Looks like someone got here before us.' Porter glanced around the apartment. Nothing out of place. Nothing obviously missing or stolen. No sight of a struggle. No forced entry. No casing.

This was a professional hit.

He pointed to the door. 'Whoever did this job, Stankovic must have known them. He just went ahead and let them walk straight in. He didn't think they were a threat. Then he turned his back on them and they popped him in the back of his head.'

Bald glanced at the door. Looked from the door to Stankovic. 'Who would have slotted him?'

Porter frowned, said nothing. He didn't know. Maybe a free-lance killer? Another kill team the Firm hadn't told them about? But whoever it is, he thought, they're one step ahead of us. And that could only mean one thing.

We're not the only ones after the names on the deathlist.

Three days later. Zlatibor, western Serbia.
1439 hours.

'Its definitely him, mucker,' said Porter.

Bald looked down at the black-and-white photograph clipped to the front of the manila folder. They were standing in the middle of a chintzy room at the Hotel Aventinus, a four-storey concrete edifice on Zlatibor's equivalent of Main Street. Bald, Porter, Devereaux and Coles, plus Ophelia and Evelyn. There was a rotary-dial telephone on a dusty bedside table and cigarette burns on the floral carpet, and a single window overlooking a derelict yard outside. The radiators in the room didn't work and they were all wearing their outer layers.

A dozen colour snaps were spread out on the lumpy bed in front of them. The photos been taken the previous morning, and they all showed the same thing: a portly man in his fifties dressed in a parka and frayed jeans, sitting on a wooden jetty by a lake. The man had a shock of grey hair tied back in a ponytail and a long white beard and thick-rimmed spectacles. He looked like a cross between a hardline Islamic cleric and Santa Claus.

Dusan Ninkovic.

Bald swung his gaze back to the black-and-white shot. A note below the pic said it had been taken in 1994. Five years ago. The guy in the photograph looked very different from the Santa Claus lookalike in the snaps laid out on the bed. He didn't have glasses or a beard, for a start. His hair was cut short and in the old photograph he was staring determinedly into the cameras, his jaw set firm and his eyes glancing up beyond the camera, as if preparing to address a large crowd. About the only similarity between the two sets of pictures was the eyes, thought Bald. They were heavy-lidded and black, and set deep into his face. Like a pair of bullet holes in a paper target. There was no mistaking that they belonged to the same person.

The team had arrived in Zlatibor eighteen hours after leaving Budapest. Bald, Porter, Coles and Devereaux had flown back to Istanbul to RV with Ophelia and Evelyn at the Marriott. Then they'd bought six tickets on a Turkish Airlines flight to Sarajevo. The sanctions against the Milosevic regime were still in place and commercial air travel direct to Belgrade was all but impossible. So they took the scenic route. From Sarajevo the team had stocked up on travel guides and rented a couple of Skoda Octavias. Then they made the two-hour drive east towards the Serbian border. Ophelia and Evelyn were staying on with the team to help with their cover story. Four middle-aged blokes entering Serbia would look suspicious. Throw in a couple of girls and they suddenly looked like a group of tourists on a trip to check out the local ruins and health spas.

From the border it was a forty-minute ride to Zlatibor. They checked into the Aventinus, the only hotel in small town, and split into two teams. Ophelia and Evelyn headed north to Belgrade to meet with a Firm handler at the British Embassy. They would get their hands on whatever int was available on Ninkovic and Brozovic. At the same time Porter, Bald, Coles and Devereaux started running an OP on the log cabin.

The place wasn't difficult to locate. There were only a few isolated cabins along the route Petrovich had described. The one they were looking for was much bigger than the rest, and the only one that had heavies guarding the approach. It was the size of a hunting lodge and situated roughly three miles south of Zlatibor on the banks of Lake Ribnica, in a clearing surrounded by a dense forest of mountain pines. The only access route was along a rocky trail that led up from the main road for seven hundred metres up a steep incline. Two bodyguards patrolled the grounds of the lodge at all times, meaning the team couldn't do a drive-past without getting spotted. Instead they carried out a 360-degree probe, getting as close as possible on foot to get eyes on the target. They worked in teams of two, in four-hour shifts. Devereaux and Porter took the first shift. Then Bald and Coles moved into position and took over.

For the past forty-eight hours they'd observed the guards from a clump of rocks by the edge of the lake, two hundred metres away from the cabin. They'd noted the movements of the bodyguards and the changeovers between the BG teams. The target himself rarely showed his face, and whenever he did he was accompanied by a couple of heavies. Porter had taken several snaps of the guy with his Nikon F90X 35mm SLR camera. Then they'd returned to the Aventinus and developed the film in the bathroom using a 'press kit' of powdered chemicals, a thermometer and a glass funnel. Then it was simply a case of comparing the developed photographs with the snap of Ninkovic attached to the folder Ophelia and Evelyn had been given.

'Christ, mate,' Bald said as he studied the two sets of pictures. 'He's changed his fucking appearance a bit.'

'More than a bit, actually,' Ophelia put in. 'Ninkovic has got himself a whole new identity.'

Bald shot her a puzzled look. She took the folder, parked her bum on the edge of the mattress and turned to the first page.

'Dusan Ninkovic. Born in Pale, Bosnia in 1947. Enlisted in the military at the age of seventeen and swiftly became one of the youngest commanding officers in the Yugoslav army. In the seventies and eighties he rose steadily through the ranks, but didn't exactly tear up any trees. When the war broke out in 1992, Brozovic issued a rallying cry to all those who wanted to defend the motherland against the Muslims. Ninkovic quit the military and was given command of one of the Red Eagles brigades. Turns out he was a lot better at killing civilians than he was at working his way up the military food chain. According to the indictment served up by the International Criminal Tribunal in the Hague, Ninkovic's brigade was responsible for burning dozens of villages and murdering thousands of Bosniaks. He's a real piece of work.'

'Could do with a few guys like that in South Africa,' said Coles. 'Put the darkies in their place.'

'What's he doing here?' Porter asked.

Ophelia brushed her hair back. She was a brunette again now. Both Evelyn and Ophelia had radically altered their appearances after the Valletta op, going back to the PhD student look.

'Laying low,' she said. 'After the indictments were served, the warlords and their lieutenants went to ground. The big cities like Belgrade are out of bounds. Too many cameras, too many spies. But out in the country, the situation is different. The people here are broadly sympathetic to the paramilitary units. That includes the local police. Even if they're aware that they have a war criminal in their midst, they're not going to report him.'

'Plus he's good at hiding,' Evelyn added. 'As you can see from the photos, Ninkovic has changed his appearance. He has a different name and profession. He's also fed a lot of misinformation to the press. Seems like every month there's been another reported sighting of him somewhere in Europe. We think Ninkovic is behind those reports. Or someone close to him.'

'To throw the authorities off the scent?' Bald asked.

Ophelia nodded. 'Besides, NATO aren't exactly pouring a lot of resources into hunting Ninkovic. They've got bigger bad guys to catch. Such as Brozovic and the other Serbian warlords. Finding a 2i/c who's off the radar isn't a big political win. Whitehall wants the celebrities. The bad guys who'll grab the headlines and earn them promotions, not their lesser-known subordinates.'

'So that's it?' Bald asked, incensed. 'He just lives freely here, and no one gives a fuck?'

'That's about the size of it,' Evelyn said. 'Plus, the Red Eagles still have a lot of clout around here. Putting up your hand and saying you know where to find Ninkovic is like signing your own death warrant.'

'Basically,' said Ophelia, 'Ninkovic is safe here as long as he doesn't venture out into the wider world. It's sort of like a drug lord going to prison. His movements are restricted, but he's still running the day-to-day business.'

Porter cocked an eyebrow at the spy. 'He's still operational?'

'As far as we can tell. But the Eagles' modus operandi has shifted. According to our intelligence, they're more like a mafia unit now. Drug smuggling, illegal guns, counterfeit cigarettes. That sort of thing. They also receive donations from wealthy Serbs.'

Evelyn said, 'Brozovic needs someone to administer his empire while he's off the grid. Obviously. From what we know, Ninkovic is the one who oversees the day-to-day running of the organisation. Anyone who wants to do business with Brozovic has to go through Ninkovic. Brozovic is more the big-picture guy.'

'So this Ninkovic fella is likely to be in contact with Brozovic?' Devereaux asked.

'More than likely,' Ophelia responded. 'I'd say it's almost certain.'

Evelyn said, 'Ninkovic is sort of like the manager of a

football club. And Brozovic is the rich chairman. He gives the orders, but Ninkovic is the guy who has to go out there and get the right men for the job.'

'All well and good,' Devereaux chipped in. 'But that still leaves us the problem of how we're gonna get to the bastard.'

'Mick's right,' said Coles. He was leaning against the wall and chewing on a wedge of tobacco. 'This prick isn't like the other guys we took care of. He's gonna be tricky to get to. Especially with those bodyguards around him twenty-four-seven. He doesn't even take a piss without those heavies by his side.'

'We could try and do him when he leaves the lodge?' Bald suggested. 'Ambush the cunt on the trail, like?'

Coles sucked his teeth. 'I don't like the sound of that, chief. He's not got a set routine, for a start. We could be sitting up on that hillside for fucking ages waiting for him to show his mug. And those bodyguards have got to be packing heat.' He glanced over at Devereaux. 'We're being paid to grab the names on the list. Not get ourselves killed.'

Bald glared at Coles. 'You're saying you give more of a shit about getting paid than nailing these fuckers?'

Devereaux stepped in, raising his palms in mock surrender. 'No one's saying anything, fella. These Serbs are animals, all right. We're bloody with you on that score. All we're saying is, they didn't kill our lot. We'll do the job, and we'll do it right. Course we will. But I'm with Davey on this one. We're not going on a fucking suicide mission.'

'Fine,' said Bald. 'We'll do a direct attack, then. Go noisy, like.'

Now Porter shook his head. 'Won't work, mucker. There's only one way in and out of the cabin. And we might be dealing with more than the two bodyguards. If Ninkovic has got the local cops in his pocket they'll have the drop on us before we can bug out of there.'

'Then how do we get to him, mate?' Devereaux asked, narrowing his eyes.

Porter considered for a beat. His eyes wandered back to one of the colour photographs of Ninkovic. In the snap the Serbian 2i/c was sitting on the wooden jetty overlooking Lake Ribnica, forty metres down from the cabin. Gripping a fishing rod. The body-guards were nowhere to be seen.

Then he looked at his muckers and said, 'I've got a plan.'

THIRTY-THREE

Two days later.
0512 hours.
Dusan Ninkovic was pissed-off and anxious.

Pissed-off, because he hated being troubled first thing in the morning. The hours immediately before and after dawn and dusk were the best time for reeling in trout, as every good fisherman knew. Something to do with behavioural drift. More insects were in the air at that time of day, so there was more food for the fish. More food meant more fish. And more fish meant a better chance of snaring a catch. Which is why Ninkovic liked to get out on the jetty early and cast his fishing line just as the sun was beginning to rise. Fly-fishing was the one time during the day when he had some peace. The one chance to get away from his bodyguards and gather his thoughts. And now this damn phone call was threatening to make him late.

He was anxious, because the call was bad news. The people beneath him knew better than to disturb Ninkovic at this hour. He had half a dozen lieutenants who were entrusted with his mobile number. Only those six men had the authority to contact him directly, and all of them knew he disliked being called at dawn or dusk. The lieutenant on the other end of the line knew this better than most. Ivanovic was his longest-serving lieutenant. The guy was loyal and efficient. And he was smart. He wouldn't have reached out to Ninkovic right now unless it was urgent. And shit, this was most definitely urgent.

'What do you mean, they're missing?' he snapped irritably. The line was secure. Ninkovic changed his number once a month, he never used the same SIM card for more than one call and his security detail conducted regular sweeps of his cabin for bugs.

There was a long pause down the other end of the line. Presumably while Ivanovic tried to think of some less damaging way of presenting the news. He obviously couldn't think of one because he said, 'They're not in the penthouse, boss. It's just like I said. Our guy went to make his regular delivery, and nobody was home.'

Ninkovic paused and rubbed his temples. This was bad news. Worse than bad. This was fucking catastrophic. The Tiger would be furious when he found out. Ninkovic was already dreading making that call.

'And there was no sign of a break-in? No disturbance, nothing unusual?'

'Nothing, boss. Our guy reckons the place was exactly the same as it was the last time he dropped by.' Ivanovic hesitated. 'Maybe they just got bored and checked out without telling anyone?'

'Impossible.'

It was a natural assumption but in this case utterly wrong. The nephew, Petrovich, he was perhaps a liability. If the kid was alone, he might have lost his nerve and gone into hiding. But not Kavlak. That guy was a true professional. A ten-year veteran of the Red Eagles and before that a shit-hot sniper in the Yugoslav Army. Ninkovic had known the guy since forever. Kavlak was as tough as they come. And loyal. He wouldn't have dared to set foot outside the penthouse. Not without Brozovic's say-so.

'You're sure they didn't leave a message? Anything at all?' he asked.

'Nothing, boss,' Ivanovic responded after a pause. 'Our guys in Valletta searched the place thoroughly. Every nook and cranny. No message. It's like they just vanished.'

But that wasn't any kind of answer, Ninkovic knew. People didn't just disappear. They were either kidnapped or murdered and dumped in rivers or mass graves. He knew, because he'd disposed of more than his fair share of dead bodies over the years. He'd wiped out entire villages.

No, he decided. Kavlak and Petrovich hadn't simply walked out.

Which could only mean one of two things.

Either they'd been taken. Or they'd been killed.

Ivanovic filled the uncomfortable silence. 'What do you want us to do, boss? I could have some of our guys put the word out. Knock on a few doors.'

Ninkovic thought for a moment. 'No. That's not a good idea. We need to keep our enquiries discreet. The less people know we're looking for them the better. Do we have any cops on the payroll down there?'

'One, boss. A sergeant. Brincat.'

'Good,' said Ninkovic. 'That's good. Reach out to him. Tell him to keep his ear close to the ground and see if he's heard anything. Maybe those idiots got drunk in a bar and tried it on with some Russian gangster's wife. Unlikely, but we shouldn't discount anything at this point.'

'Okay, boss.'

'Meanwhile I'll call the Tiger. Let him know the score. If I have anything more for you, I'll let you know.'

He killed the call. Plucked the SIM card out of the back of the Nokia and stamped it under his boot, cursing under his breath. This whole mess could have been avoided if only the Tiger had followed his advice. Right from the outset, Ninkovic had argued that the men selected to carry out the attack on the SAS should be disposed of once they'd completed their assignment. It was only logical. That would have eliminated any possibility of the attack coming back to haunt them. But Brozovic had shot that idea down. He'd insisted that he would not order the killings of his own men. And now two of the gunmen were missing.

Maybe they were dead, Ninkovic thought to himself. Or worse, they'd been arrested and were spilling their guts to some cop right at this very moment. Brozovic would be furious when he found out. He would blame Ninkovic for the fuck-up, of course.

That was inevitable. The price he had to pay for being the number-two guy in the organisation. He got all the shit that came up from the rank-and-file, and he took all the shit that came down from the top. And there was no point in trying to tell the Tiger that he'd been wrong. That would only make things worse.

He checked the clock in the cabin hallway: 0516 hours. He paced down the hallway and turned into the kitchen. One of his bodyguards was sitting at an oak table next to the window, flicking through the pages of a dirty magazine. Kezman. The bodyguard looked up.

'Where's the other one?' Ninkovic said, momentarily forgetting the guy's name. Vukic. That was it. The bodyguards rotated so frequently these days, it was hard to keep track.

'Outside, boss,' Kezman said. 'Ground patrol.'

Ninkovic nodded. 'I'm going fishing at half-past. I'm not to be disturbed. Make sure he knows.'

'Yes, boss.'

Then Ninkovic turned and headed upstairs. He felt better already. A shave, a pot of coffee and then he'd head down to the jetty. Just him and his rod and the fish. A few precious hours to forget about Petrovich and Kavlak and all the rest of it.

The call to Brozovic could wait.

Five hundred metres away, Porter and Bald prepared to dive.

They were on a small fishing boat at the edge of the lake, hidden from view of the jetty by a small island overgrown with bushes and willow trees. The boat was a battered old thing with a trolling motor and a seventeen-gallon tank, rented from the nearby marina using a fake passport and paid for in cash costing 20,000 dinars. Devereaux knew how to pilot a boat from his days in the Aussie SAS. He'd steered it into position behind the island under cover of darkness. In the summers Lake Ribnica was a popular bathing spot but in the winter months the place was deserted, especially at night. No one noticed the fishing boat motoring into position.

Porter and Bald were kitted out with Draeger closed-circuit

rebreathers. The gear had been purchased from a specialist diving outlet based in Trieste, Italy. After the team briefing Devereaux and Evelyn had made the fourteen-hour round trip up the coast in one of the rented Skodas, armed with a shopping list Porter had given them. They'd purchased two closed-circuit rebreathing systems costing three grand apiece, along with a pair of dry suits and full-face masks. They also bought a small rebreathing tank the size of a fire extinguisher. The rebreathers were essential to the op. Unlike regular scuba diving tanks, rebreathing systems recirculated exhaled air by cleaning it inside the tanks. Which meant they wouldn't produce any bubbles that would rise to the surface.

No one would see the two operators approaching the jetty underwater.

Bald and Porter double-checked each other's kit one last time and turned on the valves on their rebreathers. They were both packing Zastava CZ 99 Scorpion semi-automatic pistols strapped to holsters around their thighs. The Scorpions were Yugoslav army pieces and chambered for the .40 Smith & Wesson rounds, a slightly larger bullet than the standard 9x19mm Parabellum used in most secondary weapons. There were ten rounds to a clip and the Scorpion had an effective range of around fifty metres. The guns wouldn't be any use underwater, but if they ran into trouble at the jetty then Bald and Porter could at least reach for their pistols, shake them dry and let off a few rounds at the enemy. It would buy them a few precious seconds.

Once Porter and Bald were ready, Devereaux reached for his waterproof Motorola UHF walkie-talkie. He depressed the button, checking in with Coles. At that moment the South African was kneeling beside a clump of rocks along the southern bank of the lake, four hundred metres south of the fishing boat and two hundred metres east of the jetty. Coles was observing the jetty through a pair of Bushnell 8x42mm binoculars, checking for movement in the grounds surrounding the lodge. He would keep eyes on the jetty throughout the op. If Bald and Porter got spotted by one of the bodyguards during the approach, Coles would immediately get on the comms and raise the alarm with Devereaux.

Then the Aussie would crank up the fishing boat and speed over to the jetty to recover the divers, putting down rounds on the heavies with the Zastava M70 assault rifle that was lying next to him on the deck.

Devereaux said, 'All clear, over?'

There was a crackle and pop of static noise and then Coles replied, 'Roger, chief. Clear. The lads are good to go.'

'Roger that.'

Devereaux set down the walkie-talkie and gave the thumbs-up to Porter and Bald. Then they slid off the side of the boat and dropped into the water with a dull wet slap. Porter carried the spare air tank, along with the harness and mouthpiece attached to the end. The operators broke beneath the surface and disappeared from view beneath the murky black waters.

Heading for the jetty.

0528 hours.

He wasn't going to tell the Tiger, Ninkovic decided.

Not yet, anyway. He had thought it through, weighed up the pros and cons and decided that the best course of action would be for him to handle the situation personally. Demonstrate his leadership. Once he'd found Kavlak and Petrovich, or at least knew what had happened to them, then he would call Brozovic and explain. Even if the news was bad, the very fact that he, Ninkovic, had taken charge of the situation would present him in a better light. It might spare him from the Tiger's rage. And there was no way he was going to suffer because of the actions of two dumb fucks way down the food chain. No way at all. As soon as he was done fishing, he'd get on the blower to Ivanovic. Tell him to get to Valletta and personally find out what the hell had happened. Knock on some doors, pay some bribes, bash a few skulls. Do whatever it takes to find them.

He was feeling better already as he strolled towards the jetty with his fishing gear. As he drew near he heard a voice calling out from the direction of the grounds. He turned and saw the other bodyguard approaching him. Vukic. He was new to the job and cautious, and panicked every time Ninkovic so much as stepped outside. The 2i/c threw up his arm and motioned for Vukic to halt.

'It's okay,' he said. 'I'm going fishing for a couple of hours. Don't disturb me.'

Vukic stopped and nodded dutifully. 'Sure, boss.'

The bodyguard did a one-eighty and trudged back in the direction of the cabin, thirty metres up from the jetty. Ninkovic waited for him to leave, then swung around and made his way down the jetty. It was a rickety narrow thing that extended across the lake for twenty metres from the water's edge. Dawn had broken and there was a thin grey haze hanging just above the lake, wisps of it burning up like fumes under the rising sun. There was no sound out here except the soft slap of the water against the jetty's wooden posts and the occasional distant cry of a bittern bird. The scene had a soothing effect on Ninkovic. He soon forgot about his troubles as he set his gear down and reached for his fishing rod. The lake had been a magnet for trout and pike lately. He was confident of getting a good bite that morning.

Ninkovic took the end of his line and tied a hook onto the end of it using a simple clinch knot. He baited his hook with a worm from his bait box before casting his line into the waters. Then he sat himself down on the edge of the jetty. Stared out into the sea, and waited.

That's when he heard the splash.

It came from directly beneath the jetty. A sudden sharp noise, like something breaking through the surface of the water. Ninkovic instinctively looked down. His guts turned to ice as he saw two pairs of arms reaching out of the lake and clamping hold of both his legs. Before he could react Ninkovic felt himself being dragged off the jetty into the waters below. He released his grip on his rod and tumbled head-first into the lake, the freezing water stabbing at his exposed flesh like a million needle points. Ninkovic let out a garbled cry for help that bubbled pointlessly towards the surface. Then he caught sight of the two divers grabbing his legs and pulling him deeper, and his confusion instantly gave way to fear.

He screamed again, desperately kicking out as he tried to break away. But Bald and Porter both had a firm grip on the Serb, and the light from the surface began to fade as they dragged him deeper underwater.

Ninkovic kicked out again. But it was a weak kick. The fight was draining out of him now. Every part of his body screamed for precious oxygen. Bald kept a firm grip on him. He wrapped his arms around the guy's legs while Porter slipped his arms through the harness attached to the spare air tank he'd been carrying. Then he shoved the mouthpiece into the Serb's piehole. Ninkovic didn't resist. It was a simple survival instinct. If he spat out the mouthpiece or tried to fight back against his captors, he would drown. He had a hundred per cent chance of dying, versus a ninety-nine per cent chance if he was taken captive. Ninkovic's desire to live was stronger than his fear of whatever the two operators might have planned for him.

The plan had worked perfectly. With their rebreather systems cutting out any noise or air bubbles, Porter and Bald had been free to lurk directly under the jetty with their heads just above the water's surface, watching Ninkovic through the gaps between the wooden slats. Once the target had perched himself at the end of the jetty, the operators had made their move. Now they dragged Ninkovic back towards the fishing boat, five hundred metres to the east. It seemed to take an age to reach the boat but finally they hit the starboard side. As soon as they broke the surface Porter ripped out the Serb's mouthpiece. Ninkovic retched, coughing up mouthfuls of water and gasping for breath. Devereaux grabbed him by the scruff of his drenched parka and hauled him up onto the boat deck. Then Porter and Bald climbed onboard, turning off their rebreathers and taking out their mouthpieces. Devereaux kept his Zastava M90 aimed at Ninkovic. Both operators kept their diving kit on. They would be needing it again soon enough.

Porter dropped to one knee beside Ninkovic. The Serb was lying on his back on the deck, shivering inside his drenched clothes. His eyes frantically flicked between Porter and the business end of the M90 rifle. Porter eyeballed the Serb for a long beat.

Then he pointed to the rifle Devereaux was holding and said, 'Listen to me very carefully. If you make a single fucking sound, we'll kill you. If you try and escape, we'll kill you. If you fail to answer any of our questions, we'll kill you. Got it? Nod if you understand.'

Ninkovic steadied his erratic breathing. Confusion spread like a virus across his face.

'Who the fuck are you?'

'Us?' Bald cut in. 'We're the fuckers you'll wish you never met, pal.'

Ninkovic's expression hardened. He looked again at Porter. 'You can't arrest me like this. I have rights. Tell those fuckers at the Hague that we had a deal.'

'We're not here to arrest you,' said Porter. 'We're here because you killed our mates. Fifty-five of them.'

Something like fear flashed in Ninkovic's eyes. His face went through a bunch of different expressions. Terror, disbelief, denial. Finally it settled into pure anger. 'You're SAS?'

Porter nodded.

'What did you do to Kavlak and Petrovich?'

'They're stuffed in the back of an Alfa Romeo, mate.' Bald grinned. 'What's left of them, anyway.'

Ninkovic glowered at the Jock and spat on the deck. 'Animals! They were good men.'

'They were murdering cunts,' Bald said. 'They had it coming. Unless you want to join them, you'd better tell us what we want to know.'

Ninkovic hacked up a laugh. It sounded dusty and hoarse. Like it had been gathering dust in his throat. 'Why should I tell you anything? You'll kill me anyway. It makes no difference.'

Porter merely shrugged. Ninkovic looked left and right, like there were two piles of reasons either side of Porter and he was trying to decide which one was bigger. He closed his eyes for a long beat. Then he opened them and nodded.

'What do you want to know?'

'Brozovic,' said Porter. 'Where is he?'

Ninkovic laughed and shook his head. 'You're going after the Tiger? You're crazy. He'll kill you before you can get near him. He's got serious protection. Bodyguards, bulletproof cars. All that shit. He's worth more alive than dead.'

Porter creased his face into a deep frown. 'Brozovic?'

Ninkovic nodded. 'He's got friends.'

'What kind of friends?'

'You mean you don't know?' Ninkovic smiled triumphantly. 'You didn't think Brozovic was acting alone, did you? No. He had outside help. During the war. Funding. Intelligence. Weapons.'

Bald shook his head. 'That's a fucking lie. The weapons came from Deeds. He was smuggling them to Brozovic. We know that already.'

'Deeds?' Ninkovic laughed. 'He was just a transporter. A middleman. Nothing more. Or did you really think that a low-life British soldier would have the brains to strike a deal with Brozovic all by himself? You give him too much credit.'

'Who, then?' Porter demanded. 'Who was helping Brozovic?'

'Friends,' Ninkovic replied with a shrug. 'I don't know their names. I never meet them. All I know, I heard from Brozovic. They were big people. Important, you know. Connected. They gave the Tiger the money, guns . . . everything he needed. One of them, he was an American. Strong accent. Texan, maybe.'

Bald snorted. 'Why the fuck would the Yanks support Brozovic?'

'Because they know that Brozovic is different from the others. He's a crusader.'

'What the fuck are you talking about?' Porter said.

Ninkovic let a knowing smile play out on his thin lips. 'You still don't get it, do you? Brozovic is more than a warlord. He's a hero.'

'To the Serbs, perhaps.'

Ninkovic shook his head. 'To people in the West as well. Because he stood up to the Muslims. The Tiger saw what was happening in Kashmir. In Lebanon, in Kosovo. He could see the Muslims were taking over and if we didn't do something about it then they would conquer Europe as well. So he made a stand. That's why the people loved him for it. They saw him as a saviour.'

'Bullshit. He's just a butcher. Nothing more.'

Ninkovic smiled. 'Of course you would say that. You're fucking SAS. You betrayed us in the war. You forgot the debt you owed to Serbia.'

'What do you mean?' Porter said.

'Our fathers fought and died for the British in the Second World War.' Ninkovic's voice trembled with rage. 'The Croats, the *Ustaše*, massacred hundreds of thousands of our families. Or did you forget this while you were busy protecting the Muslim scum? We lost everything defending the West, and how did you repay us? By siding with a bunch of thieves and murderers and rapists. The Tiger told us, "Never forget this betrayal. Never forgive."'

Porter shook his head. 'I thought Brozovic attacked us because of Zvornik? Because of the bombing.'

'That was part of it. But he hated the SAS anyway. Killing his brother, that pushed the Tiger over the edge.'

'I've heard enough of this crap,' Bald snapped suddenly. 'Tell us where we can find Brozovic.'

Ninkovic fell silent for a beat. His eyes drifted to the water lapping up at the edge of the boat. In the grainy dawn the lake was dark and shiny. Like slick from an oil spill. The Serb 2i/c swung his gaze back to Porter.

'He's in Switzerland. A town called Genthod. It's a few miles north of Geneva. All the Formula One drivers and pop singers live there. He has a mansion over that way, just up from the harbour. Place is a fucking fortress. I'm talking bodyguards, cameras, fences. There's even a moat. You'll never get inside.'

Porter felt a cold sensation tingle down his spine. He'd expected Brozovic to be hiding deep inside Serbia, or maybe further east. He recalled what Deeds had said to him back at the safe house in Fuengirola. *Brozovic went deep underground after the bombing. No one's been able to find him. Not the Brits. Not the UN. Not even the Yanks.*

He's been hiding right under our bloody noses the whole time, thought Porter. *He's been here all along.*

He shook his head at Ninkovic. 'How has he managed to stay off the radar? He's in Switzerland, for fuck's sake. It's not bloody Somalia.'

'Brozovic said it was the ultimate hiding place,' Ninkovic replied simply. 'It's easy to stay anonymous there. As long as you have the money, the Swiss don't give a shit. He has fake papers and a legit business in case anyone asks questions. Some kind of an investment fund. His kids, go to school under different names.'

'Kids?' Bald asked.

Ninkovic nodded. 'A boy and a girl. They're enrolled at some rich boarding school over in Rolle. All the Russians and Saudi royals send their children there. The whole town is used to people keeping a low profile. You turn up in a motorcade with some bodyguards, nobody looks twice.' He caught his breath and blinked water out of his eyes. 'I can take you to him, if you let me go.'

Bald and Porter exchanged a quick look. Each knew what the other was thinking. They were on the same wavelength. *We don't need Ninkovic. We've got everything we need from this sack of shit.*

'I don't think so,' said Porter.

Desperation flashed in Ninkovic's eyes. 'I could set up a meeting. You could strike a deal with Brozovic. The Tiger can be very generous, you know. It wouldn't be the first time he's paid money to get someone off his back.'

'You're wasting your breath.'

'Please,' Ninkovic begged. 'I can help you. Anything you need. I know all the secrets.'

He started blabbing on about Brozovic and the Red Eagles and anyone else connected with the organisation. Anything that might allow him to barter for his life. But Bald and Porter had stopped listening. They slipped their mouthpieces back on and switched on the valves on their rebreathers to get the air circulating again. There was a brief struggle as Ninkovic backed away from them and tried to scrabble across the deck, but the floor was wet and slippery and he didn't get very far. They clamped their hands around his bicep. Porter held him in place while Bald fixed a weight belt around his waist. Then they took Ninkovic and tossed him over the side of the fishing boat.

The Serb let out a terrified scream as he hit the water, his arms flailing. Bald and Porter slipped into the water after the Serb and dragged him beneath the surface. A furious torrent of bubbles rose to the surface as Ninkovic struggled against the dragging weight of the belt strapped around him and the two killers. He thrashed about wildly, clawing at Bald and Porter and trying to kick himself up towards the light. But the combined weight kept pulling him down.

After two-and-a-half minutes, Ninkovic lost consciousness. His limbs went limp and his head sagged forward. Porter and Bald held him down for another ninety seconds. After four minutes the Serb was dead. The operators released their grip and let the weight belt slowly drag Ninkovic down towards the bottom of the lake.

Thirty minutes later Porter, Bald, Devereaux and Coles were shuttling back to Zlatibor in the two rented Skodas.

0728 hours.

The team checked out of the Aventinus two hours after the kill. Ophelia and Evelyn were waiting for them at the reception desk. They'd stayed behind at the hotel while the operators had moved in on Ninkovic. That was a basic rule of undercover ops. If you arrived as a group, you left as a group. You drew less attention to yourself that way. If the girls had checked out in advance of the others, it would have looked unusual. A member of hotel staff might have asked why. Or they might assume that there had been some falling out with the rest of the group. They might remember the detail and mention it to the police.

Porter settled their hotel bill in cash. Twenty-five thousand Serbian dinars. A hundred and fifty quid. For six people, for three nights in a shoddy hotel with no heating. The woman behind the desk didn't wish him a pleasant trip. Didn't raise so much as a smile. Hospitality in Serbia was about the same as the rest of eastern Europe. It didn't exist. Something to do with all those years living under Communism, Porter figured.

They drove west in the rented Skodas. Retracing their route to the Serbian border with Bosnia. Two and a half hours later they nosed the Skodas into the long-stay car park at Sarajevo airport and debussed. The team had agreed in advance to split up at Sarajevo. Bald, Porter, Devereaux and Coles would head on to Geneva to hunt the Tiger. Ophelia and Evelyn would return to London.

'This is where the hard part begins,' said Bald. 'It's time for the lads to take control. Shame you lasses won't be around to watch the fireworks.'

'Tragic.'

Bald grinned. 'At least you got to see a real man at work, eh? Not like those suits back in London.'

Ophelia rolled her eyes. 'You can't imagine.'

'I'll be seeing you around.'

'No,' she said. 'You really won't.'

With that, the two spies gave their backs to the operators and sauntered off towards the departure gate. Bald admired the view for a little while. The he turned to Porter and winked. 'Reckon I've got a shot at that when we get back, mate.'

Porter laughed. 'Yeah, Jock. In your dreams.'

Once the spies had thinned out the rest of the team paced over to the SwissAir desk and checked for the next available flight out of Sarajevo. There were no direct flights to Geneva from Bosnia so they bought four tickets to Zurich and paid using Porter's credit card. They could rent a motor at the airport and hammer it down to Geneva in a few hours. At 1325 they boarded the Airbus A320 bound for Zurich and settled into their seats.

Twenty-four days after the attack on Selection, they were going after the last name on the deathlist.

Radoslav Brozovic.

THIRTY-FOUR

Geneva, Switzerland.
1803 hours.

They arrived in Geneva in the fading winter light and rented a Honda Civic from one of the long line of car rental desks outside the terminal. Before they'd flown out of Sarajevo, Porter had located a bank of payphones in the departures hall and put in a call to the antique dealership in Berlin. He left a message for the Firm on the answerphone, explaining that they were heading to Geneva and that the team had int on the whereabouts of Radoslav Brozovic. He checked in on the payphones once again at Zurich, calling the numbers station in Austria. There was a new message waiting for him. Porter listened and then decoded the sequence of numbers. It simply said, *Message received.*

Geneva was a three-and-a-half-hour ride south-west on the A1 motorway, a three-lane stretch of blacktop as smooth as polished glass. The sky was cloudless and the sun was bright and cold and crisp. They shuttled past Bern and Lausanne and Nyon and hit Geneva a little before six o'clock in the evening. Porter steered the Civic south on Rue de Lausanne, motoring past the Palace of Nations and the Parc Mon Repos. Past the train station at Cornavin they arrowed onto the promenade running parallel to Lake Geneva and crossed over the Pont du Mont-Blanc bridge leading to the southern side of the city. They slid past the Jardin Anglais and took Rue d'Italie south for a hundred metres, then hung a right onto Rue de Madeline. At 1821 hours they pulled up outside the Hotel Dauphin.

The hotel was located opposite a designer clothes store, a

hundred and fifty metres south of the Promenade du Lac and the Jet d'Eau. It looked just like every other street in Geneva. Grey and cold and spotless. More like a showroom than a place where people actually lived. Bald and Porter checked into a twin room using their aliases and paid using Porter's company credit card. Devereaux and Coles paid for rooms at the Hotel Lafarge, two hundred metres further to the west. They would sit tight wait until Porter heard back from the Firm.

The twin room looked like every hotel room they'd stayed in, but cleaner. There was a TV so big Stephen Hawking probably had a theory about it, and a mini-bar stocked with miniatures of Jim Beam and Smirnoff and Johnnie Walker Black Label. A few weeks ago I'd have been all over that, Porter told himself. I'd have cleaned that bloody fridge out. now the craving was gone

Maybe when this is all over I'll crack open a bottle, he thought. Celebrate with a few measures of Bushmills.

If we ever make it that far.

He put on a pot of coffee to take his mind off the booze. Then he sparked up a cigarette and flicked through the maps of Geneva they'd purchased from a souvenir shop at Zurich airport. Genthod was a wedge of luxury mansions located four miles north of the Hotel Dauphin and less than a half a mile east of the French border. The school Ninkovic had mentioned was eighteen miles further to the north of Genthod, on the outskirts of a small town called Rolle, on the banks of Lake Geneva.

One look at the map told Porter this op was going to be tricky. First, they were going to have to get through whatever layers of security Brozovic had. Second, they would have to breach the Serb's fortress and slot the target. And they would have to do it all inside a built-up area a stone's throw from downtown Geneva. The Swiss cops wouldn't fuck about either, Porter knew. That was the deal in Switzerland. You could be a criminal or a mafia don, you could commit fraud or traffic weapons, and the Swiss would welcome you with open arms as long as you had money to burn and you didn't cause any trouble. But if you stepped out of line, the cops would be all over you like flies on shit.

Ninety minutes after they'd checked in, the phone rang.

Porter picked up the receiver. Thinking, *This must be Templar's local contact.* The team had a list of stuff they would need to source before they made an attempt on Brozovic. Cars, weapons, safe houses. He pressed the receiver to his ear and said, 'Yeah?'

A husky voice came down the line and said, 'John. We need to talk.'

Porter froze and felt a coldness rising in his guts. Cecilia Lakes. The warmth drained from his head to his toes. Porter gripped the phone tightly and thought, *How the fuck has Lakes got our hotel number? And why is she reaching out directly to us?* The standard method of comms had been through the coded messages left on the numbers station. Lakes had never reached out to them over the phone before.

'John?' Lakes asked again. 'Are you there?'

'Yeah,' he said after a beat. 'I'm here.'

'Don't act so surprised. Listen. I'm in town. We need to speak. In person.'

He felt a familiar dread rising in his guts. *Why the fuck have the Firm dispatched their agent to Switzerland at a moment's notice?* he wondered. Something was going on here. Something he didn't like.

'I got on a plane as soon as we received your message,' Lakes explained matter-of-factly. 'I just landed. Look, I can't say any more over the phone. For obvious reasons. Come and meet me.'

'Where?' Porter asked.

'The jetty next to the Jet d'Eau,' she said. 'Thirty minutes.'

2029 hours.

The jetty was mostly deserted by the time Porter and Bald made their way down Quai Gustave-Ador past the Jardin Anglais. Coles and Devereaux stayed back at the hotel, studying maps of the city and waiting to hear from Templar's local fixer. Darkness was muscling in on the city and the Jet d'Eau was lit up neon blue against the fading light. Out on the side of the lake a huge fountain of water spurted up a hundred and forty metres above the rows of moored yachts and sail boats, hissing like steam escaping a hole in a pipe. It was early February, the sky was dark and gleaming like a slit throat, and the air had a mean bite to it as Porter strolled towards the jetty. It was the kind of cold that felt like someone was scraping the blade of a rusted knife across your face.

Cecilia Lakes sat on one of the benches under a tree near the fountain. A group of Chinese tourists mingled around the stone jetty, posing in front of the huge fountain of water jetting into the sky. There were a few restaurants and coffee shops further down the promenade doing a brisk trade. A bunch of swans were feeding on scraps down by the water's edge. Porter glanced around then made his way over to the bench and pulled up a pew next to Lakes. She was dressed in a long woollen coat with a belt over her pencil skirt and she had a scarf wrapped around her neck. She was blowing out cigarette smoke and glancing up at the fountain, pretending to give a shit about the view.

'You've done well,' Lakes said. Her voice was barely audible above the hissing noise coming from the water fountain. That was deliberate, Porter figured. That was why she'd chosen the fountain as the meeting point. The noise would conceal their chatter in case anyone was listening in.

'Very well indeed,' Lakes went on. 'Everyone at Whitehall is delighted with the results you've been getting. Four targets killed in less than a month is quite remarkable. Better than we could have expected. The Prime Minister's asked me to convey his thanks. You'd be heroes back home, you know.' She pulled on her cigarette and smiled slightly. 'If it wasn't for the fact that you're both officially retired, of course.'

'Spare us the back-slapping, love,' Bald said. 'What do you want?'

Lakes took a final drag on her cancer stick then stubbed it out beneath her knee-length heeled leather boot. She stood up, pulled the coat tight around her and tipped her head at the jetty.

'Walk with me.'

The two operators stood up and paced alongside Lakes as she

wandered down the jetty. A sharp breeze picked up and blew in from the lake, seething drops of water across the stone walkway. Lakes reached into her coat pocket and pulled out a fresh pack of tabs. She tore off the cellophane and the foil wrapper and sparked up another smoke. She looked stressed, Porter thought. Tired. Like she'd aged five years in the past month.

'I'm afraid I can't stay for long,' she explained quickly. 'Really, I shouldn't even be here. I'm being vetted right now.'

'Vetted for what?'

Lakes sucked on her smoke and said, 'Chief of Six. Pettigrove's stepping down at the end of the month and I'm on the shortlist to succeed him.' She paused then added, 'It's a very short list.'

'At least someone's doing well out of this,' Bald muttered.

'We're singing from the same hymn sheet, John.'

'That'd be a first.'

Porter gritted his teeth and said, 'Just tell us why you're here.'

Lakes hesitated. She brushed back her scarf and stopped in her tracks. They were halfway up the jetty. The water from the fountain spattered the ground a couple of paces ahead of them.

She said, 'It's about the last target on the list. Radoslav Brozovic.'

Porter said, 'What about him?'

'We need him alive.'

THIRTY-FIVE

2039 hours.

There was a long pause. Porter said nothing. He listened to the seething hiss of the fountain and the sharp whip of the breeze sweeping in from the lake, rocking the boats either side of the jetty. A young couple strode past them and ambled up closer to the fountain, taking snaps on their digital camera and laughing as they got soaked. Bald just stared at Lakes. His expression shifting from puzzlement to full-blown anger.

'You want us to spare Brozovic?' he snapped quietly. 'Why the fuck would we do that?'

Lakes pursed her lips. She had one eye on the foreign couple and waited for them to wander further along the jetty. Then she turned to Bald. She had a cold, impenetrable look on her face.

'How much do you know about Brozovic?'

'He's a paramilitary leader,' Porter answered. 'One of Milosevic's thugs.'

'And he's the tosser who bankrolled the Selection attack,' Bald added in a low growl.

Lakes tipped ash onto the jetty and kind-of nodded. 'True. But that's not the whole story.'

'The fuck's that supposed to mean?' Bald asked.

'After the war ended, most of the other warlords went back to being small-time criminals. But not Brozovic. He was different. He was a national icon with an army of devoted foot soldiers willing to serve him. So he took the veterans from the Red Eagles and turned them into a highly organised criminal network. A network that stretches from Belgrade to Amsterdam. It has deep links with the Camorra in Italy and the Russian mafia. It's one of the most powerful organisations in Europe.'

'So?' Bald shrugged.

'Even in exile, Brozovic is a big deal. He has more power and influence in his little finger than any Serbian politician. Including Milosevic. He has half the security service in his pocket, and a good number of politicians too.'

There was a touch of admiration in Lakes's voice as she spoke. Porter thought back to what Ninkovic had said. *Brozovic stood up to the Muslims. He dared to make a stand against the enemy.*

'Nothing happens in Serbia without Brozovic knowing about it,' Lakes went on. 'He knows where all the bodies are buried. And it's therefore likely he knows the whereabouts of the other warlords. There are thirteen of them, all with outstanding warrants served up by the ICTY. Arresting them would be a major coup. If we take Brozovic alive, there's a chance we can find out where the other warlords are hiding and arrest them.'

'Two birds, one stone,' said Bald.

'More like fourteen birds, one stone,' said Lakes.

Porter said, 'You just said the other warlords were small-time. Why would the Firm give two shits about snatching a few Serb thugs?'

'Because this is the end game for Milosevic,' Lakes replied. 'He knows it, and so does the rest of the international community. Kosovo is his last throw of the dice. But he still has the backing of the warlords, and they have a lot of supporters across the country. Hooligans, ex-soldiers, ultra-nationalists, the local mafia. All those nice people. If he wanted to, Milosevic could drag this conflict out for a while yet. Capturing the warlords would deprive him of his last column of support. His regime would quickly crumble. That's the theory we're working on, anyway.'

'We? As in the Firm?'

Lakes said nothing. Her eyes said everything. A thought nudged at Bald.

'If that's the case, why don't you just kick down Brozovic's door and arrest him? Why bother having us lift the bastard in the middle of the city?'

Lakes flicked her cigarette butt into the water and shook her head. 'It's not that simple. If we seized Brozovic through official channels, we'd have to jump through all the usual bureaucratic hoops. He'd get lawyered up before we had a chance to question him. You don't need me to tell you what would happen next. The other warlords would hear about it and go to ground. Any hopes of bringing them to justice would be gone.'

'You couldn't arrest him formally anyway,' Porter said, following her train of thought. 'Even if you wanted to. There would be questions about how you found him, right? Questions that would make life awkward for the Firm.'

Lakes smiled uncomfortably, like she'd sat down on a bed of rusty nails. 'Precisely.'

'What happens to Brozovic?' Porter said. 'After he spills his guts?'

Lakes stuffed her hands into her coat pockets and shrugged. 'Depends. If he refuses to talk, we'll make him quietly disappear.'

'But if he agrees to cooperate?' Bald asked, his expression tightening.

Lakes shrugged again. 'That's none of your business.'

Bald took a step closer to Lakes. Porter could see the fire raging behind his eyes. 'Yes it bloody is. We're the ones putting our necks on the line here. Now you're telling us we have to hand over the guy who orchestrated the whole thing? That's a bag of bollocks, that.'

Lakes sighed. 'I'm not the one making the decisions here. I understand why you want Brozovic dead. Believe me, if I had my way we wouldn't even be having this discussion. But this order has come right from the very top. The powers that be want Brozovic alive, and there's nothing I can do to change their minds. My hands are tied.'

Lakes stared levelly at Porter as she spoke. She's telling the truth, he thought. *She doesn't want Brozovic taken alive any more than we do.*

'You'll let him off,' said Bald. 'If he cooperates. You'll let the tosser get away with it.'

Lakes hardened her expression. 'This isn't up for negotiation. Arrest Brozovic and hand him over to us once you've completed your mission. That's an order.'

'We don't work for you, remember?' Porter said. 'We're retired.'

A smile crawled out of the corner of Lakes's mouth. 'We still pay your salaries. Don't forget that. You might be off the books, but you're still answerable to Whitehall. I'd tread carefully, if I were you.'

'Are you threatening us?'

'Not at all,' Lakes replied. There was a coldness in her voice and a matching look in her pale green eyes. 'I'm just telling you how it is. You both signed the contracts. You know the score.'

Porter clenched his fists in anger. As much as he hated to admit it, Lakes was right. Trying to take on the Firm was a waste of time. The suits over at Vauxhall had long arms. Infinite resources. All they had to do was push a button, and Porter and Bald would be shafted.

He sighed and said, 'Just tell us what to do.'

Lakes relaxed her face into something approaching a smile.

'Once you have Brozovic, you'll ferry him to the pick-up point. There's an abandoned airfield ten miles outside Lausanne, at a place called Clarmont. Templar's local contact will supply you with the details. We'll have a team waiting for you at the airfield. Once you arrive, hand over the target. Our guys will safely transport Brozovic out of the country to a secure site in Britain.'

'What happens to us after all this?'

The question came from Bald. Lakes shifted on her feet. 'You'll both return to London, as previously agreed. Then our little arrangement will formally come to an end. You'll remain on the Templar payroll on full-time contracts. Your salary will be eighty thousand a year. Plus benefits and expenses.' She saw the gleam in Bald's eye and quickly added, 'But if Brozovic comes back in a body bag, the deal's off. Am I clear?'

'Crystal,' Bald replied in a low, angry voice.

'Good.' Lakes shaped to leave, then stopped. 'Oh, and before I forget. You'll be needing these.'

She reached into her tote bag and took out a padded brown envelope and passed it discreetly to Porter. It wasn't sealed. Porter popped open the envelope and looked inside. There was a bundle of receipts and train tickets inside. They were all dated a few days ago and carried addresses in Zagreb.

'Leave these behind, once you've captured Brozovic,' Lakes explained. 'The cops will find them and assume that the men who carried out the attack were Croatian Muslims looking for revenge. They'll just figure that attackers forgot to dispose of their receipts in their rush to escape.'

Porter took the envelope and stuffed it inside his jacket. Lakes shivered in the cold and straightened her back.

'Now, if you'll excuse me. I have a plane to catch.'

Bald grunted. 'Jetting in and out on the same day? Bloody hell, love. You're going up in the world.'

Lakes shot him a look. Then she turned on her heels and paced briskly down Quai Gustave-Ador. She headed south towards the roaring traffic along the wide thoroughfare on Quai du General-Guisan, hailed down a taxi and climbed inside. A few moments later the taxi took off and disappeared from view. Then Porter and Bald set off in the direction of the Hotel Dauphin, retracing their steps down Rue d'Italie. They were both fuming at the prospect of having to hand Brozovic over to the Firm. They had spent the past month tracking down the target. Porter had imagined slotting him. The look of fear in his eyes as the men of the SAS finally got their revenge. Now Lakes was taking that away from them. Porter could feel the anger calcifying in his bones.

'Fuck's sake,' Bald scowled. 'It ain't right, mucker. That warlord killed our lads, and now he's going to get a fucking free pass.'

Porter scratched the nape of his neck. 'I don't like it either. But you heard her, Jock. She's got us over a barrel. We're not in the Regiment any more. Not officially. If we go against orders, she'll sell us out. We'd be fucked then.'

'Not necessarily, mate.'

Porter stopped in his tracks and turned to Bald. 'What do you mean by that?'

There was a devious gleam in Bald's eyes. His lips parted into a sly grin. 'We've no worries on that front, mate. I've got us covered.'

Porter stared inquisitively at Bald. Waiting for the guy to explain himself. Without saying a word he reached into his jacket pocket and pulled out a mobile phone. A pre-paid Nokia handset.

A burner, Porter realised.

And then: *What's Jock Bald doing with a burner?* The orders from Lakes and Hawkridge had been clear. No one on the team was to have any contact with anyone other than through the official channels. The guys were banned from having any ties to their old lives. And that included a ban on owning a personal mobile.

'There's a number stored in the address book,' said Bald. 'This bird I know back in Hereford. Sally Higgins. I wore a wire to the meeting back at the Wainwright and gave Sally the tapes. She's got the original as well as a bunch of copies.'

Suddenly Porter understood everything. *That's who the blonde was at the Piano Bar. That's who I saw Bald giving the package to outside the safe house on Featherstone Street.* She must have slipped him the wire before the meeting. Then Bald handed it back to her afterwards. Porter was starting to see his mucker in a different light. Christ, he thought. Bald's even craftier than I'd given him credit for.

Bald said, 'If either Lakes or that tosser Hawkridge tries to pull a fast one I'll get straight on the blower to Sally. The tapes are in pre-paid envelopes addressed to every newspaper editor in London. They'll prove that the Firm was in on this thing from the beginning.'

'That's your arse covered,' said Porter, a rage building inside his chest. 'Where does that leave me?'

Bald shook his head. 'This is insurance for both of us. We're on the same side. The job's exactly the same as when it started. No one will fuck with us as long as we've got hold of them tapes.'

He tapped the burner, grinning. 'Bloody hell, mate. You didn't think I'd hang a fucking Blade out to dry, did you?'

Porter frowned. 'Why didn't you tell me this before?'

'I had to be sure you weren't on their side. With these guys, you never know what they're thinking. It pays to keep an ace up your sleeve in case they try and shaft you.'

Porter nodded slowly, letting the words sink in. He'd been wrong to doubt Bald. He saw that now. But part of him also started to wonder what other surprises his mucker might have up his sleeve. He shrugged off the thought and turned his mind back to the mission. Back to Radoslav Brozovic.

Back to the warlord they were going to capture.

THIRTY-SIX

Geneva, Switzerland.
Two days later. 0715 hours.

Radoslav Brozovic, the Tiger of the Balkans, marched angrily into the conference room and nodded at the three men seated around the table. The room was situated on the first floor of the sprawling four-storey mansion on the banks of Lake Geneva, and like every other room, no expense had been spared. The table was solid oak with a cherry veneer and the chairs were white leather and handmade in a shop in Milan. Religious art paintings hung from the walls, along with a display cabinet of antique bullets from the First World War. A tall window at the back commanded an impressive view of Brozovic's private dock and ornamental pagoda. Through the window he could see the winter sun reflecting brilliantly off the calm waters like a million gold coins, crisp and clear and cold. This view had cost him the best part of twenty million dollars, and he fucking hated it.

It had been Tatyana's idea to move to Geneva. She was a pop star back in Serbia, with pop-star tastes and pop-star needs. So when they'd been forced to leave Serbia for good, Tatyana had argued that it was better to go into hiding somewhere with good schools and high-end shopping. Plus, Tatyana sucked dick real good. Better than any whore he'd ever had. Way better. It was all in the lips, Brozovic decided. The bigger the lips, the better the blowjob. And Tatyana had huge red lips. Things were the size of inflatable dinghies. What Tatyana wanted, she got. So, Geneva it was.

But the city left Brozovic feeling cold. There were too many

Muslims, for a start. Wherever you went there were fat Saudis with their vast entourages, being driven around in their designer Italian cars. The creeping rise of Islam was everywhere he looked, and Brozovic often yearned to be back in his native Serbia. And if that wasn't bad enough, now he was being made to feel like a prisoner in his own home.

He'd first learned of the Brit's death in the papers. One of his contacts in London had alerted him to the article in the *Daily Mail*. It was only a few cursory lines, mentioning that the body of a former paratrooper had been discovered in a storm drain in Fuengirola. No suspects had been arrested but there was specula-tion that it was part of a recent spate of gangland slayings. Then Kavlak and Petrovich had disappeared from the safe house in Valletta. And two nights ago the Tiger had received a phone call from one of the cops on the organisation's payroll in Zlatibor. Ninkovic had been found drowned in Lake Ribnica, not far from his usual fishing spot. A weight belt had been tied around his waist and there were bruises on his face and neck consistent with a struggle.

The news of Ninkovic's death had struck Brozovic hard. The other guys were mere gunmen. Disposable. But Ninkovic had been a constant through the years, his right-hand man. Together they'd grown the Red Eagles from a small band of warriors into a powerful organisation with thousands of foot soldiers. And now he was gone.

Brozovic glanced around the three men at the table and noted the unease stencilled across the faces of each man. They could sense his anxiety. They could smell it. That wasn't good, Brozovic knew. An organisation like this depended on fear and loyalty. The moment you showed the first sign of weakness, you were finished.

Brozovic sat down at the head of the conference table and glanced at his Blancpain Fifty Fathoms watch. It had cost the thick end of fifteen thousand dollars. His wife had bought it for him as a present on his fortieth birthday, along with a set of gold-plated golf clubs monogrammed with his initials.

In addition to sucking dick, Tatyana was also good at spending his money.

'Let's make it quick,' Brozovic said. 'I've got fifteen minutes until I have to take my kids to school.'

The guy on the left cleared his throat and spoke first. Koroman, the Tiger's chief of security. A former cop with eyes like black studs pressed deep into his flabby face and the doughy build of a guy who had let himself go over the years. Koroman was the most nervous of the three men sitting at the table. That was not surprising. After all, he had the most to lose from this latest fuck-up. The last guy in Koroman's boots had been severely punished for failing to do his job. He'd had a bomb shoved up his arse, and his mutilated remains had been stuffed in an ice chest.

'Boss,' Koroman said. 'As you requested, we've increased your total bodyguard detail to eighteen men. Ten in the house at all times, plus eight more patrolling the grounds in two four-man teams.'

'What about the dock?' Brozovic asked. 'Is that covered too?'

'Yes, boss.' Koroman coughed. 'I've briefed our guys to keep an eye out for any intruders on the lake, after what happened to Ninkovic. We've also installed six more security cameras to cover any black spots, and upgraded the alarm system. We have the perimeter covered. No one can get within a hundred metres of the property without us knowing about it.'

'And our loose end?'

'Taken care of.'

Brozovic nodded. Killing Stankovic had been an unpleasant task, but a necessary one. Brozovic had ordered the execution as soon as he'd read about the Brit in the newspapers. He had to assume that the gunmen were spilling their guts to their captors before they died. He assumed that, because he knew more than almost anyone about the limits of human pain. If the killers were as good at torture as they were at murdering people, then it was only a matter of time before they learned about Brozovic's involvement. At least with Stankovic out of the way, it might buy him some more time before the killers tracked him down.

He smiled coldly at his chief of security. 'Let us hope your precautions are good enough, Milan.'

Silence. The Tiger turned his attention to the next man. A young guy in a tailored black suit with a dark turtleneck sweater underneath and gold rings on every finger. A big gold crucifix hung round his fat neck. Basta was his new 2i/c. Ninkovic's replacement. Brozovic could have gone for the easy option and appointed one of the older guys as a safe pair of hands, but he needed new blood in the upper ranks of the organisation. He wanted to shake things up a little. Basta was hungry and fearless, and he was desperate to prove his worth.

The Tiger routinely assessed those who worked for him by how well they would stand up to torture. He reckoned Basta could hold out for a good twelve hours. He had that hard-edged look about him. That complete lack of fear. Koroman, on the other hand, was weak. The guy wouldn't last five minutes in an interrogation. He'd start spilling his guts even before the croco- dile clips were attached to his balls. The Tiger decided there and then. He would get rid of Koroman once this mess had blown over. He visualised the ways in which he could have the guy killed. Buried alive, maybe. Or perhaps beaten to death with the golden golf clubs.

'Any word on who the fuck is behind this?'

'Not yet, boss.' Basta fiddled with his gold rings. 'I've got all my guys on it, just like you asked. They're putting the word out. Nothing's come back so far. Whoever did this, they've covered their tracks. But we'll find them.'

Brozovic nodded. It was almost certainly the British, he told himself. It had to be. Revenge for the attack on the SAS. Why else had the killers targeted the Selection gunmen? But that still left the question of who exactly was carrying out the murders. Was it an MI5 operation? MI6? SAS? Or maybe a few private individuals who'd taken the law into their own hands? Brozovic needed to know. He needed something concrete. He needed a target. He had all this muscle and firepower, and nothing to train it on. Right now he felt like a hunter without a lion.

'There are rumours it's ex-SAS men,' Koroman said.

'There are always rumours.' Brozovic, dismissed the guy with a wave of his tattooed hand. 'But you know what the problem with rumours is?'

Koroman stared blankly at the Tiger. Blanked. 'No, boss.'

'I can't fight rumours. I can't go to war with them. I can't grab rumours and put guns to their heads and blow their fucking brains out. Can I?'

'No, boss,' Koroman replied. He lowered his head in shame.

Brozovic suddenly exploded, hammering a fist down on the conference table so hard that Koroman jumped up in shock. The Tiger stared down the barrel of his thick nose at his chief of security, pulsating with rage.

'Don't give me fucking rumours! I want the sons of bitches who killed Ninkovic brought to me. I want to hear their screams as they're fed into the meat grinder. I want their faces cut off and hanging from these fucking walls.' His voice echoed like thunder through the room. Spittle flecked the table in front of him. 'I want names, I want faces. I want that information, and I want it five fucking minutes ago. Got it?'

He sat back and took a breath. No one said a word. The three guys had been stunned into silence. Basta fiddled with his tacky gold rings. Koroman stared at the floor. They were afraid now, Brozovic thought. That was good. Men worked best when they were scared, in his experience. Maybe now they would actually get some results.

'Boss. It's time,' the thickset guy on the right said.

Brozovic turned to the man. His personal bodyguard, Nastasic. The Tiger grunted and rose from his chair. He nodded at Basta and blanked Koroman.

'We'll meet again at the end of the week. I want results by then. If you still don't have anything for me, then maybe it's time we reconsidered your positions in the organisation. Understood?'

Koroman nodded meekly but said nothing. He'd been around long enough. He knew what Brozovic meant.

'We'll take care of it, boss,' Basta replied. 'Whoever did this, we'll find them.'

Brozovic turned and strode out of the room, Nastasic following close behind. He paced across the mezzanine, passing the glass elevator leading down to his garage filled with classic motors and his two prized Harleys. He walked down the spiral staircase leading to the huge living room with its high ceiling and Steinway & Sons piano, and the drinks cabinet filled with bottles of Lagavulin twenty-five-year-old whisky, and the sofa made of crocodile leather. He could hear Filip and Danica, his kids, shouting at one another across the living room. They were watched over by the other five bodyguards who would be accompanying them on the drive up to Rolle. Tatyana resented having the guards around the house twenty-four-seven, but Brozovic had put his foot down. The security was a necessity. At least for the time being.

He was the Tiger of the Balkans, decorated by the Serb government and proclaimed the saviour of the motherland by the priests of the Orthodox Church. He had built a criminal empire that had bases of operation in every major city in Europe. He had millions in the bank and millions more invested in casinos in Monte Carlo and property developments in Madrid. He even owned a football club that he'd dragged out of the Serbian fourth division and guided to the national championship and cup, which had beaten the mighty AC Milan in the Champions League. And yet Brozovic felt utterly powerless. He was gripped by the irrepressible sense that the walls were closing in around him.

Well, fuck them. The killers wouldn't get to him that easily. Not like the others. His house was impregnable, and Brozovic reassured himself with the thought that he had taken every available precaution. Nothing had been left to chance. He wasn't going down without a fight.

He took a deep breath and strode across the living room towards his children, ready for the morning school run.

0726 hours.

Two miles away, Bald and Porter sat inside the cabin of an eighteen-ton Mercedes-Benz Actros dump truck and waited.

They were parked on a potholed stretch of blacktop on the outskirts of Geneva, half a mile north of the airport and four miles from the city centre. Fifty metres ahead of them a single-lane road ran from east to west, flanked by belts of farmland and industrial warehouses. A hundred metres further to the east there was a bridge over the main road running north to south, with a dimly-lit tunnel underneath. The tunnel was fifty metres long and ten wide, and scrawled with graffiti. From where Bald and Porter were sitting they had an unobstructed view of the tunnel's western exit. The morning was grey and wet and angry and the Alps loomed in the distance, black against the rising sun. Like lumps of coal being shovelled into a furnace.

Bald said, 'How long?'

Porter checked his G-Shock and said, 'Fourteen minutes, mucker.'

'Let's hope he's not fucking late.'

'He won't be,' said Porter. 'He won't.'

The dump truck was hot. They'd stolen it from a building site in Lancy, seven miles to the south of the ambush point, at 0400 hours. The Actros had been easy enough to wire and get started, and it blended in perfectly with their surroundings. Swiss roads were under constant threat of landslides. There were roadworks in every direction. No one would give a flying monkey's about a dump truck parked up at the side of the road. By the time the construction crew turned up for work and reported the truck missing, the team would be racing towards the border.

Both operators were packing heat. Sig Sauer P226 semi-autos with thirteen-round clips of .357 SIG rounds, a necked-down version of the .40 Smith & Wesson. The Sigs were the stainless-steel variants with the heavy barrel and the polymer grip. They were instantly familiar to Bald and Porter from their days in the Regiment. Like greeting an old friend. Devereaux and Coles were also equipped with Sigs. Each man had two extra clips, giving them thirty-nine rounds of ammo per guy. Making a total of a hundred and fifty-six rounds. More than enough if things got noisy.

There was a gallon container under the seat filled with petrol, with a black pouring nozzle attached to the handle. Bald and Porter also had a steel link chain, ten metres long with grab hooks at either end, plus a Hilti cordless rotary hammer drill with a battery pack and a drill bit that was an inch in diameter. The Hilti drill was an industrial piece of kit, way more powerful than regular power tools and capable of boring through solid concrete or masonry. The hammer drill, petrol container and chain had been purchased from a hardware store in Thonex, east of Geneva and near to the French border at Ambilly. In addition Bald and Porter were wearing dark overalls with harnesses strapped around their waists, as well as knee pads and gloves and Pro-Tec crash helmets. All purchased from a shop that specialised in bikes and skateboarding equipment. Bald and Porter also wore clear plastic face masks they'd bought from a joke shop in downtown Geneva for fifteen Swiss francs a pop. They were the kind of masks that distorted your features. The ones kids wore on Halloween or to fancy dress parties. They were less obvious than the traditional ski masks. Less noticeable at a distance.

They'd made all their preparations. Sorted out their kit.

Now we've just got to get through the mission without getting killed.

For the past two days the team had been keeping eyes on Brozovic's mansion over in Genthod. Running a 360-degree probe in an exclusive neighbourhood was practically impossible without drawing serious attention to themselves. So they had created their own concealed OP instead, drilling a hole in the boot of a BMW 3 series just above the licence plate, then parking the vehicle opposite the mansion. It was an old trick they'd learned from their days running OPs in Belfast. It worked a treat. But the recce only told them what Porter had already suspected. Getting inside the mansion was a non-starter. There were bodyguards all over the place. Security cameras, regular patrols around the grounds. Even a moat. It was just like Ninkovic had said. The place was a fortress. Trying to blast their way inside would only get them killed.

Which is why they'd switched to the idea of a mobile hit. From observing the target's routine the team knew that Brozovic took his kids to their private school in Rolle every morning at 0730 hours sharp. He insisted on going with them. Six body-guards accompanied Brozovic and his kids. Two rode in the Lincoln Town Car with the principal, with the other four split in pairs between the front and rear Audi A6s. All three vehicles were armoured. Porter could tell because the blacked-out windows carried a telltale green tint. The heavy security presence would have looked conspicuous anywhere else, but not Geneva. Porter had heard of oligarchs landing their choppers on the school play-ing fields to pick up their children. No one would bat an eyelid at the two Serbian kids rocking up to the school gates in a three-car motorcade with half-a-dozen heavies in tow.

The motorcade took the same route to school each morning. Once the cars rolled out of the gates they hooked a left and rode west on Route du Creux-de-Genthod for several hundred metres. Then they took a right and arrowed north for six hundred metres until they hit Route de Valavran, exactly a mile east of the tunnel at Bald and Porter's two o'clock. On a normal day the Serb and his heavies motored down Route de Valavran for a couple of miles then fish-hooked their way around the edge of the airport before taking the slip road leading north onto the A1. But today was not going to be a normal day for Radoslav Brozovic. Today, he wasn't going to make it out of that tunnel.

Porter looked to his three o'clock. To the east. Towards the motorway bridge running over the tunnel. He could just about see the Land Rover parked on the hard shoulder. Right now Devereaux was sitting behind the Landy wheel. Watching and waiting. Five hundred metres to the east, Coles was sitting on a Yamaha R1 motorbike and doing the same. The team was ready. The trap was set.

The plan was all about timing, Porter knew. A second too early or too late, and the whole operation could go sideways. There had been little time to rehearse the attack beforehand. With the cops retrieving Ninkovic's body from the lake in Serbia, it was only a matter of time before Brozovic realised he was being targeted. If the guy didn't know already. The team had to act now, before the target went deeper underground. They had one chance to pull off the attack. One chance to lift Brozovic and end their mission.

Porter checked his G-Shock again.

0729 hours.

Eleven minutes to go.

0730 hours.

At exactly half-past seven in the morning, Radoslav Brozovic emerged from his mansion and paced across the driveway towards the fleet of cars waiting outside. He was flanked by Nastasic and his two children, Filip and Danica, with the other five bodyguards following close behind. Brozovic moved briskly past the marble statue of Poseidon that had pride of place in the middle of an expensive water feature. He strode past the perfectly manicured lawn and the Victorian lampposts lining the front drive. He followed his kids into the back of the black Lincoln Town Car, while Nastasic and one of the other bodyguards climbed into the front. At the same time the four other bodyguards swept towards the two sleek Audi A6s. They were all packing Glock 17 semi-automatic pistols clipped to their belt holsters. If anyone tried to attack Brozovic, they were going to have to get past his outer layer of security first. Even if they succeeded, they would still have to find a way inside the Lincoln, which wouldn't be easy. The windows were made of tempered bulletproof glass. The panels and floor were fitted with armour plating designed to protect against a car bomb or an RPG attack. No one was getting through the security bubble.

Thirty seconds later the wrought-iron gates at the front of the mansion whirred open and the three armoured cars slithered out in single file onto the main road. The front Audi lead the way, followed by the Lincoln, with the second Audi bringing up the rear. The motorcade slung a right onto Route du Creux-de-Genthod. Then it rumbled south, heading towards Route de Valavran.

Towards the tunnel.

0736 hours.
Four minutes to go, Devereaux finally got tired of the europop blaring out of the speakers and switched off the Land Rover radio.

He was parked on the hard shoulder of the A1 motorway, at the midway point on the bridge overlooking Route de Valavran. Devereaux had steered the Landy into position fifteen minutes earlier, turning on the hazard lights to make it look like he'd suffered an emergency breakdown. He was parallel to the section of railing immediately above the eastern entrance to the tunnel below. There was a drop of fifteen metres from the parapet to the road below. From his position Devereaux had a clear view of the approach to the tunnel from the east. The road ran straight for four hundred metres into the distance until it reached a bend and curved off to the left, disappearing behind a dense cluster of pine trees.

Now it was just a question of waiting.

There was an electric winch system fitted to the Landy's front bumper. A lot of Land Rover owners seemed to have them fitted as standard these days. Especially in the cities. Devereaux wasn't sure why. Maybe it was some kind of fashion accessory. The winch rope was thirty metres of galvanised steel, thinner than climbing rope and with a safety hook fitted to the end. The winch was plugged directly in to the Landy's battery. Devereaux could operate it using the remote control. He'd fully unwound the cable as soon as he had parked up at the side of the motorway. Right now the cable was coiled in a heap in front of the Landy, ready to be thrown over the side of the parapet at a moment's notice.

Devereaux had two jobs. The first was to coordinate the attack, observing the approach to the tunnel and watching for the motorcade. As soon as Devereaux caught sight of the target he'd get on the comms with the other guys, using the Motorola walkie-talkies they'd bought from an electronics store. His second job was to assist with the getaway. Any attack carried a certain amount of risk. But a hit in broad daylight, on a busy road in full view of potentially hundreds of witnesses, was riskier than most. Everything depended on being able to make a speedy exit. Which is where the winch came in. As soon as Bald and Porter had their hands on the principal, they would clip on to the winch with the harnesses they were wearing and Devereaux would hoist them up to the motorway. Then the team would race north, changing cars at a place called Founex, a fifteen-minute drive from the tunnel. There was a dark-blue Mercedes-Benz C-class waiting for them at an abandoned farm at Fainex. From there it was a clean ride all the way to the pick-up point at the airfield outside Lausanne.

Now Devereaux sat in tense silence, drumming his fingers on the steering wheel and listening to the snarling drone of the traffic sliding past to his left. It was still early in the morning, too early for the rush hour. There wasn't too much traffic on the roads yet. He stared out of the right passenger-side window. At the pine trees. Somewhere beyond those pines, Coles was sitting on the Yamaha motorbike, listening in to the chatter with an earpiece fitted inside his crash helmet. A hundred and fifty metres away to the west, on the other side of the tunnel, Bald and Porter were inside the dump truck.

They were all waiting for the signal.

At 0739 hours, the motorcade slid into view.

Devereaux saw the first Audi rolling down the bend. Heading straight for the tunnel. The Lincoln followed three metres behind, with the second Audi bringing up the rear. The motorcade was moving at a decent pace but keeping within the strict speed limits. Forty miles per hour, Devereaux figured. Maybe forty-five.

He grabbed the walkie-talkie and got on the comms.

'Target's just entered into sight,' he reported. 'Four hundred metres.'

The walkie-talkie crackled.

'Roger that,' came the reply from Bald.

Five hundred metres to the east, Coles heard the signal and hopped onto the Yamaha. He'd been waiting in a parking lot next to a sprawling industrial estate set back on a leafy side road. The Yamaha had been nicked, same as the truck. Stolen vehicles would make the team harder to trace. There was no paper trail, no chance of the cops somehow tracking the vehicles back to them. Coles had stolen the bike from outside a train station on the other side of Geneva, around the same time Bald and Porter were stealing the truck from the building site.

Coles glanced around, then reached into the saddlebag fixed to the back of the Yamaha and retrieved a shaped directional charge the size of a small brick. The charge was made of C4 plastic explosive, primed with a strip of det cord and lined with double-sided sticky tape on the underside. The tape would make it stick to the rear windscreen of the Audi on contact. There was a remote radio transmitter attached to the det cord. The cars were armoured and the windows bulletproofed. But more importantly, they weren't bombproof. An ounce of C4 contained enough explosive material to blow a hole through the windscreen and rip the bodyguards inside to shreds. Once Devereaux remotely activated the detonator and the charge exploded, the bodyguards sitting in the rear Audi wouldn't stand a chance.

Coles kicked the kickstand up and hit the engine switch. The Yamaha purred. He tucked the shaped charge between his legs so it was within easy reach. Then he nosed the bike out of the parking lot and leaned right onto Route de Valavran. Through his helmet visor he could see the rear Audi two hundred metres ahead of him, rolling slowly towards the tunnel under the bridge. Coles twisted the throttle.

The Yamaha growled, picking up speed.

Devereaux saw it all happening from his vantage point on the bridge above the tunnel. The front Audi was two hundred metres from the tunnel entrance, with the rear Audi sixteen metres behind. Two hundred metres further back along Route de

Valavran, Coles was bombing down the road on the Yamaha and closing in on the motorcade. First the gap was a couple of hundred metres. A few seconds later, it was down to a hundred and fifty. Five more seconds and the distance between the Yamaha and the rear Audi had narrowed to a hundred metres.

The front Audi was a hundred metres from the eastern entrance to the tunnel now. *It's time*, Devereaux thought. He got back on the walkie-talkie.

'A hundred metres,' he said. 'Get ready.'

'Roger that,' said Porter.

He set the Motorola down on the dash and turned to Bald.

'We're on, Jock.'

'At fucking last,' Bald said, grinning. 'These bastards won't know what's hit 'em.'

They put on their safety goggles over their face masks and shoved their gum shields into their mouths. They pulled their seatbelts as tight as they would go, strapping themselves into their seats. Bald gunned the engine. The Actros shuddered into life as he held the clutch to the floor and shifted into second gear. Then Bald stepped down on the accelerator and the truck started rumbling down the blacktop towards the main road, fifty metres away. He quickly shifted through the gears, picking up speed. Chewing up blacktop. After fifty metres he steered a hard right onto Route de Valavran. The truck engine was roaring like mad as he accelerated towards the tunnel entrance a hundred metres away. Now ninety metres. Now eighty.

Seventy.

Fifty metres to the east of the tunnel, Coles was breathing down the neck of the rear Audi. The target was forty metres from the tunnel entrance and twenty ahead of Coles on the Yamaha. Coles glanced up and saw the Landy parked up on the hard shoulder directly above the entrance to the tunnel. Right now Devereaux was looking down at the road, eyes on Coles. Waiting for him to place the charge. Coles figured they had ten seconds until things got noisy. He lowered his gaze to the Audi and started counting down the seconds inside his head.

He gave the throttle another twist and sped forward. On eight seconds Coles caught up with the rear Audi. His heart started to beat faster with tension. He was intensely aware that his balls were on the line here. Fail to place the charge in time, and Devereaux might trigger the detonator while it was still between Cole's legs, blowing him to shreds. The entrance to the tunnel was twenty metres ahead of Coles now. Five metres between the Audi and the tunnel. The rest of the motorcade was already moving under the bridge. On seven seconds Coles edged dangerously close to the Audi, leaving a gap of no more than an inch between the bike's front wheel and the Audi's rear bumper. He reached down with his right hand and grabbed the shaped charge from between his legs, keeping his speed steady so he remained uber close to the target car.

Five seconds to go.

Coles took the charge and slapped it on the midway point on the Audi's rear windscreen with four seconds left on the clock. The charge stuck. Coles pulled heavily on the brakes and slid back from the Audi, skidding to a halt just inside the tunnel entrance. He killed the Yamaha engine, the sweat running down his face inside his crash helmet as he watched the rear Audi carry into the gloom of the tunnel.

'Armed,' he reported down the mike. 'We're ready.'

Three seconds to go.

0740 hours.

Twenty metres west of the tunnel, Bald nudged the dump truck up to eighty miles per.

They were bulleting towards the mouth of the tunnel. Bald could see the lead Audi in the motorcade thirty metres ahead, on the other side of the road. Travelling towards the Actros Bald could see the Lincoln further back. The second Audi's brake lights flashed as it braked. The front Audi's rear-view was blocked by the Lincoln. The driver continued rolling on towards the tunnel exit at a steady fifty per. The distance between the truck and the front Audi was now twelve metres and closing. Bald yanked the wheel to the left and steered the dump truck directly into the path of the onrushing Audi. Ten metres now. Nine. Eight. Porter tensed his jaw and braced himself for impact. Seven. Six. At the very last moment Bald took his hands off the steering wheel so the impact wouldn't break his wrist joints. Five, four.

Half a second later, the dump truck ploughed into the front Audi.

The impact was catastrophic. Deafening. There was a mechanical screech and wail as the dump truck creamed into the front-end of the engine compartment. It crushed and crumpled, like an empty beer can being flattened. The windscreen shattered, spilling debris across the tarmac like cubes tumbling out of a hole in a bag of ice. Bald and Porter lurched forward. Their seat belts snapped tight across their chests, the shudder reverberating through their bones. The sheer force of the collision briefly lifted the front Audi off its wheels. Then it crashed back down to earth and skidded backwards. The dump truck jerked to a stop at a ninety-degree angle to the road, blocking the Lincoln and the second Audi from the tunnel exit.

At the same moment as the dump truck was totalling the front Audi, Devereaux finished counting to three from behind the wheel of the Landy. He depressed the remote detonator. Triggering the det cord in the shaped charge stuck to the rear windscreen of the second Audi. The driver had hit the brakes as soon as he'd clocked the Yamaha in the rear-view mirror and the motor was thirty metres from Bald and Porter when the charge exploded. A fraction of a second later a flash of brilliant orange lit up the tunnel. There was a violent boom that sounded like a jet engine during takeoff. The explosion ripped through the Audi windscreen, blasting out the windows and tearing into the two bodyguards trapped inside. White-hot smoke spewed out of the tunnel in both directions, spitting out a vicious hail of glass shards and twisted metal and burnt plastic. The Audi rolled to a stop. The Lincoln, sandwiched between the two trashed cars, hit the brakes and screeched to a sudden halt.

Porter and Bald didn't fuck about. They unbuckled their seat belts as soon as the truck had stopped, ripping off their safety goggles and Pro-Tec helmets. Porter reached down and grabbed the link chain and the petrol container. Bald seized the cordless hammer drill and a one-ounce shaped charge, identical to the one Coles had slapped on to the back of the rear Audi. Porter also grabbed a length of climbing tape from under his seat, an inch-thick nylon rope in a loop that could be used as a makeshift harness. He flung open his passenger door and dropped down to the side steps. He left a padded envelope stuffed full of Croatian receipts and currency on the dash. A parting gift for the forensics team.

The temperature was a million fucking degrees inside the tunnel. Smoke belched out from the burning rear Audi, choking the air. Porter could taste the bitter metallic tang of burnt flesh. Later on Bald and Porter would both be feeling the bruises from the collision, but right now the pair of them were running on pure adrenaline. Bald set down the drill and made straight for the wrecked Audi with the C4 charge. There was dust and glass and metal all over the place. The crumpled bonnet had lifted up. Smoke gushed out of the engine compartment. The front bumper was hanging off like a torn fingernail and the front windscreen had a spiderwebbed crack in it. There was no sign of either body-guard but Bald wasn't taking any chances. He placed the small charge on the windscreen, right over the crack. The bulletproof glass was made of layers of polycarbonate material inserted between ordinary glass. It was tough. Resilient. Even when it was cracked, Bald wouldn't be able to shoot through it. But a well-placed charge would severely fuck up the two bodyguards inside.

Bald swung around to the other side of the dump truck. Dropped down to his knee beside the wheelbase alongside Porter. Took the clacker and depressed it. The charge popped. The shock-wave tore through the glass, shredding the bodyguards in a savage hail of shrapnel before blasting out the back windscreen. The two guys inside were either dead or blinded. Bald didn't know which. He wasn't a medical professional. Either way, they were out of the picture. They wouldn't be playing the hero today.

Porter was keeping count of the bodies. Two guys dead in the front Audi. Plus the two dead guys in the rear Audi. That left Brozovic and his two kids in the Lincoln, with the two remaining bodyguards in the front seats.

Almost there.

He took one end of the link chain and clipped it to the bumper on the front of the dump truck. Then he moved past the trashed Audi and hurried towards the Lincoln, gripping the other end of the chain. There was a distance of eight metres between the Lincoln and the front end of the dump truck. Close enough for the chain to stretch between them. Porter dropped down next to the front left side of the principal car and wrapped the chain around the wheel. The strike team had done their homework on Brozovic's bodyguard detail prior to the op. They knew these guys were a cut above the average toughs. In a situation like this, any bodyguard worth his salt would go into emergency SOP mode and try to ram his way out of the trap by driving forward, then reversing into the burning Audi. If he picked up enough speed, the driver could barge the Audi out of the way and clear a path to reverse out of the tunnel. But with the chain securing the Lincoln to the dump truck, the target wasn't going anywhere.

As soon as the Lincoln was secure Bald scooped up the Hilti drill from beside the dump truck and hurried over to the principal car, while Porter grabbed the petrol container and the climbing tape. As he spun around he saw a glimmer of movement coming from the burnt-out Audi five metres to the rear of the Lincoln. Through the cobwebbed smoke Porter saw one of the bodyguards staggering out of the rear Audi. The guy was seriously fucked up. His skin was peeling and blistered. His hands and face were covered in flash burns and blood leaked out of his perforated ear drums, staining his shirt collar. Then Porter saw the Glock in the bodyguard's trembling right hand. He had the barrel trained directly at Bald. The Jock was eight metres away. Point blank. Bald was beating a rapid path towards the front of the Lincoln. He hadn't yet spotted the imminent threat at his flank.

'Mucker, look out!' Porter shouted.

Bald stopped in his tracks. Turned towards his ten o'clock. The bodyguard went to pull the trigger. A loud *ca-rack* echoed through the tunnel. The bodyguard's head snapped back as a bullet tore into the back of his skull, exiting through his jaw and painting blood and brain matter across the concrete tunnel wall. The guy hit the ground, hard and heavy and dead. Porter looked up and saw Coles standing ten metres further back from the slotted guard. He was gripping the Sig P226 he'd concealed under his leather motorcycle jacket. Coles gave the two operators a quick nod. Then he turned away to keep watch over the eastern entrance to the tunnel while Porter and Bald raced towards the Lincoln.

There was no time to lose. Porter set the petrol container down beside the front of the motor while Bald vaulted onto the Lincoln bonnet, gripping the Hilti hammer drill in his right hand. Porter consulted his G-Shock. 0742 hours. Sixty seconds since the first charge had detonated. By his reckoning the team had four minutes to lift the target before the cops rocked up. He looked back up at Bald, the clock ticking inside his head. Bald pressed the drill bit to the Lincoln roof at a point roughly over the driver's seat and began drilling. The Hilti made a high-speed whining sound as the drill bit bored through the roof, throwing up sparks in every direction.

Eighty seconds gone.

0742 hours.

Up on the bridge, Devereaux manoeuvred the Landy into position. He waited for a lull in the traffic before reversing and then steered the vehicle forward so it was at a ninety-degree angle to the hard shoulder, with the front bumper facing the metal railings head-on. The hard shoulders on Swiss roads were wider than the ones in Britain and it was just about wide enough to accommodate the Landy side-on without blocking traffic. Keeping the engine running, Devereaux debussed from the Landy. He took the remote control for the winch and his Sig Sauer P226 pistol from the glove compartment.

He hooked around to the front of the Landy, pausing to glance up and down the motorway. The motorists were speeding past, oblivious to the attack going on below. The two explosions had been contained inside the tunnel, with only a few faint threads of smoke drifting up from the entrance to the bridge. If anyone looked out of their window and saw the smoke, they'd simply assume it was a small fire or a car crash. Now Devereaux picked up the coil of extended winch cable and started paying it out over the side of the parapet so that the safety hook reached down to the road fifteen metres below, ready for the guys to clip on with their carabiners.

Devereaux finished lowering the winch cable. Lifted his gaze to the road east of the tunnel. A couple of vehicles had pulled up sixty metres short of the tunnel entrance. Civvies. Devereaux figured they must have seen the smoke, heard the gunshots and explosions, and hit their brakes. The drivers of both cars were stepping out onto the blacktop and rubbernecking the scene at the tunnel. One of the civvies reached for his mobile. Getting on the blower to the cops, no doubt. The other guy got out his handheld digital camera and started filming.

Shit, thought Devereaux. He leaned over the railings and shouted down to Coles.

'Get a fucking move on!'

His voice carried down into the tunnel, catching the South African's attention. Coles looked up at the bridge. Devereaux pointed to the cars that had stopped further along the road. 'Cops are on the way, fellas!'

Ninety seconds since the attack began.

Two-and-a-half minutes to go.

Down in the tunnel, Bald drilled.

He'd already cut an inch-wide hole through the Lincoln roof. Now he was drilling a second hole next to the first one. As he worked the Hilti a staccato series of dense thumps sounded from inside the blacked-out Lincoln. *Ker-thump! Ker-thump! Ker-thump!* Like someone striking at the roof with a hammer. The bodyguards are trying to blast away at Bald, Porter realised. The thought momentarily flashed through his head that the roof must be armoured too. That's why the shots weren't penetrating the roof. They were deflecting off the armour plating. The armour had been designed to stop anyone from shooting into the car. It would stop a bullet from shooting out of it too. But it wouldn't stop the Hilti. And once Bald had punched a larger hole in the roof, the occupants were in for a nasty shock.

Bald kept drilling. The Hilti screeched. The bodyguards kept blasting away. Bald finished putting two more identical holes in the roof next to the first one, creating a single three-inch hole. He set down the Hilti and looked down towards Porter, gesturing frantically.

A hundred and twenty seconds. Two minutes down.

Two to go.

'Now!' Bald shouted.

Porter took the petrol container and passed it up. Bald grabbed it and unscrewed the black cap, attaching the short pouring nozzle. Then he inserted the nozzle into the hole in the Lincoln roof and tipped the petrol over the heads of the two bodyguards in the front seats. Porter heard muffled screams from inside the Lincoln. Bald finished tipping the last few drops of petrol into the car. Chucked the container aside and hopped down from the Lincoln. Porter deholstered his Sig adopting a solid firing stance. He trained his semi-automatic at the passenger door. In the corner of his vision he saw Bald drawing his own weapon. He was aiming at the driver's side.

A second passed. Then another. The occupants screamed. Bald and Porter kept pointing their Sigs at the side doors. Hearts racing. The burning Audis had turned the tunnel into a sauna and Porter could feel beads of hot sweat slicking down his spine, clinging to his overalls. His hair was soaked through with sweat. His muscles pounded. After five seconds, the two bodyguards inside the Lincoln did exactly what anyone else would do when they'd just been doused in a highly flammable liquid. They panicked. They feared that Bald was going to toss a lit match into the hole and set the pair of them on fire. Nothing motivates a human being like the fear of being burned alive. The bodyguards forgot all about their SOPs and their basic training. They popped open the doors and sprang out of the Lincoln, shouting and flapping their arms and desperately trying to throw off their petrol-soaked jackets. They walked right into the line of fire. Porter had the driver lined up as soon as he set foot on the asphalt. The driver froze. Turned dumbly towards the Sig pointed at his chest. His podgy face registered something like surprise.

Then Porter squeezed the trigger.

The Sig barked. Porter could feel the moving parts of the Sig working in tandem, the slider moving backwards and then shunting forwards, ejecting the first round out of the snout and chambering the next bullet. The bullet spurted out of the pistol and hit the driver in the sternum, punching a hole clean through his heart. The driver jolted and crumpled to the ground. In the corner of his eye Porter glimpsed the second bodyguard's head jerking backwards as Bald emptied a round into a spot right between the eyes. The bodyguard went into a tailspin and then flopped backwards. He joined his mate on the ground, landing in a ragged heap and leaking blood all over the place.

Six bodyguards down, Porter thought.

Now we've just got to grab the target.

He swung around to the left side of the Lincoln and made for the open door, stepping over the slotted bodyguard. Armoured cars usually had a master-switch located on the front passenger side to control the locking mechanism on each of the individual doors. Porter ducked inside the car, eyes searching for the switch. The leather seats reeked of petrol. Porter located the master-switch and flicked it, unlocking the doors. Then he stepped out and hurried towards the rear passenger door. A hundred and forty seconds now. Bald was already beating a path towards the rear door on the opposite side of the vehicle, keeping his weapon drawn and his aim steady. Porter tugged on the handle, springing the door open and sweeping around it in a smooth motion, his Sig pointed at the figures inside and his index finger caressing the trigger.

A squat, stocky figure in a tailored suit sat in the back of the Lincoln, waving his arms at Porter. He had thick bushy eyebrows and a small mouth and a shock of balding grey hair like a bird's nest on top of his head. His eyes were narrow and black, like someone had carved them out with the point of a knife. He looked plumper than in the photographs Porter had seen, and his features were a little more haggard and worn. But it was unmistakeably him. It was the face Porter had seen staring back at him before, on wanted posters and news reports. The Tiger.

Radoslav Brozovic.

His two kids were sitting in the back either side of the warlord. A blonde-haired girl no older than nine or ten, and a dark-haired boy of around seven. Both were wearing their school uniform with the badges sewn onto the lapels of their navy-blue jackets. Their school satchels were lying next to them. Bald cranked open the opposite door. Brozovic's eyes darted from left to right as he tried to back away from the operators, holding his kids close.

'No, no!' he cried. 'Please, no!'

The warlord kept shaking his head, shielding his kids with his thick arms. Like he thought his attackers were going to kill him on the spot. Brozovic had a distinctive red cross on his neck, Porter noticed. The same one he'd seen on Bill Deeds. The images from the Brecons came flooding back to him just then. Driving like icepicks into his skull. His veins pounded. He tightened his jaw and bunched his arm muscles and felt his index finger tensing on the Sig trigger. Christ, it was tempting. *Do it*, the voice at the back of his head niggled at Porter. *Drop him now. Sod Lakes. Sod the fucking orders. Slot this bastard.*

Make him pay.

Porter shrugged off the thought. He reached out and grabbed Brozovic by the jacket and hauled him out of the Lincoln. Bald kept his aim on the Serb. The kids screamed for their father. The boy wrapped his arms around his dad's leg, clinging on to him as tears streamed down his face. Bald pulled the kid away. The girl reached out towards Brozovic as he fell to the ground outside the car. Porter pushed the girl back with his free hand, shouting at her.

'Stay where you are!'

He didn't know if the girl understood English or not. But she seemed to get the message. She retreated inside the Lincoln; silent and afraid. The boy was still bawling his eyes out, calling out to his dad. Outside the car, Brozovic tried to scrape himself off the ground but Bald was on him in a flash, sprinting around the back of the Lincoln and then booting the warlord in the small of his back. Brozovic grunted as the air exploded out of his lungs and he landed on his front. Bald grabbed the Serb's arms and pinned them behind his back. Then he dug a pair of plasticuffs out of his overalls pocket and fastened them around Brozovic's wrists. The guy swore under his breath as Bald yanked the cuffs tight. Then Porter grabbed Brozovic by his shirt collar and hauled him to his feet.

A hundred and sixty seconds gone.

Eighty seconds left.

There was no time to piss about. The clock was well and truly ticking now. Porter and Bald hustled the Tiger down the tunnel towards the eastern exit, thirty metres away. Brozovic stumbled along, moaning in pain and glancing back at the Lincoln.

'My kids,' he said in broken English. 'Please, my kids . . .'

'Shut the fuck up,' said Porter. 'Keep moving.'

He picked up the pace. Brozovic stumbled forward, snatching at the air and almost tripping over himself. They passed the burning wreckage of the rear Audi. Smoke was still seething out of the motor. Flames licked at the leather interior. The explosion had punched a huge hole through the front windscreen. Porter could see the driver slumped over the steering wheel. His head had been ripped apart literally. Bits of his jaw and the gooey residue of an eyeball were visible on the dash, amid the shards of broken glass.

The smoke cleared beyond the Audi. They were ten metres

278

from the tunnel exit now. Porter could hear Devereaux shouting down from the parapet, urging them to get a fucking move on. Coles was standing just outside the tunnel, hurriedly waving them over. Porter shoved Brozovic ahead of him, digging the Sig barrel into the nape of his neck and barking at him to hurry up. They hit the tunnel entrance in a dozen frantic strides. All three of them were covered in sweat from the heat and the fumes. Porter released his grip on Brozovic. The warlord stumbled forward a couple of steps then dropped to his knees, his fat hands splayed in front of him as he gasped frantically for breath.

Porter looked up. Half a dozen cars had halted sixty metres further back on Route de Valavran and a crowd had started to form. People were climbing out of their motors and talking into their phones, pointing out the three guys in plastic face masks. The Swiss weren't shy in coming forward and two bystanders started to approach the tunnel, gesticulating angrily at Coles and the others.

We've got to get out of here, Porter told himself.

Right fucking now.

He reached for the climbing tape he'd slung over his shoulder. At the same time Bald yanked the warlord to his feet and forced him to lift his arms behind his back. Then Porter took the length of webbing and pulled it over Brozovic's back, slipping the two ends of the loop under his armpits and bringing them across his chest. Porter took the ends and threaded them through the carabiner, locking the makeshift harness in place. The harness wasn't exactly first-class comfort but it would keep Brozovic secure. Once the harness was fastened Porter reached for the end of the steel winch cable dangling over the side of the bridge and clipped it on to the carabiner. Then Bald and Porter clipped their own harnesses onto the winch hook. The winch could handle a load up to 9,000lbs. It wouldn't have any problems hoisting all four guys simultaneously.

Coles stood by the tunnel entrance, waiting for the other three to finish clipping on to the winch cable. The two bystanders were getting dangerously close now. They were less than twenty metres away from the operators at the tunnel entrance, shouting and shaking their fists.

'Zaustavite!' Coles shouted in Croatian. 'Zaustavite!'

Meaning, *Stop*. Coles had memorised the word from a phrase-book. It would help with the team's cover posing as Croatian militants. Coles signalled with his hand for the civvies to halt, in case they didn't understand. But they kept approaching. He hefted up his Sig and fired three times in quick succession, putting down rounds on the tarmac a few metres in front of the two angry Swiss men. The bullets sparked off the ground and sent the civvies scuttling back towards their motors. Everyone else in the crowd heard the gunshots and scurried behind their cars. Coles spun away from the entrance and clipped the hook onto the harness he was wearing under his leather jacket.

'Everyone's on!' Porter shouted up at Devereaux. 'Get the fucking winch up!'

Three minutes gone. One minute left.

Up on the bridge, Devereaux operated the winch remote. The cable became taut as the electric motor whirred into action, reeling the four guys in. Suddenly their feet were leaving the ground as they were slowly lifted up towards the parapet. It would take about a minute for the winch to fully haul them up to the bridge, Porter figured. It was going to be fucking close.

Forty-five seconds to go. Porter could hear the whirr of the winch motor and the rumble of the Landy engine above the relentless buzz of traffic whizzing past above their heads. On thirty seconds the civvies started rushing back out from cover. More traffic was bottlenecking the road now and Porter could feel his heart beating erratically inside his chest. They needed to be out of here before the cops showed. The strike team would be vulnerable until they changed motors at the abandoned farm in Founex. They would have to put some serious distance between themselves and the cops before they got off the motorway.

Twenty seconds. Three minutes forty seconds since the first shaped charge had detonated. They were almost at the bridge now.

On fifteen seconds Porter caught the faint thrum of police sirens wailing in the distance. More civvies were pouring forward from behind their cars, staring towards the east. Towards the approaching cop cars. Porter willed the winch cable to reel in faster. Ten seconds later they hit the parapet. Devereaux was standing beside the railings, working the remote. Porter clambered over the metal railings and unclipped his harness. Then he and Devereaux took Brozovic by his arms and dragged the warlord over, with Bald and Coles climbing after him. The sirens were getting louder. Some of the bystanders had moved into the middle of the road and were gesturing furiously towards the motorway bridge above. Any second now the cops would be swarming over the tunnel.

'Move!' Porter boomed. 'NOW!'

Devereaux finished winding the rest of the cable back into the winch. Then he raced around to the driver's door. Coles put three more rounds down below, forcing the crowd to scatter moments before the cop cars swung into view. Then he turned and made for the front passenger door. Bald and Porter quickly disconnected Brozovic from the climbing tape harness and manhandled the warlord towards the rear of the Landy, racing like mad. Porter could feel his heart thumping inside his throat. Brozovic snarled at the operators as they bundled him into the back seat.

'You can't do this,' he said. 'I'm the fucking Tiger. Do you hear? You can't fucking do this to me.'

Porter smiled wickedly. 'You might be the Tiger, mate. But we're the fucking SAS.'

Porter clambered into the rear seat and slammed the door shut. Bald did the same, Brozovic trapping between them. Devereaux was already reversing out into traffic. There was a screech to the rear as a Volkswagen Golf slammed on the brakes and swerved into the next lane, narrowly avoiding the Landy. The sirens were deafeningly loud now. Porter could see the police lights flashing and popping on the road below as the cars tore round the bend. Devereaux put his foot to the accelerator. The Landy started pulling away from the bridge. Away from the carnage and the billowing smoke and the slotted bodyguards. Away from the cops.

Soon they were bulleting down the motorway. Heading north in the direction of Founex and the abandoned farm. The sirens faded. Devereaux kept the Landy to a steady eighty miles per. Brozovic sat in the back, silent and brooding and plasticuffed. Devereaux puffed out his cheeks and breathed a sigh of relief.

'Christ, fellas. That was fucking close.'

'We're not out of the woods yet,' Porter replied. He tore off his face mask. Blinked sweat out of his eyes. 'We've got to get this twat to the RV first and hand him over to the Firm. Then we'll get the beers in.'

THIRTY-SEVEN

0759 hours.

The team drove in silence along the A1. Devereaux stayed under the speed limit and kept flicking his eyes up at the rear-view, but there was no sign of any pursuing cops. After five miles Porter could feel the adrenaline starting to wear off. Like the comedown from a drug. A bunch of pains announced themselves across his chest. His neck muscles were stiff and sore, like rusted cables. His ribs flared up in agony every time he took in a draw of breath. Christ, Porter thought to himself. I could do with a bloody stiff drink right now.

A few more hours and I'll be sipping beers on a BA flight to Heathrow. I can't bloody wait.

After eight miles of rolling green and brown fields they passed a Best Western hotel on their right. Devereaux eased down to fifty per. They took the turn-off on Exit 10 and followed the road as it veered off to the right before merging onto Route de Divonne. After a mile Devereaux made a left onto Route de Chataigneriaz. The landscape flattened. An endless tract of farmland stretched out either side of the road, interspersed with neat terraced vineyards and the occasional farmstead. Porter looked out across the fields and for the first time in a long time started to think about the future. About how he'd get his life back on track. I'll give Diana a bell when this is over, he thought. Tell her I'm sorry. Tell her I've cleaned up my act and I want to be a part of Sandy's life again. That I'll do whatever it takes to make things right.

I'm her old man, for Christ's sake. I should be there for her.

They stayed on Route de Chataigneriaz for half a mile. There were no other cars on the road. They passed wild grasslands and vast orchards. The road got narrow and bumpy. To his right Porter could just about see Lake Geneva in the distance, a strip of silver like foil wrapping paper, backgrounded by jagged mountains. Devereaux made a series of quick turns until they hit a rutted dirt track running between a couple of barren fields. They were officially in the middle of nowhere. The Landy bounced and juddered as Devereaux steered north along the track. After two hundred metres they hit the farmhouse.

The place was a two-storey building set back from the road with a gently sloped roof and French shutters on the windows. It looked like it had stood empty for a long time. The paintwork on the shutters was peeling. The windows were filthy. The stonework was chipped and worn like enamel on a set of rotten teeth. There was a large pile of debris to the right of the farmhouse and a ramshackle barn off to the left. The team had learned about the farmhouse through their Templar contact. Templar had estate agents on its books in every major city in Europe. For a monthly retainer, the agents supplied lists of vacant properties that could be used as safe houses in an emergency. Porter and Bald had scoped the place out the previous day, checking for squatters. Then they'd stashed the second getaway motor inside the barn.

Devereaux pulled up to the side of the farmhouse. Killed the engine, got out. Coles followed him. Then Porter. Bald pressed the Sig's cold metal tip against Brozovic's flabby paunch and ordered the Serb out of the Landy. Then Devereaux hurried over to the barn and got behind the wheel of the white Mercedes-Benz C-class stowed inside. At the same time Coles retrieved a couple of three-litre plastic bottles of industrial bleach from the back of the Landy. Then he started dousing the interior of the vehicle, bleaching out any residual DNA and fingerprints the team had left inside the vehicle.

Devereaux reversed the Merc out of the barn and parked up in front of the farmhouse. He climbed out. Swung around the back of the motor and popped the boot. Then Porter and Bald hustled

Brozovic over to the rear of the Merc. The warlord staggered forwards, muttering prayers in Serbian. He had gone through a bunch of emotions since the team had captured him. First he'd been terrified. Then he got angry. Now he was just desperate.

Porter gestured to the open boot and said, 'Get in.'

Brozovic hesitated. He looked pleadingly at Bald and Porter in turn. 'Please,' he said. 'Please, no. I give you money. Women. Shit, whatever the fuck you want, it's yours. Just let me go. Eh?'

Bald pressed the cold tip of the barrel to the spot between Brozovic's eyes. Shot him a savage look and said, 'Get in the fucking boot right now, or I'll drop you faster than a sack of hammers.'

Brozovic tensed with fear. He shivered and clambered awkwardly into the back of the Merc, curling up into a ball with his knees pressed tight against his chin. Moaning, begging for his life in stunted English. Porter stuffed a gag into his mouth, shutting him up. He closed the boot. We're almost there, he told himself. Now all we've got to do is get to the RV without getting killed. The thought of handing over Brozovic still left a bad taste in his mouth, but as far as Porter was concerned they'd already had their vengeance. The gunmen behind the Selection attack were all dead. Brozovic was just the icing on the cake. If the Firm wanted the fucker alive then they were welcome to him.

Porter nodded at Bald. 'Let's get out of here, mate.'

Devereaux made for the front driver's side of the Merc. Coles was done bleaching the Land Rover. He tossed the plastic bottles aside. Bald and Porter turned away from the boot, ignoring the muffled whimpers of Brozovic inside. In a little over an hour they would reach the pick-up point at the airfield at Clarmont. Once the handover was complete they would fly back to the safe house in London for the mission debrief and their shiny new contracts with Templar. A new start, thought Porter. A clean slate. That's what I bloody need. He could finally bury his demons. Put all the shit with the Regiment behind him once and for all. Templar were offering him a decent salary and a chance to get back to doing what he did best. Being on the front line.

It's what I've been trained for. It's all I know.

As he turned away a distinct trilling reached his ears. The sound of a mobile phone ringing. Porter stopped in his tracks and looked towards Bald. The sound was coming from Bald's jacket pocket.

The burner.

Bald frowned. The first thought he had was: *Who the fuck's ringing me?* As far as he knew only one person had the number for his burner. The blonde over in Hereford. Sally Higgins. It must be her. Bald's second thought was, *Something must be wrong with the tapes.* Why else would Sally ring out of the blue? He fished the mobile out of his pocket and glanced down at the luminous green display. Unknown number. He took a few steps away from the Merc so the other lads wouldn't overhear. Tapped the answer button. Pressed the Nokia to his ear.

'Sally?' he said. 'What is it, love? What's wrong?'

There was a series of clicks and whirs down the end of the line. Then a male voice said, 'John? Are you there?'

Bald stood absolutely still. Felt the blood draining from his head to his toes. Shit. It wasn't Sally. Wasn't even close. But it was a voice Bald recognised all the same.

Hawkridge.

How did he get this number? And what the fuck does he want?

'Yeah,' Bald replied numbly. 'I'm here.'

Hawkridge sighed with relief. The sound came down the line like a shiver. 'Jesus Christ, man. Where the hell have you been? We've been trying to get hold of you for the past twenty minutes.'

'Bad reception,' said Bald. In the corner of his eye he could see Devereaux and Coles swapping questioning looks. They were both thinking the same thing, wondering why Bald had a mobile on him. 'We're out in the sticks. On our way to the RV now.'

Hawkridge took a deep breath and said, 'Listen to me, John. You're walking into a trap.'

The words moved like a knife through Bald. He stood rooted to the spot, a chill clamping around his neck. A vicious thumping triggered between his temples. He kept the phone pressed to his ear but slid his eyes across to Porter. To Devereaux, and Coles.

Thinking, *Someone's double-crossing me here.*

'John? Did you hear me? For Christ's sake, man. It's a set-up. Get the hell out of—'

There was a sudden flash of movement. Bald saw it in the corner of his eye. He looked back across to the Merc. Saw Coles retrieving his Sig Sauer P226. Drawing the weapon level with Bald's face. Bald still had the Nokia glued to his ear. He stood rooted to the spot and looked on helplessly as the South African tensed his index finger on the pistol trigger. Ready to send Bald over to the dark side.

Coles was halfway to depressing the trigger when Devereaux lunged at him. He was four metres away and shaping to tackle the South African to the ground before he could get a shot off. Coles spun towards Devereaux in a blur of motion and fired. Devereaux was less than two metres away when the pistol muzzle lit up. The bullet smacked into his upper chest and took him clean off his feet. Devereaux made a grunt then dropped and rolled away, collapsing face-down in the dirt next to the Merc.

Porter reacted in an instant and reached for his holstered Sig. Coles spotted the move and spun towards him. The Sig flashed and cracked. The round pinged off the Merc in a flurry of sparks. Porter dropped to his haunches and rolled two metres to his left, then brought his gun arm level with his shoulder. A month ago he was rusty. He'd lost his edge. But not now. Porter was sharp as fuck. He transitioned into a crouching firing stance and drew his gun arm level with his shoulder, pointing the Sig directly at Coles. The South African was slow. He was still turning when Porter pulled on the trigger.

The Sig kicked up in his grip. The bullet struck Coles several inches above his chest and buried itself in his right shoulder. His joint exploded in a gout of blood and tissue. Coles gave out a pained grunt before dropping backwards and landing on his back. The Sig tumbled out of his grip, clattering to the ground beside Devereaux. Coles clenched his jaws through the pain and rolled onto his side, reaching for the Sig with his one good arm. Now Bald burst forward and charged at the South African, kicking the gun away from him and following up with a brutal side-foot to the jaw. Coles groaned. In the same beat Porter scraped himself off the ground and moved forward, training his weapon on Coles. Devereaux lay two metres away. His left leg twitched a couple of times, then stopped. A pool of gleaming blood had formed beneath his body. Porter stared at Coles, rage brewing in his veins.

'The fuck are you doing?'

Coles said nothing. Bald glowered at him. His brow was so furrowed his whole face looked like a bunch of knots in a rope. 'Coles was flipped,' he said. 'It's a trap, mate. Hawkridge was trying to warn us.'

Coles spat out blood. His eyes were bloodshot and wide. Blood continued to disgorge from his wound, gushing down his front and staining his jacket. 'I knew the plan was blown as soon as your burner started ringing,' he said. 'You're a stupid cunt, Jock. Nobody was supposed to have a phone on the op. Nobody was supposed to be in contact with us.'

Porter scowled. 'Who the fuck are you working for?'

Coles went silent again. There was a look of fear in his eyes, but something else too. Defiance. Porter tightened his grip on the Sig and pressed the gun to Coles's stomach, digging the cold tip between his ribs.

'I said, Who are you working for?'

'Piss off.'

Porter turned to Bald and nodded. 'Get to this cunt's wound.'

Bald didn't need any encouragement. He tore off the South African's jacket and ripped open his shirt. Then he found the entry wound, a ragged hole oozing dark, greasy blood. Bald jammed his left thumb into the wound right up to the knuckle joint and rooted around inside, digging into his tendons and muscle. Coles howled in agony.

'Jesus,' he cried. 'Oh, Christ. Fucking hell, Jesus.'

Bald pulled his thumb out of the bullet wound. Tears were streaming down Coles's face. Then Bald stepped back and Porter dropped to one knee beside the South African and pressed the tip of the Sig to the wound, drawing another agonised cry from the guy.

'You're not fucking blind,' he said. 'You saw what we did to those Serbian bastards. Mark my words, we'll make sure it's a hundred times worse for you. Now, tell us who you're working for.'

Coles remained mute. Porter smashed the butt of the Sig into the South African's face. Coles groaned as the pistol slammed into his mouth, shattering a few of his front teeth. He raised a hand to try and defend himself against the next blow. Porter jabbed him in the ribs, forcing Coles to involuntarily lower his arms. Then Porter clubbed him on the temple, crashing the barrel against the side of his skull.

'Tell us what you know, and I'll make it quick. Otherwise me and Jock will make your death real fucking slow. You'll be begging us to double-tap you by the time we're done torturing you.'

'Lakes,' Coles coughed. 'I work for Lakes.'

Porter jolted. A cold fear clamped around his neck, percolating down his spine. He clenched his fists so hard his fingernails almost drew blood.

Coles went on, 'Lakes got me a spot on the team. She told me to keep a close eye on you and Jock. I had orders to stop you from handing Brozovic over to the Firm.'

'Stop us how?' Porter demanded.

Coles clamped his eyes shut for a beat. 'Lakes said I had to wait until we'd snatched Brozovic. Then I had to stop you before we made it to the RV, grab Brozovic and take him to the alternative RV. Lakes is waiting there. She was gonna put Brozovic on a plane before the Firm could get hold of him.'

Porter felt as if mice were fumbling around inside his bowels. 'The mission was to take Brozovic alive. Why would Lakes want to sabotage it?'

'They're on the same side,' Coles said. 'Her and Brozovic. She supported him back in the Bosnian war, feeding him int. Helping him stay one step ahead of NATO. Lakes was working both sides. She couldn't afford to let the Firm get to the Tiger, in case he spilled his guts and exposed her involvement.'

Bald stepped towards Coles. He made a face like he was chok-ing on someone else's spit. 'Bullshit. Why would Lakes get into bed with a fucking war criminal?'

'She's part of a movement.' Coles grimaced. He spoke through a mouthful of blood and broken teeth. 'Her and some of the Yanks over at the CIA. They supply the cash to the group. They're secretive. They've got long arms. That's how they recruited me. I was doing close protection work for a brother down in Johannesburg when they offered me a job.'

'What movement?' Porter asked.

'They're like the Crusaders. Right-wing. Hardcore. Even more than me. They think it's their mission in life to defeat Islam. Protect the West.'

A thought gripped Porter just then. The kind of thought that could make an iceberg sweat. He remembered what Ninkovic had told them on the deck of the boat back in Serbia. *Brozovic has friends*, the 2i/c had said. *There were influential people who supported the Tiger from the outside.*

He glared at Coles. 'You mean to tell me this underground move-ment was supporting our enemies, in the middle of a bloody war?'

The South African parted his lips to reveal a bloodstained smile. 'How else do you think Brozovic escaped the bombing that day in Zvornik? Someone warned him in advance. He had someone on the inside feeding him int. Lakes ... she was the one who saved his arse that day.'

'What about the Selection attack?' Bald snarled. 'Was she in on that too?'

'Nah,' said Coles. 'That was all Brozovic. But Lakes knew he'd overstepped the mark. That the security forces wouldn't stop until they'd hunted Brozovic down. That's when Keppel reached out to me and put me on the team, to make sure it never got that far. And if it did, I'd take care of it.'

Porter felt his blood run cold. *Marcus Keppel. The old Regiment CO who runs Templar.*

'He's in on it too?'

Coles swallowed blood and nodded faintly. He'd lost a shitload of blood and his skin had turned white. 'Course he fucking is. Keppel and Lakes are tight. He's the one who recommended you and Jock for the team. He reckoned you were so washed-up you didn't stand a chance of locating Brozovic.'

Porter clamped his jaws shut. *Who else is in on this thing?* he wondered. He glanced quickly at Bald. Was Jock in on it? Maybe Hawkridge too. *I don't know who to trust any more.* Then another tought jumped out at him.

'I don't understand. Lakes told us she needed Brozovic alive. Why bother getting us to kidnap him if she wanted him out of the way? She could've just given us an order to slot the bastard.'

'She couldn't,' Coles said. 'She said her orders came from the very top. She had to be seen to be following them. That's why she needed me. To get to Brozovic after the op. It was the only way.'

The sound of the Nokia ringing interrupted Porter's thoughts. Bald stared at the burner for a second. Then he took the call.

'What happened?' Hawkridge asked breathlessly.

Bald gripped the burner so tight he thought the casing might shatter. 'Next time, how about you give us some more fucking notice.'

'Calm down, old fruit,' said Hawkridge. 'We only just found out about Lakes ourselves. I tried to warn you as soon as we realised she was leading you into a trap. It's not my fault the reception where you are is dreadful.'

'Yeah, well,' said Bald. 'If you'd told us earlier then Devereaux would still be alive.'

A pause. 'He's dead?'

'Coles slotted him before we could grab the fucker.'

Hawkridge clicked his tongue. 'Pity. We knew Lakes had flipped one of the chaps on the team, but we couldn't be sure who. What about Brozovic? Is he still alive?'

'He's still breathing,' said Bald. 'For now.'

A sigh of relief came down the line. 'Thank God. Listen, John. You must keep Brozovic alive and get him to us. It's vital we find out who else was part of this secret movement along with Lakes.

She'll be finished after this. Bloody finished, I tell you. We'll crucify her.'

Hawkridge sounded enthusiastic at the prospect. No bloody wonder, thought Bald. He'll probably be next in line for the top job at Vauxhall once Lakes is out of the picture.

'What's the plan?' he said.

'The airfield's out of the question, now that we know Lakes was planning to make the intercept there. We'll divert the plane and try to find an alterative RV. Until then you're to sit tight and wait until further notice.'

'And we're just supposed to fucking trust you?'

'Right now, I'd say you don't have much of a choice, old fruit.'

Bald gritted his teeth and said, 'Fine.'

'I'll be in touch,' said Hawkridge. 'Stay low. Ciao.'

Click.

Bald stuffed the Nokia inside his jacket pocket and quickly outlined the plan to Porter. After he'd finished talking Porter glanced around the farmhouse and said, 'Well, we can't stick around here.'

'Where, then?' asked Bald.

Porter thought for a moment. 'There's a lay-by a few miles to the north. I noticed it on the map. We can go static there and sit it out until we hear back from Hawkridge.'

Bald said, 'He could be setting us up.'

'Maybe. But Hawkridge is right. We don't have any choice. We've got to get Brozovic out of the country and Hawkridge is our only ticket.'

'That just leaves us to deal with this fucking twat,' said Bald, tipping his head at Coles.

Porter glanced across at Coles. 'Leave him to me.'

He paced over to the South African and knelt down beside him, pressing the tip of the Sig Sauer to the side of the guy's head. Coles started convulsing. Blood streamed out of his nostrils and ran down his chin, mixing with the tears dried to his cheeks. He looked like shit.

'Fuck,' Coles spat, breathing hard. 'Jesus, fuck. Don't do this.'

'Time to go to the great veldt in the sky, you cunt.'

'Jesus, no—'

Porter fired once. Coles's brains exploded across the ground in a slippery red shower. The close impact shattered his temple area, leaving a crater in his skull big enough to sink an orange into. Porter stood back, watching the blood pumping out of the fuck-off huge hole in the South African's head. He felt the same as he did after crushing a cockroach, or feeding poison to a rat. He felt nothing, nothing at all. When you were dealing with vermin, there was no such thing as remorse.

He paced over to Devereaux and fished the car keys out of his trouser pocket. He took the Sigs from the two dead operators. He also took the spare clips in case they needed the extra. The way things were going he didn't want to take any chances. Then he called over Bald. They picked up Coles by his arms and legs and dragged his dead weight over to the pile of debris next to the farmhouse. Then they did the same with Devereaux. Porter and Bald laid their bodies next to the metre-high heap of smashed concrete and rotten wood and lead piping. Then they started piling the rubbish on top of Devereaux and Coles. They kept at it until both the bodies were buried under a stack of rubbish, hidden from view. It wouldn't cover the smell of decomposing flesh. And it wouldn't stop the flies from getting at the corpses. But it would keep Coles and Devereaux out of sight. Long enough, at least, to give Bald and Porter time to get out of the country.

They folded themselves into the Merc's front seats. Porter took the wheel. He arrowed out of the farmhouse and steered the motor back down the dirt track. The Merc bounced and shuddered. Thirty seconds later they were heading to the lay-by north of Founex. Porter figured they could kill a few hours there until they heard back from Hawkridge. Then we'll hand over Brozovic and get the hell out of here, he told himself.

And then Lakes is going to pay.

THIRTY-EIGHT

0837 hours.

Seventeen minutes later they reached the lay-by. It was on the side of a quiet country road surrounded by flat fields and with zero traffic in either direction. Porter parked up and turned off the engine.

Brozovic didn't make a sound in the boot. The gag in his mouth made sure of that.

As the minutes ticked by questions rattled around inside his head. How deep did this far-right movement run inside the Firm? And if Lakes and Brozovic were both on the same side, why had she allowed him to be targeted by the strike team? Why not just send a message to the Tiger in advance? Warn him that he was about to be lifted? But Porter knew the answer already.

Lakes was trying to burn the warlord too. As long as Brozovic drew breath, he represented a serious threat to her ambitions. If the authorities ever caught up with Brozovic, there was a chance he might expose his relationship with Lakes. Sell her out and cut himself a deal. With the Tiger out of the way, Lakes wouldn't have to worry about her secret being revealed.

She's getting rid of all the skeletons in her closet before she receives her promotion, Porter realised. Smart. But it's too late, now Hawkridge has rumbled her. Once we hand over Brozovic to the Firm, his evidence will bury Lakes.

It's not over yet. We've still got to make it out of here.

Two hours later, Bald's Nokia buzzed. He tossed his gum out of the window and took the call.

'The plane's off,' said Hawkridge. 'Mechanical problems. You'll have to get across the border by car instead.'

'Bloody great,' Bald replied drily. 'This just gets better and better. Remind me how you managed to wangle a job at Thames House again?'

Hawkridge ignored the last remark and said, 'There's a crossing at Premanon, west of Nyon. Make your way there now. We'll have a team in place ready to extract the target and take him back to the UK as soon as you cross the border. They'll ferry Brozovic across Calais in the back of an articulated lorry.'

'What if the border guards stop us?'

'They won't,' Hawkridge replied confidently. 'The crossing is lightly guarded. The guards usually just wave drivers through. You shouldn't encounter any problems on that front.'

'Easy for you to say,' said Bald. 'It's not your fucking neck on the line.'

'Yoga,' said Hawkridge.

'What was that?' Bald replied, frowning.

'Once this is over. I suggest you try it, old fruit. Very relaxing, you know. It could really help with your anger.'

'Thanks, but I'll stick to the Famous Grouse and Stella.'

'Your call. Our people will be waiting for you at the rendez-vous point. There's a camp site a mile south of Premanon. It'll be empty at this time of year. You'll find our chaps there.'

The line went dead. Bald listened to the dead air for a moment and imagined slogging Hawkridge in the guts. The thought pleased him. Then he put away the Nokia and filled Porter in on the details of the RV. Thirty seconds later they were pulling out of the lay-by and racing north towards Nyon.

Porter stuck to Route de Suisse, following the dual carriage-way for three miles until they hit the city outskirts. Then he made a series of turns and arrowed north-west out of the city on Route de Signy, following the road past Grens and Trelex. The Juras loomed on the horizon, a series of low rugged mountains like the knuckles on a clenched fist. On the other side of the Juras was the border with France. Porter knew the area like the back of his hand from studying the maps. He reckoned they were fifteen miles from the border now. *Not far to go until we're home and dry.*

He could almost taste that first pint. He imagined the warm feeling flowing through his veins as the booze juiced his bloodstream.

Only this time I won't be drinking myself into oblivion. I'll have one pint and bloody well savour it.

My days as a drunk are behind me.

After five miles the incline steepened as they started climbing high into the Juras. The road corkscrewed, twisting and turning through a series of bends like a snake through the long grass. Porter kept the Merc ticking along at forty miles per hour, staying under the speed limit. The road was deserted. Earlier on they'd passed a few Lycra-clad cyclists and the odd family car but now they were driving through an isolated stretch of blacktop in the middle of a large forested area, flanked by tall pine and fir trees. They kept climbing. The road kept winding. Another three or four miles and they would hit the junction at Saint-Cergue. From there it was a straight run west towards the French border.

'Almost there, mucker,' Porter said.

'Thank fuck for that,' said Bald. 'First round's on me. Celebrate getting the Firm off our backs. I've had it up to here with those backstabbing pricks, mate. I'm done with them.'

Yeah, but are they done with us? Porter wondered. Something tells me they're not gonna let us off the hook that easily. The Firm never does.

He kept his mouth shut and focused on the road. They passed a secluded gravel path at the roadside and after another hundred metres reached a dog-legged bend. There was a steep treeline to the left, and to their right the road dropped off on a heavily forested slope down the side of the mountain. Porter slowed down to twenty per as he followed the bend round. The turn was so sharp he couldn't see the other side of it. As he hit the apex the view opened up in front of Porter.

Then he saw it.

Ahead of him a BMW 5 Series had stopped in the middle of the road, blocking both lanes. The front doors were open and the hazard lights were flashing and popping. Porter hit the brakes. The Merc stopped six metres behind the Beemer.

'Fuck's sake,' Bald said. 'What now?'

'Looks like they've broken down,' said Porter.

Bald pulled a face. 'In the middle of the road?'

Before Porter could reply he heard an engine gunning at his six o'clock. He glanced up at the rear-view just in time to see a Land Rover Defender 110 hurtling out of the gravel path to the rear and rushing towards them. The Defender screeched to a halt in the middle of the road, five metres to the rear of the Merc. Blocking them in.

Shit.

Porter automatically slid a hand down to his holstered Sig. Before he could retrieve his weapon he spied movement at his three o'clock and his nine. Four figures swept forward from the treeline either side of the road. Two guys to the left. Two more to the right. They were big guys. They all had shaved heads and deep suntans and Ray-Bans. They were all packing Heckler & Koch MP5 9mm submachine guns. They didn't look like soldiers. Too flashy. Too tanned. They looked more like mercenaries coming off a job in Africa. The four gunmen converged on the Merc simultaneously, their MP5s tucked tight to their shoulders and sighted at Bald and Porter.

'Get out!' one of the gunmen shouted.

A Scouse accent. These guys were Brits, then. But definitely not from the Firm. Porter knew it was pointless to resist. It would be suicide. They'd brass him up before he could deholster his weapon.

'Fucking out!' the Scouse gunman shouted again.

Porter reached a hand down from the steering wheel and popped the handle on the door. Then he slowly stepped out of the Merc. Bald got out the other side. Two more gunmen debussed from the Defender. They looked identical to the four steroid-guzzling freaks standing either side of the treeline. They probably lifted weights together and shared spray-on tan tips. They turned towards the Beemer. Porter chased their line of sight and saw two figures stepping out of the rear passenger doors. A man and a woman. The woman dashed her cigarette and crushed the butt under her low heel. Then she paced over to the Merc, with the man at her side.

'Hello, John,' Cecilia Lakes said. She smiled. 'You didn't think you'd get away from us that easily, did you?'

Porter showed no reaction. Keppel stood next to Lakes. The former Regiment CO wore a crisp suit with the collar button popped. He had a Heckler & Koch USP pistol in his right hand. His jaw looked squarer than ever. He cocked his chin at Porter and Bald.

'Lose the weapons,' he said. 'Nice and slow.'

Six gunmen, Porter was thinking. Seven including Keppel. Against two of us. Grim odds, whichever way you looked at it. He carefully slid his pistol out of his holster, ejected the clip and shunted the round out of the chamber. So did Bald. Then the operators placed their unloaded weapons on the blacktop and kicked them across to the nearest gunman. The Scouse. He stepped forward and scooped them up.

Six miles from the border. Six miles from freedom, and now we're fucked.

Lakes ran her eyes over the Merc then looked back to Porter. 'Where's Brozovic?'

'In the boot.'

There was no point holding back. They'd find him anyway.

Keppel snapped his piercing gaze to the nearest gunman. 'What the fuck are you waiting for, man? Get him out of there.'

The gunman lowered his weapon and hurried over to the Merc, snatching the keys from the ignition. Then he swung around to the boot and unlocked it. He removed the dirty cloth from Brozovic's mouth and hauled the warlord out of the boot. He stood unsteadily on his feet, groaning and gulping down mouthfuls of air.

'A shame we'll have to kill him,' Lakes said curtly.

Porter swung his gaze back to her. He bristled with rage. 'You sold us a fucking lie.'

'I've got the eyes of the security and intelligence committees on me,' Lakes replied with a shrug. 'I had to be seen to following orders. If I'd ordered you to execute Brozovic, my bosses would have understood I had something to hide. Besides, it's clear Brozovic is too much of a liability now. He was useful once, but as long as he's alive there's a chance he may be arrested, and I can't allow that to happen. Not with my career on the line.' She smiled again. 'You see my predicament.'

Porter growled, 'I know what I see. You supported a warlord who got a kick from chopping up civvies and planned the attack on the Regiment. You're a backstabber and a fucking coward.'

Lakes smiled faintly. 'Coles told you everything before you killed him, I see. I presume you killed him, since he's not with you now.' She looked for a reaction from Porter, then went on. 'Yes. You've figured it out. I helped Brozovic during the war. With some help from our American friends, naturally. But something had to be done. We couldn't just stand back and do nothing while our governments abandoned our Christian brothers.'

'We?'

Lakes nodded. 'The movement. Look around you, John. There's an Islamic takeover of the West happening right now, in front of our very eyes. Look at the mosques. The faith schools. Multiculturalism.' Her voice trembled with anger. 'In the days of the Crusades, it was the job of the Knights Templar to fight Islam. Now it's up to those of us inside Whitehall and Washington to carry on the struggle.'

There was a fanatical look in her eyes as she spoke. Christ, Porter thought. Lakes really does believe this crap.

'You're fucking insane.'

'No. Not really. You'd be surprised how many people share my beliefs. Mine and my grandfather's. There are plenty of people inside the establishment who agree with what we're doing, even if they can't say so publicly.'

'Bullshit.'

Lakes chuckled. 'Come on, John. Do you really think a single

MI6 agent would be able to arrange an illicit deal to funnel weapons and intelligence to Brozovic, without any of her superiors taking notice?'

'Who else?' Porter said. 'Who else is in on it?'

'Too many to name. But we have friends in the cabinet. In the upper echelons of the civil service. The media. Indeed, in every corner of the establishment there are people who support our agenda. We're more powerful than you could ever imagine.'

Porter said nothing. He thought back to what Nealy had told him before the mission briefing. About Lakes's family being highly connected. About how her grandfather had been a mate of Oswald Mosley and his Blackshirts. How her father had been a top civil servant under Ted Heath. Now he wondered if they were all part of this secret movement. A state within a state. *Christ, how deep does this thing go?*

'But why support some Serb warlord on the other side of Europe?'

'Brozovic shared our beliefs. And he needed our help. He was on the frontline, and the Americans had betrayed him.'

'What do you mean?'

'The CIA was supplying weapons to the Bosnian Muslims. Unofficially, of course. When the war broke out, the Saudis wanted to help their cousins in Bosnia. So they called in their debts to Washington. The Americans owed the Saudis after the Gulf War. But supplying guns to the Bosnians was strictly illegal. We heard about it through our friends in the agency. We had no choice but to intervene. We had to support Brozovic, in whatever ways we could.'

Porter could barely believe what he was hearing. *There was a secret arms race going on in Bosnia, and no one even knew about it.*

'Then the war finished,' Lakes continued. 'We had to hide Brozovic. Keep him out of sight. In hindsight, it was a mistake. We should have simply disposed of him. Still, we'll take care of that problem now. And you two will die as well. It's all working out rather nicely, I'd say.'

'How the hell did you know where to find us?' Bald seethed.

'It was easy enough. Once you failed to show at the RV I knew the plan had been compromised, and you'd have to get out of the country by road. There are only two crossing points near Nyon. And you wouldn't have tried to cross at Geneva. Not with the heavy security presence there. This was the only route open to you. Then it was just a case of waiting until our guys in the Defender caught sight of you.'

Porter turned to Keppel and jerked a thumb at the gunmen. 'I'm guessing this lot belong to you. What'd she offer you? A lifetime of far-right bollocks? An invitation to the BNP's Christmas party?'

Porter was stalling, trying to buy himself time. He didn't know what for. But every second was another second he was still drawing breath, and kept alive his faint hope of finding some way of escaping.

Keppel raised a smile. It wrinkled his smooth face. 'Something better, actually. Contracts.'

Lakes saw the puzzled look on Porter's face and said, 'Once I'm calling the shots at Vauxhall, I'll have the final say on who gets awarded dozens of major contracts. We're talking tens of millions of pounds. Templar will be at the top of the pile. With a commission skimmed off the top for myself, of course.'

'Bastard.' Porter glared at Lakes. 'I thought the Serbs were bad enough. But you're a real fucking piece of work.'

She suppressed a laugh. 'No, John. I'm just a lot smarter than you. That's why you're in the gutter, and I'm about to become the chief of Six.' She turned to the Scouse gunman. 'You can kill them now.'

The Scouse grinned and took a step forwards. He drew up his MP5 so that the snout was level with a point between Porter's eyes. Porter stared back. He wasn't afraid of dying. But he hated the thought of getting killed while Lakes and Keppel lorded it up over at the Firm. He gritted his teeth and braced himself for the gunshot. Imagined the nine-milli round smashing into his face and tearing through his skull before punching out of his neck. Blood all over the fucking place. The last thought to enter his mind was, I never got to see my Sandy again.

I never got to see her smile one last time.

Porter closed his eyes and waited to die.

THIRTY-NINE

1142 hours.

The gunshot rang out.

Porter opened his eyes.

I'm still breathing.

The shot hadn't come from the Scouse's MP5. It sounded from further away to the right. At Porter's three o'clock. Another crack split the air, and then a third. The Scouse spun away from Porter and glanced across at the treeline. Porter looked in the same direction, just in time to see the two gunmen on the right side of the road spasming as bullets thumped into their backs. Between the gaps in the trees Porter could see half a dozen figures moving through the woods towards the road from thirty metres away. Five of them were gripping Heckler & Koch UMP submachine guns with the foldable stocks fully extended and pressed tight to their shoulders. They were pissing bullets at the mercenaries in rapid two-round bursts. The sixth shooter wielded a Colt Commando assault rifle, a cut-down and more compact version of the regular M16, with thirty rounds of 5.56x45mm in the clip. Porter recognised the operator at once.

Ophelia.

It's a counter-ambush. The Firm's here.

The two gunmen at Porter's three o'clock were already dead. They were slumped on the blacktop six metres away. The other four gunmen all turned towards the Firm operators rushing towards them from the cover of the woods. So did Keppel and Lakes. The two mercenaries over at the Defender arced their weapons towards the treeline. Ophelia got there first and squeezed off a three-round burst from the Commando. One of the mercenaries let out a throated cry as the bullets punched into his groin in a close grouping, shredding his balls. He fell away, cupping a hand to his testicles. The second gunman grabbed Brozovic and dragged him behind the Defender's front wheelbase as Ophelia unleashed another three-round burst. Bullets pinged and clattered off the Defender.

The Scouse spun away from Bald and Porter. He put down a two-round burst with his MP5 before diving for cover behind the Beemer. His mucker never made it. Two of the Firm operators had almost reached the treeline and let off a couple of bursts at the mercenary. Evelyn stood among them, brandishing a UMP. The first rounds slapped into the asphalt less than six inches from Bald and Porter, forcing them to hit the deck next to the Merc. The second burst nailed the mercenary through the upper chest, exiting through his neck and killing him instantly. He dropped four metres from Bald and Porter, four away from the Scouse. Porter glanced at his six and saw Lakes and Keppel scrambling past the Merc towards the Defender, eight metres to the rear of the Merc.

He spun around as Bald lunged forward and clasped his right hand around the UMP lying on the ground next to the slotted gunman. Bald swiftly brought the submachine gun up and took aim at the Scouse. The mercenary was still putting down suppressive fire at the treeline. He turned towards Bald. Too late. Bald fired before the Scouse could get a shot away, emptying a pair of rounds into his guts. The guy fell back, clutching his stomach and hissing sharply between his gritted teeth. There was a sudden break in the fire coming from the treeline. Bald raced forwards and jammed the barrel against the Scouse's neck and fired twice. The Scouse jerked, then went still. He was good and fucking dead. He wouldn't be claiming any more Jobseekers in this lifetime. Bald grabbed the guy's MP5 and chucked it to Porter.

'Mucker!' he shouted, nodding towards the Defender.

Porter seized the weapon. Shot to his feet and glanced at his six o'clock. Lakes and Keppel had reached the Defender. The last remaining mercenary was crouching by the wheelbase, spraying rounds wildly at the treeline and keeping the operators pinned down. Eight metres south of the Defender, Brozovic was hurrying back down the bend in the road in a lumbering gait, his hands still cuffed behind his back. Lakes yelled at Keppel. The ex-CO turned towards the warlord and raised his USP. He's going to slot Brozovic, Porter realised.

He's going to kill the target before the Firm can get their hands on him.

Porter had a second. Less than that, even. There was no time to properly aim. He had to rely on his instincts and his training, and the feel of the MP5 in his grip.

He depressed the trigger, twice. There was a bright flash and a puff of smoke as the muzzle lit up. Two jackets spat out of the ejector located on the side of the weapon. Porter's aim was surgical. Keppel jolted before he could let off a round. The bullets punched into his upper back with a deadly *whump-whump*. The ex-CO fell away. As if someone had cut the strings on him.

Three metres to the left of Keppel, the remaining mercenary heard the gunshots and swung his weapon towards Porter. He unloaded a three-round burst. Porter ducked low to his left. He felt the heat from the rounds as they grazed past him and slapped into the Beemer. The mercenary was already zeroing in on Porter before he could heft up his UMP and get a shot off. Shit, thought Porter. I'm fucked.

Then Bald sprang forward. UMP raised, the mercenary lined up in the sights. The UMP barked as the Jock fired off two rounds at the gunman. The first round missed by several inches, ricocheting off the Defender hood. The second round struck the mercenary in the throat, right on the Adam's apple. The guy made a garbled scream and went limp by the front wheel on the Defender. Blood fountained out of the hole in his neck and splashed down his front, gleaming sickly red.

Porter swung his gaze back across the road. Beyond the Defender. Brozovic had tripped and fallen to the ground. He was moaning and writhing and struggling to get to his feet. Seven metres away, Lakes had grabbed the USP pistol from beside Keppel's lifeless corpse. Now she moved towards the warlord, drawing the barrel level with his head. Porter brought up his submachine gun in an instant and trained it on Lakes, shouting at the top of his voice.

'Put the fucking gun down!'

Lakes was still holding the USP. Aiming it at Brozovic.

'I said, drop the fucking weapon,' Porter yelled.

Lakes kept her finger on the trigger. In the same moment, a figure swept into view from behind the rear of the Defender.

Ophelia.

She had the Colt Commando tight to her shoulder and her sights centred on Lakes. She unleashed a rapid burst. The rounds struck Lakes in the back of the head before she could depress the trigger. Her head snapped forward, spraying Brozovic with bits of her skull, brain and eyeball. Her fingers loosened on the USP's polymer grip. Then Lakes fell away. A second later, Evelyn and the other Firm operators were pouring forward across the road.

Porter lowered his weapon.

It was over.

He slumped to the ground. He was shattered. Never mind a beer, he thought. I need a flagon of Bushmills after that.

As soon as the firefight was over two more vehicles raced into view beyond the bend in the road and pulled up just short of the Beemer. A pair of Ford Sierras. Evelyn and Ophelia hauled Brozovic to his feet and dragged him over to the Defender. A well-dressed figure debussed from the front car and ran his eyes across the scene. Clarence Hawkridge was wearing a Barbour jacket and corduroys and Wellington boots. He looked like a banker heading down to the country for a weekend of wine-tasting and clay-pigeon shooting. He narrowed his eyes briefly at Brozovic as the two Firm lasses bundled the Serb into the boot of the other Sierra. Then he marched over to Bald and Porter. He took great care to avoid the spent brass and puddles of oily blood.

'We'll take it from here, chaps,' Hawkridge said. 'You two should get going.'

'Not even a fucking thank you,' Bald muttered under his breath. 'Bloody typical.'

Hawkridge appeared not to have heard him. Porter said, 'We're not coming back with you?'

Hawkridge rustled up a knowing smile. 'Of course not, old fruit. You don't work for the MoD, remember? No, I'm afraid you're on your own. You'll have to make your own way back. Take the Mercedes and head back down to Geneva. I'd advise taking the back route to Chamonix. Best to avoid the main roads. It's a pleasant train ride to Paris from there, I gather.'

'How did you know Lakes and Keppel were going to ambush us here?'

'We've been tracking Lakes's phone ever since we found out she was trying to lead you into a trap. As soon as the signal from her phone went static, we knew she must have set the ambush at precisely this point. Then it was simply a case of moving our chaps into position.' He glanced at the bodies slumped by the treeline and grinned smugly. 'We got here just in time, by the looks of it.'

Bald thought back to the farmhouse and the phone call, and clenched his jaw. 'Yeah, I'm beginning to think timing's not your strong point.'

Hawkridge tutted. 'Oh, no hard feelings, old fruit. It worked out for the best.'

'That's why you delayed us,' Porter replied, suddenly under-standing. 'Because you needed time to get your team together in case Lakes tried it on. But you didn't want to warn us that we might be blundering into a fucking ambush.'

Hawkridge said nothing but merely shrugged. Porter shook his head, his mind reeling. Another fucking lie. The Firm was over-flowing with them. Lies on top of lies. He couldn't wait to get away from the bastards.

He gave his back to Hawkridge. Nodded to Bald. 'Come on, mate. Let's get out of here. The stink's getting unbearable.'

'I'll see you chaps bright and early on Monday morning, then,' Hawkridge announced.

Porter stopped in his tracks. Turned slowly back to Hawkridge. The pounding between his ears returned. Mixing with the sound of the blood rushing in his ears, and the ringing echoes of the firefight. 'The fuck are you talking about? You just said that we don't work for you. We're heading back to Hereford, mate.'

'Actually,' Hawkridge adjusted his glasses, 'you're not.'

Bald and Porter looked at one another.

Looked back to Hawkridge.

'What's that supposed to mean?' said Bald.

Hawkridge smiled. 'Templar will obviously be liquidated after this. Which means your contracts are null and void. You're being transferred back to the MoD. You'll report to me.' He fixed his smile at Bald.

'You can't do that,' said Porter.

'Oh, but we can.' Hawkridge furrowed his smooth brow. 'You should be grateful, really. We're going to set up a new unit. Section 20. I'm going to be running the show, and I'll need a couple of good operators to get things done. You two have done well on this mission. I'm sure you'll prove yourself worthy of your new positions.'

Porter and Bald said nothing. They just stared at Hawkridge in disbelief. The agent stood there for a moment, basking in his new glory. Then he checked his watch and cleared his throat. 'I really must be off now. See you gents on Monday.'

Porter turned away. So did Bald.

'Oh, and one more thing,' Hawkridge called out.

Porter stopped and half-turned. Hawkridge had ditched the smile. His face was deadly serious as he looked towards Bald.

'I'll be expecting those tapes on my desk first thing, old fruit.'

'Tapes?' Bald feigned innocence. 'Don't know what the fuck you're talking about, pal.'

Hawkridge chuckled. 'Don't play games with me, John. I know you recorded the meeting.' He took a step closer. Smiled thinly. 'Remember, both of you. No matter how clever you think you are, we'll always be one step ahead of you.'

THE END